Tom Victor

About the Author

RAY BRADBURY, the author of more than thirty books, is the recipient of the National Book Foundation's 2000 Medal for Distinguished Contribution to American Letters. Some of his best-known works are *Fahrenheit 451*, *The Martian Chronicles*, *The Illustrated Man*, *Dandelion Wine*, and *Something Wicked This Way Comes*. A writer for both theater and cinema, he has adapted sixty-five of his stories for television's *The Ray Bradbury Theater*. He won an Emmy for his teleplay of *The Halloween Trees* and was nominated for an Academy Award. He lives in Los Angeles, California.

A Sound of Thunder and Other Stories

Books by Ray Bradbury

Dandelion Wine
Dark Carnival
Death Is a Lonely Business
Driving Blind
Fahrenheit 451
A Graveyard for Lunatics
Green Shadows, White Whale
The Halloween Tree
I Sing the Body Electric!
The Illustrated Man
Journey to Far Metaphor
Kaleidoscope
Long After Midnight
The Martian Chronicles
The Machineries of Joy
The October Country
One Timeless Spring
Quicker Than the Eye
R Is for Rocket
Something Wicked This Way Comes
A Sound of Thunder and Other Stories
(previously titled The Golden Apples of the Sun)
The Stories of Ray Bradbury
S Is for Space
The Toynbee Convector
When Elephants Last in the Dooryard Bloomed
Yestermorrow
Zen in the Art of Writing

A Sound of Thunder and Other Stories

Ray Bradbury

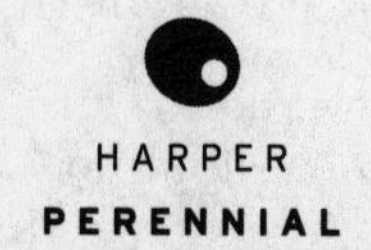

HARPER
PERENNIAL

The Golden Apples of the Sun published by Bantam 1964.

R Is for Rocket published by Bantam 1965.

A trade paperback edition of this book was published under the title *The Golden Apples of the Sun* in 1997 by Avon Books, an imprint of HarperCollins Publishers.

HarperCollins books may be purchased for educational, business, or sales promotional use. For information please write: Special Markets Department, HarperCollins Publishers Inc., 10 East 53rd Street, New York, NY 10022.

First Avon Books published in 1997.
Reprinted in Perennial 2001.
First Harper Perennial edition published 2005.

Library of Congress Cataloguing-in-Publication Data is available upon request.

ISBN-10: 0-06-078569-1 (movie tie-in)
ISBN-13: 978-0-06-078569-7 (movie tie-in)

05 06 07 08 09 ❖/RRD 10 9 8 7 6 5 4 3 2 1

acknowledgments

"The Fog Horn" copyright 1952 The Curtis Publishing Company.
"The April Witch" copyright 1951 by The Fortnightly Publishing Company.
"The Wilderness" copyright 1952 by Triangle Publications, Inc.
"The Fruit at the Bottom of the Bowl" copyright 1948 by Fiction House, Inc.
"The Flying Machine" copyright 1953 by Ray Bradbury.
"The Murderer" copyright 1953 by Ray Bradbury.
"The Golden Kite, The Silver Wind" copyright 1953 by Epoch Associates. Reprinted by permission of Epoch.
"I See You Never" copyright 1947 by The New Yorker Magazine, Inc. Reprinted by permission of The New Yorker.
"Embroidery" copyright 1951 by Stadium Publishing Corp.
"The Big Black and White Game" copyright 1945 by American Mercury, Inc.
"The Great Wide World Over There" copyright 1953 by Ray Bradbury.
"Powerhouse" copyright 1948 by Street and Smith Publications, Inc.
"En La Noche" copyright 1952 by Fawcett Publications, Inc.
"Sun and Shadow" copyright 1953 by The Fortnightly Publishing Company, Inc.
"The Meadow" copyright 1947 by Dodd, Mead & Co., Inc.
"The Garbage Collector" copyright 1953 by Ray Bradbury.
"The Great Fire" copyright 1949 by Triangle Publications, Inc.
"The Golden Apples of the Sun" copyright 1953 by Ray Bradbury.
"R Is for Rocket" copyright 1943 by Popular Publications, Inc.
"The End of the Beginning" copyright 1956 by Ray Bradbury;

contents

A Sound of Thunder and Other Stories

And this one, with love, is for Neva,
daughter of Glinda
the Good Witch of the South

. . . And pluck till time and times are done
The silver apples of the moon,
The golden apples of the sun.

W. B. YEATS

The Fog Horn

Out there in the cold water, far from land, we waited every night for the coming of the fog, and it came, and we oiled the brass machinery and lit the fog light up in the stone tower. Feeling like two birds in the gray sky, McDunn and I sent the light touching out, red, then white, then red again, to eye the lonely ships. And if they did not see our light, then there was always our Voice, the great deep cry of our Fog Horn shuddering through the rags of mist to startle the gulls away like decks of scattered cards and make the waves turn high and foam.

"It's a lonely life, but you're used to it now, aren't you?" asked McDunn.

"Yes," I said. "You're a good talker, thank the Lord."

"Well, it's your turn on land tomorrow," he said, smiling, "to dance the ladies and drink gin."

"What do you think, McDunn, when I leave you out here alone?"

"On the mysteries of the sea." McDunn lit his pipe. It was a quarter past seven of a cold November evening, the heat on, the light switching its tail in two hundred directions, the Fog Horn bumbling in the high throat of the tower. There wasn't a town for a hundred miles down the coast, just a road which came lonely through dead country to the sea, with few cars on it, a stretch of two miles of cold water out to our rock, and rare few ships.

''The mysteries of the sea,'' said McDunn thoughtfully. ''You know, the ocean's the biggest damned snowflake ever? It rolls and swells a thousand shapes and colors, no two alike. Strange. One night, years ago, I was here alone, when all of the fish of the sea surfaced out there. Something made them swim in and lie in the bay, sort of trembling and staring up at the tower light going red, white, red, white across them so I could see their funny eyes. I turned cold. They were like a big peacock's tail, moving out there until midnight. Then, without so much as a sound, they slipped away, the million of them was gone. I kind of think maybe, in some sort of way, they came all those miles to worship. Strange. But think how the tower must look to them, standing seventy feet above the water, the God-light flashing out from it, and the tower declaring itself with a monster voice. They never came back, those fish, but don't you think for a while they thought they were in the Presence?''

I shivered. I looked out at the long gray lawn of the sea stretching away into nothing and nowhere.

''Oh, the sea's full.'' McDunn puffed his pipe nervously, blinking. He had been nervous all day and hadn't said why. ''For all our engines and so-called submarines, it'll be ten thousand centuries before we set foot on the real bottom of the sunken lands, in the fairy kingdoms there, and know *real* terror. Think of it, it's still the year 300,000 Before Christ down under there. While we've paraded around with trumpets, lopping off each other's countries and heads, they have been living beneath the sea twelve miles deep and cold in a time as old as the beard of a comet.''

''Yes, it's an old world.''

''Come on. I got something special I been saving up to tell you.''

We ascended the eighty steps, talking and taking our time. At the top, McDunn switched off the room lights so there'd be no reflection in the plate glass. The great eye of the light was humming, turning easily in its oiled socket. The Fog Horn was blowing steadily, once every fifteen seconds.

''Sounds like an animal, don't it?'' McDunn nodded to himself. ''A big lonely animal crying in the night. Sitting here on the edge of ten billion years calling out to the Deeps, I'm here, I'm here, I'm here. And the Deeps do answer, yes, they do. You been here now for three months, Johnny, so I better prepare you. About this time of year," he said, studying the murk and fog, "something comes to visit the lighthouse."

"The swarms of fish like you said?"

"No, this is something else. I've put off telling you because you might think I'm daft. But tonight's the latest I can put it off, for if my calendar's marked right from last year, tonight's the night it comes. I won't go into detail, you'll have to see it yourself. Just sit down there. If you want, tomorrow you can pack your duffel and take the motorboat in to land and get your car parked there at the dinghy pier on the cape and drive on back to some little inland town and keep your lights burning nights, I won't question or blame you. It's happened three years now, and this is the only time anyone's been here with me to verify it. You wait and watch."

Half an hour passed with only a few whispers between us. When we grew tired waiting, McDunn began describing some of his ideas to me. He had some theories about the Fog Horn itself.

"One day many years ago a man walked along and stood in the sound of the ocean on a cold sunless shore and said, 'We need a voice to call across the water, to warn ships; I'll make one. I'll make a voice like all of time and all of the fog that ever was; I'll make a voice that is like an empty bed beside you all night long, and like an empty house when you open the door, and like trees in autumn with no leaves. A sound like the birds flying south, crying, and a sound like November wind and the sea on the hard, cold shore. I'll make a sound that's so alone that no one can miss it, that whoever hears it will weep in their souls, and hearths will seem warmer, and being inside will seem better to all who hear it in the distant towns. I'll make me a sound and an apparatus and they'll call it a Fog Horn and whoever hears it will know the sadness of eternity and the briefness of life.' "

The Fog Horn blew.

"I made up that story," said McDunn quietly, "to try to

explain why this thing keeps coming back to the lighthouse every year. The Fog Horn calls it, I think, and it comes. . . ."

"But——" I said.

"Sssst!" said McDunn. "There!" He nodded out to the Deeps.

Something was swimming toward the lighthouse tower.

It was a cold night, as I have said; the high tower was cold, the light coming and going, and the Fog Horn calling and calling through the raveling mist. You couldn't see far and you couldn't see plain, but there was the deep sea moving on its way about the night earth, flat and quiet, the color of gray mud, and here were the two of us alone in the high tower, and there, far out at first, was a ripple, followed by a wave, a rising, a bubble, a bit of froth. And then, from the surface of the cold sea came a head, a large head, dark-colored, with immense eyes, and then a neck. And then—not a body—but more neck and more! The head rose a full forty feet above the water on a slender and beautiful dark neck. Only then did the body, like a little island of black coral and shells and crayfish, drip up from the subterranean. There was a flicker of tail. In all, from head to tip of tail, I estimated the monster at ninety or a hundred feet.

I don't know what I said. I said something.

"Steady, boy, steady," whispered McDunn.

"It's impossible!" I said.

"No, Johnny, *we're* impossible. *It's* like it always was ten million years ago. *It* hasn't changed. It's *us* and the land that've changed, become impossible, *Us!*"

It swam slowly and with a great dark majesty out in the icy waters, far away. The fog came and went about it, momentarily erasing its shape. One of the monster eyes caught and held and flashed back our immense light, red, white, red, white, like a disk held high and sending a message in primeval code. It was as silent as the fog through which it swam.

"It's a dinosaur of some sort!" I crouched down, holding to the stair rail.

"Yes, one of the tribe."

"But they died out!"

"No, only hid away in the Deeps. Deep, deep down in the deepest Deeps. Isn't *that* a word now, Johnny, a real word, it says so much: the Deeps. There's all the coldness and darkness and deepness in a word like that."

"What'll we do?"

"Do? We got our job, we can't leave. Besides, we're safer here than in any boat trying to get to land. That thing's as big as a destroyer and almost as swift."

"But here, why does it come *here?*"

The next moment I had my answer.

The Fog Horn blew.

And the monster answered.

A cry came across a million years of water and mist. A cry so anguished and alone that it shuddered in my head and my body. The monster cried out at the tower. The Fog Horn blew. The monster roared again. The Fog Horn blew. The monster opened its great toothed mouth and the sound that came from it was the sound of the Fog Horn itself. Lonely and vast and far away. The sound of isolation, a viewless sea, a cold night, apartness. That was the sound.

"Now," whispered McDunn, "do you know why it comes here?"

I nodded.

"All year long, Johnny, that poor monster there lying far out, a thousand miles at sea, and twenty miles deep maybe, biding its time, perhaps it's a million years old, this one creature. Think of it, waiting a million years; could *you* wait that long? Maybe it's the last of its kind. I sort of think that's true. Anyway, here come men on land and build this lighthouse, five years ago. And set up their Fog Horn and sound it and sound it out toward the place where you bury yourself in sleep and sea memories of a world where there were thousands like yourself, but now you're alone, all alone in a world not made for you, a world where you have to hide.

"But the sound of the Fog Horn comes and goes, comes and goes, and you stir from the muddy bottom of the Deeps, and your eyes open like the lenses of two-foot cameras and you move, slow, slow, for you have the ocean sea on your shoulders, heavy. But that Fog Horn comes through a thousand miles of water, faint and familiar, and the furnace in your belly stokes up, and you begin to rise, slow, slow. You feed yourself on great slakes of cod and minnow, on rivers of jellyfish, and you rise slow through the autumn months, through September when the fogs started, through October with more fog and the horn still calling you on, and then, late in November, after pressurizing yourself day by day, a few feet higher every hour, you are near the surface and still alive. You've got to go slow; if you surfaced all at once you'd explode. So it takes you all of three months to surface, and then a number of days to swim through the cold waters to the lighthouse. And there you are, out there, in the night, Johnny, the biggest damn monster in creation. And here's the lighthouse calling to you, with a long neck like your neck sticking way up out of the water, and a body like your body, and, most important of all, a voice like your voice. Do you understand now, Johnny, do you understand?''

The Fog Horn blew.

The monster answered.

I saw it all, I knew it all—the million years of waiting alone, for someone to come back who never came back. The million years of isolation at the bottom of the sea, the insanity of time there, while the skies cleared of reptile-birds, the swamps dried on the continental lands, the sloths and saber-tooths had their day and sank in tar pits, and men ran like white ants upon the hills.

The Fog Horn blew.

''Last year,'' said McDunn, ''that creature swam round and round, round and round, all night. Not coming too near, puzzled, I'd say. Afraid, maybe. And a bit angry after coming all this way. But the next day, unexpectedly, the fog lifted, the sun came out fresh, the sky was as blue as a painting. And the monster swam off away from the heat and the silence and didn't come back. I suppose it's been brooding on it for a year now, thinking it over from every which way.''

The monster was only a hundred yards off now, it and the Fog Horn crying at each other. As the lights hit them, the monster's eyes were fire and ice, fire and ice.

''That's life for you,'' said McDunn. ''Someone always waiting for someone who never comes home. Always someone loving some thing more than that thing loves them. And after a while you want to destroy whatever that thing is, so it can't hurt you no more."

The monster was rushing at the lighthouse.

The Fog Horn blew.

"Let's see what happens," said McDunn.

He switched the Fog Horn off.

The ensuing minute of silence was so intense that we could hear our hearts pounding in the glassed area of the tower, could hear the slow greased turn of the light.

The monster stopped and froze. Its great lantern eyes blinked. Its mouth gaped. It gave a sort of rumble, like a volcano. It twitched its head this way and that, as if to seek the sounds now dwindled off into the fog. It peered at the lighthouse. It rumbled again. Then its eyes caught fire. It reared up, threshed the water, and rushed at the tower, its eyes filled with angry torment.

"McDunn!" I cried. "Switch on the horn!"

McDunn fumbled with the switch. But even as he flicked it on, the monster was rearing up. I had a glimpse of its gigantic paws, fishskin glittering in webs between the finger-like projections, clawing at the tower. The huge eye on the right side of its anguished head glittered before me like a caldron into which I might drop, screaming. The tower shook. The Fog Horn cried; the monster cried. It seized the tower and gnashed at the glass, which shattered in upon us.

McDunn seized my arm. "Downstairs!"

The tower rocked, trembled, and started to give. The Fog Horn and the monster roared. We stumbled and half fell down the stairs. "Quick!"

We reached the bottom as the tower buckled down toward us. We ducked under the stairs into the small stone cellar. There were a thousand concussions as the rocks rained down; the Fog Horn stopped abruptly. The monster crashed upon the tower. The tower fell. We knelt together, McDunn and I, holding tight, while our world exploded.

Then it was over, and there was nothing but darkness and the wash of the sea on the raw stones.

That and the other sound.

"Listen," said McDunn quietly. "Listen."

We waited a moment. And then I began to hear it. First a great vacuumed sucking of air, and then the lament, the bewilderment, the loneliness of the great monster, folded over and upon us, above us, so that the sickening reek of its body filled the air, a stone's thickness away from our cellar. The monster gasped and cried. The tower was gone. The light was gone. The thing that had called to it a million years was gone. And the monster was opening its mouth and sending out great sounds. The sounds of a Fog Horn, again and again. And ships far at sea, not finding the light, not seeing anything, but passing and hearing late that night, must've thought: There it is, the lonely sound, the Lonesome Bay horn. All's well. We've rounded the cape.

And so it went for the rest of that night.

The sun was hot and yellow the next afternoon when the rescuers came out to dig us from our stoned-under cellar.

"It fell apart, is all," said Mr. McDunn gravely. "We had a few bad knocks from the waves and it just crumbled." He pinched my arm.

There was nothing to see. The ocean was calm, the sky blue. The only thing was a great algaic stink from the green matter that covered the fallen tower stones and the shore rocks. Flies buzzed about. The ocean washed empty on the shore.

The next year they built a new lighthouse, but by that time I had a job in the little town and a wife and a good small warm house that glowed yellow on autumn nights, the doors locked, the chimney puffing smoke. As for McDunn, he was master of the new lighthouse, built to his own specifications, out of steel-reinforced concrete. "Just in case," he said.

The new lighthouse was ready in November. I drove down alone one evening late and parked my car and looked across the gray waters and listened to the new horn sounding, once, twice, three, four times a minute far out there, by itself.

The monster?

It never came back.

"It's gone away," said McDunn. "It's gone back to the Deeps. It's learned you can't love anything too much in this world. It's gone into the deepest Deeps to wait another million years. Ah, the poor thing! Waiting out there, and waiting out there, while man comes and goes on this pitiful little planet. Waiting and waiting.''

I sat in my car, listening. I couldn't see the lighthouse or the light standing out in Lonesome Bay. I could only hear the Horn, the Horn, the Horn. It sounded like the monster calling.

I sat there wishing there was something I could say.

The April Witch

Into the air, over the valleys, under the stars, above a river, a pond, a road, flew Cecy. Invisible as new spring winds, fresh as the breath of clover rising from twilight fields, she flew. She soared in doves as soft as white ermine, stopped in trees and lived in blossoms, showering away in petals when the breeze blew. She perched in a lime-green frog, cool as mint by a shining pool. She trotted in a brambly dog and barked to hear echoes from the sides of distant barns. She lived in new April grasses, in sweet clear liquids rising from the musky earth.

It's spring, thought Cecy. I'll be in every living thing in the world tonight.

Now she inhabited neat crickets on the tar-pool roads, now prickled in dew on an iron gate. Hers was an adaptably quick mind flowing unseen upon Illinois winds on this one evening of her life when she was just seventeen.

"I want to be in love," she said.

She had said it at supper. And her parents had widened their eyes and stiffened back in their chairs. "Patience," had been their advice. "Remember, you're remarkable. Our whole family is odd and remarkable. We can't mix or marry with ordinary folk. We'd lose our magical powers if we did. You wouldn't want to lose your ability to 'travel' by magic, would you? Then be careful. Be careful!"

But in her high bedroom, Cecy had touched perfume to her throat and stretched out, trembling and apprehensive, on her four-poster, as a moon the color of milk rose over Illinois country, turning rivers to cream and roads to platinum.

"Yes," she sighed. "I'm one of an odd family. We sleep days and fly nights like black kites on the wind. If we want, we can sleep in moles through the winter, in the warm earth. I can live in anything at all—a pebble, a crocus, or a praying mantis. I can leave my plain, bony body behind and send my mind far out for adventure. Now!"

The wind whipped her away over fields and meadows.

She saw the warm spring lights of cottages and farms glowing with twilight colors.

If I can't be in love, myself, because I'm plain and odd, then I'll be in love through someone else, she thought.

Outside a farmhouse in the spring night a dark-haired girl, no more than nineteen, drew up water from a deep stone well. She was singing.

Cecy fell—a green leaf—into the well. She lay in the tender moss of the well, gazing up through dark coolness. Now she quickened in a fluttering, invisible amoeba. Now in a water droplet! At last, within a cold cup, she felt herself lifted to the girl's warm lips. There was a soft night sound of drinking.

Cecy looked out from the girl's eyes.

She entered into the dark head and gazed from the shining eyes at the hands pulling the rough rope. She listened through the shell ears to this girl's world. She smelled a particular universe through these delicate nostrils, felt this special heart beating, beating. Felt this strange tongue move with singing.

Does she know I'm here? thought Cecy.

The girl gasped. She stared into the night meadows.

"Who's there?"

No answer.

"Only the wind," whispered Cecy.

"Only the wind." The girl laughed at herself, but shivered.

It was a good body, this girl's body. It held bones of finest slender ivory hidden and roundly fleshed. This brain was like a pink tea rose, hung in darkness, and there was cider-wine in this mouth. The lips lay firm on the white, white teeth and the brows arched neatly at the world, and the hair blew soft and fine on her milky neck. The pores knit small and close. The nose tilted at the moon and the cheeks glowed like small fires. The body drifted with feather-balances from one motion to another and seemed always singing to itself. Being in this body, this head, was like basking in a hearth fire, living in the purr of a sleeping cat, stirring in warm creek waters that flowed by night to the sea.

I'll like it here, thought Cecy.

"What?" asked the girl, as if she'd heard a voice.

"What's your name?" asked Cecy carefully.

"Ann Leary." The girl twitched. "Now why should I say *that* out loud?"

"Ann, Ann," whispered Cecy. "Ann, you're going to be in love."

As if to answer this, a great roar sprang from the road, a clatter and a ring of wheels on gravel. A tall man drove up in a rig, holding the reins high with his monstrous arms, his smile glowing across the yard.

"Ann!"

"Is that you, Tom?"

"Who else?" Leaping from the rig, he tied the reins to the fence.

"I'm not speaking to you!" Ann whirled, the bucket in her hands slopping.

"No!" cried Cecy.

Ann froze. She looked at the hills and the first spring stars. She stared at the man named Tom. Cecy made her drop the bucket.

"Look what you've done!"

Tom ran up.

"Look what you *made* me do!"

He wiped her shoes with a kerchief, laughing.

"Get away!" She kicked at his hands, but he laughed again, and gazing down on him from miles away, Cecy saw the turn of his head, the size of his skull, the flare of his nose, the shine of his eye, the girth of his shoulder, and the hard strength of his hands doing this delicate thing with the handkerchief. Peering down from the secret attic of this lovely head, Cecy yanked a hidden copper ventriloquist's wire and the pretty mouth popped wide: "Thank you!"

"Oh, so you *have* manners?" The smell of leather on his hands, the smell of the horse rose from his clothes into the tender nostrils, and Cecy, far, far away over night meadows and flowered fields, stirred as with some dream in her bed.

"Not for you, no!" said Ann.

"Hush, speak gently," said Cecy. She moved Ann's fingers out toward Tom's head. Ann snatched them back.

"I've gone mad!"

"You have." He nodded, smiling but bewildered. "Were you going to touch me then?"

"I don't know. Oh, go away!" Her cheeks glowed with pink charcoals.

"Why don't you run? I'm not stopping you." Tom got up. "Have you changed your mind? Will you go to the dance with me tonight? It's special. Tell you why later."

"No," said Ann.

"Yes!" cried Cecy. "I've never danced. I want to dance. I've never worn a long gown, all rustly. I want that. I want to dance all night. I've never known what it's like to be in a woman, dancing; Father and Mother would never permit it. Dogs, cats, locusts, leaves, everything else in the world at one time or another I've known, but never a woman in the spring, never on a night like this. Oh, please—we must go to that dance!"

She spread her thought like the fingers of a hand within a new glove.

"Yes," said Ann Leary, "I'll go. I don't know why, but I'll go to the dance with you tonight, Tom."

"Now inside, quick!" cried Cecy. "You must wash, tell your folks, get your gown ready, out with the iron, into your room!"

"Mother," said Ann, "I've changed my mind!"

The rig was galloping off down the pike, the rooms of the farmhouse jumped to life, water was boiling for a bath, the coal stove was heating an iron to press the gown, the mother was rushing about with a fringe of hairpins in her mouth. "What's come over you, Ann? You don't like Tom!"

"That's true," Ann stopped amidst the great fever.

But it's spring! thought Cecy.

"It's spring," said Ann.

And it's a fine night for dancing, thought Cecy.

". . . for dancing," murmured Ann Leary.

Then she was in the tub and the soap creaming on her white seal shoulders, small nests of soap beneath her arms, and the flesh of her warm breasts moving in her hands and Cecy moving the mouth, making the smile, keeping the actions going. There must be no pause, no hesitation, or the entire pantomime might fall in ruins! Ann Leary must be kept moving, doing, acting, wash here, soap there, now out! Rub with a towel! Now perfume and powder!

"You!" Ann caught herself in the mirror, all whiteness and pinkness like lilies and carnations. "*Who* are you tonight?"

"I'm a girl seventeen." Cecy gazed from her violet eyes. "You can't see me. Do you know I'm here?"

Ann Leary shook her head. "I've rented my body to an April witch, for sure."

"*Close,* very close!" laughed Cecy. "Now, on with your dressing."

The luxury of feeling good clothes move over an ample body! And then the halloo outside.

"Ann, Tom's back!"

"Tell him to wait." Ann sat down suddenly. "Tell him I'm not going to that dance."

"What?" said her mother, in the door.

Cecy snapped back into attention. It had been a fatal relaxing, a fatal moment of leaving Ann's body for only an instant. She had heard the distant sound of horses' hoofs and the rig rambling through moonlit spring country. For a second she thought, I'll go find Tom and sit in his head and see what it's like to be in a man of twenty-two on a night like this. And so she had started quickly across a heather field, but now, like a bird to a cage, flew back and rustled and beat about in Ann Leary's head.

"Ann!"

"Tell him to go away!"

"Ann!" Cecy settled down and spread her thoughts.

But Ann had the bit in her mouth now. "No, no, I hate him!"

I shouldn't have left—even for a moment. Cecy poured her

mind into the hands of the young girl, into the heart, into the head, softly, softly. *Stand up,* she thought.

Ann stood.

Put on your coat!

Ann put on her coat.

Now, march!

No! thought Ann Leary.

March!

"Ann," said her mother, "don't keep Tom waiting another minute. You get on out there now and no nonsense. What's come over you?"

"Nothing, Mother. Good night. We'll be home late."

Ann and Cecy ran together into the spring evening.

A room full of softly dancing pigeons ruffling their quiet, trailing feathers, a room full of peacocks, a room full of rainbow eyes and lights. And in the center of it, around, around, around, danced Ann Leary.

"Oh, it *is* a fine evening," said Cecy.

"Oh, it's a fine evening," said Ann.

"You're odd," said Tom.

The music whirled them in dimness, in rivers of song; they floated, they bobbed, they sank down, they arose for air, they gasped, they clutched each other like drowning people and whirled on again, in fan motions, in whispers and sighs, to "Beautiful Ohio."

Cecy hummed. Ann's lips parted and the music came out.

"Yes, I'm odd," said Cecy.

"You're not the same," said Tom.

"No, not tonight."

"You're not the Ann Leary I knew."

"No, not at all, at all," whispered Cecy, miles and miles away. "No, not at all," said the moved lips.

"I've the funniest feeling," said Tom.

"About what?"

"About you." He held her back and danced her and looked into her glowing face, watching for something. "Your eyes," he said, "I can't figure it."

"Do you see *me?*" asked Cecy.

"Part of you's here, Ann, and part of you's not." Tom turned her carefully, his face uneasy.

"Yes."

"Why did you come with me?"

"I didn't want to come," said Ann.

"Why, then?"

"Something made me."

"What?"

"I don't know." Ann's voice was faintly hysterical.

"Now, now, hush, hush," whispered Cecy. "Hush, that's it. Around, around."

They whispered and rustled and rose and fell away in the dark room, with the music moving and turning them.

"But you *did* come to the dance," said Tom.

"I did," said Cecy.

"Here." And he danced her lightly out an open door and walked her quietly away from the hall and the music and the people.

They climbed up and sat together in the rig.

"Ann," he said, taking her hands, trembling. "Ann." But the way he said the name it was as if it wasn't her name. He kept glancing into her pale face, and now her eyes were open again. "I used to love you, you know that," he said.

"I know."

"But you've always been fickle and I didn't want to be hurt."

"It's just as well, we're very young," said Ann.

"No, I mean to say, I'm sorry," said Cecy.

"What *do* you mean?" Tom dropped her hands and stiffened.

The night was warm and the smell of the earth shimmered up all about them where they sat, and the fresh trees breathed one leaf against another in a shaking and rustling.

"I don't know," said Ann.

"Oh, but *I* know," said Cecy. "You're tall and you're the finest-looking man in all the world. This is a good evening; this is an evening I'll always remember, being with you." She put out the alien cold hand to find his reluctant hand again and bring it back, and warm it and hold it very tight.

"But," said Tom, blinking, "tonight you're here, you're

there. One minute one way, the next minute another. I wanted to take you to the dance tonight for old times' sake. I meant nothing by it when I first asked you. And then, when we were standing at the well, I knew something had changed, really changed, about you. You were different. There was something new and soft, something . . ." He groped for a word. "I don't know, I can't say. The way you looked. Something about your voice. And I know I'm in love with you again."

"No," said Cecy. "With me, with *me*."

"And I'm afraid of being in love with you," he said. "You'll hurt me again."

"I might," said Ann.

No, no, I'd love you with all my heart! thought Cecy. Ann, say it to him, say it for me. Say you'd love him with all your heart.

Ann said nothing.

Tom moved quietly closer and put his hand up to hold her chin. "I'm going away. I've got a job a hundred miles from here. Will you miss me?"

"Yes," said Ann and Cecy.

"May I kiss you good-by, then?"

"Yes," said Cecy before anyone else could speak.

He placed his lips to the strange mouth. He kissed the strange mouth and he was trembling.

Ann sat like a white statue.

"Ann!" said Cecy. "Move your arms, *hold* him!"

She sat like a carved wooden doll in the moonlight.

Again he kissed her lips.

"I do love you," whispered Cecy. "I'm here, it's me you saw in her eyes, it's me, and I love you if she never will."

He moved away and seemed like a man who had run a long distance. He sat beside her. "I don't know what's happening. For a moment there . . ."

"Yes?" asked Cecy.

"For a moment I thought—" He put his hands to his eyes. "Never mind. Shall I take you home now?"

"Please," said Ann Leary.

He clucked to the horse, snapped the reins tiredly, and drove the rig away. They rode in the rustle and slap and motion of the moonlit rig in the still early, only eleven o'clock spring night, with the shining meadows and sweet fields of clover gliding by.

And Cecy, looking at the fields and meadows, thought, It would be worth it, it would be worth everything to be with him from this night on. And she heard her parents' voices again, faintly, "Be careful. You wouldn't want to lose your magical powers, would you—married to a mere mortal? Be careful. You wouldn't want that."

Yes, yes, thought Cecy, even that I'd give up, here and now, if he would have me. I wouldn't need to roam the spring nights then, I wouldn't need to live in birds and dogs and cats and foxes, I'd need only to be with him. Only him. Only him.

The road passed under, whispering.

"Tom," said Ann at last.

"What?" He stared coldly at the road, the horse, the trees, the sky, the stars.

"If you're ever, in years to come, at any time, in Green Town, Illinois, a few miles from here, will you do me a favor?"

"Perhaps."

"Will you do me the favor of stopping and seeing a friend of mine?" Ann Leary said this haltingly, awkwardly.

"Why?"

"She's a good friend. I've told her of you. I'll give you her address. Just a moment." When the rig stopped at her farm she drew forth a pencil and paper from her small purse and wrote in the moonlight, pressing the paper to her knee. "There it is. Can you read it?"

He glanced at the paper and nodded bewilderedly.

"Cecy Elliott, 12 Willow Street, Green Town, Illinois," he said.

"Will you vist her someday?" asked Ann.

"Someday," he said.

"Promise?"

"What has this to do with us?" he cried savagely. "What do I want with names and papers?" He crumpled the paper into a tight ball and shoved it in his coat.

"Oh, please promise!" begged Cecy.

". . . promise . . ." said Ann.

"All right, all right, now let me be!" he shouted.

I'm tired, thought Cecy. I can't stay. I have to go home. I'm weakening. I've only the power to stay a few hours out like this in the night, traveling, traveling. But before I go . . .

". . . before I go," said Ann.

She kissed Tom on the lips.

"This is *me* kissing you," said Cecy.

Tom held her off and looked at Ann Leary and looked deep, deep inside. He said nothing, but his face began to relax slowly, very slowly, and the lines vanished away, and his mouth softened from its hardness, and he looked deep again into the moonlit face held here before him.

Then he put her off the rig and without so much as a good night was driving swiftly down the road.

Cecy let go.

Ann Leary, crying out, released from prison, it seemed, raced up the moonlit path to her house and slammed the door.

Cecy lingered for only a little while. In the eyes of a cricket she saw the spring night world. In the eyes of a frog she sat for a lonely moment by a pool. In the eyes of a night bird she looked down from a tall, moon-haunted elm and saw the light go out in two farmhouses, one here, one a mile away. She thought of herself and her family, and her strange power, and the fact that no one in the family could ever marry any one of the people in this vast world out here beyond the hills.

"Tom?" Her weakening mind flew in a night bird under the trees and over deep fields of wild mustard. "Have you still got the paper, Tom? Will you come by someday, some year, sometime, to see me? Will you know me then? Will you look in my face and remember then where it was you saw me last and know that you love me as I love you, with all my heart for all time?"

She paused in the cool night air, a million miles from towns and people, above farms and continents and rivers and hills. "Tom?" Softly.

Tom was asleep. It was deep night; his clothes were hung on chairs or folded neatly over the end of the bed. And in one silent, carefully upflung hand upon the white pillow, by his head, was a small piece of paper with writing on it. Slowly,

slowly, a fraction of an inch at a time, his fingers closed down upon and held it tightly. And he did not even stir or notice when a blackbird, faintly, wondrously, beat softly for a moment against the clear moon crystals of the windowpane, then, fluttering quietly, stopped and flew away toward the east, over the sleeping earth.

The Wilderness

"Oh, the Good Time has come at last——"

It was twilight, and Janice and Leonora packed steadily in their summer house, singing songs, eating little, and holding to each other when necessary. But they never glanced at the window where the night gathered deep and the stars came out bright and cold.

"Listen!" said Janice.

A sound like a steamboat down the river, but it was a rocket in the sky. And beyond that—banjos playing? No, only the summer-night crickets in this year 2003. Ten thousand sounds breathed through the town and the weather. Janice, head bent, listened. Long, long ago, 1849, this very street had breathed the voices of ventriloquists, preachers, fortunetellers, fools, scholars, gamblers, gathered at this selfsame Independence, Missouri. Waiting for the moist earth to bake and the great tidal grasses to come up heavy enough to hold the weight of their carts, their wagons, their indiscriminate destinies, and their dreams.

"Oh, the Good Time has come at last,
To Mars we are a-going, sir,
Five Thousand Women in the sky,
That's quite a springtime sowing, sir!"

"That's an old Wyoming song," said Leonora. "Change the words and it's fine for 2003."

Janice lifted a matchbox of food pills, calculating the totals of things carried in those high-axled, tall-bedded wagons. For each man, each woman, incredible tonnages! Hams, bacon slabs, sugar, salt, flour, dried fruits, "pilot" bread, citric acid, water, ginger, pepper—a list as big as the land! Yet here, today, pills that fit a wristwatch fed you not from Fort Laramie to Hangtown, but all across a wilderness of stars.

Janice threw wide the closet door and almost screamed. Darkness and night and all the spaces between the stars looked out at her.

Long years ago two things had happened. Her sister had locked her, shrieking, in a closet. And, at a party, playing hide-and-seek, she had run through the kitchen and into a long dark hall. But it wasn't a hall. It was an unlit stairwell, a swallowing blackness. She had run out upon empty air. She had pedaled her feet, screamed, and fallen! Fallen in midnight blackness. Into the cellar. It took a long while, a heartbeat, to fall. And she had smothered in that closet a long, long time without daylight, without friends, no one to hear her screamings. Away from everything, locked in darkness. Falling in darkness. Shrieking!

The two memories.

Now, with the closet door wide, with darkness like a velvet shroud hung before her to be stroked by a trembling hand, with the darkness like a black panther breathing there, looking at her with unlit eyes, the two memories rushed out. Space and a falling. Space and being locked away, screaming. She and Leonora working steadily, packing, being careful not to glance out the window at the frightening Milky Way and the vast emptiness. Only to have the long-familiar closet, with its private night, remind them at last of their destiny.

This was how it would be, out there, sliding toward the stars, in the night, in the great hideous black closet, screaming, but no one to hear. Falling forever among meteor clouds and godless comets. Down the elevator shaft. Down the nightmare coal chute into nothingness.

She screamed. None of it came out of her mouth. It collided upon itself in her chest and head. She screamed. She slammed the closet door! She lay against it! She felt the darkness breathe and yammer at the door and she held it tight, eyes watering. She stood there a long time, until the trembling vanished, watching Leonora work. And the hysteria, thus ignored, drained away and away, and at last was gone. A wristwatch ticked, with a clean sound of normality, in the room.

"Sixty *million* miles." She moved at last to the window as if it were a deep well. "I can't believe that men on Mars, tonight, are building towns, waiting for us."

"The only thing to believe is catching our Rocket tomorrow."

Janice raised a white gown like a ghost in the room.

"Strange, strange. To marry—on another world."

"Let's get to bed."

"No! The call comes at midnight. I couldn't sleep, thinking how to tell Will I've decided to take the Mars Rocket. Oh, Leonora, think of it, my voice traveling sixty million miles on the lightphone to him. I changed my mind so quick—I'm scared!"

"Our *last* night on Earth."

Now they really knew and accepted it; now the knowledge had found them out. They were going away, and they might never come back. They were leaving the town of Independence in the state of Missouri on the continent of North America, surrounded by one ocean which was the Atlantic and another the Pacific, none of which could be put in their traveling cases. They had shrunk from this final knowledge. Now it was facing them. And they were struck numb.

"Our children, they won't be Americans, or Earth people at all. We'll all be Martians, the rest of our lives."

"I don't want to go!" cried Janice suddenly.

The panic froze her.

"I'm afraid! The space, the darkness, the Rocket, the meteors! *Everything* gone! Why should I go out there?"

Leonora took hold of her shoulders and held her close, rocking her. "It's a new world. It's like the old days. The men first and the women after."

"Why, why should I go, tell me!"

"Because," said Leonora at last, quietly, seating her on the bed, "Will is up there."

His name was good to hear. Janice quieted.

"These men make it so hard," said Leonora. "Used to be if a woman ran two hundred miles for a man it was something. Then they made it a thousand miles. And now they put a whole universe between us. But that can't stop us, can it?"

"I'm afraid I'll be a fool on the Rocket."

"I'll be a fool with you." Leonora got up. "Now, let's walk around town, let's see everything one last time."

Janice stared out at the town. "Tomorrow night this'll all be here, but we won't. People'll wake up, eat, work, sleep, wake again, but we won't know it, and they'll never miss us."

Leonora and Janice moved around each other as if they couldn't find the door.

"Come on."

They opened the door, switched off the lights, stepped out, and shut the door behind them.

In the sky there was a great coming-in and coming-in. Vast flowering motions, huge whistlings and whirlings, snowstorms falling. Helicopters, white flakes, dropping quietly. From west and east and north and south the women were arriving, arriving. Through all the night sky you saw helicopters blizzard down. The hotels were full, private homes were making accommodations, tent cities rose in meadows and pastures like strange, ugly flowers, and the town and the country were warm with more than summer tonight. Warm with women's pink faces and the sunburnt faces of new men watching the sky. Beyond the hills rockets tried their fire, and a sound like a giant organ, all its keys pressed upon at once, shuddered every crystal window and every hidden bone. You felt it in your jaw, your toes, your fingers, a shivering.

Leonora and Janice sat in the drugstore among unfamiliar women.

"You ladies look very pretty, but you sure look sad," said the soda-fountain man.

"Two chocolate malteds." Leonora smiled for both of them, as if Janice were mute.

They gazed at the chocolate drink as if it were a rare museum painting. Malts would be scarce for many years on Mars.

Janice fussed in her purse and took out an envelope reluctantly and laid it on the marble counter.

"This is from Will to me. It came in the Rocket mail two days ago. It was this that made up my mind for me, made me decide to go. I didn't tell you. I want you to see it now. Go ahead, read the note."

Leonora shook the note out of the envelope and read it aloud:

"Dear Janice: This is our house if you decide to come to Mars. Will."

Leonora tapped the envelope again, and a color photograph dropped out, glistening, on the counter. It was a picture of a house, a dark, mossy, ancient, caramel-brown, comfortable house with red flowers and green cool ferns bordering it, and a disreputably hair ivy on the porch.

"But, Janice!"

"What?"

"This is a picture of your house, here on Earth, here on Elm Street!"

"No. Look close."

And they looked again, together, and on both sides of the comfortable dark house and behind it was scenery that was not Earth scenery. The soil was a strange color of violet, and the grass was the faintest bit red, and the sky glowed like a gray diamond, and a strange crooked tree grew to one side, looking like an old woman with crystals in her white hair.

"That's the house Will's built for me," said Janice, "on Mars. It helps to look at it. All yesterday, when I had the chance, alone, and was most afraid and panicky, I took out this picture and looked at it."

They both gazed at the dark comfortable house sixty million miles away, familiar but unfamiliar, old but new, a yellow light shining in the right front parlor window.

"That man Will," said Leonora, nodding her head, "knows just what he's doing."

They finished their drinks. Outside, a vast warm crowd of

strangers wandered by and the "snow" fell steadily in the summer sky.

They bought many silly things to take with them, bags of lemon candy, glossy women's magazines, fragile perfumes; and then they walked out into the town and rented two belted jackets that refused to recognize gravity and imitated only the moth, touched the delicate controls, and felt themselves whispered like white blossom petals over the town. "Anywhere," said Leonora, "anywhere at all."

They let the wind blow them where it would; they let the wind take them through the night of summer apple trees and the night of warm preparation, over the lovely town, over the houses of childhood and other days, over schools and avenues, over creeks and meadows and farms so familiar that each grain of wheat was a golden coin. They blew as leaves must blow below the threat of a fire-wind, with warning whispers and summer lightning crackling among the folded hills. They saw the milk-dust country roads where not so long ago they had drifted in moonlit helicopters in great whirls of sound spiraling down to touch beside cool night streams with the young men who were now gone.

They floated in an immense sigh above a town already made remote by the little space between themselves and the Earth, a town receding behind them in a black river and coming up in a tidal wave of lights and color ahead, untouchable and a dream now, already smeared in their eyes with nostalgia, with a panic of memory that began before the thing itself was gone.

Blown quietly, eddying, they gazed secretly at a hundred faces of dear friends they were leaving behind, the lamp-lit people held and framed by windows which slid by on the wind, it seemed; all of Time breathing them along. There was no tree they did not examine for old confessions of love carved and whittled there, no sidewalk they did not skim across as over fields of mica-snow. For the first time they knew their town was beautiful, and the lonely lights and the ancient bricks beautiful, and they both felt their eyes grow large with the beauty of this feast they were giving themselves. All floated upon an evening carousel, with fitful drifts of music wafting up here and there, and voices calling and murmuring from houses that were whitely haunted by television.

The two women passed like needles, sewing one tree to the next with their perfume. Their eyes were too full, and yet they kept putting away each detail, each shadow, each solitary oak and elm, each passing car upon the small snaking streets below, until not only their eyes but their heads and then their hearts were too full.

I feel like I'm dead, thought Janice, and in the graveyard on a spring night and everything alive but me and everyone moving and ready to go on with life without me. It's like I felt each spring when I was sixteen, passing the graveyard and weeping for them because they were dead and it didn't seem fair, on nights as soft as that, that I was alive. I was guilty of living. And now, here, tonight, I feel they have taken me from the graveyard and let me go above the town just once more to see what it's like to be living, to be a town and a people, before they slam the black door on me again.

Softly, softly, like two white paper lanterns on a night wind, the women moved over their lifetime and their past, and over the meadows where the tent cities glowed and the highways where supply trucks would be clustered and running until dawn. They hovered above it all for a long time.

The courthouse clock was booming eleven forty-five when they came like spider webs floating from the stars, touching on the moonlit pavement before Janice's old house. The city was asleep, and Janice's house waited for them to come in searching for *their* sleep, which was not there.

"Is this *us,* here?" asked Janice. "Janice Smith and Leonora Holmes, in the year 2003?"

"Yes."

Janice licked her lips and stood straight. "I wish it was some other year."

"1492? 1612?" Leonora sighed, and the wind in the trees sighed with her, moving away. "It's always Columbus Day or Plymouth Rock Day, and I'll be darned if I know what we women can do about it."

"Be old maids."

"Or do just what we're doing."

They opened the door of the warm night house, the sounds of the town dying slowly in their ears. As they shut the door, the phone began to ring.

"The call!" cried Janice, running.

Leonora came into the bedroom after her and already Janice had the receiver up and was saying, "Hello, hello!" And the operator in a far city was readying the immense apparatus which would tie two worlds together, and the two women waited, one sitting and pale, the other standing, but just as pale, bent toward her.

There was a long pause, full of stars and time, a waiting pause not unlike the last three years for all of them. And now the moment had arrived, and it was Janice's turn to phone through millions upon millions of miles of meteors and comets, running away from the yellow sun which might boil or burn her words or scorch the meaning from them. But her voice went like a silver needle through everything, in stitches of talking, across the big night, reverberating from the moons of Mars. And then her voice found its way to a man in a room in a city there on another world, five minutes by radio away. And her message was this:

"Hello, Will. This is Janice!"

She swallowed.

"They say I haven't much time. A minute."

She closed her eyes.

"I want to talk slow, but they say talk fast and get it all in. So I want to say—I've decided. I will come up there. I'll go on the Rocket tomorrow. I *will* come up there to you, after all. And I love you. I hope you can hear me. I love you. It's been so long. . . ."

Her voice motioned on its way to that unseen world. Now, with the message sent, the words said, she wanted to call them back, to censor, to rearrange them, to make a prettier sentence, a fairer explanation of her soul. But already the words were hung between planets and if, by some cosmic radiation, they could have been illuminated, caught fire in vaporous wonder there, her love would have lit a dozen worlds and startled the night side of Earth into a premature dawn, she thought. Now the words were not hers at all, they belonged to space, they belonged to no one until they arrived, and they were traveling at one hundred and eighty-six thousand miles a second to their destination.

What will he say to me? What will he say back in *his* minute of time? she wondered. She fussed with and twisted the watch on her wrist, and the light-phone receiver on her ear crackled and space talked to her with electrical jigs and dances and audible auroras.

"Has he answered?" whispered Leonora.

"Shhh!" said Janice, bending, as if sick.

Then his voice came through space.

"I hear him!" cried Janice.

"What does he say?"

The voice called out from Mars and took itself through the places where there was no sunrise or sunset, but always the night with a sun in the middle of the blackness. And somewhere between Mars and Earth everything of the message was lost, perhaps in a sweep of electrical gravity rushing by on the flood tides of a meteor, or interfered with by a rain of silver meteors. In any event, the small words and the unimportant words of the message were washed away. And his voice came through saying only one word:

". . . love . . ."

After that there was the huge night again and the sound of stars turning and suns whispering to themselves and the sound of her heart, like another world in space, filling her earphones.

"Did you *hear* him?" asked Leonora.

Janice could only nod.

"What did he say, what did he say?" cried Leonora.

But Janice could not tell anyone; it was much too good to tell. She sat listening to that one word again and again, as her memory played it back. She sat listening, while Leonora took the phone away from her without her knowing it and put it down upon its hook.

Then they were in bed and the lights out and the night wind blowing through the rooms a smell of the long journey in darkness and stars, and their voices talking of tomorrow, and the days after tomorrow which would not be days at all, but day-nights of timeless time; their voices faded away into sleep or wakeful thinking, and Janice lay alone in her bed.

Is this how it was over a century ago, she wondered, when the women, the night before, lay ready for sleep, or not ready, in the small towns of the East, and heard the sound of horses in the night and the creak of the Conestoga wagons ready to go, and the brooding of oxen under the trees, and the cry of children already lonely before their time? All the sounds of arrivals and departures into the deep forests and fields, the blacksmiths working in their own red hells through midnight? And the smell of bacons and hams ready for the journeying, and the heavy feel of the wagons like ships foundering with goods, with water in the wooden kegs to tilt and slop across prairies, and the chickens hysterical in their slung-beneath-the-wagon crates, and the dogs running out to the wilderness ahead and, fearful, running back with a look of empty space in their eyes? Is this, then, how it was so long ago? On the rim of the precipice, on the edge of the cliff of stars. In their time the smell of buffalo, and in our time the smell of the Rocket. Is this, then, how it was?

And she decided, as sleep assumed the dreaming for her, that yes, yes indeed, very much so, irrevocably, this was as it had always been and would forever continue to be.

The Fruit at the Bottom of the Bowl

William Acton rose to his feet. The clock on the mantel ticked midnight.

He looked at his fingers and he looked at the large room around him and he looked at the man lying on the floor. William Acton, whose fingers had stroked typewriter keys and made love and fried ham and eggs for early breakfasts, had now accomplished a murder with those same ten whorled fingers.

He had never thought of himself as a sculptor and yet, in this moment, looking down between his hands at the body upon the polished hardwood floor, he realized that by some sculptural clenching and remodeling and twisting of human clay he had taken hold of this man named Donald Huxley and changed his physiognomy, the very frame of his body.

With a twist of his fingers he had wiped away the exacting glitter of Huxley's eyes; replaced it with a blind dullness of eye cold in socket. The lips, always pink and sensuous, were gaped to show the equine teeth, the yellow incisors, the nicotined canines, the gold-inlaid molars. The nose, pink also, was now mottled, pale, discolored, as were the ears. Huxley's hands, upon the floor, were open, pleading for the first time in their lives, instead of demanding.

Yes, it was an artistic conception. On the whole, the change had done Huxley a share of good. Death made him a handsomer man to deal with. You could talk to him now and he'd have to listen.

William Acton looked at his own fingers.

It was done. He could not change it back. Had anyone heard? He listened. Outside, the normal late sounds of street traffic continued. There was no banging of the house door, no shoulder wrecking the portal into kindling, no voices demanding entrance. The murder, the sculpturing of clay from warmth to coldness was done, and nobody knew.

Now what? The lock ticked midnight. His every impulse exploded him in a hysteria toward the door. Rush, get away, run, never come back, board a train, hail a taxi, get, go, run, walk, saunter, but get the blazes *out* of here!

His hands hovered before his eyes, floating, turning.

He twisted them in slow deliberation; they felt airy and feather-light. Why was he staring at them this way? he inquired of himself. Was there something in them of immense interest that he should pause now, after a successful throttling, and examine them whorl by whorl?

They were ordinary hands. Not thick, not thin, not long, not short, not hairy, not naked, not manicured and yet not dirty, not soft and yet not callused, not wrinkled and yet not smooth; not murdering hands at all—and yet not innocent. He seemed to find them miracles to look upon.

It was not the hands as hands he was interested in, nor the fingers as fingers. In the numb timelessness after an accomplished violence he found interest only in the *tips* of his fingers.

The clock ticked upon the mantel.

He knelt by Huxley's body, took a handkerchief from Huxley's pocket, and began methodically to swab Huxley's throat with it. He brushed and massaged the throat and wiped the face and the back of the neck with fierce energy. Then he stood up.

He looked at the throat. He looked at the polished floor. He bent slowly and gave the floor a few dabs with the handkerchief, then he scowled and swabbed the floor; first, near the head of the corpse; secondly, near the arms. Then he polished the floor all around the body. He polished the floor one yard from the body on all sides. Then he polished the floor two yards from the body on all sides. The he polished the floor three yards from the body in all directions. Then he——

He stopped.

* * *

There was a moment when he saw the entire house, the mirrored halls, the carved doors, the splendid furniture; and, as clearly as if it were being repeated word for word, he heard Huxley talking and himself just the way they had talked only an hour ago.

Finger on Huxley's doorbell. Huxley's door opening.

"Oh!" Huxley shocked. "It's *you*, Acton."

"Where's my wife, Huxley?"

"Do you think I'd tell you, really? Don't stand out there, you idiot. If you want to talk business, come in. Through that door. There. Into the library."

Acton had *touched* the library door.

"Drink?"

"I need one. I can't believe Lily is gone, that she—"

"There's a bottle of burgundy, Acton. Mind fetching it from that cabinet?"

Yes, fetch it. *Handle* it. *Touch* it. He did.

"Some interesting first editions there, Acton. Feel this binding. *Feel* of it."

"I didn't come to see books, I—"

He had *touched* the books and the library table and *touched* the burgundy bottle and burgundy glasses.

Now, squatting on the floor beside Huxley's cold body with the polishing handkerchief in his fingers, motionless, he stared at the house, the walls, the furniture about him, his eyes widening, his mouth dropping, stunned by what he realized and what he saw. He shut his eyes, dropped his head, crushed the handkerchief between his hands, wadding it, biting his lips with his teeth, pulling in on himself.

The fingerprints were everywhere, *everywhere!*

"Mind getting the burgundy, Acton, eh? The burgundy bottle, eh? With your fingers, eh? I'm terribly tired. You understand?"

A pair of gloves.

Before he did one more thing, before he polished another area, he must have a pair of gloves, or he might unintentionally, after cleaning a surface, redistribute his identity.

He put his hands in his pockets. He walked through the house to the hall umbrella stand, the hatrack. Huxley's overcoat. He pulled out the overcoat pockets.

No gloves.

His hands in his pockets again, he walked upstairs, moving with a controlled swiftness, allowing himself nothing frantic, nothing wild. He had made the initial error of not wearing gloves (but, after all, he hadn't *planned* a murder, and his subconscious, which may have known of the crime before its commitment, had not even hinted he might need gloves before the night was finished), so now he had to sweat for his sin of omission. Somewhere in the house there must be at least one pair of gloves. He would have to hurry; there was every chance that someone might visit Huxley, even at this hour. Rich friends drinking themselves in and out the door, laughing, shouting, coming and going without so much as hello-good-by. He would have until six in the morning, at the outside, when Huxley's friends were to pick Huxley up for the trip to the airport and Mexico City. . . .

Acton hurried about upstairs opening drawers, using the handkerchief as blotter. He untidied seventy or eighty drawers in six rooms, left them with their tongues, so to speak, hanging out, ran on to new ones. He felt naked, unable to do anything until he found gloves. He might scour the entire house with the handkerchief, buffing every possible surface where fingerprints might lie, then accidentally bump a wall here or there, thus sealing his own fate with one microscopic, whorling symbol! It would be putting his stamp of approval on the murder, that's what it would be! Like those waxen seals in the old days when they rattled papyrus, flourished ink, dusted all with sand to dry the ink, and pressed their signet rings in hot crimson tallow at the bottom. So it would be if he left one, mind you, *one* fingerprint upon the scene! His approval of the murder did not extend as far as affixing said seal.

More drawers! Be quiet, be curious, be careful, he told himself.

At the bottom of the eighty-fifth drawer he found gloves.

"Oh, my Lord, my Lord!" He slumped against the bureau, sighing. He tried the gloves on, held them up, proudly flexed them, buttoned them. They were soft, gray, thick, impregnable.

He could do all sorts of tricks with hands now and leave no trace. He thumbed his nose in the bedroom mirror, sucking his teeth.

"NO!" cried Huxley.

What a wicked plan it had been.

Huxley had fallen to the floor, *purposely!* Oh, what a wickedly clever man! Down onto the hardwood floor had dropped Huxley, with Acton after him. They had rolled and tussled and clawed at the floor, printing and printing it with their frantic fingertips! Huxley had slipped away a few feet, Acton crawling after to lay hands on his neck and squeeze until the life came out like paste from a tube!

Gloved, William Acton returned to the room and knelt down upon the floor and laboriously began the task of swabbing every wildly infested inch of it. Inch by inch, inch by inch, he polished and polished until he could almost see his intent, sweating face in it. Then he came to a table and polished the leg of it, on up its solid body and along the knobs and over the top. He came to a bowl of wax fruit, burnished the filigree silver, plucked out the wax fruit and wiped them clean, leaving the fruit at the bottom unpolished.

"I'm *sure* I didn't touch *them*," he said.

After rubbing the table he came to a picture frame hung over it.

"I'm certain I didn't touch *that*," he said.

He stood looking at it.

He glanced at all the doors in the room. Which doors had he used tonight? He couldn't remember. Polish all of them, then. He started on the doorknobs, shined them all up, and then he curried the doors from head to foot, taking no chances. Then he went to all the furniture in the room and wiped the chair arms.

"That chair you're sitting in, Acton, is an old Louis XIV piece. *Feel* that material," said Huxley.

"I didn't come to talk furniture, Huxley! I came about Lily."

"Oh, come off it, you're not that serious about her. She doesn't love you, you know. She's told me she'll go with me to Mexico City tomorrow."

"You and your money and your damned furniture!"

"It's nice furniture, Acton; be a good guest and feel of it."

Fingerprints can be found on fabric.

"Huxley!" William Acton stared at the body. "Did you guess I was going to kill you? Did your subconscious suspect, just as my subconscious suspected? And did your subconscious tell you to make me run about the house handling, touching, *fondling* books, dishes, doors, chairs? Were you *that* clever and *that* mean?"

He washed the chairs dryly with the clenched handkerchief. Then he remembered the body—he hadn't dry-washed *it.* He went to it and turned it now this way, now that, and burnished every surface of it. He even shined the shoes, charging nothing.

While shining the shoes his face took on a little tremor of worry, and after a moment he got up and walked over to that table.

He took out and polished the wax fruit at the bottom of the bowl.

"Better," he whispered, and went back to the body.

But as he crouched over the body his eyelids twitched and his jaw moved from side to side and he debated, then he got up and walked once more to the table.

He polished the picture frame.

While polishing the picture frame he discovered—

The wall.

"That," he said, "is *silly.*"

"Oh!" cried Huxley, fending him off. He gave Acton a shove as they struggled. Acton fell, got up, *touching* the wall, and ran toward Huxley again. He strangled Huxley. Huxley died.

Acton turned steadfastly from the wall, with equilibrium and decision. The harsh words and the action faded in his mind; he hid them away. He glanced at the four walls.

"Ridiculous!" he said.

From the corners of his eyes he saw something on one wall.

"I refuse to pay attention," he said to distract himself. "The next room, now! I'll be methodical. Let's see—altogether we were in the hall, the library, *this* room, and the dining room and the kitchen."

There was a spot on the wall behind him.

Well, *wasn't* there?

He turned angrily. "All right, all right, just to be *sure*," and he went over and couldn't find any spot. Oh, a *little* one, yes, right—*there.* He dabbed it. It wasn't a fingerprint anyhow. He finished with it, and his gloved hand leaned against the wall and he looked at the wall and the way it went over to his right and over to his left and how it went down to his feet and up over his head and he said softly, "No." He looked up and down and over and across and he said quietly, "That would be too much." How many square feet? "I don't give a good damn," he said. But unknown to his eyes, his gloved fingers moved in a little rubbing rhythm on the wall.

He peered at his hand and the wallpaper. He looked over his shoulder at the other room. "I must go in there and polish the essentials," he told himself, but his hand remained, as if to hold the wall, or himself, up. His face hardened.

Without a word he began to scrub the wall, up and down, back and forth, up and down, as high as he could stretch and as low as he could bend.

"Ridiculous, oh my Lord, ridiculous!"

But you must be certain, his thought said to him.

"Yes, one *must* be certain," he replied.

He got one wall finished, and then . . .

He came to another wall.

"What time *is* it?"

He looked at the mantel clock. An hour gone. It was five after one.

The doorbell rang.

Acton froze, staring at the door, the clock, the door, the clock.

Someone rapped loudly.

A long moment passed. Acton did not breathe. Without new air in his body he began to fail away, to sway; his head roared a silence of cold waves thundering onto heavy rocks.

"Hey, in there!" cried a drunken voice. "I know you're in there, Huxley! Open up, dammit! This is Billy-boy, drunk as an owl, Huxley, old pal, drunker than two owls."

"Go away," whispered Acton soundlessly, crushed.

"Huxley, you're in there, I hear you *breathing!*" cried the drunken voice.

"Yes, I'm in here," whispered Acton, feeling long and sprawled and clumsy on the floor, clumsy and cold and silent. "Yes."

"Hell!" said the voice, fading away into mist. The footsteps shuffled off. "Hell . . ."

Acton stood a long time feeling the red heart beat inside his shut eyes, within his head. When at last he opened his eyes he looked at the new fresh wall straight ahead of him and finally got courage to speak. "Silly," he said. "This wall's flawless. I won't touch it. Got to hurry. Got to hurry. Time, time. Only a few hours before those damn-fool friends blunder in!" He turned away.

From the corners of his eyes he saw the little webs. When his back was turned the little spiders came out of the woodwork and delicately spun their fragile little half-invisible webs. Not upon the wall at his left, which was already washed fresh, but upon the three walls as yet untouched. Each time he stared directly at them the spiders dropped back into the woodwork, only to spindle out as he retreated. "Those walls are all right," he insisted in a half shout. "I won't *touch* them!"

He went to a writing desk at which Huxley had been seated earlier. He opened a drawer and took out what he was looking for. A little magnifying glass Huxley sometimes used for reading. He took the magnifer and approached the wall uneasily.

Fingerprints.

"But those aren't mine!" He laughed unsteadily. "I *didn't* put them there! I'm *sure* I didn't! A servant, a butler, or a maid perhaps!"

The wall was full of them.

"Look at this one here," he said. "Long and tapered, a woman's, I'd bet money on it."

"Would you?"

"I would!"

"Are you certain?'

"Yes!"

"Positive?"

"Well—yes."

"Absolutely?"

"Yes, damn it, yes!"

"Wipe it out, anyway, why don't you?"

"There, by God!"

"Out damned spot, eh, Acton?"

"And this one, over here," scoffed Acton. "That's the print of a fat man."

"Are you sure?"

"Don't start *that* again!" he snapped, and rubbed it out. He pulled off a glove and held his hand up, trembling, in the glary light.

"Look at it, you idiot! See how the whorls go? See?"

"That proves nothing!"

"Oh, all right!" Raging, he swept the wall up and down, back and forth, with gloved hands, sweating, grunting, swearing, bending, rising, and getting redder of face.

He took off his coat, put it on a chair.

"Two o'clock," he said, finishing the wall, glaring at the clock.

He walked over to the bowl and took out the wax fruit and polished the ones at the bottom and put them back, and polished the picture frame.

He gazed up at the chandelier.

His fingers twitched at his sides.

His mouth slipped open and the tongue moved along his lips and he looked at the chandelier and looked away and looked back at the chandelier and looked at Huxley's body and then at the crystal chandelier with its long pearls of rainbow glass.

He got a chair and brought it over under the chandelier and put one foot up on it and took it down and threw the chair, violently, laughing, into a corner. Then he ran out of the room, leaving one wall as yet unwashed.

In the dining room he came to a table.

"I want to show you my Gregorian cutlery, Acton," Huxley had said. Oh, that casual, that *hypnotic* voice!

"I haven't time," Acton said. "I've got to see Lily——"

"Nonsense, look at this silver, this exquisite craftsmanship."

Acton paused over the table where the boxes of cutlery were

laid out, hearing once more Huxley's voice, remembering all the touchings and gesturings.

Now Acton wiped the forks and spoons and took down all the plaques and special ceramic dishes from the wall itself. . . .

"Here's a lovely bit of ceramics by Gertrude and Otto Natzler, Acton. Are you familiar with their work?"

"It *is* lovely."

"Pick it up. Turn it over. See the fine thinness of the bowl, hand-thrown on a turntable, thin as eggshell, incredible. And the amazing volcanic glaze. Handle it, *go* ahead. *I* don't mind."

HANDLE IT. GO AHEAD. PICK IT UP!

Acton sobbed unevenly. He hurled the pottery against the wall. It shattered and spread, flaking wildly, upon the floor.

An instant later he was on his knees. Every piece, every shard of it, must be found. Fool, fool, fool! he cried to himself, shaking his head and shutting and opening his eyes and bending under the table. Find every piece, idiot, not one fragment of it must be left behind. Fool, fool! He gathered them. Are they all here? He looked at them on the table before him. He looked under the table again and under the chairs and the service bureaus, and found one more piece by match light and started to polish each little fragment as if it were a precious stone. He laid them all out neatly upon the shining polished table.

"A lovely bit of ceramics, Acton. Go ahead—*handle* it."

He took out the linen and wiped it and wiped the chairs and tables and doorknobs and windowpanes and ledges and drapes and wiped the floor and found the kitchen, panting, breathing violently, and took off his vest and adjusted his gloves and wiped the glittering chromium. . . . "I want to show you my house, Acton," said Huxley. "Come along. . . ." And he wiped all the utensils and the silver faucets and the mixing bowls, for now he had forgotten what he had touched and what he had not. Huxley and he had lingered here, in the kitchen, Huxley prideful of its array, covering his nervousness at the presence of a potential killer, perhaps wanting to be near the knives if they were needed. They had idled, touched this, that, something else—there was no remembering what or how much or how many—and he finished the kitchen and came through the hall into the room where Huxley lay.

He cried out.

He had forgotten to wash the fourth wall of the room! And while he was gone the little spiders had popped from the fourth unwashed wall and swarmed over the already clean walls, dirtying them again! On the ceilings, from the chandelier, in the corners, on the floor, a million little whorled webs hung billowing at his scream! Tiny, tiny little webs, no bigger than, ironically, your—finger!

As he watched, the webs were woven over the picture frame, the fruit bowl, the body, the floor. Prints wielded the paper knife, pulled out drawers, touched the table top, touched, touched, touched everything everywhere.

He polished the floor wildly, wildly. He rolled the body over and cried on it while he washed it, and got up and walked over and polished the fruit at the bottom of the bowl. Then he put a chair under the chandelier and got up and polished each little hanging fire of it, shaking it like a crystal tambourine until it tilted bellwise in the air. Then he leaped off the chair and gripped the doorknobs and got up on other chairs and swabbed the walls higher and higher and ran to the kitchen and got a broom and wiped the webs down from the ceiling and polished the bottom fruit of the bowl and washed the body and doorknobs and silverware and found the hall banister and followed the banister upstairs.

Three o'clock! Everywhere, with a fierce, mechanical intensity, clocks ticked! There were twelve rooms downstairs and eight above. He figured the yards and yards of space and time needed. One hundred chairs, six sofas, twenty-seven tables, six radios. And under and on top and behind. He yanked furniture out away from walls and, sobbing, wiped them clean of years-old dust, and staggered and followed the banister up, up the stairs, handling, erasing, rubbing, polishing, because if he left one little print it would reproduce and make a million more!—and the job would have to be done all over again and now it was four o'clock!—and his arms ached and his eyes were swollen and staring and he moved sluggishly about, on strange legs, his head down, his arms moving, swabbing and rubbing, bedroom by bedroom, closet by closet. . . .

They found him at six-thirty that morning.

In the attic.

The entire house was polished to a brilliance. Vases shone like glass stars. Chairs were burnished. Bronzes, brasses, and coppers were all aglint. Floors sparkled. Banisters gleamed.

Everything glittered. Everything shone, everything was bright!

They found him in the attic, polishing the old trunks and the old frames and the old chairs and the old carriages and toys and music boxes and vases and cutlery and rocking horses and dusty Civil War coins. He was half through the attic when the police officer walked up behind him with a gun.

"Done!"

On the way out of the house Acton polished the front door-knob with his handkerchief and slammed it in triumph!

The Flying Machine

In the year A.D. 400, the Emperor Yuan held his throne by the Great Wall of China, and the land was green with rain, readying itself toward the harvest, at peace, the people in his dominion neither too happy nor too sad.

Early on the morning of the first day of the first week of the second month of the new year, the Emperor Yuan was sipping tea and fanning himself against a warm breeze when a servant ran across the scarlet and blue garden tiles, calling, "Oh, Emperor, Emperor, a miracle!"

"Yes," said the Emperor, "the air *is* sweet this morning."

"No, no, a miracle!" said the servant, bowing quickly.

"And this tea is good in my mouth, surely that is a miracle."

"No, no, Your Excellency."

"Let me guess then—the sun has risen and a new day is upon us. Or the sea is blue. *That* now is the finest of all miracles."

"Excellency, a man is flying!"

"What?" The Emperor stopped his fan.

"I saw him in the air, a man flying with wings. I heard a voice call out of the sky, and when I looked up, there he was, a dragon in the heavens with a man in its mouth, a dragon of paper and bamboo, colored like the sun and the grass."

"It is early," said the Emperor, "and you have just wakened from a dream."

"It is early, but I have seen what I have seen! Come, and you will see it too."

"Sit down with me here," said the Emperor. "Drink some tea. It must be a strange thing, if it is true, to see a man fly. You must have time to think of it, even as I must have time to prepare myself for the sight."

They drank tea.

"Please," said the servant at last, "or he will be gone."

The Emperor rose thoughtfully. "Now you may show me what you have seen."

They walked into a garden across a meadow of grass, over a small bridge, through a grove of trees, and up a tiny hill.

"There!" said the servant.

The Emperor looked into the sky.

And in the sky, laughing so high that you could hardly hear him laugh, was a man; and the man was clothed in bright papers and reeds to make wings and a beautiful yellow tail, and he was soaring all about like the largest bird in a universe of birds, like a new dragon in a land of ancient dragons.

The man called down to them from high in the cool winds of morning. "I fly, I fly!"

The servant waved to him. "Yes, *yes!*"

The Emperor Yuan did not move. Instead he looked at the Great Wall of China now taking shape out of the farthest mist in the green hills, that splendid snake of stones which writhed with majesty across the entire land. That wonderful wall which had protected them for a timeless time from enemy hordes and preserved peace for years without number. He saw the town, nestled to itself by a river and a road and a hill, beginning to waken.

"Tell me," he said to his servant, "has anyone else seen this flying man?"

"I am the only one, Excellency," said the servant, smiling at the sky, waving.

The Emperor watched the heavens another minute and then said, "Call him down to me."

"Ho, come down, come down! The Emperor wishes to see you!" called the servant, hands cupped to his shouting mouth.

The Emperor glanced in all directions while the flying man soared down the morning wind. He saw a farmer, early in his fields, watching the sky, and he noted where the farmer stood.

The flying man alit with a rustle of paper and a creak of bamboo reeds. He came proudly to the Emperor, clumsy in his rig, at last bowing before the old man.

"What have you done?" demanded the Emperor.

"I have flown in the sky, Your Excellency," replied the man.

"What *have* you done?" said the Emperor again.

"I have just told you!" cried the flier.

"You have told me nothing at all." The Emperor reached out a thin hand to touch the pretty paper and the bird-like keel of the apparatus. It smelled cool, of the wind.

"Is it not beautiful, Excellency?"

"Yes, too beautiful."

"It is the only one in the world!" smiled the man. "And I am the inventor."

"The *only* one in the world?"

"I swear it!"

"Who else knows of this?"

"No one. Not even my wife, who would think me mad with the sun. She thought I was making a kite. I rose in the night and walked to the cliffs far away. And when the morning breezes blew and the sun rose, I gathered my courage, Excellency, and leaped from the cliff. I flew! But my wife does not know of it."

"Well for her, then," said the Emperor. "Come along."

They walked back to the great house. The sun was full in the sky now, and the smell of the grass was refreshing. The Emperor, the servant, and the flier paused within the huge garden.

The Emperor clapped his hands. "Ho, guards!"

The guards came running.

"Hold this man."

The guards seized the flier.

"Call the executioner," said the Emperor.

"What's this!" cried the flier, bewildered. "What have I done?" He began to weep, so that the beautiful paper apparatus rustled.

"Here is the man who has made a certain machine," said the Emperor, "and yet asks us what he has created. He does not know himself. It is only necessary that he created, without knowing why he has done so, or what this thing will do.''

The executioner came running with a sharp silver ax. He stood with his naked, large-muscled arms ready, his face covered with a serene white mask.

''One moment,'' said the Emperor. He turned to a nearby table upon which sat a machine that he himself had created. The Emperor took a tiny golden key from his own neck. He fitted his key to the tiny, delicate machine and wound it up. Then he set the machine going.

The machine was a garden of metal and jewels. Set in motion, the birds sang in tiny metal trees, wolves walked through miniature forests, and tiny people ran in and out of sun and shadow, fanning themselves with miniature fans, listening to tiny emerald birds, and standing by impossibly small but tinkling fountains.

''Is *it* not beautiful?'' said the Emperor. ''If you asked me what I have done here, I could answer you well. I have made birds sing, I have made forests murmur, I have set people to walking in this woodland, enjoying the leaves and shadows and songs. That is what I have done.''

''But, oh, Emperor!'' pleaded the flier, on his knees, the tears pouring down his face. ''I have done a similar thing! I have found beauty. I have flown on the morning wind. I have looked down on all the sleeping houses and gardens. I have smelled the sea and even *seen* it, beyond the hills, from my high place. And I have soared like a bird; oh, I cannot say how beautiful it is up there, in the sky, with the wind about me, the wind blowing me here like a feather, here like a fan, the way the sky smells in the morning! And how free one feels! *That* is beautiful, Emperor, that is beautiful too!''

''Yes,'' said the Emperor sadly, ''I know it must be true. For I felt my heart move with you in the air and I wondered: What is it like? How does it feel? How do the distant pools look from so high? And how my houses and servants? Like ants? And how the distant towns not yet awake?''

''Then spare me!''

''But there are times,'' said the Emperor, more sadly still, ''when one must lose a little beauty if one is to keep what little beauty one already has. I do not fear you, yourself, but I fear another man."

"What man?"

"Some other man who, seeing you, will build a thing of bright papers and bamboo like this. But the other man will have an evil face and an evil heart, and the beauty will be gone. It is this man I fear."

"Why? Why?"

"Who is to say that someday just such a man, in just such an apparatus of paper and reed, might not fly in the sky and drop huge stones upon the Great Wall of China?" said the Emperor.

No one moved or said a word.

"Off with his head," said the Emperor.

The executioner whirled his silver ax.

"Burn the kite and the inventor's body and bury their ashes together," said the Emperor.

The servants retreated to obey.

The Emperor turned to his hand-servant, who had seen the man flying. "Hold your tongue. It was all a dream, a most sorrowful and beautiful dream. And that farmer in the distant field who also saw, tell him it would pay him to consider it only a vision. If ever the word passes around, you and the farmer die within the hour."

"You are merciful, Emperor."

"No, not merciful," said the old man. Beyond the garden wall he saw the guards burning the beautiful machine of paper and reeds that smelled of the morning wind. He saw the dark smoke climb into the sky. "No, only very much bewildered and afraid." he saw the guards digging a tiny pit wherein to bury the ashes. "What is the life of one man against those of a million others? I must take solace from that thought."

He took the key from its chain about his neck and once more wound up the beautiful miniature garden. He stood looking out across the land at the Great Wall, the peaceful town, the green fields, the rivers and streams. He sighed. The tiny garden whirred its hidden and delicate machinery and set itself in motion; tiny people walked in forests, tiny faces loped through sun-speckled glades in beautiful shining pelts, and among the tiny trees flew little bits of high song and bright blue and yellow color, flying, flying, flying in that small sky.

"Oh," said the Emperor, closing his eyes, "look at the birds, look at the birds!"

The Murderer

Music moved with him in the white halls. He passed an office door: "The Merry Widow Waltz." Another door: "Afternoon of a Faun." A third: "Kiss Me Again." He turned into a cross corridor: "The Sword Dance" buried him in cymbals, drums, pots, pans, knives, forks, thunder, and tin lightning. All washed away as he hurried through an anteroom where a secretary sat nicely stunned by Beethoven's Fifth. He moved himself before her eyes like a hand; she didn't see him.

His wrist radio buzzed.

"Yes?"

"This is Lee, Dad. Don't forget about my allowance."

"Yes, son, yes. I'm busy."

"Just didn't want you to forget, Dad," said the wrist radio. Tchaikovsky's "Romeo and Juliet" swarmed about the voice and flushed into the long halls.

The psychiatrist moved in the beehive of offices, in the cross-pollination of themes, Stravinsky mating with Bach, Haydn unsuccessfully repulsing Rachmaninoff, Schubert slain by Duke Ellington. He nodded to the humming secretaries and the whistling doctors fresh to their morning work. At his office he checked a few papers with his stenographer, who sang under her breath, then phoned the police captain upstairs. A few minutes later a red light blinked, a voice said from the ceiling:

"Prisoner delivered to Interview Chamber Nine."

He unlocked the chamber door, stepped in, heard the door lock behind him.

"Go away," said the prisoner, smiling.

The psychiatrist was shocked by that smile. A very sunny, pleasant warm thing, a thing that shed bright light upon the room. Dawn among the dark hills. High noon at midnight, that smile. The blue eyes sparkled serenely above that display of self-assured dentistry.

"I'm here to help you," said the psychiatrist, frowning. Something was wrong with the room. He had hesitated the moment he entered. He glanced around. The prisoner laughed. "If you're wondering why it's so quiet in here, I just kicked the radio to death."

Violent, thought the doctor.

The prisoner read this thought, smiled, put out a gentle hand. "No, only to machines that yak-yak-yak."

Bits of the wall radio's tubes and wires lay on the gray carpeting. Ignoring these, feeling that smile upon him like a heat lamp, the psychiatrist sat across from his patient in the unusual silence which was like the gathering of a storm.

"You're Mr. Albert Brock, who calls himself The Murderer?"

Brock nodded pleasantly. "Before we start . . ." He moved quietly and quickly to detach the wrist radio from the doctor's arm. He tucked it in his teeth like a walnut, gritted and heard it crack, handed it back to the appalled psychiatrist as if he had done them both a favor. "That's better."

The psychiatrist stared at the ruined machine. "You're running up quite a damage bill."

"I don't care," smiled the patient. "As the old song goes: 'Don't Care What Happens to Me!' " He hummed it.

The psychiatrist said: "Shall we start?"

"Fine. The first victim, or one of the first, was my telephone. Murder most foul. I shoved it in the kitchen Insinkerator! Stopped the disposal unit in mid-swallow. Poor thing strangled to death. After that I shot the television set!"

The psychiatrist said, "Mmm."

"Fired six shots right through the cathode. Made a beautiful tinkling crash, like a dropped chandelier."

"Nice imagery."

"Thanks, I always dreamt of being a writer."

"Suppose you tell me when you first began to hate the telephone."

"It frightened me as a child. Uncle of mine called it the Ghost Machine. Voices without bodies. Scared the living hell out of me. Later in life I was never comfortable. Seemed to me a phone was an impersonal instrument. If it *felt* like it, it let your personality go through its wires. If it didn't *want* to, it just drained your personality away until what slipped through at the other end was some cold fish of a voice all steel, copper, plastic, no warmth, no reality. It's easy to say the wrong thing on telephones; the telephone changes your meaning on you. First thing you know, you've made an enemy. Then, of course, the telephone's such a *convenient* thing; it just sits there and *demands* you call someone who doesn't want to be called. Friends were always calling, calling, calling me. Hell, I hadn't any time of my own. When it wasn't the telephone it was the television, the radio, the phonograph. When it wasn't the television or radio or the phonograph it was motion pictures at the corner theater, motion pictures projected, with commercials on low-lying cumulus clouds. It doesn't rain anymore, it rains soapsuds. When it wasn't High-Fly Cloud advertisements, it was music by Mozzek in every restaurant; music and commercials on the busses I rode to work. When it wasn't music, it was interoffice communications, and my horror chamber of a radio wristwatch on which my friends and my wife phoned every five minutes. What is there about such 'conveniences' that makes them so *temptingly* convenient? The average man thinks, Here I am, time on my hands, and there on my wrist is a wrist telephone, so why not just buzz old Joe up, eh? 'Hello, hello!' I love my friends, my wife, humanity, very much, but when one minute my wife calls to say, 'Where are you *now* dear?' and a friend calls and says, 'Got the best off-color joke to tell you. Seems there was a guy——' And a stranger calls and cries out, 'This is the Find-Fax Poll. What gum are you chewing at this very *instant!*' Well!"

"How did you feel during the week?"

"The fuse lit. On the edge of the cliff. That same afternoon I did what I did at the office."

"Which was?"

"I poured a paper cup of water into the intercommunications system."

The psychiatrist wrote on his pad.

"And the system shorted?"

"Beautifully! The Fourth of July on wheels! My God, stenographers ran around looking *lost!* What an uproar!"

"Felt better temporarily, eh?"

"Fine! Then I got the idea at noon of stomping my wrist radio on the sidewalk. A shrill voice was just yelling out of it at me, 'This is People's Poll Number Nine. What did you eat for lunch?' when I kicked the Jesus out of the wrist radio!"

"Felt even *better*, eh?"

"It *grew* on me!" Brock rubbed his hands together. "Why didn't I start a solitary revolution, deliver man from certain 'conveniences'? 'Convenient for whom?' I cried. Convenient for friends: 'Hey, Al, thought I'd call you from the locker room out here at Green Hills. Just made a sock-dolager hole in one! A hole in one, Al! A *beautiful* day. Having a shot of whiskey now. Thought you'd want to know, Al!' Convenient for my office, so when I'm in the field with my radio car there's no moment when I'm not in touch. In *touch! There's* a slimy phrase. Touch, hell. *Gripped!* Pawed, rather. Mauled and massaged and pounded by FM voices. You can't leave your car without checking in: 'Have stopped to visit gas-station men's room.' 'Okay, Brock, step on it!' 'Brock, what *took* you so long?' 'Sorry, sir.' 'Watch it next time, Brock.' *'Yes, sir!'* So, do you know what I did, Doctor? I bought a quart of French chocolate ice cream and spooned it into the car radio transmitter."

"Was there any *special* reason for selecting French chocolate ice cream to spoon into the broadcasting unit?"

Brock thought about it and smiled. "It's my favorite flavor."

"Oh," said the doctor.

"I figured, hell, what's good enough for me is good enough for the radio transmitter."

"What made you think of spooning *ice cream* into the radio?"

"It was a hot day."

The doctor paused.

"And what happened next?"

"Silence happened next. God, it was *beautiful.* That car radio cackling all day, Brock go here, Brock go there, Brock check in, Brock check out, okay Brock, hour lunch, Brock, lunch over, Brock, Brock, Brock. Well, that silence was like putting ice cream in my ears."

"You seem to like ice cream a lot."

"I just rode around feeling of the silence. It's a big bolt of the nicest, softest flannel ever made. Silence. A whole hour of it. I just sat in my car; smiling, feeling of that flannel with my ears. I felt *drunk* with Freedom!"

"Go on."

"Then I got the idea of the portable diathermy machine. I rented one, took it on the bus going home that night. There sat all the tired commuters with their wrist radios, talking to their wives, saying, 'Now I'm at Forty-third, now I'm at Forty-fourth, here I am at Forty-ninth, now turning at Sixty-first.' One husband cursing, 'Well, get *out* of that bar, damn it, and get home and get dinner started, I'm at Seventieth!' And the transit-system radio playing 'Tales from the Vienna Woods,' a canary singing words about a first-rate wheat cereal. Then—I switched on my diathermy! Static! Interference! All wives cut off from husbands grousing about a hard day at the office. All husbands cut off from wives who had just seen their children break a window! The 'Vienna Woods' chopped down, the canary mangled! *Silence!* A terrible, unexpected silence. The bus inhabitants faced with having to converse with each other. Panic! Sheer, animal panic!"

"The police seized you?"

"The bus *had* to stop. After all, the music *was* being scrambled, husbands and wives *were* out of touch with reality. Pandemonium, riot, and chaos. Squirrels chattering in cages! A trouble unit arrived, triangulated on me instantly, had me reprimanded, fined, and home, minus my diathermy machine, in jig time."

"Mr. Brock, may I suggest that so far your whole pattern here is not very—practical? If you didn't like transit radios or office radios or car business radios, why didn't you join a fraternity of radio haters, start petitions, get legal and constitutional rulings? After all, this *is* a democracy."

"And I," said Brock, "am that thing called a minority. I *did* join fraternities, picket, pass petitions, take it to court. Year after year I protested. Everyone laughed. Everyone else *loved* bus radios and commercials. *I* was out of step."

"Then you should have taken it like a good soldier, don't you think? The majority rules."

"But they went too far. If a little music and 'keeping in touch' was charming, they figured a lot would be ten times as charming. I went *wild!* I got home to find my wife hysterical. *Why?* Because she had been completely out of touch with me for half a day. Remember, I did a dance on my wrist radio? Well, that night I laid plans to murder my house.

"Are you *sure* that's how you want me to write it down?"

"That's semantically accurate. Kill it dead. It's one of those talking, singing, humming, weather-reporting, poetry-reading, novel-reciting, jingle-jangling, rockaby-crooning-when-you-go-to-bed houses. A house that screams opera to you in the shower and teaches you Spanish in your sleep. One of those blathering caves where all kinds of electronic Oracles make you feel a trifle larger than a thimble, with stoves that say, 'I'm apricot pie, and I'm *done,*' or 'I'm prime roast beef, so *baste* me!' and other nursery gibberish like that. With beds that rock you to sleep and *shake* you awake. A house that *barely* tolerates humans, I tell you. A front door that barks: 'You've mud on your feet, sir!' And an electronic vacuum hound that snuffles around after you from room to room, inhaling every fingernail or ash you drop. Jesus God, *I* say, Jesus God!"

"Quietly," suggested the psychiatrist.

"Remember that Gilbert and Sullivan song—'I've Got It on My List, It Never Will Be Missed'? All night I listed grievances. Next morning early I bought a pistol. I *purposely* muddied my feet. I stood at our front door. The front door shrilled, 'Dirty feet, muddy feet! Wipe your feet! Please be *neat!*' I shot the damn thing in its keyhole. I ran to the kitchen, where the stove was just whining, 'Turn me *over!*' In the middle of a mechanical omelet I did the stove to death. Oh, how it sizzled and screamed, 'I'm *shorted!*' Then the telephone rang like a spoiled brat. I shoved it down the Insinkerator. I must state here and now I have *nothing* whatever against the Insinkerator; it was an innocent bystander. I feel sorry for it now, a practical device indeed, which never said a word, purred like a sleepy lion most of the time, and digested our leftovers. I'll have it restored. Then I went in and shot the televisor, that insidious beast, that Medusa, which freezes a billion people to stone every night, staring fixedly, that Siren which called and sang and promised so much and gave, after all, so little, but myself always going back, going back, hoping and waiting until—bang! Like a headless turkey, gobbling, my wife whooped out the front door. The police came. Here I *am!*''

He sat back happily and lit a cigarette.

''And did you realize, in committing these crimes, that the wrist radio, the broadcasting transmitter, the phone, the bus radio, the office intercoms, all were rented or were someone else's property?''

''I would do it all over again, so help me God.''

The psychiatrist sat there in the sunshine of that beatific smile.

''You don't want any further help from the Office of Mental Health? You're ready to take the consequences?''

''This is only the beginning,'' said Mr. Brock. ''I'm the vanguard of the small public which is tired of noise and being taken advantage of and pushed around and yelled at, every moment music, every moment in touch with some voice somewhere, do this, do that, quick, quick, now here, now there. You'll see. The revolt begins. My name will go down in history!''

''Mmm.'' The psychiatrist seemed to be thinking.

''It'll take time, of course. It was all so enchanting at first. The very *idea* of these things, the practical uses, was wonderful. They were almost toys, to be played with, but the people got too involved, went too far, and got wrapped up in a pattern of social behavior and couldn't get out, couldn't admit they were *in,* even. So they rationalized their nerves as something else.

'Our modern age,' they said. 'Conditions,' they said. 'High-strung,' they said. But mark my words, the seed has been sown. I got worldwide coverage on TV, radio, films; *there's* an irony for you. That was five days ago. A billion people know about me. Check your financial columns. Any day now. Maybe today. Watch for a sudden spurt, a rise in sales for French chocolate ice cream!''

''I see,'' said the psychiatrist.

''Can I go back to my nice private cell now, where I can be alone and quiet for six months?''

''Yes,'' said the psychiatrist quietly.

''Don't worry about me,'' said Mr. Brock, rising. ''I'm just going to sit around for a long time stuffing that nice soft bolt of quiet material in both ears.''

''Mmm,'' said the psychiatrist, going to the door.

''Cheers,'' said Mr. Brock.

''Yes,'' said the psychiatrist.

He pressed a code signal on a hidden button, the door opened, he stepped out, the door shut and locked. Alone, he moved in the offices and corridors. The first twenty yards of his walk were accompanied by ''Tambourine Chinois.'' Then it was ''Tzigane,'' Bach's ''Passacaglia'' and Fugue in something Minor, ''Tiger Rag,'' ''Love Is Like a Cigarette.'' He took his broken wrist radio from his pocket like a dead praying mantis. He turned in at his office. A bell sounded; a voice came out of the ceiling, ''Doctor?''

''Just finished with Brock,'' said the psychiatrist.

''Diagnosis?''

''Seems completely disorientated, but convivial. Refuses to accept the simplest realities of his environment and work *with* them.''

''Prognosis?''

''Indefinite. Left him enjoying a piece of invisible material.''

Three phones rang. A duplicate wrist radio in his desk drawer buzzed like a wounded grasshopper. The intercom flashed a pink light and click-clicked. Three phones rang. The drawer buzzed. Music blew in through the open door. The psychiatrist, humming quietly, fitted the new wrist radio to his wrist, flipped the intercom, talked a moment, picked up one telephone, talked, picked up another telephone, talked, picked up the third telephone, talked, touched the wrist-radio button, talked calmly and quietly, his face cool and serene, in the middle of the music and the lights flashing, the two phones ringing again, and his hands moving, and his wrist radio buzzing, and the intercoms talking, and voices speaking from the ceiling. And he went on quietly this way through the remainder of a cool, air-conditioned, and long afternoon; telephone, wrist radio, intercom, telephone, wrist radio, intercom, telephone, wrist radio, intercom, telephone, wrist radio, intercom, telephone, wrist radio, intercom, telephone, wrist radio . . .

The Golden Kite, The Silver Wind

"In the shape of a *pig?*" cried the Mandarin.

"In the shape of a pig," said the messenger, and departed.

"Oh, what an evil day in an evil year," cried the Mandarin. "The town of Kwan-Si, beyond the hill, was very small in my childhood. Now it has grown so large that at last they are building a wall."

"But why should a wall two miles away make my good father sad and angry all within the hour?" asked his daughter quietly.

"They build their wall," said the Mandarin, "in the shape of a pig! Do you see? Our own city wall is built in the shape of an orange. That pig will devour us, greedily!"

"Ah."

They both sat thinking.

Life was full of symbols and omens. Demons lurked everywhere, Death swam in the wetness of an eye, the turn of a gull's wing meant rain, a fan held *so,* the tilt of a roof, and, yes, even a city wall was of immense importance. Travelers and tourists, caravans, musicians, artists, coming upon these two towns, equally judging the portents, would say, "The city shaped like an orange? No! I will enter the city shaped like a pig and prosper, eating all, growing fat with good luck and prosperity!"

The Mandarin wept. "All is lost! These symbols and signs terrify. Our city will come on evil days."

"Then," said the daughter, "call in your stonemasons and

temple builders. I will whisper from behind the silken screen and you will know the words."

The old man clapped his hands despairingly. "Ho, stonemasons! Ho, builders of towns and palaces!"

The men who knew marble and granite and onyx and quartz came quickly. The Mandarin faced them most uneasily, himself waiting for a whisper from the silken screen behind his throne. At last the whisper came.

"I have called you here," said the whisper.

"I have called you here," said the Mandarin aloud, "because our city is shaped like an orange, and the vile city of Kwan-Si has this day shaped theirs like a ravenous pig——"

Here the stonemasons groaned and wept. Death rattled his cane in the outer courtyard. Poverty made a sound like a wet cough in the shadows of the room.

"And so," said the whisper, said the Mandarin, "you raisers of walls must go bearing trowels and rocks and change the shape of *our* city!"

The architects and masons gasped. The Mandarin himself gasped at what he had said. The whisper whispered. The Mandarin went on: "And you will change our walls into a club which may beat the pig and drive it off!"

The stonemasons rose up, shouting. Even the Mandarin, delighted at the words from his mouth, applauded, stood down from his throne. "Quick!" he cried. "To work!"

When his men had gone, smiling and bustling, the Mandarin turned with great love to the silken screen. "Daughter," he whispered, "I will embrace you." There was no reply. He stepped around the screen, and she was gone.

Such modesty, he thought. She has slipped away and left me with a triumph, as if it were mine.

The news spread through the city; the Mandarin was acclaimed. Everyone carried stone to the walls. Fireworks were set off and the demons of death and poverty did not linger, as all worked together. At the end of the month the wall had been changed. It was now a mighty bludgeon with which to drive pigs, boars, even lions, far away. The Mandarin slept like a happy fox every night.

"I would like to see the Mandarin of Kwan-Si when the news is learned. Such pandemonium and hysteria; he will likely throw himself from a mountain! A little more of that wine, oh Daughter-who-thinks-like-a-son."

But the pleasure was like a winter flower; it died swiftly. That very afternoon the messenger rushed into the courtroom. "Oh, Mandarin, disease, early sorrow, avalanches, grasshopper plagues, and poisoned well water!"

The Mandarin trembled.

"The town of Kwan-Si," said the messenger, "which was built like a pig and which animal we drove away by changing our walls to a mighty stick, has now turned triumph to winter ashes. They have built their city's walls like a great bonfire to burn our stick!"

The Mandarin's heart sickened within him, like an autumn fruit upon an ancient tree. "Oh, gods! Travelers will spurn us. Tradesmen, reading the symbols, will turn from the stick, so easily destroyed, to the fire, which conquers all!"

"No," said a whisper like a snowflake from behind the silken screen.

"No," said the startled Mandarin.

"Tell my stonemasons," said the whisper that was a falling drop of rain, "to build our walls in the shape of a shining lake."

The Mandarin said this aloud, his heart warmed.

"And with this lake of water," said the whisper and the old man, "we will quench the fire and put it out forever!"

The city turned out in joy to learn that once again they had been saved by the magnificent Emperor of ideas. They ran to the walls and built them nearer to this new vision, singing, not as loudly as before, of course, for they were tired, and not as quickly, for since it had taken a month to build the wall the first time, they had had to neglect business and crops and therefore were somewhat weaker and poorer.

There then followed a succession of horrible and wonderful days, one in another like a nest of frightening boxes.

"Oh, Emperor," cried the messenger, "Kwan-Si has rebuilt their walls to resemble a mouth with which to drink all our lake!"

"Then," said the Emperor, standing very close to his silken screen, "build our walls like a needle to sew up that mouth!"

"Emperor!" screamed the messenger. "They make their walls like a sword to break your needle!"

The Emperor held, trembling, to the silken screen. "Then shift the stones to form a scabbard to sheathe that sword!"

"Mercy," wept the messenger the following morn, "they have worked all night and shaped the walls like lightning which will explode and destroy that sheath!"

Sickness spread in the city like a pack of evil dogs. Shops closed. The population, working now steadily for endless months upon the changing of the walls, resembled Death himself, clattering his white bones like musical instruments in the wind. Funerals began to appear in the streets, though it was the middle of summer, a time when all should be tending and harvesting. The Mandarin fell so ill that he had his bed drawn up by the silken screen and there he lay, miserably giving his architectural orders. The voice behind the screen was weak now, too, and faint, like the wind in the eaves.

"Kwan-Si is an eagle. Then our walls must be a net for that eagle. They are a sun to burn our net. Then we build a moon to eclipse their sun!"

Like a rusted machine, the city ground to a halt.

At last the whisper behind the screen cried out:

"In the name of the gods, send for Kwan-Si!"

Upon the last day of summer the Mandarin Kwan-Si, very ill and withered away, was carried into our Mandarin's courtroom by four starving footmen. The two mandarins were propped up, facing each other. Their breaths fluttered like winter winds in their mouths. A voice said:

"Let us put an end to this."

The old men nodded.

"This cannot go on," said the faint voice. "Our people do nothing but rebuild our cities to a different shape every day, every hour. They have no time to hunt, to fish, to love, to be good to their ancestors and their ancestors' children."

"This I admit," said the mandarins of the towns of the Cage, the Moon, the Spear, the Fire, the Sword and this, that, and other things.

"Carry us into the sunlight," said the voice.

The old men were borne out under the sun and up a little hill. In the late summer breeze a few very thin children were flying dragon kites in all the colors of the sun, and frogs and grass, the color of the sea and the color of coins and wheat.

The first Mandarin's daughter stood by his bed.

"See," she said.

"Those are nothing but kites," said the two old men.

"But what is a kite on the ground?" she said. "It is nothing. What does it need to sustain it and make it beautiful and truly spiritual?"

"The wind, of course!" said the others.

"And what do the sky and the wind need to make *them* beautiful?"

"A kite, of course—many kites, to break the monotony, the sameness of the sky. Colored kites, flying!"

"So," said the Mandarin's daughter. "You, Kwan-Si, will make a last rebuilding of your town to resemble nothing more nor less than the wind. And we shall build like a golden kite. The wind will beautify the kite and carry it to wondrous heights. And the kite will break the sameness of the wind's existence and give it purpose and meaning. One without the other is nothing. Together, all will be beauty and co-operation and a long and enduring life."

Whereupon the two mandarins were so overjoyed that they took their first nourishment in days, momentarily were given strength, embraced, and lavished praise upon each other, called the Mandarin's daughter a boy, a man, a stone pillar, a warrior, and a true and unforgettable son. Almost immediately they parted and hurried to their towns, calling out and singing, weakly but happily.

And so, in time, the towns became the Town of the Golden Kite and the Town of the Silver Wind. And harvestings were harvested and business tended again, and the flesh returned, and disease ran off like a frightened jackal. And on every night of the year the inhabitants in the Town of the Kite could hear the good clear wind sustaining them. And those in the Town of the Wind could hear the kite singing, whispering, rising, and beautifying them.

"So be it," said the Mandarin in front of his silken screen.

I See You Never

The soft knock came at the kitchen door, and when Mrs. O'Brian opened it, there on the back porch were her best tenant, Mr. Ramirez, and two police officers, one on each side of him. Mr. Ramirez just stood there, walled in and small.

"Why, Mr. Ramirez!" said Mrs. O'Brian.

Mr. Ramirez was overcome. He did not seem to have words to explain.

He had arrived at Mrs. O'Brian's rooming house more than two years earlier and had lived there ever since. He had come by bus from Mexico City to San Diego and had then gone up to Los Angeles. There he had found the clean little room, with glossy blue linoleum, and pictures and calendars on the flowered walls, and Mrs. O'Brian as the strict but kindly landlady. During the war he had worked at the airplane factory and made parts for the planes that flew off somewhere, and even now, after the war, he still held his job. From the first he had made big money. He saved some of it, and he got drunk only once a week—a privilege that, to Mrs. O'Brian's way of thinking, every good workingman deserved, unquestioned and unreprimanded.

Inside Mrs. O'Brian's kitchen, pies were baking in the oven. Soon the pies would come out with complexions like Mr. Ramirez'—brown and shiny and crisp, with slits in them for the air almost like the slits of Mr. Ramirez' dark eyes. The kitchen smelled good. The policemen leaned forward, lured by the odor.

Mr. Ramirez gazed at his feet as if they had carried him into all this trouble.

"What happened, Mr. Ramirez?" asked Mrs. O'Brian.

Behind Mrs. O'Brian, as he lifted his eyes, Mr. Ramirez saw the long table laid with clean white linen and set with a platter, cool, shining glasses, a water pitcher with ice cubes floating inside it, a bowl of fresh potato salad and one of bananas and oranges, cubed and sugared. At this table sat Mrs. O'Brian's children—her three grown sons, eating and conversing, and her two younger daughters, who were staring at the policemen as they ate.

"I have been here thirty months," said Mr. Ramirez quietly, looking at Mrs. O'Brian's plump hands.

"That's six months too long," said one policeman. "He only had a temporary visa. We've just got around to looking for him."

Soon after Mr. Ramirez had arrived he bought a radio for his little room; evenings, he turned it up very loud and enjoyed it. And he had bought a wristwatch and enjoyed that too. And on many nights he had walked silent streets and seen the bright clothes in the windows and bought some of them, and he had seen the jewels and bought some of them for his few lady friends. And he had gone to picture shows five nights a week for a while. Then, also, he had ridden the streetcars—all night some nights—smelling the electricity, his dark eyes moving over the advertisements, feeling the wheels rumble under him, watching the little sleeping houses and big hotels slip by. Besides that, he had gone to large restaurants, where he had eaten many-course dinners, and to the opera and the theater. And he had bought a car, which later, when he forgot to pay for it, the dealer had driven off angrily from in front of the rooming house.

"So here I am," said Mr. Ramirez now, "to tell you I must give up my room, Mrs. O'Brian. I come to get my baggage and clothes and go with these men."

"Back to Mexico?"

"Yes. To Lagos. That is a little town north of Mexico City."

"I'm sorry, Mr. Ramirez."

"I'm packed," said Mr. Ramirez hoarsely, blinking his dark

eyes rapidly and moving his hands helplessly before him. The policemen did not touch him. There was no necessity for that.

"Here is the key, Mrs. O'Brian," Mr. Ramirez said. "I have my bag already."

Mrs. O'Brian, for the first time, noticed a suitcase standing behind him on the porch.

Mr. Ramirez looked in again at the huge kitchen, at the bright silver cutlery and the young people eating and the shining waxed floor. He turned and looked for a long moment at the apartment house next door, rising up three stories, high and beautiful. He looked at the balconies and fire escapes and back-porch stairs, at the lines of laundry snapping in the wind.

"You've been a good tenant," said Mrs. O'Brian.

"Thank you, thank you, Mrs. O'Brian," he said softly. He closed his eyes.

Mrs. O'Brian stood holding the door half open. One of her sons, behind her, said that her dinner was getting cold, but she shook her head at him and turned back to Mr. Ramirez. She remembered a visit she had once made to some Mexican border towns—the hot days, the endless crickets leaping and falling or lying dead and brittle like the small cigars in the shop windows, and the canals taking river water out to the farms, the dirt roads, the scorched scape. She remembered the silent towns, the warm beer, the hot, thick foods each day. She remembered the slow, dragging horses and the parched jack rabbits on the road. She remembered the iron mountains and the dusty valleys and the ocean beaches that spread hundreds of miles with no sound but the waves—no cars, no buildings, nothing.

"I'm sure sorry, Mr. Ramirez," she said.

"I don't want to go back, Mrs. O'Brian," he said weakly. "I like it here, I want to stay here. I've worked, I've got money. I look all right, don't I? And I don't want to go back!"

"I'm sorry, Mr. Ramirez," she said. "I wish there was something I could do."

"Mrs. O'Brian!" he cried suddenly, tears rolling out from under his eyelids. He reached out his hand and took her hand fervently, shaking it, wringing it, holding to it. "Mrs. O'Brian, I see you never, I see you never!"

The policemen smiled at this, but Mr. Ramirez did not notice it, and they stopped smiling very soon.

"Good-by, Mrs. O'Brian. You have been good to me. Oh, good-by, Mrs. O'Brian. I see you never!"

The policemen waited for Mr. Ramirez to turn, pick up his suitcase, and walk away. Then they followed him, tipping their caps to Mrs. O'Brian. She watched them go down the porch steps. Then she shut the door quietly and went slowly back to her chair at the table. She pulled the chair out and sat down. She picked up the shining knife and fork and started once more upon her steak.

"Hurry up, Mom," said one of the sons. "It'll be cold."

Mrs. O'Brian took one bite and chewed on it for a long, slow time; then she stared at the closed door. She laid down her knife and fork.

"What's wrong, Ma?" asked her son.

"I just realized," said Mrs. O'Brian—she put her hand to her face—"I'll never see Mr. Ramirez again."

Embroidery

The dark porch air in the late afternoon was full of needle flashes, like a movement of gathered silver insects in the light. The three women's mouths twitched over their work. Their bodies lay back and then imperceptibly forward, so that the rocking chairs tilted and murmured. Each woman looked to her own hands, as if quite suddenly she had found her heart beating there.

"What time is it?"

"Ten minutes to five."

"Got to get up in a minute and shell those peas for dinner."

"But——" said one of them.

"Oh yes, I forgot. How foolish of me. . . ." the first woman paused, put down her embroidery and needle, and looked through the open porch door, through the warm interior of the quiet house, to the silent kitchen. There upon the table, seeming more like symbols of domesticity than anything she had ever seen in her life, lay the mound of fresh-washed peas in their neat, resilient jackets, waiting for her fingers to bring them into the world.

"Go hull them if it'll make you feel good," said the second woman.

"No," said the first. "I won't. I just won't."

The third woman sighed. She embroidered a rose, a leaf, a daisy on a green field. The embroidery needle rose and vanished.

The second woman was working on the finest, most delicate piece of embroidery of them all, deftly poking, finding, and returning the quick needle upon innumerable journeys. Her quick black glance was on each motion. A flower, a man, a road, a sun, a house; the scene grew under hand, a miniature beauty, perfect in every threaded detail.

"It seems at times like this that it's always your hands you turn to," she said, and the others nodded enough to make the rockers rock again.

"I believe," said the first lady, "that our souls are in our hands. For we do *everything* to the world with our hands. Sometimes I think we don't use our hands half enough; it's certain we don't use our heads."

They all peered more intently at what their hands were doing. "Yes," said the third lady, "when you look back on a whole lifetime, it seems you don't remember faces so much as hands and what they did."

They recounted to themselves the lids they had lifted, the doors they had opened and shut, the flowers they had picked, the dinners they had made, all with slow or quick fingers, as was their manner or custom. Looking back, you saw a flurry of hands, like a magician's dream, doors popping wide, taps turned, brooms wielded, children spanked. The flutter of pink hands was the only sound; the rest was a dream without voices.

"No supper to fix tonight or tomorrow night or the next night after that," said the third lady.

"No windows to open or shut."

"No coal to shovel in the basement furnace next winter."

"No papers to clip cooking articles out of."

And suddenly they were crying. The tears rolled softly down their faces and fell into the material upon which their fingers twitched.

"This won't help things," said the first lady at last, putting the back of her thumb to each under-eyelid. She looked at her thumb and it was wet.

"Now look what I've done!" cried the second lady, exasperated. The others stopped and peered over. The second lady held out her embroidery. There was the scene, perfect except that while the embroidered yellow sun shone down upon the embroidered green field, and the embroidered brown road curved toward an embroidered pink house, the man standing on the road had something wrong with his face.

"I'll just have to rip out the whole pattern, practically, to fix it right," said the second lady.

"What a shame." They all stared intently at the beautiful scene with the flaw in it.

The second lady began to pick away at the thread with her little deft scissors flashing. The pattern came out thread by thread. She pulled and yanked, almost viciously. The man's face was gone. She continued to seize at the threads.

"What are you *doing?*" asked the other women.

They leaned and saw what she had done.

The man was gone from the road. She had taken him out entirely.

They said nothing but returned to their own tasks.

"What time is it?" asked someone.

"Five minutes to five."

"Is it supposed to happen at five o'clock?"

"Yes."

"And they're not sure what it'll do to anything, really, when it happens?"

"No, not sure."

"Why didn't we stop them before it got this far and this big?"

"It's twice as big as ever before. No, ten times, maybe a thousand."

"This isn't like the first one or the dozen later ones. This is different. Nobody knows what it might do when it comes."

They waited on the porch in the smell of roses and cut grass.
"What time is it now?"

"One minute to five."

The needles flashed silver fire. They swam like a tiny school of metal fish in the darkening summer air.

Far away a mosquito sound. Then something like a tremor of drums. The three women cocked their heads, listening.

"We won't hear anything, will we?"

"They say not."

"Perhaps we're foolish. Perhaps we'll go right on, after five o'clock, shelling peas, opening doors, stirring soups, washing dishes, making lunches, peeling oranges. . . ."

"My, how we'll laugh to think we were frightened by an old experiment!" They smiled a moment at each other.

"It's five o'clock."

At these words, hushed, they all busied themselves. Their fingers darted. Their faces were turned down to the motions they made. They made frantic patterns. They made lilacs and grass and trees and houses and rivers in the embroidered cloth. They said nothing, but you could hear their breath in the silent porch air.

Thirty seconds passed.

The second woman sighed finally and began to relax.

"I think I just *will* go shell those peas for supper," she said. "I—"

But she hadn't time even to lift her head. Somewhere, at the side of her vision, she saw the world brighten and catch fire. She kept her head down, for she knew what it was. She didn't look up, nor did the others, and in the last instant their fingers were flying; they didn't glance about to see what was happening to the country, the town, this house, or even this porch. They were only staring down at the design in their flickering hands.

The second woman watched an embroidered flower go. She tried to embroider it back in, but it went, and then the road vanished, and the blades of grass. She watched a fire, in slow motion almost, catch upon the embroidered house and unshingle it, and pull each threaded leaf from the small green tree in the hoop, and she saw the sun itself pulled apart in the design. Then the fire caught upon the moving point of the needle while still it flashed; she watched the fire come along her fingers and arms and body, untwisting the yarn of her being so painstakingly that she could see it in all its devilish beauty, yanking out the pattern from the material at hand. What it was doing to the other women or the furniture or the elm tree in the yard, she never knew. For now, yes, now! it was plucking at the white embroidery of her flesh, the pink thread of her cheeks, and at last it found her heart, a soft red rose sewn with fire, and it burned the fresh, embroidered petals away, one by delicate one. . . .

The Big Black and White Game

The people filled the stands behind the wire screen, waiting. Us kids, dripping from the lake, ran between the white cottages, past the resort hotel, screaming, and sat on the bleachers, making wet bottom marks. The hot sun beat down through the tall oak trees around the baseball diamond. Our fathers and mothers, in golf pants and light summer dresses, scolded us and made us sit still.

We looked toward the hotel and the back door of the vast kitchen, expectantly. A few colored women began walking across the shade-freckled area between, and in ten minutes the far left section of the bleachers was mellow with the color of their fresh-washed faces and arms. After all these years, whenever I think back on it, I can still hear the sounds they made. The sound on the warm air was like a soft moving of dove voices each time they talked among themselves.

Everybody quickened into amusement, laughter rose right up into the clear blue Wisconsin sky, as the kitchen door flung wide and out ran the big and little, the dark and high-yellar uniformed Negro waiters, janitors, bus boys, boatmen, cooks, bottle washers, soda jerks, gardeners, and golf-links tenders. They came capering, showing their fine white teeth, proud of their new red-striped uniforms, their shiny shoes rising and coming down on the green grass as they skirted the bleachers and drifted with lazy speed out on the field, calling to everybody and everything.

Us kids squealed. There was Long Johnson, the lawn-cutting man, and Cavanaugh, the soda-fountain man, and Shorty Smith and Pete Brown and Jiff Miller!

And *there* was Big Poe! Us kids shouted, applauded!

Big Poe was the one who stood so tall by the popcorn machine every night in the million-dollar dance pavilion farther down beyond the hotel on the lake rim. Every night I bought popcorn from Big Poe and he poured lots of butter all over it for me.

I stomped and yelled, "Big Poe! Big Poe!"

And he looked over at me and stretched his lips to bring out his teeth, waved, and shouted a laugh.

And Mama looked to the right, to the left, and back of us with worried eyes and nudged my elbow. "Hush," she said. "Hush."

"Land, land," said the lady next to my mother, fanning herself with a folded paper. "This is quite a day for the colored servants, ain't it? Only time of year they break loose. They look forward all summer to the big Black and White game. But this ain't nothing. You seen their Cakewalk Jamboree?"

"We got tickets for it," said Mother. "For tonight at the pavilion. Cost us a dollar each. That's pretty expensive, I'd say."

"But I always figure," said the woman, "once a year you got to spend. And it's really something to watch them dance. They just naturally got . . ."

"Rhythm," said Mother.

"That's the word," said the lady. "Rhythm. That's what they got. Land, you should see the colored maids up at the hotel. They been buying satin yardage in at the big store in Madison for a month now. And every spare minute they sit sewing and laughing. And I seen some of the feathers they bought for their hats. Mustard and wine ones and blue ones and violet ones. Oh, it'll be a sight!"

"They been airing out their tuxedos," I said. "I saw them hanging on lines behind the hotel all last week!"

"Look at them prance," said Mother. "You'd think they thought they were going to win the game from our men."

The colored men ran back and forth and yelled with their

high, fluting voices and their low, lazy, interminable voices. Way out in center field you could see the flash of teeth, their upraised naked black arms swinging and beating their sides as they hopped up and down and ran like rabbits, exuberantly.

Big Poe took a double fistful of bats, bundled them on his huge bull shoulder, and strutted along the first-base line, head back, mouth smiling wide open, his tongue moving, singing:

> *"—gonna dance out both of my shoes,*
> *When they play those Jelly Roll Blues;*
> *Tomorrow night at the Dark Town Strutters' Ball!"*

Up went his knees and down and out, swinging the bats like musical batons. A burst of applause and soft laughter came from the left-hand grandstands, where all the young, ripply colored girls with shiny brown eyes sat eager and easy. They made quick motions that were graceful and mellow because, maybe, of their rich coloring. Their laughter was like shy birds; they waved at Big Poe, and one of them with a high voice cried, "Oh, Big Poe! Oh, Big Poe!"

The white section joined politely in the applause as Big Poe finished his cakewalk. "Hey, Poe!" I yelled again.

"Stop that, Douglas!" said Mother, straight at me.

Now the white men came running between the trees with their uniforms on. There was a great thunder and shouting and rising up in our grandstand. The white men ran across the green diamond, flashing white.

"Oh, there's Uncle George!" said Mother. "My, doesn't he look nice?" And there was my Uncle George toddling along in his outfit which didn't quite fit because Uncle has a potbelly, and jowls that sit out over any collar he puts on. He was hurrying along, trying to breathe and smile at the same time, lifting up his pudgy little legs. "My, they look *so* nice," enthused Mother.

I sat there, watching their movements. Mother sat beside me, and I think she was comparing and thinking, too, and what she saw amazed and disconcerted her. How easily the dark people had come running first, like those slow-motion deer and buck antelopes in those African moving pictures, like things in dreams. They came like beautiful brown, shiny animals that didn't know they were alive, but lived. And when they ran and put their easy, lazy, timeless legs out and followed them with their big, sprawling arms and loose fingers and smiled in the blowing wind, their expressions didn't say, "Look at *me* run, look at *me* run!" No, not at all. Their faces dreamily said, "Lord, but it's sure nice to run. See the ground swell soft under me? Gosh, I feel good. My muscles are moving like oil on my bones and it's the best pleasure in the world to run." And they ran. There was no purpose to their running but exhilaration and living.

The white men worked at their running as they worked at everything. You felt embarrassed for them because they were alive too much in the wrong way. Always looking from the corners of their eyes to see if you were watching. The Negroes didn't care if you watched or not; they went on living, moving. They were so sure of playing that they didn't have to think about it anymore.

"My, but our men look so nice," said my mother, repeating herself rather flatly. She had seen, compared the teams. Inside, she realized how laxly the colored men hung swaying in their uniforms, and how tensely, nervously, the white men were crammed, shoved, and belted into *their* outfits.

I guess the tenseness began then.

I guess everybody saw what was happening. They saw how the white men looked like senators in sun suits. And they admired the graceful unawareness of the colored men. And, as is always the case, that admiration turned to envy, to jealousy, to irritation. It turned to conversation like:

"That's my husband, Tom, on third base. Why doesn't he pick up his feet? He just *stands* there."

"Never you mind, never you mind. He'll pick 'em up when the time comes!"

"That's what *I* say! Now, take my Henry, for instance. Henry mightn't be active all the time, but when there's a crisis—just you *watch* him. Uh—I do wish he'd wave or something, though. Oh, *there!* Hello, Henry!"

"Look at that Jimmie Cosner playing around out there!"

I looked. A medium-sized white man with a freckled face

and red hair was clowning on the diamond. He was balancing a bat on his forehead. There was laughter from the white grandstand. But it sounded like the kind of laughter you laugh when you're embarrassed for someone.

"Play ball!" said the umpire.

A coin was flipped. The colored men batted first.

"Darn it," said my mother.

The colored men ran in from the field happily.

Big Poe was first to bat. I cheered. He picked up the bat in one hand like a toothpick and idled over to the plate and laid the bat on his thick shoulder, smiling along its polished surface toward the stands where the colored women sat with their fresh flowery cream dresses stirring over their legs, which hung down between the seat intervals like crisp new sticks of ginger; their hair was all fancily spun and hung over their ears. Big Poe looked in particular at the little, dainty-as-a-chicken-bone shape of his girl friend Katherine. She was the one who made the beds at the hotel and cottages every morning, who tapped on your door like a bird and politely asked if you was done dreaming, 'cause if you was she'd clean away all them old nightmares and bring in a fresh batch—please use them *one* at a time, thank yoah. Big Poe shook his head, looking at her, as if he couldn't believe she was there. Then he turned, one hand balancing the bat, his left hand dangling free at his side, to await the trial pitches. They hissed past, spatted into the open mouth of the catcher's mitt, were hurled back. The umpire grunted. The next pitch was the starter.

Big Poe let the first ball go by him.

"Stee-rike!" announced the umpire. Big Poe winked good-naturedly at the white folks. Bang! "Stee-rike two!" cried the umpire.

The ball came for the third time.

Big Poe was suddenly a greased machine pivoting; the dangling hand swept up to the butt end of the bat, the bat swiveled, connected with the ball——*Whack!* The ball shot up into the sky, away down toward the wavering line of oak trees, down toward the lake, where a white sailboat slid silently by. The crowd yelled, me loudest! There went Uncle George, running on his stubby, wool-stockinged legs, getting smaller with distance.

Big Poe stood for a moment watching the ball go. Then he began to run. He went around the bases, loping, and on the way home from third base he waved to the colored girls naturally and happily and they waved back, standing on their seats and shrilling.

Ten minutes later, with the bases loaded and run after run being driven in, and Big Poe coming to bat again, my mother turned to me. "They're the most inconsiderate people," she said.

"But that's the game," I said. "They've only got two outs."

"But the score's seven to nothing," my mother protested.

"Well, just you wait until *our* men come to bat," said the lady next to my mother, waving away a fly with a pale blue-veined hand. "Those Negroes are too big for their britches."

"Stee-rike two!" said the umpire as Big Poe swung.

"All the past week at the hotel," said the woman next to my mother, staring out at Big Poe steadily, "the hotel service has been simply terrible. Those maids don't talk about a thing save the Cakewalk Jamboree, and whenever you want ice water it takes half an hour to fetch it, they're so busy sewing."

"Ball one!" said the umpire.

The woman fussed. "I'll be glad when this week's over, that's what I got to say," she said.

"Ball two!" said the umpire to Big Poe.

"Are they going to *walk* him?" asked my mother of me. "Are they *crazy?*" To the woman next to her: "That's right. They been acting funny all week. Last night I had to tell Big Poe twice to put extra butter on my popcorn. *I* guess he was trying to save money or something."

"Ball three!" said the umpire.

The lady next to my mother cried out suddenly and fanned herself furiously with her newspaper. "Land, I just *thought.* Wouldn't it be awful if they *won* the game? They *might,* you know. They might do it."

My mother looked at the lake, at the trees, at her hands. "I don't know why Uncle George had to play. Make a fool of himself. Douglas, you run tell him to quit right now. It's bad on his heart."

"You're out!" cried the umpire to Big Poe.

''Ah,'' sighed the grandstand.

The side was retired. Big Poe laid down his bat gently and walked along the base line. The white men pattered in from the field looking red and irritable, with big islands of sweat under their armpits. Big Poe looked over at me. I winked at him. He winked back. Then I knew he wasn't so dumb.

He'd struck out on purpose.

Long Johnson was going to pitch for the colored team.

He ambled out to the rubber, worked his fingers around in his fists to limber them up.

First white man to bat was a man named Kodimer, who sold suits in Chicago all year round.

Long Johnson fed them over the plate with tired, unassuming, controlled accuracy.

Mr. Kodimer chopped. Mr. Kodimer swatted. Finally Mr. Kodimer bunted the ball down the third-base line.

''Out at first base,'' said the umpire, an Irishman named Mahoney.

Second man up was a young Swede named Moberg. He hit a high fly to center field which was taken by a little plump Negro who didn't look fat because he moved around like a smooth, round glob of mercury.

Third man up was a Milwaukee truck driver. He whammed a line drive to center field. It was good. Except that he tried to stretch it into a two-bagger. When he pulled up at second base, there was Emancipated Smith with a white pellet in his dark, dark hand, waiting.

My mother sank back in her seat, exhaling. ''Well, I *never!*''

''It's getting hotter,'' said the lady elbow-next. ''Think I'll go for a stroll by the lake soon. It's too hot to sit and watch a silly game today. Mightn't you come along with me, missus?'' she asked Mother.

It went on that way for five innings.

It was eleven to nothing and Big Poe had struck out three times on purpose, and in the last half of the fifth was when Jimmie Cosner came to bat for our side again. He'd been trying all afternoon, clowning, giving directions, telling everybody just where he was going to blast that pill once he got hold of it. He swaggered up toward the plate now, confident and bugle-voiced. He swung six bats in his thin hands, eying them critically with his shiny green little eyes. He chose one, dropped the others, ran to the plate, chopping out little islands of green fresh lawn with his cleated heels. He pushed his cap back on his dusty red hair. "Watch this!" he called out loud to the ladies. "You watch me show these dark boys! Ya-hah!"

Long Johnson on the mound did a slow serpentine windup. It was like a snake on a limb of a tree, uncoiling, suddenly darting at you. Instantly Johnson's hand was in front of him, open, like black fangs, empty. And the white pill slashed across the plate with a sound like a razor.

"Stee-rike!"

Jimmie Cosner put his bat down and stood glaring at the umpire. He said nothing for a long time. Then he spat deliberately near the catcher's foot, took up the yellow maple bat again, and swung it so the sun glinted the rim of it in a nervous halo. He twitched and sidled it on his thin-boned shoulder, and his mouth opened and shut over his long nicotined teeth.

Clap! went the catcher's mitt.

Cosner turned, stared.

The catcher, like a black magician, his white teeth gleaming, opened up his oily glove. There, like a white flower growing, was the baseball.

"Stee-rike two!" said the umpire, far away in the heat.

Jimmie Cosner laid his bat across the plate and hunched his freckled hands on his hips. "You mean to tell me that was a strike?"

"That's what I said," said the umpire. "Pick up the bat."

"To hit you on the head with," said Cosner sharply.

"Play ball or hit the showers!"

Jimmie Cosner worked his mouth to collect enough saliva to spit, then angrily swallowed it, swore a bitter oath instead. Reaching down, he raised the bat, poised it like a musket on his shoulder.

And here came the ball! It started out small and wound up big in front of him. Powie! An explosion off the yellow bat. The ball spiraled up and up. Jimmie lit out for first base. The ball paused, as if thinking about gravity up there in the sky. A wave came in on the shore of the lake and fell down. The crowd yelled. Jimmie ran. The ball made its decision, came down. A lithe high-yellar was under it, fumbled it. The ball spilled to the turf, was plucked up, hurled to first base.

Jimmie saw he was going to be out. So he jumped feet-first at the base.

Everyone saw his cleats go into Big Poe's ankle. Everybody saw the red blood. Everybody heard the shout, the shriek, saw the heavy clouds of dust rising.

"I'm safe!" protested Jimmie two minutes later.

Big Poe sat on the ground. The entire dark team stood around him. The doctor bent down, probed Big Poe's ankle, saying, "Mmmm," and "Pretty bad. Here." And he swabbed medicine on it and put a white bandage on it.

The umpire gave Cosner the cold-water eye. "Hit the showers!"

"Like hell!" said Cosner. And he stood on that first base, blowing his cheeks out and in, his freckled hands swaying at his sides. "I'm safe. I'm stayin' right here, by God! No nigger put *me* out!"

"No," said the umpire. "A white man did. *Me. Get!*"

"He dropped the ball! Look up the rules! I'm safe!"

The umpire and Cosner stood glaring at each other.

Big Poe looked up from having his swollen ankle tended. His voice was thick and gentle and his eyes examined Jimmie Cosner gently.

"Yes, he's safe, Mr. Umpire. Leave him stay. He's safe."

I was standing right there. I heard the whole thing. Me and some other kids had run out on the field to see. My mother kept calling me to come back to the stands.

"Yes, he's safe," said Big Poe again.

All the colored men let out a yell.

"What'sa matter with you, black boy? You get hit in the head?"

"You heard me," replied Big Poe quietly. He looked at the doctor bandaging him. "He's safe. Leave him stay."

The umpire swore.

"Okay, okay. So he's safe!"

The umpire stalked off, his back stiff, his neck red.

Big Poe was helped up. "Better not walk on that," cautioned the doctor.

"I can walk," whispered Big Poe carefully.

"Better not play."

"I can play," said Big Poe gently, certainly, shaking his head, wet streaks drying under his white eyes. "I'll play *good*." He looked no place at all. "I'll play plenty good."

"Oh," said the second-base colored man. It was a funny sound.

All the colored men looked at each other, at Big Poe, then at Jimmie Cosner, at the sky, at the lake, the crowd. They walked off quietly to take their places. Big Poe stood with his bad foot hardly touching the ground, balanced. The doctor argued. But Big Poe waved him away.

"Batter up!" cried the umpire.

We got settled in the stands again. My mother pinched my leg and asked me why I couldn't sit still. It got warmer. Three or four more waves fell on the shore line. Behind the wire screen the ladies fanned their wet faces and the men inched their rumps forward on the wooden planks, held papers over their scowling brows to see Big Poe standing like a redwood tree out there on first base, Jimmie Cosner standing in the immense shade of that dark tree.

Young Moberg came up to bat for our side.

"Come on, Swede, come on, Swede!" was the cry, a lonely cry, like a dry bird, from out on the blazing green turf. It was Jimmie Cosner calling. The grandstand stared at him. The dark heads turned on their moist pivots in the outfield; the black faces came in his direction, looking him over, seeing his thin, nervously arched back. He was the center of the universe.

"Come on, Swede! Let's show these black boys!" laughed Cosner.

He trailed off. There was a complete silence. Only the wind came through the high, glittering trees.

"Come on, Swede, hang one on that old pill. . . ."

Long Johnson, on the pitcher's mound, cocked his head. Slowly, deliberately, he eyed Cosner. A look passed between him and Big Poe, and Jimmie Cosner saw the look and shut up and swallowed, hard.

Long Johnson took his time with his windup.

Cosner took a lead off base.

Long Johnson stopped loading his pitch.

Cosner skipped back to the bag, kissed his hand, and patted the kiss dead center on the bag. Then he looked up and smiled around.

Again the pitcher coiled up his long, hinged arm, curled loving dark fingers on the leather pellet, drew it back and—Cosner danced off first base. Cosner jumped up and down like a monkey. The pitcher did not look at him. The pitcher's eyes watched secretively, slyly, amusedly, sidewise. Then, snapping his head, the pitcher scared Cosner back to the bag. Cosner stood and jeered.

The third time Long Johnson made as if to pitch, Cosner was far off the bag and running toward second.

Snap went the pitcher's hand. *Boom* went the ball in Big Poe's glove at first base.

Everything was sort of frozen. Just for a second.

There was the sun in the sky, the lake and the boats on it, the grandstands, the pitcher on his mound standing with his hand out and down after tossing the ball; there was Big Poe with the ball in his mighty black hand; there was the infield staring, crouching in at the scene, and there was Jimmie Cosner running, kicking up dirt, the only moving thing in the entire summer world.

Big Poe leaned forward, sighted toward second base, drew back his mighty right hand, and hurled that white baseball straight down along the line until it reached Jimmie Cosner's head.

Next instant, the spell was broken.

Jimmie Cosner lay flat on the burning grass. People boiled out of the grandstands. There was swearing, and women screaming, a clattering of wood as the men rushed down the wooden boards of the bleachers. The colored team ran in from the field, Jimmie Cosner lay there. Big Poe, no expression on his face, limped off the field, pushing white men away from him like clothespins when they tried stopping him. He just picked them up and threw them away.

"Come on, Douglas!" shrieked Mother, grabbing me. "Let's get home! They might have razors! Oh!"

That night, after the near riot of the afternoon, my folks stayed home reading magazines. All the cottages around us were lighted. Everybody was home. Distantly I heard music. I slipped out the back door into the ripe summer-night darkness and ran toward the dance pavilion. All the lights were on, and music played.

But there were no white people at the tables. Nobody had come to the Jamboree.

There were only colored folks. Women in bright red and blue satin gowns and net stockings and soft gloves, with wine-plume hats, and men in glossy tuxedos. The music crashed out, up, down, and around the floor. And laughing and stepping high, flinging their polished shoes out and up in the cakewalk, were Long Johnson and Cavanaugh and Jiff Miller and Pete Brown, and—limping—Big Poe and Katherine, his girl, and all the other lawn-cutters and boatmen and janitors and chambermaids, all on the floor at one time.

It was so dark all around the pavilion; the stars shone in the black sky, and I stood outside, my nose against the window, looking in for a long, long time, silently.

I went to bed without telling anyone what I'd seen.

I just lay in the dark smelling the ripe apples in the dimness and hearing the lake at night and listening to that distant, faint and wonderful music. Just before I slept I heard those last strains again:

"—gonna dance out both of my shoes,
When they play those Jelly Roll Blues;
Tomorrow night at the Dark Town Strutters' Ball!"

The Great Wide World Over There

It was a day to be out of bed, to pull curtains and fling open windows. It was a day to make your heart bigger with warm mountain air.

Cora, feeling like a young girl in a wrinkled old dress, sat up in bed.

It was early, the sun barely on the horizon, but already the birds were stirring from the pines and ten billion red ants milled free from their bronze hills by the cabin door. Cora's husband Tom slept like a bear in a snowy hibernation of bedclothes beside her. Will my heart wake him up? she wondered.

And then she knew why this seemed a special day.

"Benjy's coming!"

She imagined him far off, leaping green meadows, fording streams where spring was pushing itself in cool colors of moss and clear water toward the sea. She saw his great shoes dusting and flicking the stony roads and paths. She saw his freckled face high in the sun looking giddily down his long body at his distant hands flying out and back behind him.

Benjy, come on! she thought, opening a window swiftly. Wind blew her hair like a gray spider web about her cold ears. Now Benjy's at Iron Bridge, now at Meadow Pike, now up Creek Path, over Chesley's Field . . .

Somewhere in those Missouri mountains was Benjy. Cora blinked. Those strange high hills beyond which twice a year she and Tom drove their horse and wagon to town, and through which, thirty years ago, she had wanted to run forever, saying, "Oh, Tom, let's just drive and drive until we reach the sea." But Tom had looked at her as if she had slapped his face, and he had turned the wagon around and driven on home, talking to the mare. And if people lived by shores where the sea came like a storm, now louder, now softer, every day, she did not know it. And if there were cities where neons were like pink ice and green mint and red fireworks each evening, she didn't know that either. Her horizon, north, south, east, west, was this valley, and had never been anything else.

But now, today, she thought, Benjy's coming from that world out there; he's seen it, smelt it; he'll tell me about it. And he can write. She looked at her hands. He'll be here a whole month and teach me. Then I can write out into that world and bring it here to the mailbox I'll make Tom build today. "Get up, Tom! You *hear?*"

She put her hand out to push the bank of sleeping snow.

By nine o'clock the valley was full of grasshoppers flinging themselves through the blue, piney air, while smoke curled into the sky.

Cora, singing into her pots and pans as she polished them, saw her wrinkled face bronzed and freshened in the copper bottoms. Tom was grumbling the sounds of a sleepy bear at his mush breakfast, while her singing moved all about him, like a bird in a cage.

"*Someone's* mighty happy," said a voice.

Cora made herself into a statue. From the corners of her eyes she saw a shadow cross the room.

"Mrs. Brabbam?" asked Cora of her scouring cloth.

"That's who it is!" And there stood the Widow Lady, her gingham dress dragging the warm dust, her letters in her chickeny hand. "Morning! I just been to my mailbox. Got me a real beauty of a letter from my Uncle George in Springfield." Mrs. Brabbam fixed Cora with a gaze like a silver needle. "How long since you got a letter from your uncle, missus?"

"My uncles are all dead." It was not Cora herself, but her tongue, that lied. When the time came, she knew, it would be her tongue alone that must take communion and confess earthly sinning.

"It's certainly *nice,* getting mail." Mrs. Brabbam waved her letters in a straight flush on the morning air.

Always twisting the knife in the flesh. How many years, thought Cora, had this run on, Mrs. Brabbam and her smily eyes, talking loud of how she got mail; implying that nobody else for miles around could read? Cora bit her lip and almost threw the pot, but set it down, laughing. "I forgot to tell you. My nephew Benjy's coming; his folks are poorly, and he's here for the summer today. He'll teach me to write. And Tom's building us a postal box, aren't you, Tom?"

Mrs. Brabbam clutched her letters. "Well, isn't that fine! You *lucky* lady." And suddenly the door was empty. Mrs. Brabbam was gone.

But Cora was after her. For in that instant she had seen something like a scarecrow, something like a flicker of pure sunlight, something like a brook trout jumping upstream, leap a fence in the yard below. She saw a huge hand wave and birds flush in terror from a crabapple tree.

Cora was rushing, the world rushing back of her, down the path. "Benjy!"

They ran at each other like partners in a Saturday dance, linked arms, collided, and waltzed, jabbering. "Benjy!"

She glanced swiftly behind his ear.

Yes, *there* was the yellow pencil.

"Benjy, welcome!"

"Why, ma'am!" He held her off at arm's length. "Why, ma'am, you're *crying.*"

"Here's my nephew," said Cora.

Tom scowled up from spooning his corn-meal mush.

"Mighty glad," smiled Benjy.

Cora held his arm tight so he couldn't vanish. She felt faint, wanting to sit, stand, run, but she only beat her heart fast and laughed at strange times. Now, in an instant, the far countries were brought near; here was this tall boy, lighting up the room like a pine torch, this boy who had seen cities and seas and been places when things had been better for his parents.

"Benjy, I got peas, corn, bacon, mush, soup, and beans for breakfast."

"Hold on!" said Tom.

"Hush, Tom, the boy's down to the bone with walking." She turned to the boy. "Benjy, tell me all about yourself. You *did* go to school?"

Benjy kicked off his shoes. With one bare foot he traced a word in the hearth ashes.

Tom scowled. "What's it say?"

"It says," said Benjy, "C and O and R and A. *Cora*."

"*My* name, Tom, see it! Oh, Benjy, it's good you really write, child. We had one cousin here, long ago, claimed he could spell upside down and backwards. So we fattened him up and he wrote letters but we never got answers. Come to find out he knew just enough spelling to mail letters to the dead-letter office. Lord, Tom knocked two months' worth of vittles out of that boy, batting him up the road with a piece of fence."

They laughed anxiously.

"I write fine," said the serious boy.

"That's all we want to know." She shoved a cut of berry pie at him. "Eat."

By ten-thirty, with the sun riding higher, after watching Benjy devour heaped platters of food, Tom thundered from the cabin; jamming his cap on. "I'm going out, by God, and cut down half the forest!" he said angrily.

But no one heard. Cora was seated in a breathless spell. She was watching the pencil behind Benjy's peach-fuzz ear. She saw him finger it casually, lazily, indifferently. Oh, not so casual, Benjy, she thought. Handle it like a spring robin's egg. She wanted to touch the pencil, but hadn't touched one in years because it made her feel foolish and then angry and then sad. Her hand twitched in her lap.

"You got some paper?" asked Benjy.

"Oh, land, I never thought," she wailed, and the room walls darkened. "What'll we do?"

"Just happens I brought some." He fetched a tablet from his little bag. "You want to write a letter somewhere?"

She smiled outrageously. "I want to write a letter to . . . to . . ." Her face fell apart. She looked around for someone in the distance. She looked at the mountains in the morning sunshine. She heard the sea rolling off on yellow shores a thousand miles away. The birds were coming north over the valley, on their way to multitudes of cities indifferent to her need at this instant.

"Benjy, why, I never thought until this moment. I don't know anybody in all the world out there. Nobody but my aunt. And if I wrote her it'd make her feel bad, a hundred miles from here, to have to find someone else to read the letter to her. She's got a whale-boned-corset sort of pride. Make her nervous the next ten years, that letter setting in her house on the mantel. No, no letter to her." Cora's eyes moved from the hills and the unseen ocean. "Who then? Where? Someone. I just've got to get me some letters."

"Hold on." Benjy fished a dime magazine from his coat. It had a red cover of an undressed lady screaming away from a green monster. "All sorts of addresses in here."

They leafed the pages together. "What's this?" Cora tapped an ad.

" 'HERE'S YOUR *Power Plus* FREE MUSCLE CHART. Send name, address,' " read Benjy, " 'to Dept. M-3 for Free Health Map!' "

"And what about *this* one?"

" 'DETECTIVES MAKE SECRET INVESTIGATIONS, PARTICULARS FREE. WRITE G.D.M. DETECTIVE SCHOOL——' "

"Everything's free. Well, Benjy." She looked at the pencil in his hand. He drew up his chair. She watched him turn the pencil in his fingers, making minor adjustments. She saw him bite his tongue softly. She saw him squint his eyes. She held her breath. She bent forward. She squinted her own eyes and clamped her tongue.

Now, now Benjy raised his pencil, licked it, and set it down to the paper.

There it is, thought Cora.

The first words. They formed themselves slowly on the incredible paper.

Dear Power Plus Muscle Company
Sirs, [he wrote].

The morning blew away on a wind, the morning flowed down the creek, the morning flew off with some ravens, and the sun burned on the cabin roof. Cora didn't turn when she heard a shuffle at the blazing, sun-filled door. Tom was there, but not there; nothing was before her but a series of filled pages, a whispering pencil, and Benjy's Palmer Penmanship hand. Cora moved her head around, around, with each *o,* each *l,* with each small hill of an *m*; each tiny dot made her head peck like a chicken; each crossed *t* made her tongue lick across her upper lip.

"It's noon and I'm hungry!" said Tom almost behind her.

But Cora was a statue now, watching the pencil as one watches a snail leaving an exceptional trail across a flat stone in the early morning.

"It's noon!" cried Tom again.

Cora glanced up, stunned.

"Why, it seems only a moment ago we wrote to that Philadelphia Coin Collecting Company, ain't that right, Benjy?" Cora smiled a smile much too dazzling for a woman fifty-five years old. "While you wait for your vittles, Tom, just can't you build that mailbox? Bigger than Mrs. Brabbam's, please?"

"I'll nail up a shoe box."

"Tom Gibbs." She rose pleasantly. Her smile said, Better run, better work, better *do!* "I want a big, pretty mailbox. All white, for Benjy to paint our name on in black spelling. I won't have a shoe box for my very first real letter."

And it was done.

Benjy lettered the finished mailbox: MRS. CORA GIBBS, while Tom stood grumbling behind him.

"What's it say?"

" 'MR. TOM GIBBS,' " said Benjy quietly, painting.

Tom blinked at it for a minute, quietly, and then said, "I'm *still* hungry. Someone light the fire."

There were no stamps. Cora turned white. Tom was made to hitch up the horse and drive to Green Fork to buy some red ones, a green, and ten pink stamps with dignified gentlemen printed on them. But Cora rode along to be certain Tom didn't hurl these first letters in the creek. When they rode home, the first thing Cora did, face glowing, was poke in the new mailbox.

"You crazy?" said Tom.

"No harm looking."

That afternoon she visited the mailbox six times. On the seventh, a woodchuck jumped out. Tom stood laughing in the door, pounding his knees. Cora chased him out of the house, still laughing.

Then she stood in the window looking down at her mailbox right across from Mrs. Brabbam's. Ten years ago the Widow Lady had plunked her letter box right under Cora's nose, almost, when she could as easily have built it up nearer her own cabin. But it gave Mrs. Brabbam an excuse to float like a flower on a river down the hill path, flip the box wide with a great coughing and rustling, from time to time spying to see if Cora was watching. Cora always was. When caught, she pretended to sprinkle flowers with an empty watering can, or pick mushrooms in the wrong season.

Next morning Cora was up before the sun had warmed the strawberry patch or the wind had stirred the pines.

Benjy was sitting up in his cot when Cora returned from the mailbox. "Too early," he said. "Postman won't drive by yet."

"*Drive* by?"

"They come in cars this far out."

"Oh." Cora sat down.

"You sick, Aunt Cora?"

"No, no." She blinked. "It's just, I don't recall in twenty years seeing no mail truck whistle by here. It just came to me. All this time, I never seen no mailman at all."

"Maybe he comes when you're not around."

"I'm up with the fog spunks, down with the chickens. I never really gave it a thought, of course, but——" She turned to look out the window, up at Mrs. Brabbam's house. "Benjy, I got a kind of sneaking hunch." She stood up and walked straight out of the cabin, down the dust path, Benjy following, across the thin road to Mrs. Brabbam's mailbox. A hush was on the fields and hills. It was so early it made you whisper.

"Don't break the law, Aunt Cora!"

"Shh! Here." She opened the box, put her hand in like someone fumbling in a gopher hole. "And here, and here." She rattled some letters into his cupped hands.

"Why, these been opened already! You open these, Aunt Cora?"

"Child, I never touched them." Her face was stunned. "This is the first time in my life I ever even let my shadow touch this box."

Benjy turned the letters around and around, cocking his head. "Why, Aunt Cora, these letters, they're ten years old!"

"What!" Cora grabbed at them.

"Aunt Cora, that lady's been getting the same mail every day for years. And they're not even addressed to Mrs. Brabbam, they're to some woman named Ortega in Green Fork."

"Ortega, the Mexican grocery woman! All these years," whispered Cora, staring at the worn mail in her hands. "All these years."

They gazed up at Mrs. Brabbam's sleeping house in the cool quiet morning.

"Oh, that sly woman, making a commotion with her letters, making me feel small. All puffed out she was, swishing along, reading her mail."

Mrs. Brabbam's front door opened.

"Put them back, Aunt Cora!"

Cora slammed the mailbox shut with time to spare.

Mrs. Brabbam drifted down the path, stopping here or there, quietly, to peer at the opening wild flowers.

"Morning," she said sweetly.

"Mrs. Brabbam, this is my nephew Benjy."

"How nice." Mrs. Brabbam, with a great swivel of her body, a flourish of her flour-white hands, rapped the mailbox as if to shake the letters loose inside, flipped the lid, and extracted the mail, covering her actions with her back. She made motions, and spun about merrily, winking. "Wonderful! Why, just look at this letter from dear Uncle George!"

"Well, ain't that *nice!*" said Cora.

Then the breathless summer days of waiting. The butterflies jumping orange and blue on the air, the flowers nodding about the cabin, and the hard, constant sound of Benjy's pencil scribbling through the afternoons. Benjy's mouth was always packed with food, and Tom was always stomping in, to find lunch or supper late, cold, or both, or none at all.

Benjy handled the pencil with a delicious spread of his bony hands, lovingly inscribing each vowel and consonant as Cora hovered about him, making up words, rolling them on her tongue, delighted each time she saw them roll out on the paper. But she wasn't learning to write. "It's so much fun watching you write, Benjy. Tomorrow I'll start learning. Now take another letter!"

They worked their way through ads about Asthma, Trusses and Magic, they joined the Rosicrucians, or at least sent for a free Sealed Book all about the Knowledge that had been damned to oblivion, Secrets from Hidden ancient temples and buried sanctuaries. Then there were free packets of Giant Sunflower seeds, and something about HEARTBURN. They had worked back to page 127 of *Quarter Murder Magazine* on a bright summer morning when . . .

"Listen!" said Cora.

They listened.

"A car," said Benjy.

And up the blue hills and through the tall fiery green pines and along the dusty road, mile by mile, came the sound of a car riding along and along, until finally, at the bend, it came full thundering, and in an instant Cora was out of the door running, and as she ran she heard and saw and felt many things. First, from the corner of her eye, she saw Mrs. Brabbam gliding down the road from the other direction. Mrs. Brabbam froze when she saw the bright green car boiling on the grade, and there was the whistle of a silver whistle and the old man in the car leaned out just before Cora arrived and said, "Mrs. Gibbs?" "Yes!" she cried. "Mail for you, ma'am," he said, and held it toward her. She put out her hand, then drew it back, remembering. "Oh," she said, "please, would you mind, would you put it, please . . . in my mailbox?" The old man squinted at her, at the mailbox, back at her, and laughed. "Don't mind," he said, and did just that, put the mail in the box.

Mrs. Brabbam stood where she was, not moving, eyes wild.
"Any mail for Mrs. Brabbam?" asked Cora.

"That's all." And the car dusted away down the road.

Mrs. Brabbam stood with her hands clenched together. Then, without looking in her own letter box, turned and rustled swiftly up her path, out of sight.

Cora walked around her mailbox twice, not touching it for a long time. "Benjy, I've got me some letters!" She reached in delicately and took them out and turned them over. She put them quietly in his hand. "Read them to me. Is my name on the front?"

"Yes'm." He opened the first letter with due carefulness and read it aloud in the summer morning:

" 'Dear Mrs. Gibbs . . .' "

He stopped and let her savor it, her eyes half shut, her mouth moving the words. He repeated it for artistic emphasis and then went on: " 'We are sending you our free folder, enclosed, from the Intercontinental Mailing Schools concerning full particulars on how you, too, can take our Correspondence Course in Sanitary Engineering——' "

"Benjy, Benjy, I'm so happy! Start over again!"

" 'Dear Mrs. Gibbs,' " he read.

After that the mailbox was never empty. The world came rushing and crowding in, all the places she had never seen or heard about or been to. Travel folders, spice cake recipes, and even a letter from an elderly gentleman who wished for a lady "—fifty years old, gentle disposition, money; object matrimony." Benjy wrote back, "I am already married, but thank you for your kind and thoughtful consideration. Yours truly, Cora Gibbs."

And the letters continued to pour across the hills, coin collectors' catalogues, Dime Novelty books, Magic List Numbers, Arthritis Charts, Flea Killer Samples. The world filled up her letter box, and suddenly she was not alone or remote from people. If a man wrote a form letter to Cora about the Mysteries of Ancient Maya Revealed, he was likely as not to receive three letters from Cora in the next week, budding out their formal meeting into a warm friendship. After one particularly hard day of writing, Benjy was forced to soak his hand in Epsom salts.

By the end of the third week Mrs. Brabbam no longer came down to her mailbox. She didn't even come out the front door of her cabin to get the air, for Cora was always down at the road, leaning out, smiling for the mailman.

All too quickly the summer was at an end, or, at least, that part of the summer that counted most, anyway; Benjy's visit. There was his red bandanna handkerchief on the cabin table, sandwiches folded fresh and oniony in it, tied with a mint sprig to keep it clean to the smell; there on the floor, freshly polished, were his shoes to get into, and there on the chair, with his pencil which had once been long and yellow but was now stubby and chewed, sat Benjy. Cora took hold of his chin and tilted his head, as if she were testing a summer squash of an unfamiliar variety.

"Benjy, I owe you an apology. I don't think I looked at your face once in all this time. Seems I know every wart on your hand, every hangnail, every bump and every crinkle, but I might pass your face in a crowd and miss you."

"It's no face to look at," said Benjy shyly.

"But I'd know that hand in a million hands," Cora said. "Let anyone shake my hand in a dark room, a thousand people, and out of all those I'd say, 'Well, this one's Benjy.' " She smiled quietly and walked away to the open door. "I been thinking." She looked up at a distant cabin. "Ain't seen Mrs. Brabbam in weeks. Stays in all the time now. I've got a guilty feeling. I've done a prideful thing, a thing more sinful than she ever done me. I took the bottom out of her life. It was a mean and spiteful thing and I'm ashamed." She gazed up the hill toward that silent, locked place. "Benjy, would you do me one last favor?"

"Yes'm."

"Write a letter for Mrs. Brabbam."

"Ma'am?"

"Yes, write one of those companies for a free chart, a sample, something, and sign Mrs. Brabbam's name."

"All right," said Benjy.

"That way, in a week or a month the postman'll come by

and whistle, and I'll tell him to go up to her door, special, and deliver it. And I'll be sure and be out in my front yard where I can see and Mrs. Brabbam can see I see. And I'll wave my letters to her and she'll wave her letters to me, and everybody'll smile."

"Yes'm," said Benjy.

He wrote three letters, licked the envelopes carefully, stuck them in his pocket. "I'll mail them when I get to St. Louis."

"It's been a fine summer," she said.

"It sure has."

"But, Benjy, I didn't learn to write, did I? I was after the letters and made you write late nights, and we were so busy sending labels and getting samples, land, it seemed there wasn't time to learn. And that means . . ."

He knew what it meant. He shook her hand. They stood in the cabin door. "Thanks," she said, "for everything."

Then he was running off. He ran as far as the meadow fence, leaped it easily, and the last she saw of him he was still running, waving the special letters, off into the great world over the hills.

The letters kept coming for some six months after Benjy went away. There would be the postman's little green car and the sharp ice-rimed shout of good morning, or the whistle, as he clapped two or three pink or blue envelopes into that fine mailbox.

And there was that special day when Mrs. Brabbam received her first real letter.

After that the letters were spaced a week apart, then a month, and finally the postman didn't say hello at all, there was no sound of a car coming up that lonely mountain road. First a spider moved into the mailbox, then a sparrow.

And Cora, while the letters still lasted, would clutch them in her bewildered hands, staring at them quietly until the pressure of her face muscles squeezed clear round shiny drops of water from her eyes. She'd hold up one blue envelope. "Who's this from?"

"Don't know," said Tom.

"What's it say?" she wailed.

"Don't know," said Tom.

"What's going on in that world out there, oh, I'll never know, I'll never know now," she said. "And this letter, and this one, and *this!*" She tumbled the stacks and stacks of letters that had come since Benjy ran off. "All the world and all the people and all the happenings, and me not knowing. All that world and people waiting to hear from us, and us not writing, and them not ever writing back!"

And at last the day came when the wind blew the mailbox over. In the mornings again, Cora would stand at the open door of her cabin, brushing her gray hair with a slow brush, not speaking, looking at the hills. And in all the years that followed she never passed the fallen mailbox without stooping aimlessly to fumble inside and take her hand out with nothing in it before she wandered on again into the fields.

Powerhouse

The horses moved gently to a stop, and the man and his wife gazed down into a dry, sandy valley. The woman sat lost in her saddle; she hadn't spoken for hours, didn't know a good word to speak. She was trapped somewhere between the hot, dark pressure of the storm-clouded Arizona sky and the hard, granite pressure of the wind-blasted mountains. A few drops of cool rain fell on her trembling hands.

She looked over at her husband wearily. He sat his dusty horse easily, with a firm quietness. She closed her eyes and thought of how she had been all of these mild years until today. She wanted to laugh at the mirror she was holding up to herself, but there was no way of doing even that; it would be somewhat insane. After all, it might just be the pushing of this dark weather, or the telegram they had taken from the messenger on horseback this morning, or the long journey now to town.

There was still an empty world to cross, and she was cold.

"I'm the lady who was never going to need religion," she said quietly, her eyes shut.

"What?" Berty, her husband, glanced over at her.

"Nothing," she whispered, shaking her head. In all the years, how *certain* she had been. Never, never would she have need of a church. She had heard fine people talk on and on of religion and waxed pews and calla lilies in great bronze buckets and vast bells of churches in which the preacher rang like a clapper. She had heard the shouting kind and the fervent, whispery kind, and they were all the same. Hers was simply not a pew-shaped spine.

"I just never had a reason ever to sit in a church," she had told people. She wasn't vehement about it. She just walked around and lived and moved her hands that were pebble-smooth and pebble-small. Work had polished the nails of those hands with a polish you could never buy in a bottle. The touching of children had made them soft, and the raising of children had made them temperately stern, and the loving of a husband had made them gentle.

And now, death made them tremble.

"Here," said her husband. And the horses dusted down the trail to where an odd brick building stood beside a dry wash. The building was all glazed green windows, blue machinery, red tile, and wires. The wires ran off on high-tension towers to the farthest directions of the desert. She watched them go, silently, and, still held by her thoughts, turned her gaze back to the strange storm-green windows and the burning-colored bricks.

She had never slipped a ribbon in a Bible at a certain significant verse, because though her life in this desert was a life of granite, sun, and the steaming away of the waters of her flesh, there had never been a threat in it to her. Always things had worked out before the necessity had come for sleepless dawns and wrinkles in the forehead. Somehow, the very poisonous things of life had passed her. Death was a remote storm rumor beyond the farthest range.

Twenty years had blown in tumbleweeds, away, since she'd come West, worn this lonely trapping man's gold ring, and taken the desert as a third, and constant, partner to their living. None of their four children had ever been fearfully sick or near death. She had never had to get down on her knees except for the scrubbing of an already well-scrubbed floor.

Now all that was ended. Here they were riding toward a remote town because a simple piece of yellow paper had come and said very plainly that her mother was dying.

And she could not imagine it—no matter how she turned her head to see or turned her mind to look in on itself. There were no rungs anywhere to hold to, going either up *or* down, and her mind, like a compass left out in a sudden storm of sand, was suddenly blown free of all its once-clear directions, all points of reference worn away, the needle spinning without purpose, around, around. Even with Berty's arms on her back it wasn't enough. It was like the end of a good play and the beginning of an evil one. Someone she loved was actually going to die. This was impossible!

"I've got to stop," she said, not trusting her voice at all, so she made it sound irritated to cover her fear.

Berty knew her as no irritated woman, so the irritation did not carry over and fill him up. He was a capped jug; the contents there for sure. Rain on the outside didn't stir the brew. He side-ran his horse to her and took her hand gently. "Sure," he said. He squinted at the eastern sky. "Some clouds piling up black there. We'll wait a bit. It might rain. I wouldn't want to get caught in it."

Now she was irritated at her own irritation, one fed upon the other, and she was helpless. But rather than speak and risk the cycle's commencing again, she slumped forward and began to sob, allowing her horse to be led until it stood and tramped its feet softly beside the red brick building.

She slid down like a parcel into his arms, and he held her as she turned in on his shoulder; then he set her down and said, "Don't look like there's people here." He called, "Hey, there!" and looked at the sign on the door: *Danger. Bureau of Electric Power.*

There was a great insect humming all through the air. It sang in a ceaseless, bumbling tone, rising a bit, perhaps falling just a bit, but keeping the same pitch. Like a woman humming between pressed lips as she makes a meal in the warm twilight over a hot stove. They could see no movement within the building; there was only the gigantic humming. It was the sort of noise you would expect the sun-shimmer to make rising from hot railroad ties on a blazing summer day, when there is that flurried silence and you see the air eddy and whorl and ribbon, and expect a sound from the process but get nothing but an arched tautness of the eardrums and the tense quiet.

The humming came up through her heels, into her medium-slim legs, and thence to her body. It moved to her heart and touched it, as the sight of Berty just sitting on a top rail of the corral often did. And then it moved on to her head and the slenderest niches in the skull and set up a singing, as love songs and good books had done once on a time.

The humming was everywhere. It was as much a part of the soil as the cactus. It was as much a part of the air as the heat.

''What is it?'' she asked, vaguely perplexed, looking at the building.

''I don't know much about it except it's a powerhouse,'' said Berty. He tried the door. ''It's open,'' he said, surprised. ''I wish someone was around.'' The door swung wide and the pulsing hum came out like a breath of air over them, louder.

They entered together into the solemn, singing place. She held him tightly, arm in arm.

It was a dim undersea place, smooth and clean and polished, as if something or other was always coming through and coming through and nothing ever stayed, but always there was motion and motion, invisible and stirring and never settling. On each side of them as they advanced were what first appeared to be people standing quietly, one after the other, in a double line. But these resolved into round, shell-like machines from which the humming sprang. Each black and gray and green machine gave forth golden cables and lime-colored wires, and there were silver metal pouches with crimson tabs and white lettering, and a pit like a washtub in which something whirled as if rinsing unseen materials at invisible speeds. The centrifuge raced so fast it stood still. Immense snakes of copper lopped down from the twilight ceiling, and vertical pipes webbed up from cement floor to fiery brick wall. And the whole of it was as clean as a bolt of green lightning and smelled similarly. There was a crackling, eating sound, a dry rustling as of paper; flickers of blue fire shuttled, snapped, sparked, hissed where wires joined porcelain bobbins and green glass insulation.

Outside, in the real world, it began to rain.

She didn't want to stay in this place; it was no place to stay, with its people that were not people but dim machines and its music like an organ caught and pressed on a low note and a high note. But the rain washed every window and Berty said,

"Looks like it'll last. Might have to stay the night here. It's late, anyhow. I'd better get the stuff in."

She said nothing. She wanted to be getting on. Getting on to what thing in what place, there was really no way of knowing. But at least in town she would hold onto the money and buy the tickets and hold them tight in her hand and hold onto a train which would rush and make a great noise, and get off the train, and get another horse, or get into a car hundreds of miles away and ride again, and stand at last by her dead or alive mother. It all depended on time and breath. There were many places she would pass through, but none of them would offer a thing to her except ground for her feet, air for her nostrils, food for her numb mouth. And these were worse than nothing. Why go to her mother at all, say words, and make gestures? she wondered. What would be the use?

The floor was clean as a solid river under her. When she moved forward on it, it sent echoes cracking back and forth like small, faint gunshots through the room. Any word that was spoken came back as from a granite cavern.

Behind her, she heard Berty setting down the equipment. He spread two gray blankets and put out a little collection of tinned foods.

It was night. The rain still streamed on the high green-glazed windows, rinsing and making patterns of silk that flowed and intermingled in soft clear curtains. There were occasional thunderclaps which fell and broke upon themselves in avalanches of cold rain and wind hitting sand and stone.

Her head lay upon a folded cloth, and no matter how she turned it, the humming of the immense powerhouse worked up through the cloth into her head. She shifted, shut her eyes, and adjusted herself, but it went on and on. She sat up, patted the cloth, lay back down.

But the humming was there.

She knew without looking, by some sense deep in herself, that her husband was awake. There was no year she could remember when she hadn't known. It was some subtle difference in his breathing. It was the absence of sound, rather; no sound of breathing at all, save at long carefully thought-out intervals.

She knew then that he was looking at her in the rainy darkness, concerned with her, taking great care of his breath.

She turned in the darkness. "Berty?"

"Yes?"

"I'm awake too," she said.

"I know," he said.

They lay, she very straight, very rigid, he in a half curl, like a hand relaxed, half bent inward. She traced this dark, easy curve and was filled with incomprehensible wonder.

"Berty," she asked, and paused a long while, "how . . . how are you like you are?"

He waited a moment. "How do you mean?" he said.

"How do you *rest?*" She stopped. It sounded very bad. It sounded so much like an accusation, but it was not, really. She knew him to be a man concerned with all things, a man who could see in darknesses and who was not conceited because of his ability. He was worried for her now, and for her mother's life or death, but he had a way of worrying that seemed indifferent and irresponsible. It was neither of the two. His concern was all in him, deep; but it lay side by side with some faith, some belief that accepted it, made it welcome, and did not fight it. Something in him took hold of the sorrow first, got acquainted with it, knew each of its traceries before passing the message on to all of his waiting body. His body held a faith like a maze, and the sorrow that struck into him was lost and gone before it finally reached where it wanted to hurt him. Sometimes this faith drove her into a senseless anger, from which she recovered quickly, knowing how useless it was to criticize something as contained as a stone in a peach.

"Why didn't I ever catch it from you?" she said at last.

He laughed a little bit, softly. "Catch what?"

"I caught everything else. You shook me up and down in other ways. I didn't know anything but what you taught me." She stopped. It was hard to explain. Their life had been like the warm blood in a person passing through tissues quietly, both ways.

"Everything but religion," she said. "I never caught that from you."

"It's not a catching thing," he said. "Someday you just relax. And there it is."

Relax, she thought. Relax what? The body. But how to relax the mind? Her fingers twitched beside her. Her eyes wandered idly about the vast interior of the powerhouse. The machines stood over her in dark silhouettes with little sparkles crawling on them. The humming-humming-humming crept along her limbs.

Sleepy. Tired. She drowsed. Her eyes lidded and opened and lidded and opened. The humming-humming filled her marrow as if small hummingbirds were suspended in her body and in her head.

She traced the half-seen tubing up and up into the ceiling, and she saw the machines and heard the invisible whirlings. She suddenly became very alert in her drowsiness. Her eyes moved swiftly up and up and then down and across, and the humming-singing of the machines grew louder and louder, and her eyes moved, and her body relaxed; and on the tall, green windows she saw the shadows of the high-tension wires rushing off into the raining night.

Now the humming was in her, her eyes jerked, she felt herself yanked violently upright. She felt seized by a whirling dynamo, around, around in a whirl, out, out, into the heart of whirling invisibilities, fed into, accepted by a thousand copper wires, and shot, in an instant, over the earth!

She was everywhere at once!

Streaking along high monster towers in instants, sizzling between high poles where small glass knobs sat like crystal-green birds holding the wires in their nonconductive beaks, branching in four directions, eight secondary directions, finding towns, hamlets, cities, racing on to farms, ranches, haciendas, she descended gently like a widely filamented spider web upon a thousand square miles of desert!

The earth was suddenly more than many separate things, more than houses, rocks, concrete roads, a horse here or there, a human in a shallow, boulder-topped grave, a prickling of cactus, a town invested with its own light surrounded by night, a million apart things. Suddenly it all had one pattern encompassed and held by the pulsing electric web.

She spilled out swiftly into rooms where life was rising from a slap on a naked child's back, into rooms where life was leaving bodies like the light fading from an electric bulb—the filament glowing, fading, finally colorless. She was in every town, every room, making light-patterns over hundreds of miles of land; seeing, hearing everything, not alone anymore, but one of thousands of people, each with his ideas and his faiths.

Her body lay, a lifeless reed, pale and trembling. Her mind, in all its electric tensity, was flung about this way, that, down vast networks of powerhouse tributary.

Everything balanced. In one room she saw life wither; in another, a mile away, she saw wineglasses lifted to the newborn, cigars passed, smiles, handshakes, laughter. She saw the pale, drawn faces of people at white deathbeds, heard how they understood and accepted death, saw their gestures, felt their feelings, and saw that they, too, were lonely in themselves, with no way to get to the world to see the balance, see it as she was seeing it now.

She swallowed. Her eyelids flickered and her throat burned under her upraised fingers.

She was not alone.

The dynamo had whirled and flung her with centrifugal force out along a thousand lines into a million glass capsules screwed into ceilings, plucked into light by a pull of a cord or a twist of a knob or a flick of a switch.

The light could be in *any* room; all that was needed was to touch the switch. All rooms were dark until light came. And here she was, in all of them at once. And she was not alone. Her grief was but one part of a vast grief, her fear only one of countless others. And this grief was only a half thing. There was the other half; of things born, of comfort in the shape of a new child, of food in the warmed body, of colors for the eye and sounds in the awakened ear, and spring wild flowers for the smelling.

Whenever a light blinked out, life threw another switch; rooms were illumined afresh.

She was with those named Clark and those named Gray and the Shaws and Martins and Hanfords, the Fentons, the Drakes, the Shattucks, the Hubbells, and the Smiths. Being alone was not alone, except in the mind. You had all sorts of peekholes in your head. A silly, strange way to put it, perhaps, but there were the holes; the ones to see through and see that the world was there and people in it, as hard put to and uneasy as yourself; and there were the holes for hearing, and the one for speaking out your grief and getting rid of it, and the holes for knowing the changes of season through the scents of summer grain or winter ice or autumn fires. They were there to be used so that one was not alone. Loneliness was a shutting of the eyes. Faith was a simple opening.

The light-net fell upon all the world she had known for twenty years, herself blended with every line. She glowed and pulsed and was gentled in the great easy fabric. It lay across the land, covering each mile like a gentle, warm, and humming blanket. She was everywhere.

In the powerhouse the turbines whirled and hummed and the electric sparks, like little votive candles, jumped and clustered upon bent elbows of electric piping and glass. And the machines stood like saints and choruses, haloed now yellow, now red, now green, and a massed singing beat along the roof hollows and echoed down in endless hymns and chants. Outside, the wind clamored at the brick walls and drenched the glazed windows with rain; inside, she lay upon her small pillow and suddenly began to cry.

Whether it was with understanding, acceptance, joy, resignation, she couldn't know. The singing went on, higher and higher, and she was everywhere. She put out her hand, caught hold of her husband, who was still awake, his eyes fixed at the ceiling. Perhaps he had run everywhere, too, in this instant, through the network of light and power. But then, he had always been everywhere at once. He felt himself a unit of a whole and therefore he was stable; to her, unity was new and shaking. She felt his arms suddenly around her and she pressed her face into his shoulder for a long while, hard, while the humming and the humming climbed higher, and she cried freely, achingly, against him. . . .

In the morning the desert sky was very clear. They walked from the powerhouse quietly, saddled their horses, cinched on all of the equipment, and mounted.

She settled herself and sat there under the blue sky. And

slowly she was aware of her back, and her back was straight, and she looked at her alien hands on the reins, and they had ceased trembling. And she could see the far mountains; there was no blur nor a running-of-color to things. All was solid stone touching stone, and stone touching sand, and sand touching wild flower, and wild flower touching the sky in one continuous clear flow, everything definite and of a piece.

"Wope!" cried Berty, and the horses walked slowly off, away from the brick building, through the cool sweet morning air.

She rode handsomely and she rode well, and in her, like a stone in a peach, was a peacefulness. She called to her husband as they slowed on a rise, "Berty!"

"Yes?"

"Can we . . ." she asked.

"Can we what?" he said, not hearing the first time.

"Can we come here again sometime?" she asked, nodding back toward the powerhouse. "Once in a while? Some Sunday?"

He looked at her and nodded slowly. "I reckon. Yes. Sure. I reckon so."

And as they rode on into town she was humming, humming a strange soft tune, and he glanced over and listened to it, and it was the sound you would expect to hear from sun-warmed railroad ties on a hot summer day when the air rises in a shimmer, flurried and whorling; a sound in one key, one pitch, rising a little, falling a little, humming, humming, but constant, peaceful, and wondrous to hear.

En La Noche

All night Mrs. Navarrez moaned, and these moans filled the tenement like a light turned on in every room so no one could sleep. All night she gnashed her white pillow and wrung her thin hands and cried, "My Joe!" The tenement people, at 3 A.M., finally discouraged that she would *never* shut her painted red mouth, arose, feeling warm and gritty, and dressed to take the trolley downtown to an all-night movie. There Roy Rogers chased bad men through veils of stale smoke and spoke dialogue above the soft snorings in the dark night theater.

By dawn Mrs. Navarrez was still sobbing and screaming.

During the day it was not so bad. Then the massed choir of babies crying here or there in the house added the saving grace of what was almost a harmony. There was also the chugging thunder of the washing machines on the tenement porch, and chenille-robed women standing on the flooded, soggy boards of the porch, talking their Mexican gossip rapidly. But now and again, above the shrill talk, the washing, the babies, one could hear Mrs. Navarrez like a radio tuned high. "My Joe, oh, my poor Joe!" she screamed.

Now, at twilight, the men arrived with the sweat of their work under their arms. Lolling in cool bathtubs all through the cooking tenement, they cursed and held their hands to their ears.

"Is she *still* at it!" they raged helplessly. One man even kicked her door. "Shut *up,* woman!" But this only made Mrs. Navarrez shriek louder. "Oh, ah! Joe, Joe!"

"Tonight we eat out!" said the men to their wives. All through the house, kitchen utensils were shelved and doors locked as men hurried their perfumed wives down the halls by their pale elbows.

Mr. Villanazul, unlocking his ancient, flaking door at midnight, closed his brown eyes and stood for a moment, swaying. His wife Tina stood beside him with their three sons and two daughters, one in arms.

"Oh God," whispered Mr. Villanazul. "Sweet Jesus, come down off the cross and silence that woman." They entered their dim little room and looked at the blue candlelight flickering under a lonely crucifix. Mr. Villanazul shook his head philosophically. "He is still on the cross."

They lay in their beds like burning barbecues, the summer night basting them with their own liquors. The house flamed with that ill woman's cry.

"I am stifled!" Mr. Villanazul fled through the tenement, downstairs to the front porch with his wife, leaving the children, who had the great and miraculous talent of sleeping through all things.

Dim figures occupied the front porch, a dozen quiet men crouched with cigarettes fuming and glowing in their brown fingers, women in chenille wrappers taking what there was of the summer-night wind. They moved like dream figures, like clothes dummies worked stiffly on wires and rollers. Their eyes were puffed and their tongues thick.

"Let us go to her room and strangle her," said one of the men.

"No, that would not be right," said a woman. "Let us throw her from the window."

Everyone laughed tiredly.

Mr. Villanazul stood blinking bewilderedly at all the people. His wife moved sluggishly beside him.

"You would think Joe was the only man in the world to join the Army," someone said irritably. "Mrs. Navarrez, *pah!* This Joe-husband of hers will peel potatoes; the safest man in the infantry!"

"Something *must* be done." Mr. Villanazul had spoken. He

was startled at the hard firmness of his own voice. Everyone glanced at him.

"We can't go on another night," Mr. Villanazul continued bluntly.

"The more we pound her door, the more she cries," explained Mr. Gomez.

"The priest came this afternoon," said Mrs. Gutierrez. "We sent for him in desperation. But Mrs. Navarrez would not even let him in the door, no matter how he pleaded. The priest went away. We had Officer Gilvie yell at her, too, but do you think she listened?"

"We must try some other way, then," mused Mr. Villanazul. "Someone must be—sympathetic—with her."

"What other way is there?" asked Mr. Gomez.

"If only," figured Mr. Villanazul after a moment's thought, "if only there was a *single* man among us."

He dropped that like a cold stone into a deep well. He let the splash occur and the ripples move gently out.

Everybody sighed.

It was like a little summer-night wind arisen. The men straightened up a bit; the women quickened.

"But," replied Mr. Gomez, sinking back, "we are all married. There is no single man."

"Oh," said everyone, and settled down into the hot, empty river bed of night, smoke rising, silent.

"Then," Mr. Villanazul shot back, lifting his shoulders, tightening his mouth, "it must be one of *us!*"

Again the night wind blew, stirring the people in awe.

"This is no time for selfishness!" declared Villanazul. "One of us must *do* this thing! That, or roast in hell another night!"

Now the people on the porch separated away from him, blinking. "*You* will do it, of course, Mr. Villanazul?" they wished to know.

He stiffened. The cigarette almost fell from his fingers. "Oh, but I——" he objected.

"You," they said. "Yes?"

He waved his hands feverishly. "I have a wife and five children, one in arms!"

"But none of us are single, and it is your idea and you

must have the courage of your convictions, Mr. Villanazul!'' everyone said.

He was very frightened and silent. He glanced with startled flashes of his eyes at his wife.

She stood wearily weaving on the night air, trying to see him.

''I'm so *tired,*'' she grieved.

''Tina,'' he said.

''I will die if I do not sleep,'' she said.

''Oh, but, Tina,'' he said.

''I will die and there will be many flowers and I will be buried if I do not get some rest,'' she murmured.

''She looks very bad,'' said everyone.

Mr. Villanazul hesitated only a moment longer. He touched his wife's slack hot fingers. He touched her hot cheek with his lips.

Without a word he walked from the porch.

They could hear his feet climbing the unlit stairs of the house, up and around to the third floor where Mrs. Navarrez wailed and screamed.

They waited on the porch.

The men lit new cigarettes and flicked away the matches, talking like the wind, the women wandering around among them, all of them coming and talking to Mrs. Villanazul, who stood, lines under her tired eyes, leaning against the porch rail.

''*Now,*'' whispered one of the men quietly. ''Mr. Villanazul is at the top of the house!''

Everybody quieted.

''Now,'' hissed the man in a stage whisper. ''Mr. Villanazul taps at her door! Tap, tap.''

Everyone listened, holding his breath.

Far away there was a gentle tapping sound.

''Now, Mrs. Navarrez, at this intrusion, breaks out anew with crying!''

At the top of the house came a scream.

''Now,'' the man imagined, crouched, his hand delicately weaving on the air, ''Mr. Villanazul pleads and pleads, softly, quietly, to the locked door.''

The people on the porch lifted their chins tentatively, trying to see through three flights of wood and plaster to the third floor, waiting.

The screaming faded.

"Now, Mr. Villanazul talks quickly, he pleads, he whispers, he promises," cried the man softly.

The screaming settled to a sobbing, the sobbing to a moan, and finally all died away into breathing and the pounding of hearts and listening.

After about two minutes of standing, sweating, waiting, everyone on the porch heard the door far away upstairs rattle its lock, open, and, a second later, with a whisper, close.

The house was silent.

Silence lived in every room like a light turned off. Silence flowed like a cool wine in the tunnel halls. Silence came through the open casements like a cool breath from the cellar. They all stood breathing the coolness of it.

"Ah," they sighed.

Men flicked away cigarettes and moved on tiptoe into the silent tenement. Women followed. Soon the porch was empty. They drifted in cool halls of quietness.

Mrs. Villanazul, in a drugged stupor, unlocked her door.

"We must give Mr. Villanazul a banquet," a voice whispered.

"Light a candle for him tomorrow."

The doors shut.

In her fresh bed Mrs. Villanazul lay. He is a thoughtful man, she dreamed, eyes closed. For such things, I love him.

The silence was like a cool hand, stroking her to sleep.

Sun and Shadow

The camera clicked like an insect. It was blue and metallic, like a great fat beetle held in the man's precious and tenderly exploiting hands. It winked in the flashing sunlight.

"Hsst, Ricardo, come away!"

"You down there!" cried Ricardo out the window.

"Ricardo, stop!"

He turned to his wife. "Don't tell me to stop, tell them to stop. Go down and tell them, or are you afraid?"

"They aren't hurting anything," said his wife patiently.

He shook her off and leaned out the window and looked down into the alley. "You there!" he cried.

The man with the black camera in the alley glanced up, then went on focusing his machine at the lady in the salt-white beach pants, the white bra, and the green checkered scarf. She leaned against the cracked plaster of the building. Behind her a dark boy smiled, his hand to his mouth.

"Tomás!" yelled Ricardo. He turned to his wife. "Oh, Jesus the Blessed, Tomás is in the street, my own son laughing there." Ricardo started out the door.

"Don't do anything!" said his wife.

"I'll cut off their heads!" said Ricardo, and was gone.

In the street the lazy woman was lounging now against the peeling blue paint of a banister. Ricardo emerged in time to see her doing this. "That's my banister!" he said.

The cameraman hurried up. ''No, no, we're taking pictures. Everything's all right. We'll be moving on.''

''Everything's not all right,'' said Ricardo, his brown eyes flashing. He waves a wrinkled hand. ''She's on my house.''

''We're taking fashion pictures,'' smiled the photographer.

''*Now* what am I to do?'' said Ricardo to the blue sky. ''Go mad with this news? Dance around like an epileptic saint?''

''If it's money, well, here's a five-peso bill,'' smiled the photographer.

Ricardo pushed the hand away. ''I *work* for my money. You don't understand. Please go.''

The photographer was bewildered. ''Wait . . .''

''Tomás, get in the house!''

''But, Papa . . .''

''Gahh!'' bellowed Ricardo.

The boy vanished.

''This has *never* happened before,'' said the photographer.

''It is long past time! What are we? Cowards?'' Ricardo asked the world.

A crowd was gathering. They murmured and smiled and nudged each other's elbows. The photographer with irritable good will snapped his camera shut, said over his shoulder to the model, ''All right, we'll use that other street. I saw a nice cracked wall there and some nice deep shadows. If we hurry . . .''

The girl, who had stood during the exchange nervously twisting her scarf, now seized her make-up kit and darted by Ricardo, but not before he touched at her arm. ''Do not misunderstand,'' he said quickly. She stopped, blinked at him. He went on. ''It is not you I am mad at. Or you.'' He addressed the photographer.

''Then why——'' said the photographer.

Ricardo waved his hand. ''You are employed; I am employed. We are all people employed. We must understand each other. But when you come to my house with your camera that looks like the complex eye of a black horsefly, then the understanding is over. I will not have my alley used because of its pretty shadows, or my sky used because of its sun, or my house used because there is an interesting crack in the wall, here! You *see!* Ah, how beautiful! Lean here! Stand there! Sit here! Crouch there! Hold it! Oh, I *heard* you. Do you think I am stupid? I have books up in my room. You see that window? Maria!''

His wife's head popped out. ''Show them my books!'' he cried.

She fussed and muttered, but a moment later she held out one, then two, then half a dozen books, eyes shut, head turned away, as if they were old fish.

''And two dozen more like them upstairs!'' cried Ricardo. ''You're not talking to some cow in the forest, you're talking to a man!''

''Look,'' said the photographer, packing his plates swiftly. ''We're going. Thanks for nothing.''

''Before you go, you must see what I am getting at,'' said Ricardo. ''I am not a mean man. But I *can* be a very angry man. Do I look like a cardboard cutout?''

''Nobody said anybody looked like anything.'' The photographer hefted his case and started off.

''There is a photographer two blocks over,'' said Ricardo, pacing him. ''They have cutouts. You stand in front of them. It says 'GRAND HOTEL.' They take a picture of you and it looks like you are in the Grand Hotel. Do you see what I mean? My alley is my alley, my life is my life, my son is my son. My son is not cardboard! I saw you putting my son against the wall, so, and thus, in the background. What do you call it—for the correct air? To make the whole attractive, and the lovely lady in front of him?''

''It's getting late,'' said the photographer, sweating. The model trotted along on the other side of him.

''We are poor people,'' said Ricardo. ''Our doors peel paint, our walls are chipped and cracked, our gutters fume in the street, the alleys are all cobbles. But it fills me with a terrible rage when I see you make over these things as if I had *planned* it this way, as if I had years ago induced the wall to crack. Did you think I knew you were coming and aged the paint? Or that I knew you were coming and put my boy in his dirtiest clothes? We are *not* a studio! We are people and must be given attention as people. Have I made it clear?''

"With abundant detail," said the photographer, not looking at him, hurrying.

"Now that you know my wishes and my reasoning, you will do the friendly thing and go home?"

"You are a hilarious man," said the photographer. "Hey!" They had joined a group of five other models and a second photographer at the base of a vast stone stairway which in layers, like a bridal cake, led up to the white town square. "How you doing, Joe?"

"We got some beautiful shots near the Church of the Virgin, some statuary without any noses, lovely stuff," said Joe. "What's the commotion?"

"Pancho here got in an uproar. Seems we leaned against his house and knocked it down."

"My name is Ricardo. My house is completely intact."

"We'll shoot it *here,* dear," said the first photographer. "Stand by the archway of that store. There's a nice antique wall going up there." He peered into the mysteries of his camera.

"So!" A dreadful quiet came upon Ricardo. He watched them prepare. When they were ready to take the picture he hurried forward, calling to a man in a doorway. "Jorge! What are you *doing?*"

"I'm standing here," said the man.

"Well," said Ricardo, "isn't that *your* archway? Are you going to let them *use* it?"

"I'm not bothered," said Jorge.

Ricardo shook his arm. "They're treating your property like a movie actor's place. Aren't you insulted?"

"I haven't thought about it." Jorge picked his nose.

"Jesus upon earth, man, *think!*"

"I can't see any harm," said Jorge.

"Am I the *only* one in the world with a tongue in my mouth?" said Ricardo to his empty hands. "And taste on my tongue? Is this a town of backdrops and picture sets? Won't *anyone* do something about this except me?"

The crowd had followed them down the street, gathering others to it as it came; now it was of a fair size and more were coming, drawn by Ricardo's bullish shouts. He stomped his feet. He made fists. He spat. The cameraman and the models watched him nervously. "Do you want a *quaint* man in the background?" he said wildly to the cameraman. "I'll pose back here. Do you want me near this wall, my hat *so,* my feet *so,* the light so and thus on my sandals which I made myself? Do you want me to rip this hole in my shirt a bit larger, eh, like *this? So!* Is my face smeared with enough perspiration? Is my hair long enough, kind sir?"

"Stand there if you want," said the photographer.

"I won't look in the camera," Ricardo assured him.

The photographer smiled and lifted his machine. "Over to your left one step, dear." The model moved. "Now turn your right leg. That's fine. Fine, fine. *Hold* it!"

The model froze, chin tilted up.

Ricardo dropped his pants.

"Oh, my God!" said the photographer.

Some of the models squealed. The crowd laughed and pummeled each other a bit. Ricardo quietly raised his pants and leaned against the wall.

"Was that quaint enough?" he said.

"Oh, my God!" muttered the photographer.

"Let's go down to the docks," said his assistant.

"I think *I'll* go there too," Ricardo smiled.

"Good God, what can we do with the idiot?" whispered the photographer.

"Buy him off!"

"I *tried* that!"

"You didn't go high enough."

"Listen, you run get a policeman. I'll put a stop to this."

The assistant ran. Everyone stood around smoking cigarettes nervously, eyeing Ricardo. A dog came by and briefly made water against the wall.

"Look at that!" cried Ricardo. "What art! What a pattern! Quick, before the sun dries it!"

The cameraman turned his back and looked out to sea.

The assistant came rushing along the street. Behind him, a native policeman strolled quietly. The assistant had to stop and run back to urge the policeman to hurry. The policeman assured him with a gesture, at a distance, that the day was not yet over and in time they would arrive at the scene of whatever disaster lay ahead.

The policeman took up a position behind the two cameramen. "What seems to be the trouble?"

"That man up there. We want him removed."

"That man up there seems only to be leaning against a wall," said the officer.

"No, no, it's not the leaning, he—— Oh hell," said the cameraman. "The only way to explain is to show you. Take your pose, dear."

The girl posed. Ricardo posed, smiling casually.

"Hold it!"

The girl froze.

Ricardo dropped his pants.

Click went the camera.

"Ah," said the policeman.

"Got the evidence right in this old camera if you need it!" said the cameraman.

"Ah," said the policeman, not moving, hand to chin. "So." He surveyed the scene like an amateur photographer himself. He saw the model with the flushed, nervous marble face, the cobbles, the wall, and Ricardo. Ricardo magnificently smoking a cigarette there in the noon sunlight under the blue sky, his pants where a man's pants rarely are.

"Well, officer?" said the cameraman, waiting.

"Just what," said the policeman, taking off his cap and wiping his dark brow, "do you want me to do?"

"Arrest that man! Indecent exposure!"

"Ah," said the policeman.

"Well?" said the cameraman.

The crowd murmured. All the nice lady models were looking out at the sea gulls and the ocean.

"That man up there against the wall," said the officer, "I know him. His name is Ricardo Reyes."

"Hello, Esteban!" called Ricardo.

The officer called back at him, "Hello, Ricardo."

They waved at each other.

"He's not doing anything *I* can see," said the officer.

"What do you mean?" asked the cameraman. "He's as naked as a rock. It's immoral!"

"That man is doing nothing immoral. He's just standing there," said the policeman. "Now if he were *doing* something with his hands or body, something terrible to view, I would act upon the instant. However, since he is simply leaning against the wall, not moving a single limb or muscle, there *is* nothing wrong."

"He's naked, *naked!*" screamed the cameraman.

"I don't understand." The officer blinked.

"You just don't go around naked, that's all!"

"There are naked people and naked people," said the officer. "Good and bad. Sober and with drink in them. I judge this one to be a man with no drink in him, a good man by reputation; naked, yes, but doing nothing with this nakedness in any way to offend the community."

"What *are* you, his *brother?* What are you, his confederate?" said the cameraman. It seemed that at any moment he might snap and bite and bark and woof and race around in circles under the blazing sun. "Where's the justice? What's going *on* here? Come on, girls, we'll go somewhere else!"

"France," said Ricardo.

"What!" The photographer whirled.

"I said France, or Spain," suggested Ricardo. "Or Sweden. I have seen some nice pictures of walls in Sweden. But not many cracks in them. Forgive my suggestion."

"We'll get pictures in spite of you!" The cameraman shook his camera, his fist.

"I will be there," said Ricardo. "Tomorrow, the next day, at the bullfights, at the market, anywhere, everywhere you go I go, quietly, with grace. With dignity, to perform my necessary task."

Looking at him, they knew it was true.

"Who are you—who in hell do you think you are?" cried the photographer.

"I have been waiting for you to ask me," said Ricardo. "Consider me. Go home and think of me. As long as there is one man like me in a town of ten thousand, the world will go on. Without me, all would be chaos."

"Good night, nurse," said the photographer, and the entire swarm of ladies, hatboxes, cameras, and make-up kits retreated down the street toward the docks. "Time out for lunch, dears. We'll figure something later!"

Ricardo watched them go, quietly. He had not moved from his position. The crowd still looked upon him and smiled.

Now, Ricardo thought, I will walk up the street to my house, which has paint peeling from the door where I have brushed it a thousand times in passing, and I shall walk over the stones I have worn down in forty-six years of walking, and I shall run my hand over the crack in the wall of my own house, which is the crack made by the earthquake in 1930. I remember well the night, us all in bed, Tomás as yet unborn, and Maria and I much in love, and thinking it was our love which moved the house, warm and great in the night; but it was the earth trembling, and in the morning, that crack in the wall. And I shall climb the steps to the lacework-grille balcony of my father's house, which grillwork he made with his own hands, and I shall eat the food my wife serves me on the balcony, with the books near at hand. And my son Tomás, whom I created out of whole cloth, yes, bed sheets, let us admit it, with my good wife. And we shall sit eating and talking, not photographs, not backdrops, not paintings, not stage furniture, any of us. But actors, all of us, very fine actors indeed.

As if to second this last thought, a sound startled his ear. He was in the midst of solemnly, with great dignity and grace, lifting his pants to belt them around his waist, when he heard this lovely sound. It was like the winging of soft doves in the air. It was applause.

The small crowd, looking up at him, enacting the final scene of the play before the intermission for lunch, saw with what beauty and gentlemanly decorum he was elevating his trousers. The applause broke like a brief wave upon the shore of the nearby sea.

Ricardo gestured and smiled to them all.

On his way home up the hill he shook hands with the dog that had watered the wall.

The Meadow

A wall collapses, followed by another and another; with dull thunder, a city falls into ruin.

The night wind blows.

The world lies silent.

London was torn down during the day. Port Said was destroyed. The nails were pulled out of San Francisco. Glasgow is no more.

They are gone, forever.

Boards clatter softly in the wind, sand whines and trickles in small storms upon the still air.

Along the road toward the colorless ruins comes the old night watchman to unlock the gate in the high barbed-wire fence and stand looking in.

There in the moonlight lie Alexandria and Moscow and New York. There in the moonlight lie Johannesburg and Dublin and Stockholm. And Clearwater, Kansas, and Provincetown, and Rio de Janeiro.

Just this afternoon the old man saw it happen, saw the car roaring outside the barbed-wire fence, saw the lean, sun-tanned men in that car, the men with their luxurious charcoal-flannel suits, and winking gold-mask cuff links, and their burning-gold wristwatches, and eye-blinding rings, lighting their cork-tipped cigarettes with engraved lighters. . . .

"There it is, gentlemen. What a mess. Look what the weather's done to it."

"Yes, sir, it's bad, Mr. Douglas!"

"We just *might* save Paris."

"Yes, *sir!*"

"But, hell! The rain's warped it. That's Hollywood for you! Tear it down! Clear it out! We can use that land. Send a wrecking crew in today!"

"Yes, *sir,* Mr. Douglas!"

The car roaring off and gone away.

And now it is night. And the old night watchman stands inside the gate.

He remembers what happened this same still afternoon when the wreckers came.

A hammering, ripping, clattering; a collapse and a roar. Dust and thunder, thunder and dust!

And the whole of the entire world shook loose its nails and lath and plaster and sill and celluloid window as town after town following town banged over flat and lay still.

A shuddering, a thunder fading away, and then, once more, only the quiet wind.

The night watchman now walks slowly forward along the empty streets.

And one moment he is in Baghdad, and beggars loll in wondrous filth, and women with clear sapphire eyes give veiled smiles from high thin windows.

The wind blows sand and confetti.

The women and beggars vanish.

And it is all strutworks again, it is all papier-mâché and oil-painted canvas and props lettered with the name of this studio, and there is nothing behind any of the building fronts but night and space and stars.

The old man pulls a hammer and a few long nails from his tool chest; he peers around in the junk until he finds a dozen good strong boards and some untorn canvas. And he takes the bright steel nails in his blunt fingers, and they are single-headed nails.

And he begins to put London back together again, hammering and hammering, board by board, wall by wall, window by window, hammering, hammering, louder, louder, steel on steel,

steel in wood, wood against sky, working the hours toward midnight, with no end to his striking and fixing and striking again.

"Hey there, *you!*"

The old man pauses.

"You, night *watchman!*"

Out of the shadows hurries a stranger in overalls, calling:

"Hey, what's-your-name!"

The old man turns. "The name's Smith."

"Okay, Smith, what in hell's the idea!"

The watchman eyes the stranger quietly. "Who are *you?*"

"Kelly, foreman of the wrecking gang."

The old man nods. "Ah. The ones who tear everything down. You've done plenty today. Why aren't you home bragging about it?"

Kelly hawks and spits. "There was some machinery over on the Singapore set I had to check." He wipes his mouth. . . . "Now, Smith, what in Christ's name you think you're doing? Drop that hammer. You're building it all up again! We tear it down and you put it up. You crazy?"

The old man nods. "Maybe I am. But somebody has to put it up again."

"Look, Smith. I do *my* work, you do yours, everyone's happy. But I can't have you messing, see? I'm turning you in to Mr. Douglas."

The old man goes on with his hammering. "Call him up. Send him around. I want to talk to him. *He's* the crazy one."

Kelly laughs. "You kidding? Douglas don't see nobody." He jerks his hand, then bends to examine Smith's newly finished work. "Hey, wait a minute! What *kind* of nails you using? Single-heads! Now, *cut that!* It'll be hell to pay tomorrow, trying to pull 'em out!"

Smith turns his head and looks for a moment at the other man swaying there. "Well, it stands to reason you can't put the world together with double-headed nails. They're too easy to yank out. You got to use single-headed nails and hammer 'em way in. Like *this!*"

He gives a steel nail one tremendous blow that buries it completely in the wood.

Kelly works his hands on his hips. "I'll give you one more chance. Quit putting things back together and I'll play ball with you."

"Young man," says the night watchman, and keeps on hammering while he talks, and thinks about it, and talks some more, "I was here long before you were born. I was here when all *this* was only a meadow. And there was a wind set the meadow running in waves. For more than thirty years I watched it grow, until it was all of the world together. I lived here *with* it. I lived nice. This is the *real* world to me now. That world out there, beyond the fence, is where I spend time sleeping. I got a little room on a little street, and I see headlines and read about wars and strange, bad people. But here? Here I have the whole world together and it's all peace. I been walking through the cities of *this* world since 1920. Any night I feel like it, I have a one-o'clock snack at a bar on the Champs Élysées! I can get me some fine amontillado sherry at a sidewalk café in Madrid, if I want. Or else me and the stone gargoyles, high up there—you *see* them, on top Notre Dame?—we can turn over great state matters and reach big political decisions!"

"Yeah, Pop, sure." Kelly waves impatiently.

"And now you come and kick it down and leave only that world out there which hasn't learned the *first thing* about peace that I know from seeing this land here inside the barbed wire. And so you come and rip it up and there's no peace anymore, anywhere. You and your wreckers so proud of your wrecking. Pulling down towns and cities and whole lands!"

"A guy's got to live," says Kelly. "I got a wife and kids."

"That's what they all say. They got wives and kids. And they go on, pulling apart, tearing down, killing. They had *orders!* Somebody *told* them. They *had* to do it!"

"Shut up and gimme that hammer!"

"Don't come any closer!"

"Why, you crazy old——"

"This hammer's good for more than nails!" The old man whistles the hammer through the air; the wrecker jumps back.

"Hell," says Kelly, "you're insane! I'm putting a call through to the main studio; we'll get some cops here quick. My God, one minute you're building things up and talking crazy, but how do I know two minutes from now you won't run wild and start pouring kerosene and lighting matches!"

"I wouldn't harm the smallest piece of kindling in this place, and you know it," says the old man.

"Might burn the whole goddam place down, hell," says Kelly. "Listen, old man, you just wait right *there!*"

The wrecker spins about and runs off into the villages and the ruined cities and the sleeping two-dimensional towns of this night world, and after his footsteps fade there is a music that the wind plays on the long silver barbed wires of the fence, and the old man hammering and hammering and selecting long boards and rearing walls until a time finally comes when his mouth is gasping, his heart is exploding; the hammer drops from his open fingers, steel nails tinkle like coins on the pavement, and the old man cries out to himself alone:

"It's no use, no use. I can't put it all back up before they come. I need so very much help I don't know what to do."

The old man leaves his hammer lying on the road and begins to walk with no direction, with no purpose, it seems, save that he is thinking to make one last round and take one last look at everything and say good-by to whatever there is or was in this world to say good-by to. And so he walks with the shadows all around and the shadows all through this land where time has grown late indeed, and the shadows are of all kinds and types and sizes, shadows of buildings, and shadows of people. And he doesn't look straight *at* them, no, because if he looked at them straight, they would all blow away. No, he just walks, down the middle of Piccadilly Circus . . . the echo of his steps . . . or the Rue de la Paix . . . the sound of him clearing his throat . . . or Fifth Avenue . . . and he doesn't look right or left. And all around him, in dark doorways and empty windows, are his many friends, his good friends, his *very* good friends. Far away there are the hiss and steam and soft whispering of a *caffè espresso* machine, all silver and chrome, and soft Italian singing . . . the flutter of hands in darkness over the open mouths of balalaikas, the rustle of palm trees, a touching of drums with the chimes chiming and small bells belling, and a sound of summer apples dropped in soft night grass which are not apples at all but the motion of women's bared feet slowly dancing a circle to the chimes' faint chiming and the belling of the tiny golden bells. There is the munch of maize kernels crushed on black volcanic stone, the sizzle of tortillas drowned in hot fat, the whisk of charcoals tossing up a thousand fireflies of spark at the blowing of a mouth and the wave of a papaya frond; everywhere faces and forms, everywhere stirs and gestures and ghost fires which float the magical torch-colored faces of Spanish gypsies in air as on a fiery water, the mouths crying out the songs that tell of the oddness and the strangeness and the sadness of living. Everywhere shadows and people, everywhere people and shadows and singing to music.

Just that very trite thing—the wind?

No. The people are all here. They have been here for many years. And tomorrow?

The old man stops, presses his hands to his chest.

They will not be here anymore.

A horn blows!

Outside the barbed-wire gate—the enemy! Outside the gate a small black police car and a large black limousine from the studio itself, three miles away.

The horn blares!

The old man seizes the rungs of a ladder and climbs, the sound of the horn pushing him higher and higher. The gate crashes wide; the enemy roars in.

"There he goes!"

The glaring lights of the police shine in upon the cities of the meadow; the lights reveal the stark canvas set-pieces of Manhattan, Chicago, and Chungking! The light glitters on the imitation stone towers of Notre Dame Cathedral, fixes on a tiny figure balancing on the catwalks of Notre Dame, climbing and climbing up where the night and the stars are turning slowly by.

"There he is, Mr. Douglas, at the top!"

"Good God. It's getting so a man can't spend an evening at a quiet party without——"

"He's striking a match! Call the fire department!"

On top of Notre Dame, the night watchman, looking down, shielding the match from the softly blowing wind, sees the police, the workmen, and the producer in a dark suit, a big man, gazing up at him. Then the night watchman slowly turns the match, cupping it, applies it to the tip of his cigar. He lights the cigar in slow puffs.

He calls: "Is Mr. Douglas down there?"

A voice calls back: "What do you want with me?"

The old man smiles. "Come up, alone! Bring a gun if you want! I just want a little talk!"

The voices echo in the vast churchyard:

"Don't *do* it, Mr. Douglas!"

"Give me your gun. Let's get this *over* with so I can get back to the party. Keep me covered, I'll play it safe. I don't want these sets burned. There's two million dollars in lumber alone here. *Ready?* I'm on my way."

The producer climbs high on the night ladders, up through the half shell of Notre Dame to where the old man leans against a plaster gargoyle, quietly smoking a cigar. The producer stops, gun pointed, half through an open trap door.

"All right, Smith. Stay where you are."

Smith removes the cigar from his mouth quietly. "Don't you be afraid of me. I'm all right."

"I wouldn't bet money on that."

"Mr. Douglas," says the night watchman, "did you ever read that story about the man who traveled to the future and found everyone there insane? *Everyone.* But since they were all insane they didn't *know* they were insane. They all acted alike and so they thought themselves normal. And since our hero was the only sane one among them, he was abnormal; therefore, *he* was the insane one. To *them,* at least. Yes, Mr. Douglas, insanity is relative. It depends on who has who locked in what cage."

The producer swears under his breath. "I didn't climb up here to talk all night. What do you want?"

"I want to talk with the Creator. That's you, Mr. Douglas. You created all this. You came here one day and struck the earth with a magical checkbook and cried, 'Let there be Paris!' And there *was* Paris: streets, bistros, flowers, wine, outdoor bookshops and all. And you clapped your hands again: 'Let there be Constantinople!' And there *it* was! You clapped your hands a thousand times, and each time made something new, and now you think just by clapping your hands one *last* time you can drop it all down in ruins. But, Mr. Douglas, it's not as easy as that!"

"I own fifty-one percent of the stock in this studio!"

"But did the studio ever belong to you, really? Did you ever think to drive here late some night and climb up on this cathedral and see what a *wonderful* world you created? Did you ever wonder if it might not be a good idea for you to sit up here with me and my friends and have a cup of amontillado sherry with us? All right—so the amontillado smells and looks and tastes like coffee. Imagination, Mr. Creator, imagination. But no, you never came around, you never climbed up, you never looked or listened or cared. There was always a party somewhere else. And now, very late, without asking us, you want to destroy it all. You may own fifty-one percent of the studio stock, but you don't own *them.*"

"Them!" cries the producer. "What's all this business about 'them'?"

"It's hard to put in words. The people who *live* here." The night watchman moves his hand in the empty air toward the half-cities and the night. "So many films were made here in all the long years. Extras moved in the streets in costumes, they talked a thousand tongues, they smoked cigarettes and meerschaums and Persian hookahs, even. Dancing girls danced. They *glittered,* oh, how they glittered! Women with veils smiled down from high balconies. Soldiers marched. Children played. Knights in silver armor fought. There were orange-tea shops. People sipped tea in them and dropped their *h*'s. Gongs were beaten. Viking ships sailed the inland seas."

The producer lifts himself up through the trap door and sits on the plankings, the gun cradled more easily in his hand. He seems to be looking at the old man first with one eye, then the other, listening to him with one ear, then the other, shaking his head a little to himself.

The night watchman continues:

"And somehow, after the extras and the men with the cameras and microphones and all the equipment walked away and the gates were shut and they drove off in big cars, somehow something of all those thousands of different people remained. The things they had been, or *pretended* to be, stayed on. The foreign languages, the costumes, the things they did, the things they thought about, their religions and their music, all those little things and big things stayed on. The sights of far places. The smells. The salt wind. The sea. It's all here tonight if you *listen.*''

The producer listens and the old man listens in the drafty strutworks of the cathedral, with the moonlight blinding the eyes of the plaster gargoyles and the wind making the false stone mouths to whisper, and the sound of a thousand lands within a land below blowing and dusting and leaning in that wind, a thousand yellow minarets and milk-white towers and green avenues yet untouched among the hundred new ruins, and all of it murmuring its wires and lathings like a great steel-and-wooden harp touched in the night, and the wind bringing that self-made sound high up here in the sky to these two men who stand listening and apart.

The producer laughs shortly and shakes his head.

''You *heard,*'' says the night watchman. ''You *did* hear, didn't you? I see it in your face.''

Douglas shoves the gun in his coat pocket. ''Anything you listen for you can hear. I made the mistake of listening. You should have been a writer. You could throw six of my best ones out of work. Well, what about it—are you ready to come down out of here now?''

''You sound almost polite,'' says the night watchman.

''Don't know why I should. You ruined a good evening for me.''

''Did I? It hasn't been that bad, has it? A bit different, I should say. Stimulating, maybe.''

Douglas laughs quietly. ''You're not dangerous at all. You just need company. It's your job and everything going to hell and you're lonely. I can't quite figure you, though.''

''Don't tell me I've got you thinking?'' asks the old man.

Douglas snorts. ''After you've lived in Hollywood long enough, you meet all kinds. Besides, I've never been up here before. It's a real view, like you say. But I'll be damned if I can figure why you should worry about all this junk. What's it to you?''

The night watchman gets down on one knee and taps one

hand into the palm of the other, illustrating his points. "Look. As I said before, you came here years ago, clapped your hands, and three hundred cities jumped up! Then you added a half-thousand other nations, and states and peoples and religions and political setups inside the barbed-wire fence. And there was trouble! Oh, nothing you could see. It was all in the wind and the spaces between. But it was the same kind of trouble the world out there beyond the fence has—squabbles and riots and invisible wars. But at last the trouble died out. You want to know why?"

"If I didn't, I wouldn't be sitting up here freezing."

A little night music, please, thinks the old man, and moves his hand on the air like someone playing the proper and beautiful music to background all that he has to tell. . . .

"Because you got Boston joined to Trinidad," he says softly, "part of Trinidad poking out of Lisbon, part of Lisbon leaning on Alexandria, Alexandria tacked onto Shanghai, and a lot of little pegs and nails between, like Chattanooga, Oshkosh, Oslo, Sweet Water, Soissons, Beirut, Bombay, and Port Arthur. You shoot a man in New York and he stumbles forward and drops dead in Athens. You take a political bribe in Chicago and somebody in London goes to jail. You hang a Negro man in Alabama and the people of Hungary have to bury him. The dead Jews of Poland clutter the streets of Sydney, Portland, and Tokyo. You push a knife into a man's stomach in Berlin and it comes out the back of a farmer in Memphis. It's all so *close,* so very *close*. That's why we have peace here. We're all so crowded there *has got to be peace,* or nothing would be left! One fire would destroy all of us, no matter who started it, for what reason. So all of the people, the memories, whatever you want to call them, that are here, have settled down, and this is their world, a good world, a fine world."

The old man stops and licks his lips slowly and takes a breath. "And tomorrow," he says, "you're going to stomp it down."

The old man crouches there a moment longer, then gets to his feet and gazes out at the cities and the thousand shadows in those cities. The great plaster cathedral whines and sways in the night air, back and forth, rocking on the summer tides.

"Well," says Douglas at last, "shall—shall we go down now?"

Smith nods. "I've had my say."

Douglas vanishes, and the watchman listens to the younger man going down and down through the ladders and catwalks of the night. Then, after a reasonable hesitation, the old man takes hold of the ladder, breathes something to himself, and begins the long descent in shadow.

The studio police and the few workers and some minor executives all drive away. Only one large dark car waits outside the barbed-wire gate as the two men stand talking in the cities of the meadow.

"What are you going to do now?" asks Smith.

"Go back to my party, I suppose," says the producer.

"Will it be fun?"

"Yes." The producer hesitates. "Sure, it'll be fun!" He glances at the night watchman's right hand. "Don't tell me you've found that hammer Kelly told me you were using? You going to start building again? You don't give up, do you?"

"Would you, if you were the last builder and everybody else was a wrecker?"

Douglas starts to walk with the old man. "Well, maybe I'll see you again, Smith."

"No," says Smith, "I won't be here. This all won't be here. If you come back again, it'll be too late."

Douglas stops. "Hell, hell! What do you want me to do?"

"A simple thing. Leave all this standing. Leave these cities up."

"I can't do that! Damn it. Business reasons. It has to go."

"A man with a real nose for business and some imagination could think up a profitable reason for it to stay," says Smith.

"My car's waiting! How do I get out of here?"

The producer strikes off over a patch of rubble, cuts through half of a tumbled ruin, kicking boards aside, leaning for a moment on plaster façades and strutworks. Dust rains from the sky.

"Watch out!"

The producer stumbles in a thunder of dust and avalanching

brick; he gropes, he topples, he is seized upon by the old man and yanked forward.

"Jump!"

They jump, and half the building slides to ruin, crashes into hills and mountains of old paper and lathing. A great bloom of dust strikes out upon the air.

"You all right?"

"Yes. Thanks. Thanks." The producer looks at the fallen building. The dust clears. "You probably saved my life."

"Hardly that. Most of those are papier-mâché bricks. You might have been cut and bruised a little."

"Nevertheless, thanks. What building was that that fell?"

"Norman village tower, built in 1925. Don't get near the rest of it; it might go down."

"I'll be careful." The producer moves carefully in to stand by the set-piece. "Why—I could push this whole damn building over with one hand." He demonstrates; the building leans and quivers and groans. The producer steps quickly back. "I could knock it down in a second."

"But you wouldn't want to do that," says the watchman.

"Oh, wouldn't I? What's one French house more or less, this late in the day?"

The old man takes his arm. "Walk around here to the other side of the house."

They walk to the other side.

"Read that sign," says Smith.

The producer flicks his cigarette lighter, holds the fire up to help him squint, and reads:

" 'THE FIRST NATIONAL BANK, MELLIN TOWN.' " He pauses. " 'ILLINOIS,' " he says, very slowly.

The building stands there in the sharp light of the stars and the bland light of the moon.

"On one side"—Douglas balances his hands like a scales—"a French tower. On the other side—" He walks seven steps to the right, seven steps to the left, peering. " 'THE FIRST NATIONAL BANK.' Bank. Tower. Tower. Bank. Well, I'll be *damned.*"

Smith smiles and says, "Still want to push the French tower down, Mr. Douglas?"

"Wait a minute, wait a minute, hold on, hold on," says Douglas, and suddenly begins to see the buildings that stand before him. He turns in a slow circle; his eyes move up and down and across and over; his eyes flick here, flick there, see this, see that, examine, file, put away, and re-examine. He begins to walk in silence. They move in the cities of the meadow, over grasses and wild flowers, up to and into and through ruins and half-ruins and up to and into and through complete avenues and villages and towns.

They begin a recital which goes on and on as they walk, Douglas asking, the night watchman answering, Douglas asking, the night watchman answering.

"What's this over here?"

"A Buddhist temple."

"And on the other side of it?"

"The log cabin where Lincoln was born."

"And here?"

"St. Patrick's church, New York."

"And on the reverse?"

"A Russian Orthodox church in Rostov!"

"What's *this?*"

"The door of a castle on the Rhine!"

"And *inside?*"

"A Kansas City soda fountain!"

"And here? And here? And over *there?* And what's *that?*" asks Douglas. "What's this! What about that one! And over *there!*"

It seems as if they are running and rushing and yelling all through the cities, here, there, everywhere, up, down, in, out, climbing, descending, poking, stirring, opening-shutting doors.

"And this, and this, and this, and *this!*"

The night watchman tells all there is to tell.

Their shadows run ahead in narrow alleys, and avenues as broad as rivers made of stone and sand.

They make a great talking circle; they hurry all around and back to where they started.

They are quiet again. The old man is quiet from having said what there was to say, and the producer is quiet from listening and remembering and fitting it all together in his mind. He stands, absentmindedly fumbling for his cigarette case. It takes him a full minute to open it, examining every action, thinking about it, and to offer the case to the watchman.

"Thanks."

They light up thoughtfully. They puff on their cigarettes and watch the smoke blow away.

Douglas says, "Where's that damned hammer of yours?"

"Here," says Smith.

"You got your nails with you?"

"Yes, sir."

Douglas takes a deep drag on his cigarette and exhales. "Okay, Smith, get to work."

"What?"

"You heard me. Nail what you can back up, on your own time. Most of the stuff that's already torn down is a complete loss. But any bits and pieces that fit and will look decent, put 'em together. Thank God there's a lot still standing. It took me a long time to get it through my head. A man with a nose for business and some imagination, you said. That *is* the world, you said. I should have seen it years ago. Here it all is inside the fence, and me too blind to see what could be done with it. The World Federation in my own back yard and me kicking it over. So help me God, we need more crazy people and night watchmen."

"You know," says the night watchman, "I'm getting old and I'm getting strange. You wouldn't be fooling an old and strange man, would you?"

"I'll make no promises I can't keep," says the producer. "I'll only promise to try. There's a good chance we can go ahead. It would make a beautiful film, there's no doubt of that. We could make it all here, inside the fence, photograph it ten ways from Christmas. There's no doubt about a story, either. You provided it. It's yours. It wouldn't be hard to put some writers to work on it. Good writers. Perhaps only a short subject, twenty minutes, but we could show all the cities and countries here, leaning on and holding each other up. I *like* the idea. I like it very much, believe me. We could show a film like that to anyone anywhere in the world and they'd like it. They couldn't pass it up, it would be too important."

"It's good to hear you talk this way."

"I hope I keep on talking this way," says the producer. "I can't be trusted. I don't trust myself. Hell, I get excited, up one day, down the next. Maybe you'll have to hit me on the head with that hammer to keep me going."

"I'd be pleased," says Smith.

"And *if* we do the film," says the younger man, "I suppose you could help. You know the sets, probably better than anyone. Any suggestions you might want to make, we'd be glad to have. Then, after we do the film, I suppose you won't mind letting us tear the rest of the world down, right?"

"I'd give my permission," says the watchman.

"Well, I'll call off the hounds for a few days and see what happens. Send out a camera crew tomorrow to see what we can line up for shots. Send out some writers. Maybe you can *all* gab. Hell, hell. We'll work it out." Douglas turns toward the gate. "In the meantime, use your hammer all you want. I'll be seeing you. My God, I'm *freezing!*"

They hurry toward the gate. On the way, the old man finds his lunch box where he abandoned it some hours ago. He picks it up, takes out the thermos, and shakes it. "How about a drink before you go?"

"What've you got? Some of that amontillado you were yelling about?"

"1876."

"Let's have some of that, sure."

The thermos is opened and the liquid poured steaming from it into the cup.

"There you are," says the old man.

"Thanks. Here's to you." The producer drinks. "That's good. Ah, that's damned good!"

"It might taste like coffee, but I tell you it's the finest amontillado ever put under a cork."

"You can say *that* again."

The two of them stand among the cities of the world in the moonlight, drinking the hot drink, and the old man remembers something: "There's an old song fits here, a drinking song, I think, a song that all of us who live inside the fence sing, when we're of a mind, when I listen right, and the wind's just right in the telephone wires. It goes like this:

''We all go the same way home,
All the same collection, in the same direction,
All go the same way home.
So there's no need to part at all,
And we'll all cling together like the ivy on the old garden wall . . .''

They finish drinking the coffee in the middle of Port-au-Prince.

''Hey!'' says the producer suddenly. ''Take it easy with that cigarette! You want to burn down the whole darn *world?*''

They both look at the cigarette and smile.

''I'll be careful,'' says Smith.

''So long,'' says the producer. ''I'm *really* late for that party.''

''So long, Mr. Douglas.''

The gate hasp clicks open and shut, the footsteps die away, the limousine starts up and drives off in the moonlight, leaving behind the cities of the world and an old man standing in the middle of these cities of the world raising his hand to wave.

''So long,'' says the night watchman.

And then there is only the wind.

The Garbage Collector

This is how his work was: He got up at five in the cold dark morning and washed his face with warm water if the heater was working and cold water if the heater was not working. He shaved carefully, talking out to his wife in the kitchen, who was fixing ham and eggs or pancakes or whatever it was that morning. By six o'clock he was driving on his way to work alone, and parking his car in the big yard where all the other men parked their cars as the sun was coming up. The colors of the sky that time of morning were orange and blue and violet and sometimes very red and sometimes yellow or a clear color like water on white rock. Some mornings he could see his breath on the air and some mornings he could not. But as the sun was still rising he knocked his fist on the side of the green truck, and his driver, smiling and saying hello, would climb in the other side of the truck and they would drive out into the great city and go down all the streets until they came to the place where they started work. Sometimes, on the way, they stopped for black coffee and then went on, the warmness in them. And they began the work which meant that he jumped off in front of each house and picked up the garbage cans and brought them back and took off their lids and knocked them against the bin edge, which made the orange peels and canta-loupe rinds and coffee grounds fall out and thump down and begin to fill the empty truck. There were always steak bones and the heads of fish and pieces of green onion and stale celery.

If the garbage was new it wasn't so bad, but if it was very old it was bad. He was not sure if he liked the job or not, but it was a job and he did it well, talking about it a lot at some times and sometimes not thinking of it in any way at all. Some days the job was wonderful, for you were out early and the air was cool and fresh until you had worked too long and the sun got hot and the garbage steamed early. But mostly it was a job significant enough to keep him busy and calm and looking at the houses and cut lawns he passed by and seeing how everybody lived. And once or twice a month he was surprised to find that he loved the job and that it was the finest job in the world.

It went on just that way for many years. And then suddenly the job changed for him. It changed in a single day. Later he often wondered how a job could change so much in such a few short hours.

He walked into the apartment and did not see his wife or hear her voice, but she was there, and he walked to a chair and let her stand away from him, watching him as he touched the chair and sat down in it without saying a word. He sat there for a long time.

''What's wrong?'' At last her voice came through to him. She must have said it three or four times.

''Wrong?'' He looked at this woman and yes, it was his wife all right, it was someone he knew, and this was their apartment with the tall ceilings and the worn carpeting.

''Something happened at work today,'' he said.

She waited for him.

''On my garbage truck, something happened.'' His tongue moved dryly on his lips and his eyes shut over his seeing until there was all blackness and no light of any sort and it was like standing alone in a room when you got out of bed in the middle of a dark night. ''I think I'm going to quit my job. Try to understand.''

''Understand!'' she cried.

''It can't be helped. This is all the strangest damned thing that ever happened to me in my life.'' He opened his eyes and sat there, his hands feeling cold when he rubbed his thumb and forefingers together. ''The thing that happened was strange.''

''Well, don't just *sit* there!''

He took part of a newspaper from the pocket of his leather jacket. ''This is today's paper,'' he said. ''December 10, 1951. Los Angeles *Times*. Civil Defense Bulletin. It says they're buying radios for our garbage trucks.''

''Well, what's so bad about a little music?''

''No music. You don't understand. No music.''

He opened his rough hand and drew with one clean fingernail, slowly, trying to put everything there where he could see it and she could see it. ''In this article the mayor says they'll put sending and receiving apparatus on every garbage truck in town.'' He squinted at his hand. ''After the atom bombs hit our city, those radios will talk to us. And then our garbage trucks will go pick up the bodies.''

''Well, that seems practical. When——''

''The garbage trucks,'' he said, ''go out and pick up all the bodies.''

''You can't just leave bodies around, can you? You've got to take them and——'' His wife shut her mouth very slowly. She blinked, one time only, and she did this very slowly also. He watched that one slow blink of her eyes. Then, with a turn of her body, as if someone else had turned it for her, she walked to a chair, paused, thought how to do it, and sat down, very straight and stiff. She said nothing.

He listened to his wristwatch ticking, but with only a small part of his attention.

At last she laughed. ''They were joking!''

He shook his head. He felt his head moving from left to right and from right to left, as slowly as everything else had happened. ''No. They put a receiver on my truck today. They said, at the alert, if you're working, dump your garbage anywhere. When we radio you, get *in* there and haul out the dead.''

Some water in the kitchen boiled over loudly. She let it boil for five seconds and then held the arm of the chair with one hand and got up and found the door and went out. The boiling sound stopped. She stood in the door and then walked back to where he still sat, not moving, his head in one position only.

"It's all blueprinted out. They have squads, sergeants, captains, corporals, everything," he said. "We even know where to *bring* the bodies."

"So you've been thinking about it all day," she said.

"All day since this morning. I thought: Maybe now I don't want to be a garbage collector anymore. It used to be Tom and me had fun with a kind of game. You got to do that. Garbage is bad. But if you work at it you can make a game. Tom and me did that. We watched people's garbage. We saw what kind they had. Steak bones in rich houses, lettuce and orange peel in poor ones. Sure it's silly, but a guy's got to make his work as good as he can and worthwhile or why in hell do it? And you're your own boss, in a way, on a truck. You get out early in the morning and it's an outdoor job, anyway; you see the sun come up and you see the town get up, and that's not bad at all. But now, today, all of a sudden it's not the kind of job for me anymore."

His wife started to talk swiftly. She named a lot of things and she talked about a lot more, but before she got very far he cut gently across her talking. "I know, I know, the kids and school, our car, I know," he said. "And bills and money and credit. But what about that farm Dad left us? Why can't we move there, away from cities? I know a little about farming. We could stock up, hole in, have enough to live on for months if anything happened."

She said nothing.

"Sure, all of our friends are here in town," he went on reasonably. "And movies and shows and the kids' friends, and . . ."

She took a deep breath. "Can't we think it over a few more days?"

"I don't know. I'm afraid of that. I'm afraid if I think it over, about my truck and my new work, I'll get used to it. And, oh Christ, it just doesn't seem right a man, a human being, should ever let himself get used to any idea like that."

She shook her head slowly, looking at the windows, the gray walls, the dark pictures on the walls. She tightened her hands. She started to open her mouth.

"I'll think tonight," he said. "I'll stay up a while. By morning I'll know what to do."

"Be careful with the children. It wouldn't be good, their knowing all this."

"I'll be careful."

"Let's not talk anymore, then. I'll finish dinner!" She jumped up and put her hands to her face and then looked at her hands and at the sunlight in the windows. "Why, the kids'll be home any minute."

"I'm not very hungry."

"You got to eat, you just got to keep on going." She hurried off, leaving him alone in the middle of a room where not a breeze stirred the curtains, and only the gray ceiling hung over him with a lonely bulb unlit in it, like an old moon in a sky. He was quiet. He massaged his face with both hands. He got up and stood alone in the dining-room door and walked forward and felt himself sit down and remain seated in a dining-room chair. He saw his hands spread on the white tablecloth, open and empty.

"All afternoon," he said, "I've thought."

She moved through the kitchen, rattling silverware, crashing pans against the silence that was everywhere.

"Wondering," he said, "if you put the bodies in the trucks lengthwise or endwise, with the heads on the right, or the *feet* on the right. Men and women together, or separated? Children in one truck, or mixed with men and women? Dogs in special trucks, or just let them lay? Wondering how *many* bodies one garbage truck can hold. And wondering if you stack them on top of each other and finally knowing you must just have to. I can't figure it. I can't work it out. I try, but there's no guessing, no guessing at all how many you could stack in one single truck."

He sat thinking of how it was late in the day at his work, with the truck full and the canvas pulled over the great bulk of garbage so the bulk shaped the canvas in an uneven mound. And how it was if you suddenly pulled the canvas back and looked in. And for a few seconds you saw the white things like macaroni or noodles, only the white things were alive and boiling up, millions of them. And when the white things felt the hot sun on them they simmered down and burrowed and were gone in the lettuce and the old ground beef and the coffee grounds and the heads of white fish. After ten seconds of sunlight the white things that looked like noodles or macaroni were gone and the great bulk of garbage silent and not moving, and you drew the canvas over the bulk and looked at how the canvas folded unevenly over the hidden collection, and underneath you knew it was dark again, and things beginning to move as they must always move when things get dark again.

He was still sitting there in the empty room when the front door of the apartment burst wide. His son and daughter rushed in, laughing, and saw him sitting there, and stopped.

Their mother ran to the kitchen door, held to the edge of it quickly, and stared at her family. They saw her face and they heard her voice:

"Sit down, children, sit down!" She lifted one hand and pushed it toward them. "You're just in time."

The Great Fire

The morning the great fire started, nobody in the house could put it out. It was Mother's niece, Marianne, living with us while her parents were in Europe, who was all aflame. So nobody could smash the little window in the red box at the corner and pull the trigger to bring the gushing hoses and the hatted firemen. Blazing like so much ignited cellophane, Marianne came downstairs, plumped herself with a loud cry or moan at the breakfast table, and refused to eat enough to fill a tooth cavity.

Mother and Father moved away, the warmth in the room being excessive.

"Good morning, Marianne."

"What?" Marianne looked beyond people and spoke vaguely. "Oh, good morning."

"Did you sleep well last night, Marianne?"

But they knew she hadn't slept. Mother gave Marianne a glass of water to drink, and everyone wondered if it would evaporate in her hand. Grandma, from her table chair, surveyed Marianne's fevered eyes. "You're sick, but it's no microbe," she said. "They couldn't find it under a microscope."

"What?" said Marianne.

"Love is godmother to stupidity," said Father detachedly.

"She'll be all right," Mother said to Father. "Girls only seem stupid because when they're in love they can't hear."

"It affects the semicircular canals," said Father. "Making many girls fall right into a fellow's arms. I *know*. I was almost crushed to death once by a falling woman, and let me tell you——"

"Hush." Mother frowned, looking at Marianne.

"She can't hear what we're saying; she's cataleptic right now."

"He's coming to pick her up this morning," whispered Mother to Father, as if Marianne wasn't even in the room. "They're going riding in his jalopy."

Father patted his mouth with a napkin. "Was our daughter like this, Mama?" he wanted to know. "She's been married and gone so long, I've forgotten. I don't recall she was so foolish. One would never know a girl had an ounce of sense at a time like this. That's what fools a man. He says, Oh, what a lovely brainless girl, she loves me, I think I'll marry her. He marries her and wakes up one morning and all the dreaminess is gone out of her and her intellect has returned, unpacked, and is hanging up undies all about the house. The man begins running into ropes and lines. He finds himself on a little desert isle, a little living room alone in the midst of a universe, with a honeycomb that has turned into a bear trap, with a butterfly metamorphosed into a wasp. He then immediately takes up a hobby: stamp collecting, lodge meetings, or——"

"How you *do* run on," cried Mother. "Marianne, tell us about this young man. What was his name again? Was it Isak Van Pelt?"

"What? Oh—Isak, yes." Marianne had been roving about her bed all night, sometimes flipping poetry books and reading incredible lines, sometimes lying flat on her back, sometimes on her tummy looking out at dreaming moonlit country. The smell of jasmine had touched the room all night and the excessive warmth of early spring (the thermometer read fifty-five degrees) had kept her awake. She looked like a dying moth, if anyone had peeked through the keyhole.

This morning she had clapped her hands over her head in the mirror and come to breakfast, remembering just in time to put on a dress.

Grandma laughed quietly all during breakfast. Finally she said, "You must eat, child, you *must*." So Marianne played with her toast and got half a piece down. Just then there was a loud honk outside. That was Isak! In his jalopy!

"Whoop!" cried Marianne, and ran upstairs quickly.

The young Isak Van Pelt was brought in and introduced around.

When Marianne was finally gone, Father sat down, wiping his forehead. "I don't know. This is too much."

"You were the one who suggested she start going out," said Mother.

"And I'm sorry I suggested it," he said. "But she's been visiting us for six months now, and six more months to go. I thought if she met some nice young man——"

"And they were married," husked Grandma darkly, "Why, Marianne might move out almost immediately—is *that* it?"

"Well," said Father.

"Well," said Grandma.

"But now it's worse than before," said Father. "She floats around singing with her eyes shut, playing those infernal love records and talking to herself. A man can stand so much. She's getting so she laughs all the time, too. Do eighteen-year-old girls often wind up in the booby hatch?"

"He seems a nice young man," said Mother.

"Yes, we can always pray for that," said Father, taking out a little shot glass. "Here's to an early marriage."

The second morning Marianne was out of the house like a fireball when first she heard the jalopy horn. There was no time for the young man even to come to the door. Only Grandma saw them roar off together, from the parlor window.

"She almost knocked me down." Father brushed his mustache. "What's *that?* Brained eggs? Well."

In the afternoon, Marianne, home again, drifted about the living room to the phonograph records. The needle hiss filled the house. She played "That Old Black Magic" twenty-one times, going "la la la" as she swam with her eyes closed in the room.

"I'm afraid to go in my own parlor," said Father. "I retired from business to smoke cigars and enjoy living, not to have a limp relative humming about under the parlor chandelier."

"Hush," said Mother.

"This is a crisis," announced Father, "in my life. After all, she's just visiting."

"You know how visiting girls are. Away from home they think they're in Paris, France. She'll be gone in October. It's not so dreadful."

"Let's see," figured Father slowly. "I'll have been buried just about one hundred and thirty days out at Green Lawn Cemetery by then." He got up and threw his paper down into a little white tent on the floor. "By George, Mother, I'm talking to her right *now!*"

He went and stood in the parlor door, peering through it at the waltzing Marianne. "La," she sang to the music.

Clearing his throat, he stepped through.

"Marianne," he said.

" 'That old black magic . . .' " sang Marianne. "Yes?"

He watched her hands swinging in the air. She gave him a sudden fiery look as she danced by.

"I want to talk to you." He straightened his tie.

"Dah dum dee dum dum dee dum dee dum dum," she sang.

"Did you *hear* me?" he demanded.

"He's *so* nice," she said.

"Evidently."

"Do you know, he bows and opens doors like a doorman and plays a trumpet like Harry James and brought me daisies this morning?"

"I wouldn't doubt."

"His eyes are blue." She looked at the ceiling.

He could find nothing at all on the ceiling to look at.

She kept looking, as she danced, at the ceiling as he came over and stood near her, looking up, but there wasn't a rain spot or a settling crack there, and he sighed, "Marianne."

"And we ate lobster at that river café."

"Lobster. I know, but we don't want you breaking down, getting weak. One day, tomorrow, you must stay home and help your aunt Math make her doilies——"

"Yes, sir." She dreamed around the room with her wings out.

"Did you *hear* me?" he demanded.

"Yes," she whispered. "Yes." Her eyes shut. "Oh yes,

yes.'' Her skirts whished around. ''Uncle,'' she said, her head back, lolling.

''You'll help your aunt with her doilies?'' he cried.

''—with her doilies,'' she murmured.

''There!'' He sat down in the kitchen, plucking up the paper. ''I guess *I* told her!''

But next morning he was on the edge of his bed when he heard the hot-rod's thunderous muffler and heard Marianne fall downstairs, linger two seconds in the dining room for breakfast, hesitate by the bathroom long enough to consider whether she would be sick, and then the slam of the front door, the sound of the jalopy banging down the street, two people singing off key in it.

Father put his head in his hands, ''Doilies,'' he said.

''What?'' said Mother.

''Dooley's,'' said Father. ''I'm going down to Dooley's for a morning visit.''

''But Dooley's isn't open until ten.''

''I'll wait,'' decided Father, eyes shut.

That night and seven other wild nights the porch swing sang a little creaking song, back and forth, back and forth. Father, hiding in the living room, could be seen in fierce relief whenever he drafted his ten-cent cigar and the cherry light illumined his immensely tragic face. The porch swing creaked. He waited for another creak. He heard little butterfly-soft sounds from outside, little palpitations of laughter and sweet nothings in small ears. ''My porch,'' said Father. ''My swing,'' he whispered to his cigar, looking at it. ''My house.'' He listened for another creak. ''My God,'' he said.

He went to the tool shed and appeared on the dark porch with a shiny oil can. ''No, don't get up. Don't bother. There, and there.'' He oiled the swing joints. It was dark. He couldn't see Marianne; he could smell her. The perfume almost knocked him off into the rosebush. He couldn't see her gentleman friend, either. ''Good night,'' he said. He went in and sat down and there was no more creaking. Now all he could hear was something that sounded like the mothlike flutter of Marianne's heart.

''He must be very nice,'' said Mother in the kitchen door, wiping a dinner dish.

"That's what I'm hoping," whispered Father. "That's why I let them have the porch every night!"

"So many days in a row," said Mother. "A girl doesn't go with a nice young man that many times unless he's serious."

"Maybe he'll propose tonight!" was Father's happy thought.

"Hardly so soon. And she is so young."

"Still," he ruminated, "it might happen. It's *got* to happen, by the Lord Harry."

Grandma chuckled from her corner easy chair. It sounded like someone turning the pages of an ancient book.

"What's so funny?" said Father.

"Wait and see," said Grandma. "Tomorrow."

Father stared at the dark, but Grandma would say no more.

"Well, well," said Father at breakfast. He surveyed his eggs with a kindly, paternal eye. "Well, well, by gosh, last night, on the porch, there was *more whispering*. What's his name? Isak? Well, now, if I'm any judge at all, I think he proposed to Marianne last night; yes, I'm positive of it!"

"It would be nice," said Mother. "A spring marriage. But it's so *soon*."

"Look," said Father with full-mouthed logic. "Marianne's the kind of girl who marries quick and young. We can't stand in her way, can we?"

"For once I think you're right," said Mother. "A marriage would be fine. Spring flowers, and Marianne looking nice in that gown I saw at Haydecker's last week."

They all peered anxiously at the stairs, waiting for Marianne to appear.

"Pardon me," rasped Grandma, sighting up from her morning toast. "But I wouldn't talk of getting rid of Marianne just yet if I were you."

"And why not?"

"Because."

"Because why?"

"I hate to spoil your plans," rustled Grandma, chuckling. She gestured with her little vinegary head. "But while you people were worrying about getting Marianne married, I've been keeping tab on her. Seven days now I've been watching this young fellow each day he came in his car and honked his horn outside. He must be an actor or a quick-change artist or something."

"What?" asked Father.

"Yep," said Grandma. "Because one day he was a young blond fellow, and next day he was a tall dark fellow, and Wednesday he was a chap with a brown mustache, and Thursday he had wavy red hair, and Friday he was shorter, with a Chevrolet stripped down instead of a Ford."

Mother and Father sat for a minute as if hit with hammers right behind the left ear.

At last Father, his face exploding with color, shouted, "Do you mean to *say!* You *sat* there, woman, you say; all those men, and you——"

"You were always hiding," snapped Grandma. "So you wouldn't spoil things. If you'd come out in the open you'd have seen the same as I. I never said a word. She'll simmer down. It's just her time of life. Every woman goes through it. It's hard, but they can survive. A new man every day does wonders for a girl's ego!"

"You, you, you, you, *you!*" Father choked on it, eyes wild, throat gorged too big for his collar. He fell back in his chair, exhausted. Mother sat, stunned.

"Good morning, everyone!" Marianne raced downstairs and popped into a chair. Father stared at her.

"You, you, you, you, you," he accused Grandma.

I shall run down the street shouting, thought Father wildly, and break the fire-alarm window and pull the lever and bring the fire engines and the hoses. Or perhaps there will be a late snowstorm and I shall set Marianne out in it to cool.

He did neither. The heat in the room being excessive, according to the wall calendar, everyone moved out onto the cool porch while Marianne sat looking at her orange juice.

The Golden Apples of the Sun

"South," said the captain.

"But," said his crew, "there simply *aren't* any directions out here in space."

"When you travel on down toward the sun," replied the captain, "and everything gets yellow and warm and lazy, then you're going in one direction only." He shut his eyes and thought about the smoldering, warm, faraway land, his breath moving gently in his mouth. "South." He nodded slowly to himself. "South."

Their rocket was the *Copa de Oro,* also named the *Prometheus* and the *Icarus,* and their destination in all reality was the blazing noonday sun. In high good spirits they had packed along two thousand sour lemonades and a thousand white-capped beers for this journey to the wide Sahara. And now as the sun boiled up at them they remembered a score of verses and quotations:

" 'The golden apples of the sun'?"

"Yeats."

" 'Fear no more the heat of the sun'?"

"Shakespeare, of course!"

Cup of Gold? Steinbeck. *The Crock of Gold?* Stephens. And what about the pot of gold at the rainbow's end? *There's* a name for our trajectory, by God. Rainbow!

"Temperature?"

"One thousand degrees Fahrenheit!"

The captain stared from the huge dark-lensed port, and there indeed was the sun, and to go to that sun and touch it and steal part of it forever away was his quiet and single idea. In this ship were combined the coolly delicate and the coldly practical. Through corridors of ice and milk-frost, ammoniated winter and storming snowflakes blew. Any spark from that vast hearth burning out there beyond the callous hull of this ship, any small firebreath that might seep through would find winter, slumbering here like all the coldest hours of February.

The audio-thermometer murmured in the arctic silence: "Temperature: two thousand degrees!"

Falling, thought the captain, like a snowflake into the lap of June, warm July, and the sweltering dog-mad days of August.

"Three thousand degrees Fahrenheit!"

Under the snow fields engines raced, refrigerants pumped ten thousand miles per hour in rimed boa-constrictor coils.

"Four thousand degrees Fahrenheit."

Noon. Summer. July.

"Five thousand Fahreheit!"

And at last the captain spoke with all the quietness of the journey in his voice:

"Now, we are touching the sun."

Their eyes, thinking it, were melted gold.

"Seven thousand degrees!"

Strange how a mechanical thermometer could sound excited, though it possessed only an emotionless steel voice.

"What *time* is it?" asked someone.

Everyone had to smile.

For now there was only the sun and the sun and the sun. It was every horizon, it was every direction. It burned the minutes, the seconds, the hourglasses, the clocks; it burned all time and eternity away. It burned the eyelids and the serum of the dark world behind the lids, the retina, the hidden brain; and it burned sleep and the sweet memories of sleep and cool nightfall.

"Watch it!"

"Captain!"

Bretton, the first mate, fell flat to the winter deck. His protective suit whistled where, burst open, his warmness, his oxygen, and his life bloomed out in a frosted steam.

"Quick!"

Inside Bretton's plastic face-mask, milk crystals had already gathered in blind patterns. They bent to see.

"A structural defect in his suit, Captain. Dead."

"Frozen."

They stared at that other thermometer which showed how winter lived in this snowing ship. One thousand degrees below zero. The captain gazed down upon the frosted statue and the twinkling crystals that iced over it as he watched. Irony of the coolest sort, he thought; a man afraid of fire and killed by frost.

The captain turned away. "No time. No time. Let him lie." He felt his tongue move. "Temperature?"

The dials jumped four thousand degrees.

"Look. Will you look? Look."

Their icicle was melting.

The captain jerked his head to look at the ceiling.

As if a motion picture projector had jammed a single clear memory frame in his head, he found his mind focused ridiculously on a scene whipped out of childhood.

Spring mornings as a boy he had leaned from his bedroom window into the snow-smelling air to see the sun sparkle the last icicle of winter. A dripping of white wine, the blood of cool but warming April fell from that clear crystal blade. Minute by minute, December's weapon grew less dangerous. And then at last the icicle fell with the sound of a single chime to the graveled walk below.

"Auxiliary pump's broken, sir. Refrigeration. We're losing our ice!"

A shower of warm rain shivered down upon them. The captain jerked his head right and left. "Can you see the trouble? Christ, don't stand there, we haven't time!"

The men rushed; the captain bent in the warm rain, cursing, felt his hands run over the cold machine, felt them burrow and search, and while he worked he saw a future which was removed from them by the merest breath. He was the skin peel from the rocket beehive, men, thus revealed, running, running, mouths shrieking, soundless. Space was a black mossed well where life drowned its roars and terrors. Scream a big scream, but space snuffed it out before it was half up your throat. Men scurried, ants in a flaming matchbox; the ship was dripping lava, gushing steam, nothing!

"Captain?"

The nightmare flicked away.

"Here." He worked in the soft warm rain that fell from the upper decks. He fumbled at the auxiliary pump. "Damn it!" He jerked the feed line. When it came, it'd be the quickest death in the history of dying. One moment, yelling; a warm flash later only the billion, billion tons of space-fire would whisper, unheard, in space. Popped like strawberries in a furnace, while their thoughts lingered on the scorched air a long breath after their bodies were charred roast and fluorescent gas.

"Damn!" He stabbed the auxiliary pump with a screwdriver. "Jesus!" He shuddered. The complete annihilation of it. He clamped his eyes tight, teeth tight. God, he thought, we're used to more leisurely dyings, measured in minutes and hours. Even twenty seconds now would be a slow death compared to this hungry idiot thing waiting to eat us!

"Captain, do we pull out or stay?"

"Get the Cup ready. Take over, finish this. "Now!"

He turned and put his hand to the working mechanism of the huge Cup; shoved his fingers into the robot Glove. A twitch of his hand here moved a gigantic hand, with gigantic metal fingers, from the bowels of the ship. Now, now, the great metal hand slid out holding the huge *Copa de Oro,* breathless, into the iron furnace, the bodiless body and the fleshless flesh of the sun.

A million years ago, thought the captain, quickly, quickly, as he moved the hand and the Cup, a million years ago a naked man on a lonely northern trail saw lightning strike a tree. And while his clan fled, with bare hands he plucked a limb of fire, broiling the flesh of his fingers, to carry it, running in triumph, shielding it from the rain with his body, to his cave, where he shrieked out a laugh and tossed it full on a mound of leaves and gave his people summer. And the tribe crept at last, trembling, near the fire, and they put out their flinching hands and felt the new season in their cave, this small yellow spot of changing weather, and they, too, at last, nervously, smiled. And the gift of fire was theirs.

"Captain!"

It took all of four seconds for the huge hand to push the empty Cup to the fire. So here we are again, today, on another trail, he thought, reaching for a cup of precious gas and vacuum, a handful of different fire with which to run back up cold space, lighting our way, and take to Earth a gift of fire that might burn forever. Why?

He knew the answer before the question.

Because the atoms we work with our hands, on Earth, are pitiful; the atomic bomb is pitiful and small and our knowledge is pitiful and small, and only the sun really knows what we want to know, and only the sun has the secret. And besides, it's fun, it's a chance, it's a great thing coming here, playing tag, hitting and running. There is no reason, really, except the pride and vanity of little insect men hoping to sting the lion and escape the maw. My God, we'll say, we *did* it! And here is our cup of energy, fire, vibration, call it what you will, that may well power our cities and sail our ships and light our libraries and tan our children and bake our daily breads and simmer the knowledge of our universe for us for a thousand years until it is well done. Here, from this cup, all good men of science and religion: drink! Warm yourselves against the night of ignorance, the long snows of superstition, the cold winds of disbelief, and from the great fear of darkness in each man. So: we stretch our hand with the beggar's cup. . . .

"Ah."

The Cup dipped into the sun. It scooped up a bit of the flesh of God, the blood of the universe, the blazing thought, the blinding philosophy that set out and mothered a galaxy, that idled and swept planets in their fields and summoned or laid to rest lives and livelihoods.

"Now, *slow,*" whispered the captain.

"What'll happen when we pull it inside? That extra heat now, at this time, Captain?"

"God knows."

"Auxiliary pump all repaired, sir."

"Start it!"

The pump leaped on.

"Close the lid of the Cup and inside now, slow, slow."

The beautiful hand outside the ship trembled, a tremendous image of his own gesture, sank with oiled silence into the ship body. The Cup, lid shut, dripped yellow flowers and white stars, slid deep. The audiothermometer screamed. The refrigerator system kicked; ammoniated fluids banged the walls like blood in the head of a shrieking idiot.

He shut the outer air-lock door.

"Now."

They waited. The ship's pulse ran. The heart of the ship rushed, beat, rushed, the Cup of Gold in it. The cold blood raced around about down through, around about down through.

The captain exhaled slowly.

The ice stopped dripping from the ceiling. It froze again.

"Let's get out of here."

The ship turned and ran.

"Listen!"

The heart of the ship was slowing, slowing. The dials spun on down through the thousands; the needles whirred, invisible. The thermometer voice chanted the change of seasons. They were all thinking now, together: Pull away and away from the fire and the flame, the heat and the melting, the yellow and the white. Go on out now to cool and dark. In twenty hours perhaps they might even dismantle some refrigerators, let winter die. Soon they would move in night so cold it might be necessary to use the ship's new furnace, draw heat from the shielded fire they carried now like an unborn child.

They were going home.

They were going home and there was some little time, even as he tended to the body of Bretton lying in a bank of white winter snow, for the captain to remember a poem he had written many years before:

Sometimes I see the sun a burning Tree,
Its golden fruit swung bright in airless air,
Its apples wormed with man and gravity,
Their worship breathing from them everywhere,
As man sees Sun as burning Tree . . .

The captain sat for a long while by the body, feeling many separate things. I feel sad, he thought, and I feel good, and I feel like a boy coming home from school with a handful of dandelions.

''Well,'' said the captain, sitting, eyes shut, sighing. ''Well, where do we go now, eh, where are we going?'' He felt his men sitting or standing all about him, the terror dead in them, their breathing quiet. ''When you've gone a long, long way down to the sun and touched it and lingered and jumped around and streaked away from it, where are you going then? When you go away from the heat and the noonday light and the laziness, where do you go?''

His men waited for him to say it out. They waited for him to gather all of the coolness and the whiteness and the welcome and refreshing climate of the word in his mind, and they saw him settle the word, like a bit of ice cream, in his mouth, rolling it gently.

''There's only one direction in space from here on out,'' he said at last.

They waited. They waited as the ship moved swiftly into cold darkness away from the light.

''North,'' murmured the captain. ''North.''

And they all smiled, as if a wind had come up suddenly in the middle of a hot afternoon.

When I was a boy in the Midwest I used to go out and look at the stars at night and wonder about them.

I guess every boy has done that.

When I wasn't looking at the stars, I was running in my old or my brand-new tennis shoes, on my way to swing in a tree, swim in a lake, or delve in the town library to read about dinosaurs or Time Machines.

I guess every boy has done that, too.

This is a book about those stars and those tennis shoes. Mainly about the stars, because that is the way I grew up, getting more and more involved with rockets and space as I moved toward my twelfth, thirteenth, and fourteenth years.

Not that I have forgotten the tennis shoes and their powerful magic, as you will see in the last story here, which I have included not because it concerns the Future, but because it gives you some sort of idea of the kind of boy I was when I was looking at the stars and thinking of the Years Ahead.

Nor have I forgotten the dinosaurs that all boys love; they are here, too, along with a Machine that travels back in Time to step on a butterfly.

This is a book then by a boy who grew up in a small Illinois town and lived to see the Space Age arrive, as he hoped and dreamt it would.

I dedicate these stories to all boys who wonder about the Past, run swiftly in the Present, and have high hopes for our Future.

The stars are yours, if you have the head, the hands, and the heart for them.

RAY BRADBURY
Los Angeles
March 28, 1962

R Is for Rocket

There was this fence where we pressed our faces and felt the wind turn warm and held to the fence and forgot who we were or where we came from but dreamed of who we might be and where we might go. . . .

Yet we were boys and liked being boys and lived in a Florida town and liked the town and went to school and fairly liked the school and climbed trees and played football and liked our mothers and fathers. . . .

But some time every hour of every day of every week for a minute or a second when we thought on fire and stars and the fence beyond which they waited . . . we liked the rockets more.

The fence. The rockets.

Every Saturday morning . . .

The guys met at my house . . .

With the sun hardly up, they yelled until the neighbors were moved to brandish paralysis guns out their ventilators commanding the guys to shut up or they'd be frozen statues for the next hour and *then* where would they be?

Aw, climb a rocket, stick your head in the main-jet! the kids always yelled back, but yelled this safe behind our garden fence. Old Man Wickard, next door, is a great shot with the para-gun.

This one dim cool Saturday morning I was lying in bed thinking about how I had flunked my semantics exam the day before at formula-school, when I heard the gang yelling below. It was hardly 7 A.M. and there was still a lot of fog roaming in off the Atlantic, and only now were the weather-control vibrators at each corner starting to hum and shoot out rays to get rid of the stuff; I heard them moaning soft and nice.

I padded to the window and stuck my head out.

"Okay, space-pirates! Motors off!"

"Hey!" shouted Ralph Priory. "We just heard, there's a new schedule today! The Moon Job, the one with the new XL3-motor, is cutting gravity in an *hour!*"

"Buddha, Muhammad, Allah, and other real and semimythological figures," I said, and went away from the window so fast the concussion laid all the boys out on my lawn.

I zippered myself into a jumper, yanked on my boots, clipped my food-capsules to my hip-pocket, for I knew there'd be no food or even thought of food today, we'd just stuff with pills when our stomachs barked, and fell down the two-story vacuum elevator.

On the lawn, all five of the guys were chewing their lips, bouncing around, scowling.

"Last one," said I, passing them at 5000 mph, "to the monorail is a bug-eyed Martian!"

On the monorail, with the cylinder hissing us along to Rocket Port, twenty miles from town—a few minutes' ride—I had bugs in my stomach. A guy fifteen doesn't get to see the big stuff often enough, mostly every week it was the small continental cargo rockets coming and going on schedule. But this was big, among the biggest . . . the Moon and beyond. . . .

"I'm sick," said Priory, and hit me on the arm.

I hit him back. "Me, too. Boy, ain't Saturday the best day in the week!?"

Priory and I traded wide, understanding grins. We got along all Condition Go. The other pirates were okay. Sid Rossen, Mac Leslyn, Earl Marnee, they knew how to jump around like all the kids, and they loved the rockets, too, but I had the feeling they wouldn't be doing what Ralph and I would do someday. Ralph and I wanted the stars for each of us, more than we would want a fistful of clear-cut blue-white diamonds.

We yelled with the yellers, we laughed with the laughers, but at the middle of it all, we were still, Ralph and I, and the cylinder whispered to a stop and we were outside yelling, laughing, running, but quiet and almost in slow motion, Ralph ahead of me, and all of us pointed one way, at the observation fence and grabbing hold, yelling for the slowpokes to catch up, but not looking back for them, and then we were all there together and the big rocket came out of its plastic work canopy like a great interstellar circus tent and moved along its gleaming track out toward the fire point, accompanied by the gigantic gantry like a gathering of prehistoric reptile birds which kept and preened and fed this one big fire monster and led it toward its seizure and birth into a suddenly blast-furnace sky.

I quit breathing. I didn't even suck another breath it seemed until the rocket was way out on the concrete meadow, followed by water-beetle tractors and great cylinders bearing hidden men, and all around, in asbestos suits, praying-mantis mechanics fiddled with machines and buzzed and cawwed and gibbered to each other on invisible, unhearable radiophones, but we could hear it all, in our heads, our minds, our hearts.

"Lord," I said at last.

"The very good Lord," said Ralph Priory at my elbow.

The others said this, too, over and over.

It was something to "good Lord" about. It was a hundred years of dreaming all sorted out and chosen and put together to make the hardest, prettiest, swiftest dream of all. Every line was fire solidified and made perfect, it was flame frozen, and ice waiting to thaw there in the middle of a concrete prairie, ready to wake with a roar, jump high and knock its silly fine great head against the Milky Way and knock the stars down in a full return of firefall meteors. You felt it could kick the Coal Sack Nebula square in the midriff and make it stand out of the way.

It got me in the midriff, too—it gripped me in such a way I knew the special sickness of longing and envy and grief for lack of accomplishment. And when the astronauts patrolled the field in the final silent mobile-van, my body went with them in their strange white armor, in their bubble-helmets and insouciant pride, looking as if they were team-parading to a magnetic football game at one of the local mag-fields, for mere practice. But they were going to the Moon, they went every month now, and the crowds that used to come to watch were no longer there, there was just us kids to worry them up and worry them off.

''Gosh,'' I said. ''What wouldn't I give to go with them. What wouldn't I give.''

''Me,'' said Mac, ''I'd give my one-year monorail privileges.''

''Yeah. Oh, very much yeah.''

It was a big feeling for us kids caught half between this morning's toys and this afternoon's very real and powerful fireworks.

And then the preliminaries got over with. The fuel was in the rocket and the men ran away from it on the ground like ants running lickety from a metal god—and the Dream woke up and gave a yell and jumped into the sky. And then it was gone, all the vacuum shouting of it, leaving nothing but a hot trembling in the air, through the ground, and up our legs to our hearts. Where it had been was a blazed, seared pock and a fog of rocket smoke like a cumulus cloud banked low.

''It's gone!'' yelled Priory.

And we all began to breathe fast again, frozen there on the ground as if stunned by the passing of a gigantic paralysis gun.

''I want to grow up quick,'' I said, then. ''I want to grow up quick so I can take that rocket.''

I bit my lips. I was so darned young, and you cannot apply for space work. You have to be *chosen.* Chosen.

Finally somebody, I guess it was Sidney, said:

''Let's go to the tele-show now.''

Everyone said yeah, except Priory and myself. We said no, and the other kids went off laughing breathlessly, talking, and left Priory and me there to look at the spot where the ship had been.

It spoiled everything else for us—that takeoff.

Because of it, I flunked my semantics test on Monday.

I didn't care.

At times like that I thanked Providence for concentrates. When your stomach is nothing but a coiled mass of excitement, you hardly feel like drawing a chair to a full hot dinner. A few concen-tabs swallowed did wonderfully well as substitution, without the urge of appetite.

I got to thinking about it, tough and hard, all day long and late at night. It got so bad I had to use sleep-massage mechs every night, coupled with some of Tschaikovsky's quieter music to get my eyes shut.

"Good Lord, young man," said my teacher, that Monday at class. "If this keeps up I'll have you reclassified at the next psych-board meeting."

"I'm sorry," I replied.

He looked hard at me. "What sort of block have you got? It must be a very simple, and also a conscious, one."

I winced. "It's conscious, sir; but it's not simple. It's multi-tentacular. In brief, though—it's rockets."

He smiled. "R is for Rocket, eh?"

"I guess that's it, sir."

"We can't let it interfere with your scholastic record, though, young man."

"Do you think I need hypnotic suggestion, sir?"

"No, no." He flipped through a small tab of records with my name blocked on it. I had a funny stone in my stomach, just lying there. He looked at me. "You know, Christopher, you're king-of-the-hill here; head of the class." He closed his eyes and mused over it. "We'll have to see about a lot of other things," he concluded. Then he patted me on the shoulder. "Well—get on with your work. Nothing to worry about."

He walked away.

I tried to get back to work, but I couldn't. During the rest of the day the teacher kept watching me and looking at my tab-record and chewing his lip. About two in the afternoon he dialed a number on his desk-audio and discussed something with somebody for about five minutes.

I couldn't hear what was said.

But when he set the audio into its cradle, he stared straight at me with the funniest light in his eyes.

It was envy and admiration and pity all in one. It was a little sad and it was much of happiness. It had a lot in it, just in his eyes. The rest of his face said nothing.

It made me feel like a saint and a devil sitting there.

* * *

Ralph Priory and I slid home from formula-school together early that afternoon. I told Ralph what had happened and he frowned in the dark way he always frowns.

I began to worry. And between the two of us we doubled and tripled the worry.

"You don't think you'll be sent away, do you, Chris?"

Our monorail car hissed. We stopped at our station. We got out. We walked slow. "I don't know," I said.

"That would be plain dirty," said Ralph.

"Maybe I need a good psychiatric laundering, Ralph. I can't go on flubbing my studies this way."

We stopped outside my house and looked at the sky for a long moment. Ralph said something funny.

"The stars aren't out in the daytime, but we can see 'em, can't we, Chris?"

"Yeah," I said. "Darn rights."

"We'll stick it together, huh, Chris? Blast them, they can't take you away now. We're pals. It wouldn't be fair."

I didn't say anything because there was no room in my throat for anything but a hectagonal lump.

"What's the matter with your eyes?" asked Priory.

"Aw, I looked at the sun too long. Come on inside, Ralph."

We yelled under the shower spray in the bath-cubicle, but our yells weren't especially convincing, even when we turned on the ice-water.

While we were standing in the warm-air dryer, I did a lot of thinking. Literature, I figured, was full of people who fought battles against hard, razor-edged opponents. They pitted brain and muscle against obstacles until they won out or were themselves defeated. But here I was with hardly a sign of any outward conflict. It was all running around in spiked boots inside my head, making cuts and bruises where no one could see them except me and a psychologist. But it was just as bad.

"Ralph," I said, as we dressed, "I got a war on."

"All by yourself?" he asked.

"I can't include you," I said. "Because this is personal. How many times has my mother said, 'Don't eat so much, Chris, your eyes are bigger than your stomach?' "

"A million times."

"*Two* million. Well, paraphrase it, Ralph. Change it to 'Don't *see* so much, Chris, your mind is too big for your body.' I got a war on between a mind that wants things my body can't give it."

Priory nodded quietly. "I see what you mean about its being a personal war. In that case, Christopher, I'm at war, too."

"I knew you were," I said. "Somehow I think the other kids'll grow out of it. But I don't think we will, Ralph. I think we'll keep waiting."

We sat down in the middle of the sunlit upper deck of the house, and started checking over some homework on our formula-pads. Priory couldn't get his. Neither could I. Priory put into words the very thing I didn't dare say out loud.

"Chris, the Astronaut Board *selects.* You can't apply for it, You *wait.*"

"I know."

"You wait from the time you're old enough to turn cold in the stomach when you see a Moon rocket, until all the years go by, and every month that passes you hope that one morning a blue Astronaut helicopter will come down out of the sky, land on your lawn, and that a neat-looking engineer will ease out, walk up the rampway briskly, and touch the bell.

"You keep waiting for that helicopter until you're twenty-one. And then, on the last day of your twentieth year you drink and laugh a lot and say what the heck, you didn't really care about it, anyway."

We both just sat there, deep in the middle of his words. We both just sat there. Then:

"I don't want that disappointment, Chris. I'm fifteen, just like you. But if I reach my twenty-first year without an Astronaut ringing the bell where I live at the ortho-station, I—"

"I know," I said. "I know. I've talked to men who've waited, all for nothing. And if it happens that way to us, Ralph, well—we'll get good and drunk together and then go out and take jobs loading cargo on a Europe-bound freighter."

Ralph stiffened and his face went pale. "Loading cargo."

There was a soft, quick step on the ramp and my mother was there. I smiled. "Hi, lady!"

"Hello. Hello, Ralph."

''Hello, Jhene.''

She didn't look much older than twenty-five, in spite of having birthed and raised me and worked at the Government Statistics House. She was light and graceful and smiled a lot, and I could see how father must have loved her very much when he was alive. One parent is better than none. Poor Priory now, raised in one of those orthopedical stations. . . .

Jhene walked over and put her hand on Ralph's face. ''You look ill,'' she said. ''What's wrong?''

Ralph managed a fairly good smile. ''Nothing—at all.''

Jhene didn't need prompting. She said, ''You can stay here tonight, Priory. We want you. Don't we, Chris?''

''Heck, yes.''

''I should get back to the station,'' said Ralph, rather feebly, I observed. ''But since you asked and Chris here needs help on his semantics for tomorrow, I'll stick and help him.''

''Very generous,'' I observed.

''First, though, I've a few errands. I'll take the 'rail and be back in an hour, people.''

When Ralph was gone my mother looked at me intently, then brushed my hair back with a nice little move of her fingers.

''Something's happening, Chris.''

My heart stopped talking because it didn't want to talk anymore for a while. It waited.

I opened my mouth, but Jhene went on:

''Something's up somewhere. I had two calls at work today. One from your teacher. One from—I can't say. I don't *want* to say until things happen—''

My heart started talking again, slow and warm.

''Don't tell me, then, Jhene. Those calls—''

She just looked at me. She took my hand between her two soft warm ones. ''You're so young, Chris. You're so awfully young.''

I didn't speak.

Her eyes brightened. ''You never knew your father. I wish you had. You know what he was, Chris?''

I said, ''Yeah. He worked in a Chemistry Lab, deep underground most of the time.''

And, my mother added, strangely, "He worked deep under the ground, Chris, and never saw the stars."

My heart yelled in my chest. Yelled loud and hard.

"Oh, Mother. Mother—"

It was the first time in years I had called her mother.

When I woke the next morning there was a lot of sunlight in the room, but the cushion where Priory slept when he stayed over was vacant. I listened. I didn't hear him splashing in the shower-cube, and the dryer wasn't humming. He was gone.

I found his note pinned on the sliding door.

"See you at formula at noon. Your mother wanted me to do some work for her. She got a call this morning, and said she needed me to help. So long. Priory."

Priory out running errands for Jhene. Strange. A call in the early morning to Jhene. I went back and sat down on the cushion.

While I was sitting there a bunch of the kids yelled down on the lawn-court. "Hey, Chris! You're late!"

I stuck my head out the window. "Be right down!"

"No, Chris."

My mother's voice. It was quiet and it had something funny in it. I turned around. She was standing in the doorway behind me, her face pale, drawn, full of some small pain. "No, Chris," she said again, softly. "Tell them to go on to formula without you—today."

The kids were still making noise downstairs, I guess, but I didn't hear them. I just felt myself and my mother, slim and pale and restrained in my room. Far off, the weather-control vibrators started to hum and throb.

I turned slowly and looked down at the kids. The three of them were looking up, lips parted casually, half-smiling, semantic-tabs in their knotty fingers. "Hey—" one of them said. Sidney, it was.

"Sorry, Sid. Sorry, gang. Go on without me. I can't go to formula today. See you later, huh?"

"Aw, Chris!"

"Sick?"

"No. Just— Just go on without me, gang. I'll see you."

I felt numb. I turned away from their upturned, questioning

faces and glanced at the door. Mother wasn't there. She had gone downstairs, quietly. I heard the kids moving off, not quite as boisterously, toward the monorail station.

Instead of using the vac-elevator, I walked slowly downstairs. "Jhene," I said, "where's Ralph?"

Jhene pretended to be interested in combing her long light hair with a vibro-toothed comb. "I sent him off. I didn't want him here this morning."

"Why am I staying home from formula, Jhene?"

"Chris, please don't ask."

Before I could say anything else, there was a sound in the air. It cut through the very soundproofed wall of the house, and hummed in my marrow, quick and high as an arrow of glittering music.

I swallowed. All the fear and uncertainty and doubt went away, instantly.

When I heard that note, I thought of Ralph Priory. *Oh, Ralph, if you could be here now.* I couldn't believe the truth of it. Hearing that note and hearing it with my whole body and soul as well as with my ears.

It came closer, that sound. I was afraid it would go away. But it didn't go away. It lowered its pitch and came down outside the house in great whirling petals of light and shadow and I knew it was a helicopter the color of the sky. It stopped humming, and in the silence my mother tensed forward, dropped the vibro-comb and took in her breath.

In that silence, too, I heard booted footsteps walking up the ramp below. Footsteps that I had waited for a long time.

Footsteps I was afraid would never come.

Somebody touched the bell.

And I *knew* who it was.

And all I could think was, Ralph, why in heck did you have to go away now, when all this is happening? Blast it, Ralph, why did you?

The man looked as if he had been born in his uniform. It fitted like a second layer of salt-colored skin, touched here and there with a line, a dot of blue. As simple and perfect a uniform as could be made, but with all the muscled power of the universe behind it.

His name was Trent. He spoke firmly, with a natural round perfection, directly to the subject.

I stood there, and my mother was on the far side of the room, looking like a bewildered little girl. I stood listening.

Out of all the talking I remember some of the snatches:

". . . highest grades, high IQ. Perception A-1, curiosity Triple-A. Enthusiasm necessary to the long, eight-year educational grind. . . ."

"Yes, sir."

". . . talks with your semantics and psychology teachers—"

"Yes, sir."

". . . and don't forget, Mr. Christopher . . ."

Mister Christopher!

". . . and don't forget, Mr. Christopher, nobody is to know you have been selected by the Astronaut Board."

"No one?"

"Your mother and teacher know, naturally. But no other person must know. Is that perfectly understood?"

"Yes, sir."

Trent smiled quietly, standing there with his big hands at his sides. "You want to ask why, don't you? Why you can't tell your friends? I'll explain.

"It's a form of psychological protection. We select about ten thousand young men each year from the earth's billions. Out of that number three thousand wind up, eight years later, as spacemen of one sort or another. The others must return to society. They've flunked out, but there's no reason for everyone to know. They usually flunk out, if they're going to flunk, in the first six months. And it's tough to go back and face your friends and say you couldn't make the grade at the biggest job in the world. So we make it easy to go back.

"But there's still another reason. It's psychological, too. Half the fun of being a kid is being able to lord it over the other guys, by being superior in some way. We take half the fun out of Astronaut selection by strictly forbidding you to tell your pals. Then, we'll know if you wanted to go into space for frivolous reasons, or for space itself. If you're in it for personal conceit—you're damned. If you're in it because you can't help being in it and *have* to be in it—you're blessed."

He nodded to my mother. "Thank you, Mrs. Christopher."

"Sir," I said. "A question. I have a friend. Ralph Priory. He lives at an ortho-station—"

Trent nodded. "I can't tell you his rating, of course, but he's on our list. He's your buddy? You want him along, of course. I'll check his record. Station-bred, you say? That's not good. But—we'll see."

"If you would, please, thanks."

"Report to me at the Rocket Station Saturday afternoon at five, Mr. Christopher. Meantime: silence."

He saluted. He walked off. He went away in the helicopter into the sky, and Mother was beside me quickly, saying, "Oh, Chris, Chris," over and over, and we held to each other and whispered and talked and she said many things, how good this was going to be for us, but especially for me, how fine, what an honor it was, like the old old days when men fasted and took vows and joined churches and stopped up their tongues and were silent and prayed to be worthy and to live well as monks and priests of many churches in far places, and came forth and moved in the world and lived as examples and taught well. It was no different now, this was a greater priesthood, in a way, she said, she inferred, she knew, and I was to be some small part of it, I would not be hers anymore, I would belong to all the worlds, I would be all the things my father wanted to be and never lived or had a chance to be. . . .

"Darn rights, darn rights," I murmured. "I will, I promise I will . . ."

I caught my voice. "Jhene—how—how will we tell Ralph? What about him?"

"You're going away, that's all, Chris. Tell him that. Very simply. Tell him no more. He'll understand."

"But, Jhene, *you*—"

She smiled softly. "Yes, I'll be lonely, Chris. But I'll have my work and I'll have Ralph."

"You mean . . ."

"I'm taking him from the ortho-station. He'll live here, when you're gone. That's what you *wanted* me to say, isn't it, Chris?"

I nodded, all paralyzed and strange inside.

"That's exactly what I wanted you to say."

"He'll be a good son, Chris. *Almost* as good as you."

"He'll be *fine!*"

We told Ralph Priory. How I was going away maybe to school in Europe for a year and how Mother wanted him to come live as her son, now, until such time as I came back. We said it quick and fast, as if it burned our tongues. And when we finished, Ralph came and shook my hand and kissed my mother on the cheek and he said:

"I'll be proud. I'll be very proud."

It was funny, but Ralph didn't even ask any more about why I was going, or where, or how long I would be away. All he would say was, "We had a lot of fun, didn't we?" and let it go at that, as if he didn't dare say any more.

It was Friday night, after a concert at the amphitheater in the center of our public circle, and Priory and Jhene and I came home, laughing, ready to go to bed.

I hadn't packed anything. Priory noted this briefly, and let it go. All of my personal supplies for the next eight years would be supplied by someone else. No need for packing.

My semantics teacher called on the audio, smiling and saying a very brief, pleasant good-bye.

Then, we went to bed, and I kept thinking in the hour before I lolled off, about how this was the last night with Jhene and Ralph. The very last night.

Only a kid of fifteen—me.

And then, in the darkness, just before I went to sleep, Priory twisted softly on his cushion, turned his solemn face to me, and whispered, "Chris?" A pause. "Chris. You still awake?" It was like a faint echo.

"Yes," I said.

"Thinking?"

A pause.

"Yes."

He said, "You're— You're not *waiting* anymore, are you, Chris?"

I knew what he meant. I couldn't answer.

I said, "I'm awfully tired, Ralph."

He twisted back and settled down and said, "That's what I thought. You're not *waiting* anymore. Gosh, but that's good, Chris. That's good."

He reached out and punched me in the arm-muscle, lightly. Then we both went to sleep.

It was Saturday morning. The kids were yelling outside. Their voices filled the seven o'clock fog. I heard Old Man Wickard's ventilator flip open and the zip of his para-gun playfully touching around the kids.

"Shut up!" I heard him cry, but he didn't sound grouchy. It was a regular Saturday game with him. And I heard the kids giggle.

Priory woke up and said, "Shall I tell them, Chris, you're not going with them today?"

"Tell them nothing of the sort." Jhene moved from the door. She bent out the window, her hair all light against a ribbon of fog. "Hi, gang! Ralph and Chris will be right down. Hold gravity!"

"Jhene!" I cried.

She came over to both of us. "You're going to spend your Saturday the way you always spend it—with the gang!"

"I planned on sticking with you, Jhene."

"What sort of holiday would *that* be, now?"

She ran us through our breakfast, kissed us on the cheeks, and forced us out the door into the gang's arms.

"Let's not go out to the Rocket Port today, guys."

"Aw, Chris—why not?"

Their faces did a lot of changes. This was the first time in history I hadn't wanted to go. "You're kidding, Chris."

"Sure he is."

"No, he's not. He means it," said Priory. "And I don't want to go either. We go *every* Saturday. It gets tiresome. We can go next week instead."

"Aw . . ."

They didn't like it, but they didn't go off by themselves. It was no fun, they said, without us.

"What the heck—we'll go next week."

"Sure we will. What do you want to do, Chris?"

I told them.

We spent the morning playing Kick the Can and some games we'd given up a long time ago, and we hiked out along some old rusty and abandoned railroad tracks and walked in a small woods outside town and photographed some birds and went swimming raw, and all the time I kept thinking—this is the last day.

We did everything we had ever done before on Saturday. All the silly crazy things, and nobody knew I was going away except Ralph, and five o'clock kept getting nearer and nearer.

At four, I said good-bye to the kids.

"Leaving so soon, Chris? What about tonight?"

"Call for me at eight," I said. "We'll go see the new Sally Gibberts picture!"

"Swell."

"Cut gravity!"

And Ralph and I went home.

Mother wasn't there, but she had left part of herself, her smile and her voice and her words on a spool of audio-film on my bed. I inserted it in the viewer and threw the picture on the wall. Soft yellow hair, her white face and her quiet words:

"I hate good-byes, Chris. I've gone to the laboratory to do some extra work. Good luck. All of my love. When I see you again—you'll be a man."

That was all.

Priory waited outside while I saw it over four times. "I hate good-byes, Chris. I've gone . . . work . . . luck. All . . . my love. . . ."

I had made a film-spool myself the night before. I spotted it in the viewer and left it there. It only said good-bye.

Priory walked halfway with me. I wouldn't let him get on the Rocket Port Monorail with me. I just shook his hand, tight, and said, "It was fun today, Ralph."

"Yeah. Well, see you next Saturday, huh, Chris?"

"I wish I could say yes."

"Say yes anyway. Next Saturday—the woods, the gang, the rockets, and Old Man Wickard and his trusty para-gun."

We laughed. "Sure. Next Saturday, early. Take— Take care of *our* mother, will you, Priory?"

"That's a silly question, you nut," he said.

"It is, isn't it?"

He swallowed. "Chris."

"Yeah?"

"I'll be waiting. Just like you waited and don't have to wait anymore. I'll *wait.*"

"Maybe it won't be long, Priory. I hope not."

I jabbed him, once, in the arm. He jabbed back.

The monorail door sealed. The car hurled itself away, and Priory was left behind.

I stepped out at the Port. It was a five-hundred-yard walk down to the Administration building. It took me ten years to walk it.

"Next time I see you you'll be a man—"

"Don't tell anybody—"

"I'll wait, Chris—"

It was all choked in my heart and it wouldn't go away and it swam around in my eyes.

I thought about my dreams. The Moon Rocket. It won't be part of me, part of my *dream* any longer. I'll be part of *it.*

I felt small there, walking, walking, walking.

The afternoon rocket to London was just taking off as I went down the ramp to the office. It shivered the ground and it shivered and thrilled my heart.

I was beginning to grow up awfully fast.

I stood watching the rocket until someone snapped their heels, cracked me a quick salute.

I was numb.

"C.M. Christopher?"

"Yes, sir. Reporting, sir."

"This way, Christopher. Through that gate."

Through that gate and beyond *the* fence . . .

This fence where we had pressed our faces and felt the wind turn warm and held to the fence and forgot who we were or where we came from but dreamed of who we might be and where we might go . . .

This fence where had stood the boys who liked being boys who lived in a town and liked the town and fairly liked school and liked football and liked their fathers and mothers . . .

The boys who some time every hour of every day of every

week thought on fire and stars and the fence beyond which they waited. . . . The boys who liked the rockets *more.*

Mother, Ralph, I'll see you. I'll be back.

Mother!

Ralph!

And, walking, I went beyond the fence.

The End of the Beginning

He stopped the lawn mower in the middle of the yard, because he felt that the sun at just that moment had gone down and the stars come out. The fresh-cut grass that had showered his face and body died softly away. Yes, the stars were there, faint at first, but brightening in the clear desert sky. He heard the porch screen door tap shut and felt his wife watching him as he watched the night.

''Almost time,'' she said.

He nodded; he did not have to check his watch. In the passing moments he felt very old, then very young, very cold, then very warm, now this, now that. Suddenly he was miles away. He was his own son talking steadily, moving briskly to cover his pounding heart and the resurgent panics as he felt himself slip into fresh uniform, check food supplies, oxygen flasks, pressure helmet, space-suiting, and turn as every man on earth tonight turned, to gaze at the swiftly filling sky.

Then, quickly, he was back, once more the father of the son, hands gripped to the lawn-mower handle. His wife called, ''Come sit on the porch.''

''I've got to keep busy!''

She came down the steps and across the lawn. ''Don't worry about Robert; he'll be all right.''

''But it's all so new,'' he heard himself say. ''It's never been done before. Think of it—a manned rocket going up tonight to build the first space station. Good Lord, it can't be done, it doesn't exist, there's no rocket, no proving ground, no takeoff time, no technicians. For that matter, I don't even have a son named Bob. The whole thing's too much for me!''

''Then what are you doing out here, staring?''

He shook his head. ''Well, late this morning, walking to the office, I heard someone laugh out loud. It shocked me, so I froze in the middle of the street. It was *me,* laughing! Why? Because finally I really *knew* what Bob was going to do tonight; at last I *believed* it. Holy is a word I never use, but that's how I felt stranded in all that traffic. Then, middle of the afternoon I caught myself humming. You know the song. 'A wheel in a wheel. Way in the middle of the air.' I laughed again. The space station, of course, I thought. The big wheel with hollow spokes where Bob'll live six or eight months, then get on back. Walking home, I remembered more of the song. 'Little wheel run by faith, Big wheel run by the grace of God.' I wanted to jump, yell, and flame-out myself!''

His wife touched his arm. ''If we stay out here, let's at least be comfortable.''

They placed two wicker rockers in the center of the lawn and sat quietly as the stars dissolved out of darkness in pale crushings of rock salt strewn from horizon to horizon.

''Why,'' said his wife, at last, ''it's like waiting for the fireworks at Sisley Field every year.''

''Bigger crowd tonight . . .''

''I keep thinking—a billion people watching the sky right now, their mouths all open at the same time.''

They waited, feeling the earth move under their chairs.

''What time is it now?''

''Eleven minutes to eight.''

''You're always right; there must be a clock in your head.''

''I can't be wrong, tonight. I'll be able to tell you one second before they blast off. Look! The ten-minute warning!''

On the western sky they saw four crimson flares open out, float shimmering down the wind above the desert, then sink silently to the extinguishing earth.

In the new darkness the husband and wife did not rock in their chairs.

After a while he said, "Eight minutes." A pause. "Seven minutes." What seemed a much longer pause. "Six . . ."

His wife, her head back, studied the stars immediately above her and murmured, "Why?" She closed her eyes. "Why the rockets, why tonight? Why all this? I'd like to know."

He examined her face, pale in the vast powdering light of the Milky Way. He felt the stirring of an answer, but let his wife continue.

"I mean it's not that old thing again, is it, when people asked why men climbed Mt. Everest and they said, 'Because it's there.' I never understood. That was no answer to me."

Five minutes, he thought. Time ticking . . . his wristwatch . . . a wheel in a wheel . . . little wheel run by . . . big wheel run by . . . way in the middle of . . . four minutes! . . . The men snug in the rocket by now, the hive, the control board flickering with light. . . .

His lips moved.

"All I know is it's really the end of the beginning. The Stone Age, Bronze Age, Iron Age; from now on we'll lump all those together under one big name for when we walked on Earth and heard the birds at morning and cried with envy. Maybe we'll call it the Earth Age, or maybe the Age of Gravity. Millions of years we fought gravity. When we were amoebas and fish we struggled to get out of the sea without gravity crushing us. Once safe on the shore we fought to stand upright without gravity breaking our new invention, the spine, tried to walk without stumbling, run without falling. A billion years Gravity kept us home, mocked us with wind and clouds, cabbage moths and locusts. That's what's so really big about tonight . . . it's the end of old man Gravity and the age we'll remember him by, for once and all. I don't know where they'll divide the ages, at the Persians, who dreamt of flying carpets, or the Chinese, who all unknowing celebrated birthdays and New Years with strung ladyfingers and high skyrockets, or some minute, some incredible second in the next hour. But we're in at the end of a billion years trying, the end of something long and to us humans, anyway, honorable."

Three minutes . . . two minutes fifty-nine seconds . . . two minutes fifty-eight seconds . . .

"But," said his wife, "I still don't know why."

Two minutes, he thought. *Ready? Ready? Ready?* The far radio voice calling. *Ready! Ready! Ready!* The quick, faint replies from the humming rocket. *Check! Check! Check!*

Tonight, he thought, even if we fail with this first, we'll send a second and a third ship and move on out to all the planets and later, all the stars. We'll just keep going until the big words like immortal and forever take on meaning. Big words, yes, that's what we want. Continuity. Since our tongues first moved in our mouths we've asked, What does it all mean? No other question made sense, with death breathing down our necks. But just let us settle in on ten thousand worlds spinning around ten thousand alien suns and the question will fade away. Man will be endless and infinite, even as space is endless and infinite. Man will go on, as space goes on, forever. Individuals will die as always, but our history will reach as far as we'll ever need to see into the future, and with the knowledge of our survival for all time to come, we'll know security and thus the answer we've always searched for. Gifted with life, the least we can do is preserve and pass on the gift to infinity. That's a goal worth shooting for.

The wicker chairs whispered ever so softly on the grass.

One minute.

"One minute," he said aloud.

"Oh!" His wife moved suddenly to seize his hands. "I hope that Bob . . ."

"He'll be all right!"

"Oh, God, take care . . ."

Thirty seconds.

"Watch now."

Fifteen, ten, five . . .

"Watch!"

Four, three, two, one.

"There! There! Oh, there, there!"

They both cried out. They both stood. The chairs toppled back, fell flat on the lawn. The man and his wife swayed, their hands struggled to find each other, grip, hold. They saw the brightening color in the sky and, ten seconds later, the great uprising comet burn the air, put out the stars, and rush away in fire flight to become another star in the returning profusion of the Milky Way. The man and wife held each other as if they had stumbled on the rim of an incredible cliff that faced an abyss so deep and dark there seemed no end to it. Staring up, they heard themselves sobbing and crying. Only after a long time were they able to speak.

"It got away, it did, *didn't* it?"

"Yes . . ."

"It's all right, isn't it?"

"Yes . . . yes . . ."

"It didn't fall back . . . ?"

"No, no, it's all right. Bob's all right, it's all right."

They stood away from each other at last.

He touched his face with his hand and looked at his wet fingers. "I'll be," he said, "I'll be. . . ."

They waited another five and then ten minutes until the darkness in their heads, the retina, ached with a million specks of fiery salt. Then they had to close their eyes.

"Well," she said, "now let's go in."

He could not move. Only his hand reached a long way out by itself to find the lawn-mower handle. He saw what his hand had done and said, "There's just a little more to do. . . ."

"But you can't see."

"Well enough," he said. "I must finish this. Then we'll sit on the porch awhile before we turn in."

He helped her put the chairs on the porch and sat her down and then walked back out to put his hands on the guide bar of the lawn mower. The lawn mower. A wheel in a wheel. A simple machine which you held in your hands, which you sent on ahead with a rush and a clatter while you walked behind with your quiet philosophy. Racket, followed by warm silence. Whirling wheel, then soft footfall of thought.

I'm a billion years old, he told himself; I'm one minute old. I'm one inch, no, ten thousand *miles,* tall. I look down and can't see my feet they're so far off and gone away below.

He moved the lawn mower. The grass showering up fell softly around him; he relished and savored it and felt that he was all mankind bathing at last in the fresh waters of the fountain of youth.

Thus bathed, he remembered the song again about the wheel and the faith and the grace of God being way up there in the middle of the sky where that single star, among a million motionless stars, dared to move and keep on moving.

Then he finished cutting the grass.

The Rocket

Many nights Fiorello Bodoni would awaken to hear the rockets sighing in the dark sky. He would tiptoe from bed, certain that his kind wife was dreaming, to let himself out into the night air. For a few moments he would be free of the smells of old food in the small house by the river. For a silent moment he would let his heart soar alone into space, following the rockets.

Now, this very night, he stood half naked in the darkness, watching the fire fountains murmuring in the air. The rockets on their long wild way to Mars and Saturn and Venus!

"Well, well, Bodoni."

Bodoni started.

On a milk crate, by the silent river, sat an old man who also watched the rockets through the midnight hush.

"Oh, it's you, Bramante!"

"Do you come out every night, Bodoni?"

"Only for the air."

"So? I prefer the rockets myself," said old Bramante. "I was a boy when they started. Eighty years ago, and I've never been on one yet."

"I will ride up in one someday," said Bodoni.

"Fool!" cried Bramante. "You'll never go. This is a rich man's world." He shook his gray head, remembering. "When I was young they wrote it in fiery letters: THE WORLD OF THE FUTURE! Science, Comfort, and New Things for All! Ha! Eighty years. The Future becomes Now! Do *we* fly rockets? No! We live in shacks like our ancestors before us."

"Perhaps my *sons—*" said Bodoni.

"No, nor *their* sons!" the old man shouted. "It's the rich who have dreams and rockets!"

Bodoni hesitated. "Old man, I've saved three thousand dollars. It took me six years to save it. For my business, to invest in machinery. But every night for a month now I've been awake. I hear the rockets. I think. And tonight I've made up my mind. One of us will fly to Mars!" His eyes were shining and dark.

"Idiot," snapped Bramante. "How will you choose? Who will go? If you go, your wife will hate you, for you will be just a bit nearer God, in space. When you tell your amazing trip to her, over the years, won't bitterness gnaw at her?"

"No, no!"

"Yes! And your children? Will their lives be filled with the memory of Papa, who flew to Mars while they stayed here? What a senseless task you will set your boys. They will think of the rocket all their lives. They will lie awake. They will be sick with wanting it. Just as you are sick now. They will want to die if they cannot go. Don't set that goal, I warn you. Let them be content with being poor. Turn their eyes down to their hands and to your junkyard, not up to the stars."

"But—"

"Suppose your wife went? How would you feel, knowing she had *seen* and you had not? She would become holy. You would think of throwing her in the river. No, Bodoni, buy a new wrecking machine, which you need, and pull your dreams apart with it, and smash them to pieces."

The old man subsided, gazing at the river in which, drowned, images of rockets burned down the sky.

"Good night," said Bodoni.

"Sleep well," said the other.

When the toast jumped from its silver box, Bodoni almost screamed. The night had been sleepless. Among his nervous children, beside his mountainous wife, Bodoni had twisted and stared at nothing. Bramante was right. Better to invest the money. Why save it when only one of the family could ride the rocket, while the others remained to melt in frustration?

"Fiorello, eat your toast," said his wife, Maria.

"My throat is shriveled," said Bodoni.

The children rushed in, the three boys fighting over a toy rocket, the two girls carrying dolls which duplicated the inhabitants of Mars, Venus, and Neptune, green mannequins with three yellow eyes and twelve fingers.

"I saw the Venus rocket!" cried Paolo.

"It took off, *whoosh!*" hissed Antonello.

"Children!" shouted Bodoni, hands to his ears.

They stared at him. He seldom shouted.

Bodoni arose. "Listen, all of you," he said. "I have enough money to take one of us on the Mars rocket."

Everyone yelled.

"You understand?" he asked. "Only *one* of us. Who?"

"Me, me, me!" cried the children.

"You," said Maria.

"You," said Bodoni to her.

They all fell silent.

The children reconsidered. "Let Lorenzo go—he's oldest."

"Let Miriamne go—she's a girl!"

"Think what you would see," said Bodoni's wife to him. But her eyes were strange. Her voice shook. "The meteors, like fish. The universe. The Moon. Someone should go who could tell it well on returning. You have a way with words."

"Nonsense. So have you," he objected.

Everyone trembled.

"Here," said Bodoni unhappily. From a broom he broke straws of various lengths. "The short straw wins." He held out his tight fist. "Choose."

Solemnly each took his turn.

"Long straw."

"Long straw."

Another.

"Long straw."

The children finished. The room was quiet.

Two straws remained. Bodoni felt his heart ache in him. "Now," he whispered. "Maria."

She drew.

''The short straw,'' she said.

''Ah,'' sighed Lorenzo, half happy, half sad. ''Mama goes to Mars.''

Bodoni tried to smile. ''Congratulations. I will buy your ticket today.''

''Wait, Fiorello—''

''You can leave next week,'' he murmured.

She saw the sad eyes of her children upon her, with the smiles beneath their straight, large noses. She returned the straw slowly to her husband. ''I cannot go to Mars.''

''But why not?''

''I will be busy with another child.''

''What!''

She would not look at him. ''It wouldn't do for me to travel in my condition.''

He took her elbow. ''Is this the truth?''

''Draw again. Start over.''

''Why didn't you tell me before?'' he said incredulously.

''I didn't remember.''

''Maria, Maria,'' he whispered, patting her face. He turned to the children. ''Draw again.''

Paolo immediately drew the short straw.

''I go to Mars!'' He danced wildly. ''Thank you, Father!''

The other children edged away. ''That's swell, Paolo.''

Paolo stopped smiling to examine his parents and his brothers and sisters. ''I *can* go, can't I?'' he asked uncertainly.

''Yes.''

''And you'll *like* me when I come back?''

''Of course.''

Paolo studied the precious broomstraw on his trembling hand and shook his head. He threw it away. ''I forgot. School starts. I can't go. Draw again.''

But no one would draw. A full sadness lay on them.

''None of us will go,'' said Lorenzo.

''That's best,'' said Maria.

''Bramante was right,'' said Bodoni.

* * *

With his breakfast curdled within him, Fiorello Bodoni worked in his junkyard, ripping metal, melting it, pouring out usable ingots. His equipment flaked apart; competition had kept him on the insane edge of poverty for twenty years.

It was a very bad morning.

In the afternoon a man entered the junkyard and called up to Bodoni on his wrecking machine. ''Hey, Bodoni, I got some metal for you!''

''What is it, Mr. Mathews?'' asked Bodoni, listlessly.

''A rocket ship. What's wrong? Don't you want it?''

''Yes, yes!'' He seized the man's arm, and stopped, bewildered.

''Of course,'' said Mathews, ''it's only a mockup. *You* know. When they plan a rocket they build a full-scale model first, of aluminum. You might make a small profit boiling her down. Let you have her for two thousand—''

Bodoni dropped his hand. ''I haven't the money.''

''Sorry. Thought I'd help you. Last time we talked you said how everyone outbid you on junk. Thought I'd slip this to you on the q.t. Well—''

''I need new equipment. I saved money for that.''

''I understand.''

''If I bought your rocket, I wouldn't even be able to melt it down. My aluminum furnace broke down last week—''

''Sure.''

''I couldn't possibly use the rocket if I bought it from you.''

''I know.''

Bodoni blinked and shut his eyes. He opened them and looked at Mr. Mathews. ''But I am a great fool. I will take my money from the bank and give it to you.''

''But if you can't melt the rocket down—''

''Deliver it,'' said Bodoni.

''All right, if you say so. Tonight?''

''Tonight,'' said Bodoni, ''would be fine. Yes, I would like to have a rocket ship tonight.''

There was a moon. The rocket was white and big in the junkyard. It held the whiteness of the moon and the blueness of the stars. Bodoni looked at it and loved all of it. He wanted to pet it and lie against it, pressing it with his cheek, telling it all the secret wants of his heart.

He stared up at it. "You are all mine," he said. "Even if you never move or spit fire, and just sit there and rust for fifty years, you are mine."

The rocket smelled of time and distance. It was like walking into a clock. It was finished with Swiss delicacy. One might wear it on one's watch fob. "I might even sleep here tonight," Bodoni whispered excitedly.

He sat in the pilot's seat.

He touched a lever.

He hummed in his shut mouth, his eyes closed.

The humming grew louder, louder, higher, higher, wilder, stranger, more exhilarating, trembling in him and leaning him forward and pulling him and the ship in a roaring silence and in a kind of metal screaming, while his fists flew over the controls, and his shut eyes quivered, and the sound grew and grew until it was a fire, a strength, a lifting and a pushing of power that threatened to tear him in half. He gasped. He hummed again and again, and did not stop, for it could not be stopped, it could only go on, his eyes tighter, his heart furious. "Taking off!" he screamed. *The jolting concussion! The thunder!* "The Moon!" he cried, eyes blind, tight. "The meteors!" *The silent rush in volcanic light. "Mars.* Oh, yes! Mars! Mars!"

He fell back, exhausted and panting. His shaking hands came loose of the controls and his head tilted wildly. He sat for a long time, breathing out and in, his heart slowing.

Slowly, slowly, he opened his eyes.

The junkyard was still there.

He sat motionless. He looked at the heaped piles of metal for a minute, his eyes never leaving them. Then, leaping up, he kicked the levers. "Take off, blast you!"

The ship was silent.

"I'll show you!" he cried.

Out in the night air, stumbling, he started the fierce motor of his terrible wrecking machine and advanced upon the rocket. He maneuvered the massive weights into the moonlit sky. He readied his trembling hands to plunge the weights, to smash, to rip apart this insolently false dream, this silly thing for which he had paid his money, which would not move, which would not do his bidding. "I'll teach you!" he shouted.

But his hand stayed.

The silver rocket lay in the light of the moon. And beyond the rocket stood the yellow lights of his home, a block away, burning warmly. He heard the family radio playing some distant music. He sat for half an hour considering the rocket and the house lights, and his eyes narrowed and grew wide. He stepped down from the wrecking machine and began to walk, and as he walked he began to laugh, and when he reached the back door of his house he took a deep breath and called, "Maria, Maria, start packing. We're going to Mars!"

"Oh!"

"Ah!"

"I can't *believe* it!"

"You will, you will."

The children balanced in the windy yard, under the glowing rocket, not touching it yet. They started to cry.

Maria looked at her husband. "What have you done?" she said. "Taken our money for this? It will never fly."

"It will fly," he said, looking at it.

"Rocket ships cost millions. Have you millions?"

"It will fly," he repeated steadily. "Now, go to the house, all of you. I have phone calls to make, work to do. Tomorrow we leave! Tell no one, understand? It is a secret."

The children edged off from the rocket, stumbling. He saw their small, feverish faces in the house windows, far away.

Maria had not moved. "You have ruined us," she said. "Our money used for this—this thing. When it should have been spent on equipment."

"You will see," he said.

Without a word she turned away.

"God help me," he whispered, and started to work.

Through the midnight hours trucks arrived, packages were delivered, and Bodoni, smiling, exhausted his bank account. With blowtorch and metal stripping he assaulted the rocket, added, took away, worked fiery magics and secret insults upon it. He bolted nine ancient automobile motors into the rocket's empty engine room. Then he welded the engine room shut, so none could see his hidden labor.

At dawn he entered the kitchen. "Maria," he said, "I'm ready for breakfast."

She would not speak to him.

At sunset he called to the children. "We're ready! Come on!" The house was silent.

"I've locked them in the closet," said Maria.

"What do you mean?" he demanded.

"You'll be killed in that rocket," she said. "What kind of rocket can you buy for two thousand dollars? A bad one!"

"Listen to me, Maria."

"It will blow up. Anyway, you are no pilot."

"Nevertheless, I can fly *this* ship. I have fixed it."

"You have gone mad," she said.

"Where is the key to the closet?"

"I have it here."

He put out his hand. "Give it to me."

She handed it to him. "You will kill them."

"No, no."

"Yes, you will. I *feel* it."

He stood before her. "You won't come along?"

"I'll stay here," she said.

"You will understand; you will see then," he said, and smiled. He unlocked the closet. "Come, children. Follow your father."

"Good-bye, good-bye, Mama!"

She stayed in the kitchen window, looking out at them, very straight and silent.

At the door of the rocket the father said, "Children, this is a swift rocket. We will be gone only a short while. You must come back to school, and I to my business." He took each of their hands in turn. "Listen. This rocket is very old and will fly only *one* more journey. It will not fly again. This will be the one trip of your life. Keep your eyes wide."

"Yes, Papa."

"Listen, keep your ears clean. Smell the smells of a rocket.

Feel. Remember. So when you return you will talk of it all the rest of your lives.''

''Yes, Papa.''

The ship was quiet as a stopped clock. The airlock hissed shut behind them. He strapped them all, like tiny mummies, into rubber hammocks. ''Ready? he called.

''Ready!'' all replied.

''Blast-off!'' He jerked ten switches. The rocket thundered and leaped. The children danced in their hammocks, screaming. ''We're moving! We're off! Look!''

''Here comes the Moon!''

The moon dreamed by. Meteors broke into fireworks. Time flowed away in a serpentine of gas. The children shouted. Released from their hammocks, hours later, they peered from the ports. ''There's Earth!'' ''There's Mars!''

The rocket dropped pink petals of fire while the hour dials spun; the child eyes dropped shut. At last they hung like drunken moths in their cocoon hammocks.

''Good,'' whispered Bodoni, alone.

He tiptoed from the control room to stand for a long moment, fearful, at the airlock door.

He pressed a button. The airlock door swung wide. He stepped out. Into space? Into the inky tides of meteor and gaseous torch? Into swift mileages and infinite dimensions?

No. Bodoni smiled.

All about the quivering rocket lay the junkyard.

Rusting, unchanged, there stood the padlocked junkyard gate, the little silent house by the river, the kitchen window lighted, and the river going down to the same sea. And in the center of the junkyard, manufacturing a magic dream, lay the quivering, purring rocket. Shaking and roaring, bouncing the netted children like flies in a web.

Maria stood in the kitchen window.

He waved to her and smiled.

He could not see if she waved or not. A small wave, perhaps. A small smile.

The sun was rising.

Bodoni withdrew hastily into the rocket. Silence. All still slept. He breathed easily. Tying himself into a hammock, he closed his eyes. To himself he prayed, Oh, let nothing happen to the illusion in the next six days. Let all of space come and go, and red Mars come up under our ship, and the moons of Mars, and let there be no flaws in the color film. Let there be three dimensions; let nothing go wrong with the hidden mirrors and screens that mold the fine illusion. Let time pass without crisis.

He awoke.

Red Mars floated near the rocket.

"Papa!" The children thrashed to be free.

Bodoni looked and saw red Mars and it was good and there was no flaw in it and he was very happy.

At sunset on the seventh day the rocket stopped shuddering.

"We are home," said Bodoni.

They walked across the junkyard from the open door of the rocket, their blood singing, their faces glowing. Perhaps they knew what he had done. Perhaps they guessed his wonderful magic trick. But if they knew, if they guessed, they never said. Now they only laughed and ran.

"I have ham and eggs for all of you," said Maria, at the kitchen door.

"Mama, Mama, you should have come, to see it, to see Mars, Mama, and meteors, and everything!"

"Yes," she said.

At bedtime the children gathered before Bodoni. "We want to thank you, Papa."

"It was nothing."

"We will remember it for always, Papa. We will never forget."

Very late in the night Bodoni opened his eyes. He sensed that his wife was lying beside him, watching him. She did not move for a very long time, and then suddenly she kissed his cheeks and his forehead. "What's this?" he cried.

"You're the best father in the world," she whispered.

"Why?"

"Now I see," she said. "I understand."

She lay back and closed her eyes, holding his hand. "Is it a very lovely journey?" she asked.

"Yes," he said.

"Perhaps," she said, "perhaps, some night, you might take me on just a little trip, do you think?"

"Just a little one, perhaps," he said.

"Thank you," she said. "Good night."

"Good night," said Fiorello Bodoni.

The Rocket Man

The electrical fireflies were hovering above Mother's dark hair to light her path. She stood in her bedroom door looking out at me as I passed in the silent hall. "You *will* help me keep him here this time, won't you?" she asked.

"I guess so," I said.

"Please." The fireflies cast moving bits of light on her white face. "This time he mustn't go away again."

"All right," I said, after standing there a moment. "But it won't do any good; it's no use."

She went away, and the fireflies, on their electric circuits, fluttered after her like an errant constellation, showing her how to walk in darkness. I heard her say, faintly, "We've got to try, anyway."

Other fireflies followed me to my room. When the weight of my body cut a circuit in the bed, the fireflies winked out. It was midnight, and my mother and I waited, our rooms separated by darkness, in bed. The bed began to rock me and sing to me. I touched a switch; the singing and rocking stopped. I didn't want to sleep. I didn't want to sleep at all.

This night was no different from a thousand others in our time. We would wake nights and feel the cool air turn hot, feel the fire in the wind, or see the walls burned a bright color for an instant, and then we knew *his* rocket was over our house—his rocket, and the oak trees swaying from the concussion. And

I would lie there, eyes wide, panting, and Mother in her room. Her voice would come to me over the interroom radio:

"Did you feel it?"

And I would answer, "That was him, all right."

That was my father's ship passing over our town, a small town where space rockets never came, and we would lie awake for the next two hours, thinking. "Now Dad's landed in Springfield, now he's on the tarmac, now he is signing the papers, now he's in the helicopter, now he's over the river, now the hills, now he's settling the helicopter in at the little airport at Green Village here. . . ." And the night would be half over when, in our separate cool beds, Mother and I would be listening, listening. "Now he's walking down Bell Street. He always walks . . . never takes a cab . . . now across the park, now turning the corner of Oakhurst and *now*. . . ."

I lifted my head from my pillow. Far down the street, coming closer and closer, smartly, quickly, briskly—footsteps. Now turning in at our house, up the porch steps. And we were both smiling in the cool darkness, Mom and I, when we heard the front door open in recognition, speak a quiet word of welcome, and shut, downstairs. . . .

Three hours later I turned the brass knob to their room quietly, holding my breath, balancing in a darkness as big as the space between the planets, my hand out to reach the small black case at the foot of my parents' sleeping bed. Taking it, I ran silently to my room, thinking. He won't tell me, he doesn't want me to *know*.

And from the opened case spilled his black uniform, like a black nebula, stars glittering here or there, distantly, in the material. I kneaded the dark stuff in my warm hands; I smelled the planet Mars, an iron smell, and the planet Venus, a green ivy smell, and the planet Mercury, a scent of sulfur and fire; and I could smell the milky moon and the hardness of stars. I pushed the uniform into a centrifuge machine I'd built in my ninth-grade shop that year, set it whirling. Soon a fine powder precipitated into a retort. This I slid under a microscope. And while my parents slept unaware and while our house was asleep, all the automatic bakers and servers and robot cleaners in an electric slumber, I stared down upon brilliant motes of meteor dust, comet tail, and loam from far Jupiter glistening like worlds themselves which drew me down the tube a billion miles into space, at terrific accelerations.

At dawn, exhausted with my journey and fearful of discovery, I returned the boxed uniform to their sleeping room.

Then I slept, only to waken at the sound of the horn of the dry-cleaning car which stopped in the yard below. They took the black uniform box with them. It's good I didn't wait, I thought. For the uniform would be back in an hour, clean of all its destiny and travel.

I slept again, with the little vial of magical dust in my pajama pocket, over my beating heart.

When I came downstairs, there was Dad at the breakfast table, biting into his toast. "Sleep good, Doug?" he said, as if he had been here all the time, and hadn't been gone for three months.

"All right," I said.

"Toast?"

He pressed a button and the breakfast table made me four pieces, golden brown.

I remember my father that afternoon, digging and digging in the garden, like an animal after something, it seemed. There he was with his long dark arms moving swiftly, planting, tamping, fixing, cutting, pruning, his dark face always down to the soil, his eyes always down to what he was doing, never up to the sky, never looking at me, or Mother, even, unless we knelt with him to feel the earth soak up through the overalls at our knees, to put our hands into the black dirt and not look at the bright, crazy sky. Then he would glance to either side, to Mother or me, and give us a gentle wink, and go on, bent down, face down, the sky staring at his back.

That night we sat on the mechanical porch swing which swung us and blew a wind upon us and sang to us. It was summer and moonlight and we had lemonade to drink, and we held the cold glasses in our hands, and Dad read the stereo-newspapers inserted into the special hat you put on your head and which turned the microscopic page in front of the magnifying lens if you blinked three times in succession. Dad smoked cigarettes and told me about how it was when he was a boy in the year 1997. After a while he said, ''Why aren't you out playing kick-the-can, Doug?''

I didn't say anything, but Mom said, ''He does, on nights when you're not here.''

Dad looked at me and then, for the first time that day, at the sky. Mother always watched him when he glanced at the stars. The first day and night when he got home he wouldn't look at the sky much. I thought about him gardening and gardening so furiously, his face almost driven into the earth. But the second night he looked at the stars a little more. Mother wasn't afraid of the sky in the day so much, but it was the night stars that she wanted to turn off, and sometimes I could almost see her reaching for a switch in her mind, but never finding it. And by the third night maybe Dad'd be out here on the porch until way after we were all ready for bed, and then I'd hear Mom call him in, almost like she called me from the street at times. And then I would hear Dad fitting the electric-eye door lock in place, with a sigh. And the next morning at breakfast I'd glance down and see his little black case near his feet as he buttered his toast and Mother slept late.

''Well, be seeing you, Doug,'' he'd say, and we'd shake hands.

''In about three months?''

''Right.''

And he'd walk away down the street, not taking a helicopter or beetle or bus, just walking with his uniform hidden in his small underarm case; he didn't want anyone to think he was vain about being a Rocket Man.

Mother would come out to eat breakfast, one piece of dry toast, about an hour later.

But now it was tonight, the first night, the good night, and he wasn't looking at the stars much at all.

''Let's go to the television carnival,'' I said.

''Fine,'' said Dad.

Mother smiled at me.

And we rushed off to town in a helicopter and took Dad through a thousand exhibits, to keep his face and head down with us and not looking anywhere else. And as we laughed at the funny things and looked serious at the serious ones, I thought, My father goes to Saturn and Neptune and Pluto, but he never brings me presents. Other boys whose fathers go into space bring back bits of ore from Callisto and hunks of black meteor or blue sand. But I have to get my own collection, trading from other boys, the Martian rocks and Mercurian sands which filled my room, but about which Dad would never comment.

On occasion, I remembered, he brought something for Mother. He planted some Martian sunflowers once in our yard, but after he was gone a month and the sunflowers grew large, Mom ran out one day and cut them all down.

Without thinking, as we paused at one of the three-dimensional exhibits, I asked Dad the question I always asked:

"What's it like, out in space?"

Mother shot me a frightened glance. It was too late.

Dad stood there for a full half minute trying to find an answer, then he shrugged.

"It's the best thing in a lifetime of best things." Then he caught himself. "Oh, it's really nothing at all. Routine. You wouldn't like it." He looked at me, apprehensively.

"But *you* always go back."

"Habit."

"Where're you going next?"

"I haven't decided yet. I'll think it over."

He always thought it over. In those days rocket pilots were rare and he could pick and choose, work when he liked. On the third night of his homecoming you could see him picking and choosing among the stars.

"Come on," said Mother, "let's go home."

It was still early when we got home. I wanted Dad to put on his uniform. I shouldn't have asked—it always made Mother unhappy—but I could not help myself. I kept at him though he had always refused. I had never seen him in it, and at last he said, "Oh, all right."

We waited in the parlor while he went upstairs in the air flue. Mother looked at me dully, as if she couldn't believe that her own son could do this to her. I glanced away. "I'm sorry," I said.

"You're not helping at all," she said. "At all."

There was a whisper in the air flue a moment later.

"Here I am," said Dad quietly.

We looked at him in his uniform.

It was glossy black with silver buttons and silver rims to the heels of the black boots, and it looked as if someone had cut the arms and legs and body from a dark nebula, with little faint stars glowing through it. It fit as close as a glove fits to a slender long hand, and it smelled like cool air and metal and space. It smelled of fire and time.

Father stood, smiling awkwardly, in the center of the room.

"Turn around," said Mother.

Her eyes were remote, looking at him.

When he was gone, she never talked of him. She never said anything about anything but the weather or the condition of my neck and the need of a washcloth for it, or the fact that she didn't sleep nights. Once she said the light was too strong at night.

"But there's no moon this week," I said.

"There's starlight," she said.

I went to the store and bought her some darker, greener shades. As I lay in bed at night, I could hear her pull them down tight to the bottom of the windows. It made a long rustling noise.

Once I tried to mow the lawn.

"No." Mom stood in the door. "Put the mower away."

So the grass went three months at a time without cutting. Dad cut it when he came home.

She wouldn't let me do anything else either, like repairing the electrical breakfast maker or the mechanical book reader. She saved everything up, as if for Christmas. And then I would see Dad hammering or tinkering, and always smiling at his work, and Mother smiling over him, happy.

No, she never talked of him when he was gone. And as for Dad, he never did anything to make a contact across the millions of miles. He said once, "If I called you, I'd want to be with you. I wouldn't be happy."

Once Dad said to me, "Your mother treats me, sometimes, as if I weren't here—as if I were invisible."

I had seen her do it. She would look just beyond him, over his shoulder, at his chin or hands, but never into his eyes. If she did look at his eyes, her eyes were covered with a film, like an animal going to sleep. She said yes at the right times, and smiled, but always a half second later than expected.

"I'm not there for her," said Dad.

But other days she would be there and he would be there for her, and they would hold hands and walk around the block, or take rides, with Mom's hair flying like a girl's behind her, and she would cut off all the mechanical devices in the kitchen and bake him incredible cakes and pies and cookies, looking deep into his face, her smile a real smile. But at the end of such days when he was there to her, she would always cry. And Dad would stand helpless, gazing about the room as if to find the answer but never finding it.

Dad turned slowly, in his uniform, for us to see.

"Turn around again," said Mom.

The next morning Dad came rushing into the house with handfuls of tickets. Pink rocket tickets for California, blue tickets for Mexico.

"Come on!" he said. "We'll buy disposable clothes and burn them when they're soiled. Look, we take the noon rocket to L.A., the two-o'clock helicopter to Santa Barbara, the nine-o'clock plane to Ensenada, sleep overnight!"

And we went to California and up and down the Pacific Coast for a day and a half, settling at last on the sands of Malibu to cook wieners at night. Dad was always listening or singing or watching things on all sides of him, holding onto things as if the world were a centrifuge going so swiftly that he might be flung off away from us at any instant.

The last afternoon at Malibu Mom was up in the hotel room. Dad lay on the sand beside me for a long time in the hot sun. "Ah," he sighed, "this is it." His eyes were gently closed; he lay on his back, drinking the sun. "You *miss* this," he said.

He meant "on the rocket," of course. But he never said "the rocket" or mentioned the rocket and all the things you couldn't have on the rocket. You couldn't have a salt wind on the rocket or a blue sky or a yellow sun or Mom's cooking. You couldn't talk to your fourteen-year-old boy on a rocket.

"Let's hear it," he said at last.

And I knew that now we would talk, as we had always talked, for three hours straight. All afternoon we would murmur back and forth in the lazy sun about my school grades, how high I could jump, how fast I could swim.

Dad nodded each time I spoke and smiled and slapped my chest lightly in approval. We talked. We did not talk of rockets or space, but we talked of Mexico, where we had driven once in an ancient car, and of the butterflies we had caught in the rain forests of green warm Mexico at noon, seeing the hundred butterflies sucked to our radiator, dying there, beating their blue and crimson wings, twitching, beautiful, and sad. We talked of such things instead of the things I wanted to talk about. And he listened to me. That was the thing he did, as if he was trying to fill himself up with all the sound he could hear. He listened to the wind and the falling ocean and my voice, always with a rapt attention, a concentration that almost excluded physical bodies themselves and kept only the sounds. He shut his eyes to listen. I would see him listening to the lawn mower as he cut the grass by hand instead of using the remote-control device, and I would see him smelling the cut grass as it sprayed up at him behind the mower in a green fount.

"Doug," he said, about five in the afternoon, as we were picking up our towels and heading back along the beach near the surf, "I want you to promise me something."

"What?"

"Don't ever be a Rocket Man."

I stopped.

"I mean it," he said. "Because when you're out there you want to be here, and when you're here you want to be out there. Don't start that. Don't let it get hold of you."

"But—"

"You don't know what it is. Every time I'm out there I think, 'If I ever get back to Earth I'll stay there; I'll never go out again.' But I go out, and I guess I'll always go out."

"I've thought about being a Rocket Man for a long time," I said.

He didn't hear me. "I *try* to stay here. Last Saturday when I got home I started trying so darned hard to *stay* here."

I remembered him in the garden, sweating, and all the traveling and doing and listening, and I knew that he did this to convince himself that the sea and the towns and the land and his family were the only real things and the good things. But I knew where he would be tonight: looking at the jewelry in Orion from our front porch.

"Promise you won't be like me," he said.

I hesitated awhile. "Okay," I said.

He shook my hand. "Good boy," he said.

The dinner was fine that night. Mom had run about the kitchen with handfuls of cinnamon and dough and pots and pans tinkling, and now a great turkey fumed on the table, with dressing, cranberry sauce, peas, and pumpkin pie.

"In the middle of August?" said Dad, amazed.

"You won't be here for Thanksgiving."

"So I won't."

He sniffed it. He lifted each lid from each tureen and let the flavor steam over his sunburned face. He said "Ah" to each. He looked at the room and his hands. He gazed at the pictures on the wall, the chairs, the table, me, and Mom. He cleared his throat. I saw him make up his mind. "Lilly?"

"Yes?" Mom looked across her table which she had set like a wonderful silver trap, a miraculous gravy pit into which, like a struggling beast of the past caught in a tar pool, her husband might at last be caught and held, gazing out through a jail of wishbones, safe forever. Her eyes sparkled.

"Lilly," said Dad.

Go on, I thought crazily. Say it quick: say you'll stay home this time, for good, and never go away; say it!

Just then a passing helicopter jarred the room and the windowpane shook with a crystal sound. Dad glanced at the window.

The blue stars of evening were there, and the red planet Mars was rising in the East.

Dad looked at Mars a full minute. Then he put his hand out blindly toward me. "May I have some peas," he said.

"Excuse me," said Mother. "I'm going to get some bread."

She rushed out into the kitchen.

"But there's bread on the table," I said.

Dad didn't look at me as he began his meal.

I couldn't sleep that night. I came downstairs at one in the morning and the moonlight was like ice on all the housetops, and dew glittered in a snow field on our grass. I stood in the doorway in my pajamas, feeling the warm night wind, and then I knew that Dad was sitting in the mechanical porch swing, gliding gently. I could see his profile tilted back, and he was watching the stars wheel over the sky. His eyes were like gray crystal there, the moon in each one.

I went out and sat beside him.

We glided awhile in the swing.

At last I said, "How many ways are there to die in space?"

"A million."

"Name some."

"The meteors hit you. The air goes out of your rocket. Or comets take you along with them. Concussion. Strangulation. Explosion. Centrifugal force. Too much acceleration. Too little. The heat, the cold, the sun, the moon, the stars, the planets, the asteroids, the planetoids, radiation . . ."

"And do they bury you?"

"They never find you."

"Where do you go?"

"A billion miles away. Traveling graves, they call them. You become a meteor or a planetoid traveling forever through space."

I said nothing.

"One thing," he said later, "it's quick in space. Death. It's over like that. You don't linger. Most of the time you don't even know it. You're dead and that's it."

We went up to bed.

It was morning.

Standing in the doorway, Dad listened to the yellow canary singing in its golden cage.

"Well, I've decided," he said. "Next time I come home, I'm home to stay."

"Dad!" I said.

"Tell your mother that when she gets up," he said.

"You *mean* it!"

He nodded gravely. "See you in about three months."

And there he went off down the street, carrying his uniform in its secret box, whistling and looking at the tall green trees and picking chinaberries off the chinaberry bush as he brushed by, tossing them ahead of him as he walked away into the bright shade of early morning. . . .

I asked Mother about a few things that morning after Father had been gone a number of hours. "Dad said that sometimes you don't act as if you hear or see him," I said.

And then she explained everything to me quietly.

"When he went off into space ten years ago, I said to myself, 'He's dead.' Or as good as dead. So think of him dead. And when he comes back, three or four times a year, it's not him at all, it's only a pleasant little memory or a dream. And if a memory stops or a dream stops, it can't hurt half as much. So most of the time I think of him dead—"

"But other times—"

"Other times I can't help myself. I bake pies and treat him as if he were alive, and then it hurts. No, it's better to think he hasn't been here for ten years and I'll never see him again. It doesn't hurt as much."

"Didn't he say next time he'd settle down?"

She shook her head slowly. "No, he's dead. I'm very sure of that."

"He'll come alive again, then," I said.

"Ten years ago," said Mother, "I thought, What if he dies on Venus? Then we'll never be able to see Venus again. What if he dies on Mars? We'll never be able to look at Mars again, all red in the sky, without wanting to go in and lock the door. Or what if he dies on Jupiter or Saturn or Neptune? On those nights when those planets were high in the sky, we wouldn't want to have anything to do with the stars."

"I guess not," I said.

* * *

The message came the next day.

The messenger gave it to me and I read it standing on the porch. The sun was setting. Mom stood in the screen door behind me, watching me fold the message and put it in my pocket.

''Mom,'' I said.

''Don't tell me anything I don't already know,'' she said.

She didn't cry.

Well, it wasn't Mars, and it wasn't Venus, and it wasn't Jupiter or Saturn that killed him. We wouldn't have to think of him every time Jupiter or Saturn or Mars lit up the evening sky.

This was different.

His ship had fallen into the sun.

And the sun was big and fiery and merciless, and it was always in the sky and you couldn't get away from it.

So for a long time after my father died my mother slept through the days and wouldn't go out. We had breakfast at midnight and lunch at three in the morning, and dinner at the cold dim hour of 6 A.M. We went to all-night shows and went to bed at sunrise, with all the green dark shades pulled tight down on all the windows.

And, for a long while, the only days we ever went out to walk were the days when it was raining and there was no sun.

A Sound of Thunder

The sign on the wall seemed to quaver under a film of sliding warm water. Eckels felt his eyelids blink over his stare, and the sign burned in this momentary darkness:

TIME SAFARI, INC.
SAFARIS TO ANY YEAR IN THE PAST.
YOU NAME THE ANIMAL.
WE TAKE YOU THERE.
YOU SHOOT IT.

A warm phlegm gathered in Eckels' throat; he swallowed and pushed it down. The muscles around his mouth formed a smile as he put his hand slowly out upon the air, and in that hand waved a check for ten thousand dollars to the man behind the desk.

"Does this safari guarantee I come back alive?"

"We guarantee nothing," said the official, "except the dinosaurs." He turned. "This is Mr. Travis, your Safari Guide in the Past. He'll tell you what and where to shoot. If he says no shooting, no shooting. If you disobey instructions, there's a stiff penalty of another ten thousand dollars, plus possible government action, on your return."

Eckels glanced across the vast office at a mass and tangle, a snaking and humming of wires and steel boxes, at an aurora that flickered now orange, now silver, now blue. There was a sound like a gigantic bonfire burning all of Time, all the years and all the parchment calendars, all the hours piled high and set aflame.

A touch of the hand and this burning would, on the instant, beautifully reverse itself. Eckels remembered the wording in the advertisements to the letter. Out of chars and ashes, out of dust and coals, like golden salamanders, the old years, the green years, might leap; roses sweeten the air, white hair turn Irish-black, wrinkles vanish; all, everything fly back to seed, flee death, rush down to their beginnings, suns rise in western skies and set in glorious easts, moons eat themselves opposite to the custom, all and everything cupping one in another like Chinese boxes, rabbits into hats, all and everything returning to the fresh death, the seed death, the green death, to the time before the beginning. A touch of a hand might do it, the merest touch of a hand.

"Unbelievable." Eckels breathed, the light of the Machine on his thin face. "A real Time Machine." He shook his head. "Makes you think. If the election had gone badly yesterday, I might be here now running away from the results. Thank God Keith won. He'll make a fine President of the United States."

"Yes," said the man behind the desk. "We're lucky. If Deutscher had gotten in, we'd have the worst kind of dictatorship. There's an anti-everything man for you, a militarist, anti-Christ, anti-human, anti-intellectual. People called us up, you know, joking but not joking. Said if Deutscher became President they wanted to go live in 1492. Of course it's not our business to conduct Escapes, but to form Safaris. Anyway, Keith's President now. All you got to worry about is—"

"Shooting my dinosaur," Eckels finished it for him.

"A *Tyrannosaurus rex.* The Tyrant Lizard, the most incredible monster in history. Sign this release. Anything happens to you, we're not responsible. Those dinosaurs are hungry."

Eckels flushed angrily. "Trying to scare me!"

"Frankly, yes. We don't want anyone going who'll panic at the first shot. Six Safari leaders were killed last year, and a dozen hunters. We're here to give you the severest thrill a *real* hunter ever asked for. Traveling you back sixty million years to bag the biggest game in all of Time. Your personal check's still there. Tear it up."

Mr. Eckels looked at the check. His fingers twitched.

"Good luck," said the man behind the desk. "Mr. Travis, he's all yours."

They moved silently across the room, taking their guns with them, toward the Machine, toward the silver metal and the roaring light.

First a day and then a night and then a day and then a night, then it was day-night-day-night-day. A week, a month, a year, a decade! A.D. 2055 A.D. 2019. 1999! 1957! Gone! The Machine roared.

They put on their oxygen helmets and tested the intercoms.

Eckels swayed on the padded seat, his face pale, his jaw stiff. He felt the trembling in his arms and he looked down and found his hands tight on the new rifle. There were four other men in the Machine. Travis, the Safari Leader, his assistant, Lesperance, and two other hunters, Billings and Kramer. They sat looking at each other, and the years blazed around them.

"Can these guns get a dinosaur cold?" Eckels felt his mouth saying.

"If you hit them right," said Travis on the helmet radio. "Some dinosaurs have two brains, one in the head, another far down the spinal column. We stay away from those. That's stretching luck. Put your first two shots into the eyes, if you can, blind them, and go back into the brain."

The Machine howled. Time was a film run backward. Suns fled and ten million moons fled after them. "Think," said Eckels. "Every hunter that ever lived would envy us today. This makes Africa seem like Illinois."

The Machine slowed; its scream fell to a murmur. The Machine stopped.

The sun stopped in the sky.

The fog that had enveloped the Machine blew away and they were in an old time, a very old time indeed, three hunters and two Safari Heads with their blue metal guns across their knees.

"Christ isn't born yet," said Travis. "Moses has not gone to the mountain to talk with God. The Pyramids are still in the earth, waiting to be cut out and put up. *Remember* that. Alexander, Caesar, Napoleon, Hitler—none of them exists.''

The men nodded.

''That''—Mr. Travis pointed—''is the jungle of sixty million two thousand and fifty-five years before President Keith.''

He indicated a metal path that struck off into green wilderness, over streaming swamp, among giant ferns and palms.

''And that,'' he said, ''is the Path, laid by Time Safari for your use. It floats six inches above the earth. Doesn't touch so much as one grass blade, flower, or tree. It's an anti-gravity metal. Its purpose is to keep you from touching this world of the past in any way. Stay on the Path. Don't go off it. I repeat. *Don't go off.* For *any* reason! If you fall off, there's a penalty. And don't shoot any animals we don't okay.''

''Why?'' asked Eckels.

They sat in the ancient wilderness. Far birds' cries blew on a wind, and the smell of tar and old salt sea, moist grasses, and flowers the color of blood.

''We don't want to change the Future. We don't belong here in the Past. The government doesn't *like* us here. We have to pay big graft to keep our franchise. A Time Machine is finicky business. Not knowing it, we might kill an important animal, a small bird, a roach, a flower even, thus destroying an important link in a growing species.''

''That's not clear,'' said Eckels.

''All right,'' Travis continued, ''say we accidentally kill one mouse here. That means all the future families of this one particular mouse are destroyed, right?''

''Right.''

''And all the families of the families of the families of that one mouse! With a stamp of your foot, you annihilate first one, then a dozen, then a thousand, a million, a *billion* possible mice!''

''So they're dead,'' said Eckels. ''So what?''

''So what?'' Travis snorted quietly. ''Well, what about the foxes that'll need those mice to survive? For want of ten mice, a fox dies. For want of ten foxes, a lion starves. For want of a lion, all manner of insects, vultures, infinite billions of life forms are thrown into chaos and destruction. Eventually it all boils down to this: fifty-nine million years later, a caveman, one of a dozen on the *entire world,* goes hunting wild boar, or saber-toothed tiger for food. But you, friend, have *stepped* on all the tigers in that region. By stepping on *one* single mouse. So the caveman starves. And the caveman, please note, is not just *any* expendable man, no! He is an *entire future nation.* From his loins would have sprung ten sons. From *their* loins one hundred sons, and thus onward to a civilization. Destroy this one man, and you destroy a race, a people, an entire history of life. It is comparable to slaying some of Adam's grandchildren. The stomp of your foot, on one mouse, could start an earthquake, the effects of which could shake our earth and destinies down through Time, to their very foundations. With the death of that one caveman, a billion others yet unborn are throttled in the womb. Perhaps Rome never rises on its seven hills. Perhaps Europe is forever a dark forest, and only Asia waxes healthy and teeming. Step on a mouse and you crush the Pyramids. Step on a mouse and you leave your print, like a Grand Canyon, across Eternity. Queen Elizabeth might never be born. Washington might not cross the Delaware, there might never be a United States at all. So be careful. Stay on the Path. *Never* step off!"

"I see," said Eckels. "Then it wouldn't pay for us even to touch the *grass?*"

"Correct. Crushing certain plants could add up infinitesimally. A little error here would multiply in sixty million years, all out of proportion. Of course maybe our theory is wrong. Maybe Time *can't* be changed by us. Or maybe it can be changed only in little subtle ways. A dead mouse here makes an insect imbalance there, a population disproportion later, a bad harvest further on, a depression, mass starvation, and, finally, a change in *social* temperament in far-flung countries. Something much more subtle, like that. Perhaps only a soft breath, a whisper, a hair, pollen on the air, such a slight, slight change that unless you looked close you wouldn't see it. Who knows? Who really can say he knows? We don't know. We're guessing. But until we do know for certain whether our messing around in Time *can* make a big roar or a little rustle in history, we're being careful. This Machine, this Path, your clothing and bodies, were sterilized, as you know, before the journey. We wear these oxygen helmets so we can't introduce our bacteria into an ancient atmosphere."

"How do we know which animals to shoot?"

"They're marked with red paint," said Travis. "Today, before our journey, we sent Lesperance here back with the Machine. He came to this particular era and followed certain animals."

"Studying them?"

"Right," said Lesperance. "I track them through their entire existence, noting which of them lives longest. Very few. How many times they mate. Not often. Life's short. When I find one that's going to die when a tree falls on him, or one that drowns in a tar pit, I note the exact hour, minute, and second. I shoot a paint bomb. It leaves a red patch on his side. We can't miss it. Then I correlate our arrival in the Past so that we meet the Monster not more than two minutes before he would have died anyway. This way, we kill only animals with no future, that are never going to mate again. You see how *careful* we are?"

"But if you came back this morning in Time," said Eckels eagerly, "you must've bumped into *us,* our Safari! How did it turn out? Was it successful? Did all of us get through—alive?"

Travis and Lesperance gave each other a look.

"That'd be a paradox," said the latter. "Time doesn't permit that sort of mess—a man meeting himself. When such occasions threaten, Time steps aside. Like an airplane hitting an air pocket. You felt the Machine jump just before we stopped? That was us passing ourselves on the way back to the Future. We saw nothing. There's no way of telling *if* this expedition was a success, *if we* got our monster, or whether all of us—meaning *you,* Mr. Eckels—got out alive."

Eckels smiled palely.

"Cut that," said Travis sharply. "Everyone on his feet!"

They were ready to leave the Machine.

The jungle was high and the jungle was broad and the jungle was the entire world forever and forever. Sounds like music and sounds like flying tents filled the sky, and those were pterodactyls soaring with cavernous gray wings, gigantic bats of delirium and night fever. Eckels, balanced on the narrow Path, aimed his rifle playfully.

"Stop that!" said Travis. "Don't even aim for fun, blast you! If your guns should go off—"

Eckels flushed. "Where's our *Tyrannosaurus?*"

Lesperance checked his wristwatch. "Up ahead. We'll bisect his trail in sixty seconds. Look for the red paint! Don't shoot till we give the word. Stay on the path. *Stay on the Path!*"

They moved forward in the wind of morning.

"Strange," murmured Eckels. "Up ahead, sixty million years, Election Day over. Keith made President. Everyone celebrating. And here we are, a million years lost, and they don't exist. The things we worried about for months, a lifetime, not even born or thought of yet."

"Safety catches off, everyone!" ordered Travis. "You, first shot, Eckels. Second, Billings. Third, Kramer."

"I've hunted tiger, wild boar, buffalo, elephant, but now, this is *it,*" said Eckels. "I'm shaking like a kid."

"Ah," said Travis.

Everyone stopped.

Travis raised his hand. "Ahead," he whispered. "In the mist. There he is. There's His Royal Majesty now."

The jungle was wide and full of twitterings, rustlings, murmurs, and sighs.

Suddenly it all ceased, as if someone had shut a door.

Silence.

A sound of thunder.

Out of the mist, one hundred yards away, came *Tyrannosaurus rex.*

"It," whispered Eckels. "It . . ."

"Sh!"

It came on great oiled, resilient, striding legs. It towered thirty feet above half of the trees, a great evil god, folding its delicate watchmaker's claws close to its oily reptilian chest. Each lower leg was a piston, a thousand pounds of white bone, sunk in thick ropes of muscle, sheathed over in a gleam of pebbled skin like the mail of a terrible warrior. Each thigh was a ton of meat, ivory, and steel mesh. And from the great breathing cage of the upper body those two delicate arms dangled out front, arms with hands which might pick up and examine men like toys, while the snake neck coiled. And the head itself, a ton of sculptured stone, lifted easily upon the sky. Its mouth gaped, exposing a fence of teeth like daggers. Its eyes rolled, ostrich eggs, empty of all expression save hunger. It closed its mouth in a death grin. It ran, its pelvic bones crushing aside trees and bushes, its taloned feet clawing damp earth, leaving prints six inches deep wherever it settled its weight. It ran with a gliding ballet step, far too poised and balanced for its ten tons. It moved into a sunlit arena warily, its beautifully reptilian hands feeling the air.

"Why, why," Eckels twitched his mouth. "It could reach up and grab the moon."

"Sh!" Travis jerked angrily. "He hasn't seen us yet."

"It can't be killed." Eckels pronounced his verdict quietly, as if there could be no argument. He had weighed the evidence and this was his considered opinion. The rifle in his hands seemed a cap gun. "We were fools to come. This is impossible."

"Shut up!" hissed Travis.

"Nightmare."

"Turn around," commanded Travis. "Walk quietly to the Machine. We'll remit one half your fee."

"I didn't realize it would be this *big,*" said Eckels. "I miscalculated, that's all. And now I want out."

"It *sees* us!"

"There's the red paint on its chest!"

The Tyrant Lizard raised itself. Its armored flesh glittered like a thousand green coins. The coins, crusted with slime, steamed. In the slime, tiny insects wriggled, so that the entire body seemed to twitch and undulate, even while the monster itself did not move. It exhaled. The stink of raw flesh blew down the wilderness.

"Get me out of here," said Eckels. "It was never like this before. I was always sure I'd come through alive. I had good guides, good safaris, and safety. This time, I figured wrong. I've met my match and admit it. This is too much for me to get hold of."

"Don't run," said Lesperance. "Turn around. Hide in the Machine."

"Yes." Eckels seemed to be numb. He looked at his feet as if trying to make them move. He gave a grunt of helplessness.

"Eckels!"

He took a few steps, blinking, shuffling.

"Not *that* way!"

The Monster, at the first motion, lunged forward with a terrible scream. It covered one hundred yards in six seconds. The rifles jerked up and blazed fire. A windstorm from the beast's mouth engulfed them in the stench of slime and old blood. The Monster roared, teeth glittering with sun.

Eckels, not looking back, walked blindly to the edge of the Path, his gun limp in his arms, stepped off the Path, and walked, not knowing it, in the jungle. His feet sank into green moss. His legs moved him, and he felt alone and remote from the events behind.

The rifles cracked again. Their sound was lost in shriek and lizard thunder. The great level of the reptile's tail swung up, lashed sideways. Trees exploded in clouds of leaf and branch. The Monster twitched its jeweler's hands down to fondle at the men, to twist them in half, to crush them like berries, to cram them into its teeth and its screaming throat. Its boulder-stone eyes leveled with the men. They saw themselves mirrored. They fired at the metallic eyelids and the blazing black iris.

Like a stone idol, like a mountain avalanche, *Tyrannosaurus* fell. Thundering, it clutched trees, pulled them with it. It wrenched and tore the metal Path. The men flung themselves back and away. The body hit, ten tons of cold flesh and stone. The guns fired. The Monster lashed its armored tail, twitched its snake jaws, and lay still. A fount of blood spurted from its throat. Somewhere inside, a sac of fluids burst. Sickening gushes drenched the hunters. They stood, red and glistening.

The thunder faded.

The jungle was silent. After the avalanche, a green peace. After the nightmare, morning.

Billings and Kramer sat on the pathway and threw up. Travis and Lesperance stood with smoking rifles, cursing steadily.

In the Time Machine, on his face, Eckels lay shivering. He had found his way back to the Path, climbed into the Machine.

Travis came walking, glanced at Eckels, took cotton gauze from a metal box, and returned to the others, who were sitting on the Path.

"Clean up."

They wiped the blood from their helmets. They began to curse too. The Monster lay, a hill of solid flesh. Within, you could hear the sighs and murmurs as the furthest chambers of it died, the organs malfunctioning, liquids running a final instant from pocket to sac to spleen, everything shutting off, closing up forever. It was like standing by a wrecked locomotive or a steam shovel at quitting time, all valves being released or levered tight. Bones cracked; the tonnage of its own flesh, off balance, dead weight, snapped the delicate forearms, caught underneath. The meat settled, quivering.

Another cracking sound. Overhead, a gigantic tree branch broke from its heavy mooring, fell. It crashed upon the dead beast with finality.

"There." Lesperance checked his watch. "Right on time. That's the giant tree that was scheduled to fall and kill this animal originally." He glanced at the two hunters. "You want the trophy picture?"

"What?"

"We can't take a trophy back to the Future. The body has to stay right here where it would have died originally, so the insects, birds, and bacteria can get at it, as they were intended to. Everything in balance. The body stays. But we *can* take a picture of you standing near it."

The two men tried to think, but gave up, shaking their heads.

They let themselves be led along the metal Path. They sank wearily into the Machine cushions. They gazed back at the ruined Monster, the stagnating mound, where already strange reptilian birds and golden insects were busy at the steaming armor.

A sound on the floor of the Time Machine stiffened them. Eckels sat there, shivering.

"I'm sorry," he said at last.

"Get up!" cried Travis.

Eckels got up.

"Go out on that Path alone," said Travis. He had his rifle pointed. "You're not coming back in the Machine. We're leaving you here!"

Lesperance seized Travis's arm. "Wait—"

"Stay out of this!" Travis shook his hand away. "This fool nearly killed us. But it isn't *that* so much, no. It's his *shoes!* Look at them! He ran off the Path. That *ruins* us! We'll forfeit! Thousands of dollars of insurance! We guarantee no one leaves the Path. He left it. Oh, the fool! I'll have to report to the government. They might revoke our license to travel. Who knows *what* he's done to Time, to History!"

"Take it easy, all he did was kick up some dirt."

"How do we *know?*" cried Travis. "We don't know anything! It's all a mystery! Get out of here, Eckels!"

Eckels fumbled his shirt. "I'll pay anything. A hundred thousand dollars!"

Travis glared at Eckels' checkbook and spat. "Go out there. The Monster's next to the Path. Stick your arms up to your elbows in his mouth. Then you can come back with us."

"That's unreasonable!"

"The Monster's dead, you idiot. The bullets! The bullets can't be left behind. They don't belong in the Past; they might change anything. Here's my knife. Dig them out!"

The jungle was alive again, full of the old tremorings and bird cries. Eckels turned slowly to regard the primeval garbage dump, that hill of nightmares and terror. After a long time, like a sleepwalker he shuffled out along the Path.

He returned, shuddering, five minutes later, his arms soaked and red to the elbows. He held out his hands. Each held a number of steel bullets. Then he fell. He lay where he fell, not moving.

"You didn't have to make him do that," said Lesperance.

"Didn't I? It's too early to tell." Travis nudged the still body. "He'll live. Next time he won't go hunting game like this. Okay." He jerked his thumb wearily at Lesperance. "Switch on. Let's go home."

1492. 1776. 1812.

They cleaned their hands and faces. They changed their caking shirts and pants. Eckels was up and around again, not speaking. Travis glared at him for a full ten minutes.

"Don't look at me," cried Eckels. "I haven't done anything."

"Who can tell?"

"Just ran off the Path, that's all, a little mud on my shoes—what do you want me to do—get down and pray?"

"We might need it. I'm warning you, Eckels, I might kill you yet. I've got my gun ready."

"I'm innocent. I've done nothing!"

1999. 2000. 2055.

The Machine stopped.

"Get out," said Travis.

The room was there as they had left it. But not the same as they had left it. The same man sat behind the same desk. But the same man did not quite sit behind the same desk.

Travis looked around swiftly. "Everything okay here?" he snapped.

"Fine. Welcome home!"

Travis did not relax. He seemed to be looking at the very atoms of the air itself, at the way the sun poured through the one high window.

"Okay, Eckels, get out. Don't ever come back."

Eckels could not move.

"You heard me," said Travis. "What're you *staring* at?"

Eckels stood smelling of the air, and there was a thing to the air, a chemical taint so subtle, so slight, that only a faint cry of his sublimal senses warned him it was there. The colors, white, gray, blue, orange, in the wall, in the furniture, in the sky beyond the window, were . . . were . . . And there was a *feel.* His flesh twitched. His hands twitched. He stood drinking the oddness with the pores of his body. Somewhere, someone must have been screaming one of those whistles that only a dog can hear. His body screamed silence in return. Beyond this room, beyond this wall, beyond this man who was not quite the same man seated at this desk that was not quite the same desk . . . lay an entire world of streets and people. What sort of world it was now, there was no telling. He could feel them moving there, beyond the walls, almost, like so many chess pieces blown in a dry wind. . . .

But the immediate thing was the sign painted on the office wall, the same sign he had read earlier today on first entering.

Somehow, the sign had changed:

TYME SEFARI INC.
SEFARIS TU ANY YEER EN THE PAST.
YU NAIM THE ANIMALL.
WEE TAEKYUTHAIR.
YU SHOOT ITT.

Eckels felt himself fall into a chair. He fumbled crazily at the thick slime on his boots. He held up a clod of dirt, trembling. "No, it *can't* be. Not a *little* thing like that. No!"

Embedded in the mud, glistening green and gold and black, was a butterfly, very beautiful and very dead.

"Not a little thing like *that!* Not a butterfly!" cried Eckels.

It fell to the floor, an exquisite thing, a small thing that could upset balances and knock down a line of small dominoes and then big dominoes and then gigantic dominoes, all down the years across Time. Eckels' mind whirled. It *couldn't* change things. Killing one butterfly couldn't be *that* important! Could it?

His face was cold. His mouth trembled, asking: "Who—Who won the presidential election yesterday?"

The man behind the desk laughed. "You joking? You know very well. Deutscher, of course! Who else? Not that fool weakling Keith. We got an iron man now, a man with guts!" The official stopped. "What's wrong?"

Eckels moaned. He dropped to his knees. He scrabbled at the golden butterfly with shaking fingers. "Can't we," he pleaded to the world, to himself, to the officials, to the Machine, "can't we take it *back,* can't we *make* it alive again? Can't we start over? Can't we—"

He did not move. Eyes shut, he waited, shivering. He heard Travis breathe loud in the room; he heard Travis shift his rifle, click the safety catch, and raise the weapon.

There was a sound of thunder.

The Long Rain

The rain continued. It was a hard rain, a perpetual rain, a sweating and steaming rain; it was a mizzle, a downpour, a fountain, a whipping at the eyes, an undertow at the ankles; it was a rain to drown all rains and the memory of rains. It came by the pound and the ton, it hacked at the jungle and cut the trees like scissors and shaved the grass and tunneled the soil and molted the bushes. It shrank men's hands into the hands of wrinkled apes; it rained a solid glassy rain, and it never stopped.

"How much farther, Lieutenant?"

"I don't know. A mile, ten miles, a thousand."

"Aren't you sure?"

"How can I be sure?"

"I don't like this rain. If we only knew how far it is to the Sun Dome, I'd feel better."

"Another hour or two from here."

"You really think so, Lieutenant?"

"Of course."

"Or are you lying to keep us happy?"

"I'm lying to keep you happy. Shut up!"

The two men sat together in the rain. Behind them sat two other men who were wet and tired and slumped like clay that was melting.

The lieutenant looked up. He had a face that once had been brown and now the rain had washed it pale, and the rain had washed the color from his eyes and they were white, as were his teeth, and as was his hair. He was all white. Even his uniform was beginning to turn white, and perhaps a little green with fungus.

The lieutenant felt the rain on his cheeks. ''How many million years since the rain stopped raining here on Venus.''

''Don't be crazy,'' said one of the two other men. ''It never stops raining on Venus. It just goes on and on. I've lived here for ten years and I never saw a minute, or even a second, when it wasn't pouring.''

''It's like living under water,'' said the lieutenant, and rose up, shrugging his guns into place. ''Well, we'd better get going. We'll find that Sun Dome yet.''

''Or we won't find it,'' said the cynic.

''It's an hour or so.''

''Now you're lying to me, Lieutenant.''

''No, now I'm lying to myself. This is one of those times when you've got to lie. I can't take much more of this.''

They walked down the jungle trail, now and then looking at their compasses. There was no direction anywhere, only what the compass said. There was a gray sky and rain falling and jungle and a path, and, far back behind them somewhere, a rocket in which they had ridden and fallen. A rocket in which lay two of their friends, dead and dripping rain.

They walked in single file, not speaking. They came to a river which lay wide and flat and brown, flowing down to the great Single Sea. The surface of it was stippled in a billion places by the rain.

''All right, Simmons.''

The lieutenant nodded and Simmons took a small packet from his back which, with a pressure of hidden chemical, inflated into a large boat. The lieutenant directed the cutting of wood and the quick making of paddles and they set out into the river, paddling swiftly across the smooth surface in the rain.

The lieutenant felt the cold rain on his cheeks and on his neck and on his moving arms. The cold was beginning to seep into his lungs. He felt the rain on his ears, on his eyes, on his legs.

''I didn't sleep last night,'' he said.

''Who could? Who has? When? How many nights have we

slept? Thirty nights, thirty days! Who can sleep with rain slamming their head, banging away. . . . I'd give anything for a hat. Anything at all, just so it wouldn't hit my head anymore. I get headaches. My head is sore; it hurts all the time."

"I'm sorry I came to China," said one of the others.

"First time I ever heard Venus called China."

"Sure, China. Chinese water cure. Remember the old torture? Rope you against a wall. Drop one drop of water on your head every half-hour. You go crazy waiting for the next one. Well, that's Venus, but on a big scale. We're not made for water. You can't sleep, you can't breathe right, and you're crazy from just being soggy. If we'd been ready for a crash, we'd have brought waterproofed uniforms and hats. It's this beating rain on your head gets you, most of all. It's so heavy. It's like BB shot. I don't know how long I can take it."

"Boy, me for the Sun Dome! The man who thought *them* up, thought of something."

They crossed the river, and in crossing they thought of the Sun Dome, somewhere ahead of them, shining in the jungle rain. A yellow house, round and bright as the sun. A house forty feet high by one hundred feet in diameter, in which was warmth and quiet and hot food and freedom from rain. And in the center of the Sun Dome, of course, was a sun. A small floating free globe of yellow fire, drifting in a space at the top of the building where you could look at it from where you sat, smoking or reading a book or drinking your hot chocolate crowned with marshmallow dollops or drinking something else. There it would be, the yellow sun, just the size of the Earth sun, and it was warm and continuous, and the rain world of Venus would be forgotten as long as you stayed in that house and idled your time.

The lieutenant turned and looked back at the three men using their oars and gritting their teeth. They were as white as mushrooms, as white as he was. Venus bleached everything away in a few months. Even the jungle was an immense cartoon nightmare, for how could the jungle be green with no sun, with always rain falling and always dusk? The white, white jungle with the pale cheese-colored leaves, and the earth carved of wet Camembert, and the tree boles like immense toadstools—

everything black and white. And how often could you see the soil itself? Wasn't it mostly a creek, a stream, a puddle, a pool, a lake, a river, and then, at last, the sea?

"Here we are!"

They leaped out on the farthest shore, splashing and sending up showers. The boat was deflated and stored in a cigar-box packet. Then, standing on the rainy shore, they tried to light up a few smokes for themselves, and it was five minutes or so before, shuddering, they worked the inverted lighter and, cupping their hands, managed a few drags upon cigarettes that all too quickly were limp and beaten away from their lips by a sudden slap of rain.

They walked on.

"Wait just a moment," said the lieutenant. "I thought I saw something ahead."

"The Sun Dome?"

"I'm not sure. The rain closed in again."

Simmons began to run. "The Sun Dome!"

"Come back, Simmons!"

"The Sun Dome!"

Simmons vanished in the rain. The others ran after him.

They found him in a little clearing, and they stopped and looked at him and what he had discovered.

The rocket ship.

It was lying where they had left it. Somehow they had circled back and were where they had started. In the ruin of the ship green fungus was growing out of the mouths of the two dead men. As they watched, the fungus took flower, the petals broke away in the rain, and the fungus died.

"How did we do it?"

"An electrical storm must be nearby. Threw our compasses off. That explains it."

"You're right."

"What'll we do now?"

"Start out again."

"Good Lord, we're not any closer to anywhere!"

"Let's try to keep calm about it, Simmons."

"Calm, calm! This rain's driving me wild!"

"We've enough food for another two days if we're careful."

The rain danced on their skin, on their wet uniforms; the rain streamed from their noses and ears, from their fingers and knees. They looked like stone fountains frozen in the jungle, issuing forth water from every pore.

And, as they stood, from a distance they heard a roar.

And the monster came out of the rain.

The monster was supported upon a thousand electric blue legs. It walked swiftly and terribly. It struck down a leg with a driving blow. Everywhere a leg struck a tree fell and burned. Great whiffs of ozone filled the rainy air, and smoke blew away and was broken up by the rain. The monster was a half mile wide and a mile high and it felt of the ground like a great blind thing. Sometimes, for a moment, it had no legs at all. And then, in an instant, a thousand whips would fall out of its belly, white-blue whips, to sting the jungle.

"There's the electrical storm," said one of the men. "There's the thing ruined our compasses. And it's coming this way."

"Lie down, everyone," said the lieutenant.

"Run!" cried Simmons.

"Don't be a fool. Lie down. It hits the highest points. We may get through unhurt. Lie down about fifty feet from the rocket. It may very well spend its force there and leave us be. Get down!"

The men flopped.

"Is it coming?" they asked each other, after a moment.

"Coming."

"Is it nearer?"

"Two hundred yards off."

"Nearer?"

"Here she is!"

The monster came and stood over them. It dropped down ten blue bolts of lightning which struck the rocket. The rocket flashed like a beaten gong and gave off a metal ringing. The monster let down fifteen more bolts which danced about in a ridiculous pantomime, feeling of the jungle and the watery soil.

"No, no!" One of the men jumped up.

"Get down, you fool!" said the lieutenant.

"No!"

The lightning struck the rocket another dozen times. The lieutenant turned his head on his arm and saw the blue blazing flashes. He saw trees split and crumple into ruin. He saw the monstrous dark cloud turn like a black disk overhead and hurl down a hundred other poles of electricity.

The man who had leaped up was now running, like someone in a great hall of pillars. He ran and dodged between the pillars and then at last a dozen of the pillars slammed down and there was the sound a fly makes when landing upon the grill wires of an exterminator. The lieutenant remembered this from his childhood on a farm. And there was a smell of a man burned to a cinder.

The lieutenant lowered his head. ''Don't look up,'' he told the others. He was afraid that he too might run at any moment.

The storm above them flashed down another series of bolts and then moved on away. Once again there was only the rain, which rapidly cleared the air of the charred smell, and in a moment the three remaining men were sitting and waiting for the beat of their hearts to subside into quiet once more.

They walked over to the body, thinking that perhaps they could still save the man's life. They couldn't believe that there wasn't some way to help the man. It was the natural act of men who have not accepted death until they have touched it and turned it over and made plans to bury it or leave it there for the jungle to bury in an hour of quick growth.

The body was twisted steel, wrapped in burned leather. It looked like a wax dummy that had been thrown into an incinerator and pulled out after the wax had sunk to the charcoal skeleton. Only the teeth were white, and they shone like a strange white bracelet dropped half through a clenched black fist.

''He shouldn't have jumped up.'' They said it almost at the same time.

Even as they stood over the body it began to vanish, for the vegetation was edging in upon it, little vines and ivy and creepers, and even flowers for the dead.

At a distance the storm walked off on blue bolts of lightning and was gone.

* * *

They crossed a river and a creek and a stream and a dozen other rivers and creeks and streams. Before their eyes rivers appeared, rushing, new rivers, while old rivers changed their courses—rivers the color of mercury, rivers the color of silver and milk.

They came to the sea.

The Single Sea. There was only one continent on Venus. This land was three thousand miles long by a thousand miles wide, and about this island was the Single Sea, which covered the entire raining planet. The Single Sea, which lay upon the pallid shore with little motion . . .

"This way." The lieutenant nodded south. "I'm sure there are two Sun Domes down that way."

"While they were at it, why didn't they build a hundred more?"

"There're a hundred and twenty of them now, aren't there?"

"One hundred and twenty-six, as of last month. They tried to push a bill through Congress back on Earth a year ago to provide for a couple dozen more, but oh no, you know how *that* is. They'd rather a few men went crazy with the rain."

They started south.

The lieutenant and Simmons and the third man, Pickard, walked in the rain, in the rain that fell heavily and lightly, heavily and lightly; in the rain that poured and hammered and did not stop falling upon the land and the sea and the walking people.

Simmons saw it first. "There it is!"

"There's what?"

"The Sun Dome!"

The lieutenant blinked the water from his eyes and raised his hands to ward off the stinging blows of the rain.

At a distance there was a yellow glow on the edge of the jungle by the sea. It was, indeed, the Sun Dome.

The men smiled at each other.

"Looks like you were right, Lieutenant."

"Luck."

"Brother, that puts muscle in me, just seeing it. Come on!" Simmons began to trot. The others automatically fell in with this, gasping, tired, but keeping pace.

"A big pot of coffee for me," panted Simmons, smiling. "And a pan of cinnamon buns. Boy! And just lie there and let the old sun hit you. The guy that invented the Sun Domes, he should have got a medal!"

They ran faster. The yellow glow grew brighter.

"Guess a lot of men went crazy before they figured out the cure. Think it'd be obvious! Right off." Simmons panted the words in cadence to his running. "Rain, rain! Years ago. Found a friend. Of mine. Out in the jungle. Wandering around. In the rain. Saying over and over, 'Don't know enough, to come in, outta the rain. Don't know enough, to come in, outta the rain. Don't know enough—' On and on. Like that. Poor crazy fool."

"Save your breath!"

They ran.

They all laughed. They reached the door of the Sun Dome, laughing.

Simmons yanked the door wide. "Hey!" he yelled. "Bring on the coffee!"

There was no reply.

They stepped through the door.

The Sun Dome was empty and dark. There was no synthetic yellow sun floating in a high gaseous whisper at the center of the blue ceiling. There was no food waiting. It was cold as a vault. And through a thousand holes which had been newly punctured in the ceiling water streamed, the rain fell down, soaking into the thick rugs and the heavy modern furniture and splashing on the glass tables. The jungle was growing up like a moss in the room, on top of the bookcases and the divans. The rain slashed through the holes and fell upon the three men's faces.

Pickard began to laugh quietly.

"Shut up, Pickard!"

"Ye gods, look what's here for us—no food, no sun, nothing. The Venusians—they did it! Of course!"

Simmons nodded, with the rain funneling down on his face. The water ran in his silvered hair and on his white eyebrows. "Every once in a while the Venusians come up out of the sea and attack a Sun Dome. They know if they ruin the Sun Domes they can ruin us."

"But aren't the Sun Domes protected with guns?"

"Sure." Simmons stepped aside to a place that was relatively dry. "But it's been five years since the Venusians tried anything. Defense relaxes. They caught this Dome unaware."

"Where are the bodies?"

"The Venusians took them all down into the sea. I hear they have a delightful way of drowning you. It takes about eight hours to drown the way they work it. Really delightful."

"I bet there isn't any food here at all." Pickard laughed.

The lieutenant frowned at him, nodded at him so Simmons could see. Simmons shook his head and went back to a room at one side of the oval chamber. The kitchen was strewn with soggy loaves of bread, and meat that had grown a faint green fur. Rain came through a hundred holes in the kitchen roof.

"Brilliant." The lieutenant glanced up at the holes. "I don't suppose we can plug up all those holes and get snug here."

"Without food, sir?" Simmons snorted. "I notice the sun machine's dismantled. Our best bet is to make our way to the next Sun Dome. How far is that from here?"

"Not far. As I recall, they built two rather close together here. Perhaps if we waited, a rescue mission from the other might—"

"It's probably been here and gone already, some days ago. They'll send a crew to repair this place in about six months, when they get the money from Congress. I don't think we'd better wait."

"All right then, we'll eat what's left of our rations and get on to the next Dome."

Pickard said, "If only the rain wouldn't hit my head, just for a few minutes. If I could only remember what it's like not to be bothered." He put his hands on his skull and held it tight. "I remember when I was in school a bully used to sit in back of me and pinch me and pinch me and pinch me every five minutes, all day long. He did that for weeks and months. My arms were sore and black and blue all the time. And I thought I'd go crazy from being pinched. One day I must have gone a little mad from being hurt and hurt, and I turned around and took a metal trisquare I used in mechanical drawing and I almost cut his lousy head off. I almost scalped him before they dragged me out of the room, and I kept yelling, 'Why don't he leave me alone? Why don't he leave me alone?' Brother!'' His hands clenched the bone of his head, shaking, tightening, his eyes shut. ''But what do I do *now?* Who do I hit, who do I tell to lay off, stop bothering me, this damn rain, like the pinching, always *on* you, that's all you hear, that's all you feel!''

''We'll be at the other Sun Dome by four this afternoon.''

''Sun Dome? Look at this one! What if all the Sun Domes on Venus are gone? What then? What if there are holes in all the ceilings, and the rain coming in!''

''We'll have to chance it.''

''I'm tired of chancing it. All I want is a roof and some quiet. I want to be alone.''

''That's only eight hours off, if you hold on.''

''Don't worry, I'll hold on all right.'' And Pickard laughed, not looking at them.

''Let's eat,'' said Simmons, watching him.

They set off down the coast, southward again. After four hours they had to cut inland to go around a river that was a mile wide and so swift it was not navigable by boat. They had to walk inland six miles to a place where the river boiled out of the earth, suddenly, like a mortal wound. In the rain, they walked on solid ground and returned to the sea.

''I've got to sleep,'' said Pickard at last. He slumped. ''Haven't slept in four weeks. Tried, but couldn't. Sleep here.''

The sky was getting darker. The night of Venus was setting in and it was so completely black that it was dangerous to move. Simmons and the lieutenant fell to their knees also, and the lieutenant said, ''All right, we'll see what we can do. We've tried it before, but I don't know. Sleep doesn't seem one of the things you can get in this weather.''

They lay out full, propping their heads so the water wouldn't come to their mouths, and they closed their eyes.

The lieutenant twitched.

He did not sleep.

There were things that crawled on his skin. Things grew upon him in layers. Drops fell and touched other drops and they became streams that trickled over his body, and while these moved down his flesh, the small growths of the forest took root in his clothing. He felt the ivy cling and make a second garment over him; he felt the small flowers bud and open and petal away, and still the rain pattered on his body and on his head. In the luminous night—for the vegetation glowed in the darkness—he could see the other two men outlined, like logs that had fallen and taken upon themselves velvet coverings of grass and flowers. The rain hit his face. He covered his face with his hands. The rain hit his neck. He turned over on his stomach in the mud, on the rubbery plants, and the rain hit his back and hit his legs.

Suddenly he leaped up and began to brush the water from himself. A thousand hands were touching him and he no longer wanted to be touched. He no longer could stand being touched. He floundered and struck something else and knew that it was Simmons, standing up in the rain, sneezing moisture, coughing and choking. And then Pickard was up, shouting, running about.

"Wait a minute, Pickard!"

"Stop it, stop it!" Pickard screamed. He fired his gun six times at the night sky. In the flashes of powdery illumination they could see armies of raindrops, suspended as in a vast motionless amber, for an instant, hesitating as if shocked by the explosion, fifteen billion droplets, fifteen billion tears, fifteen billion ornaments, jewels standing out against a white velvet viewing board. And then, with the light gone, the drops which had waited to have their pictures taken, which had suspended their downward rush, fell upon them, stinging, in an insect cloud of coldness and pain.

"Stop it! Stop it!"

"Pickard!"

But Pickard was only standing now, alone. When the lieutenant switched on a small hand lamp and played it over Pickard's wet face, the eyes of the man were dilated, and his mouth was open, his face turned up, so the water hit and splashed on his tongue, and hit and drowned the wide eyes, and bubbled in a whispering froth on the nostrils.

"Pickard!"

The man would not reply. He simply stood there for a long while with the bubbles of rain breaking out in his whitened hair and manacles of rain jewels dropping from his wrists and his neck.

"Pickard! We're leaving. We're going on. Follow us."

The rain dripped from Pickard's ears.

"Do you hear me, Pickard!"

It was like shouting down a well.

"Pickard!"

"Leave him alone," said Simmons.

"We can't go on without him."

"What'll we do, carry him?" Simmons spat. "He's no good to us or himself. You know what he'll do? He'll just stand here and drown."

"What?"

"You ought to know that by now. Don't you know the story? He'll just stand here with his head up and let the rain come in his nostrils and his mouth. He'll breathe the water."

"No."

"That's how they found General Mendt that time. Sitting on a rock with his head back, breathing the rain. His lungs were full of water."

The lieutenant turned the light back to the unblinking face. Pickard's nostrils gave off a tiny whispering wet sound.

"Pickard!" The lieutenant slapped the face.

"He can't even feel you," said Simmons. "A few days in this rain and you don't have any face or any legs or hands."

The lieutenant looked at his own hand in horror. He could no longer feel it.

"But we can't leave Pickard here."

"I'll show you what we can do." Simmons fired his gun.

Pickard fell into the raining earth.

Simmons said, "Don't move, Lieutenant. I've got my gun ready for you too. Think it over; he would only have stood or sat there and drowned. It's quicker this way."

The lieutenant blinked at the body. "But you killed him."

"Yes, because he'd have killed us by being a burden. You saw his face. Insane."

After a moment the lieutenant nodded.

They walked off into the rain.

It was dark and their hand lamps threw a beam that pierced

the rain for only a few feet. After a half hour they had to stop and sit through the rest of the night, aching with hunger, waiting for the dawn to come; when it did come it was gray and continually raining as before, and they began to walk again.

''We've miscalculated,'' said Simmons.

''No. Another hour.''

''Speak louder. I can't hear you.'' Simmons stopped and smiled. He touched his ears. ''My ears. They've gone out on me. All the rain pouring finally numbed me right down to the bone.''

''Can't you hear anything?'' said the lieutenant.

''What?'' Simmons' eyes were puzzled.

''Nothing. Come on.''

''I think I'll wait here. You go on ahead.''

''You can't do that.''

''I can't hear you. You go on. I'm tired. I don't think the Sun Dome is down this way. And, if it is, it's probably got holes in the roof, like the last one. I think I'll just sit here.''

''Get up from there!''

''So long, Lieutenant.''

''You can't give up now.''

''I've got a gun here that says I'm staying. I just don't care anymore. I'm not crazy yet, but I'm the next thing to it. I don't want to go out that way. As soon as you get out of sight I'm going to use this gun on myself.''

''Simmons!''

''You said my name. I can read that much off your lips.''

''Simmons.''

''Look, it's a matter of time. Either I die now or in a few hours. Wait'll you get to that next Dome, if you ever get there, and find rain coming in through the roof. Won't that be nice?''

The lieutenant waited and then splashed off in the rain. He turned and called back once, but Simmons was only sitting there with the gun in his hands, waiting for him to get out of sight. He shook his head and waved the lieutenant on.

The lieutenant didn't even hear the sound of the gun.

He began to eat the flowers as he walked. They stayed down for a time, and weren't poisonous; neither were they particularly sustaining, and he vomited them up, sickly, a minute or so later.

Once he took some leaves and tried to make himself a hat, but he had tried that before; the rain melted the leaves from his head. Once picked, the vegetation rotted quickly and fell away into gray masses in his fingers.

"Another five minutes," he told himself. "Another five minutes and then I'll walk into the sea and keep walking. We weren't made for this; no Earthman was or ever will be able to take it. Your nerves, your nerves."

He floundered his way through a sea of slush and foliage and came to a small hill.

At a distance there was a faint yellow smudge in the cold veils of water.

The next Sun Dome.

Through the trees, a long round yellow building, far away. For a moment he only stood, swaying, looking at it.

He began to run and then he slowed down, for he was afraid. He didn't call out. What if it's the same one? What if it's the dead Sun Dome, with no sun in it? he thought.

He slipped and fell. Lie here, he thought; it's the wrong one. Lie here. It's no use. Drink all you want.

But he managed to climb to his feet again and crossed several creeks, and the yellow light grew very bright, and he began to run again, his feet crashing into mirrors and glass, his arms flailing at diamonds and precious stones.

He stood before the yellow door. The printed letters over it said THE SUN DOME. He put his numb hand up to feel it. Then he twisted the doorknob and stumbled in.

He stood for a moment looking about. Behind him the rain whirled at the door. Ahead of him, upon a low table, stood a silver pot of hot chocolate, steaming, and a cup, full, with a marshmallow in it. And beside that, on another tray, stood thick sandwiches of rich chicken meat and fresh-cut tomatoes and green onions. And on a rod just before his eyes was a great thick green Turkish towel, and a bin in which to throw wet clothes, and, to his right, a small cubicle in which heat rays might dry you instantly. And upon a chair, a fresh change of uniform, waiting for anyone—himself, or any lost one—to make use of it. And farther over, coffee in steaming copper urns, and a phonograph from which music would soon play quietly, and books bound in red and brown leather. And near the books a cot, a soft deep cot upon which one might lie, exposed and bare, to drink in the rays of the one great bright thing which dominated the long room.

He put his hands to his eyes. He saw other men moving toward him, but said nothing to them. He waited, and opened his eyes, and looked. The water from his uniform pooled at his feet, and he felt it drying from his hair and his face and his chest and his arms and his legs.

He was looking at the sun.

It was hung in the center of the room, large and yellow and warm. It made not a sound, and there was no sound in the room. The door was shut and the rain only a memory to his tingling body. The sun hung high in the blue sky of the room, warm, hot, yellow, and very fine.

He walked forward, tearing off his clothes as he went.

The Exiles

Their eyes were fire and the breath flamed out the witches' mouths as they bent to probe the caldron with greasy stick and bony finger.

"When shall we three meet again
In thunder, lightning, or in rain?"

They danced drunkenly on the shore of an empty sea, fouling the air with their three tongues, and burning it with their cats' eyes malevolently aglitter:

"Round about the cauldron go:
In the poison'd entrails throw. . . .
Double, double toil and trouble;
Fire burn and cauldron bubble."

They paused and cast a glance about. "Where's the crystal? Where the needles?"

"Here!"

"Good!"

"Is the yellow wax thickened?"

"Yes!"

"Pour it in the iron mold!"

"Is the wax figure done?" They shaped it like molasses adrip on their green hands.

"Shove the needle through the heart!"

"The crystal, the crystal; fetch it from the tarot bag. Dust it off; have a look!"

They bent to the crystal, their faces white.

"See, see, see . . ."

A rocket ship moved through space from the planet Earth to the planet Mars. On the rocket ship men were dying.

The captain raised his head, tiredly. "We'll have to use the morphine."

"But, Captain—"

"You see yourself this man's condition." The captain lifted the wool blanket and the man restrained beneath the wet sheet moved and groaned. The air was full of sulfurous thunder.

"I saw it—I saw it." The man opened his eyes and stared at the port where there were only black spaces, reeling stars, Earth far removed, and the planet Mars rising large and red. "I saw it—a bat, a huge thing, a bat with a man's face, spread over the front port. Fluttering and fluttering, fluttering and fluttering."

"Pulse?" asked the captain.

The orderly measured it. "One hundred and thirty."

"He can't go on with that. Use the morphine. Come along, Smith."

They moved away. Suddenly the floor plates were laced with bone and white skulls that screamed. The captain did not dare look down, and over the screaming he said, "Is this where Perse is?" turning in at a hatch.

A white-smocked surgeon stepped away from a body. "I just don't understand it."

"How did Perse die?"

"We don't know, Captain. It wasn't his heart, his brain, or shock. He just—died."

The captain felt the doctor's wrist, which changed to a hissing snake and bit him. The captain did not flinch. "Take care of yourself. You've a pulse too."

The doctor nodded. "Perse complained of pains—needles, he said—in his wrists and legs. Said he felt like wax, melting. He fell. I helped him up. He cried like a child. Said he had a silver needle in his heart. He died. Here he is. We can repeat the autopsy for you. Everything's physically normal."

"That's impossible! He died of *something!*"

The captain walked to a port. He smelled of menthol and iodine and green soap on his polished and manicured hands. His white teeth were dentrificed, and his ears scoured to a pinkness, as were his cheeks. His uniform was the color of new salt, and his boots were black mirrors shining below him. His crisp crew-cut hair smelled of sharp alcohol. Even his breath was sharp and new and clean. There was no spot to him. He was a fresh instrument, honed and ready, still hot from the surgeon's oven.

The men with him were from the same mold. One expected huge brass keys spiraling slowly from their backs. They were expensive, talented, well-oiled toys, obedient and quick.

The captain watched the planet Mars grow very large in space.

"We'll be landing in an hour on that blasted place. Smith, did you see any bats, or have other nightmares?"

"Yes, sir. The month before our rocket took off from New York, sir. White rats biting my neck, drinking my blood. I didn't tell. I was afraid you wouldn't let me come on this trip."

"Never mind," sighed the captain. "I had dreams too. In all of my fifty years I never had a dream until that week before we took off from Earth. And then every night I dreamed I was a white wolf. Caught on a snowy hill. Shot with a silver bullet. Buried with a stake in my heart." He moved his head toward Mars. "Do you think, Smith, *they* know we're coming?"

"We don't know if there *are* Martian people, sir."

"Don't we? They began frightening us off eight weeks ago, before we started. They've killed Perse and Reynolds now. Yesterday they made Grenville go blind. How? I don't know. Bats, needles, dreams, men dying for no reason. I'd call it witchcraft in another day. But this is the year 2120, Smith. We're rational men. This all can't be happening. But it is! Whoever they are, with their needles and their bats, they'll try to finish us all." He swung about. "Smith, fetch those books from my file. I want them when we land."

Two hundred books were piled on the rocket deck.

"Thank you, Smith. Have you glanced at them? Think I'm insane? Perhaps. It's a crazy hunch. At that last moment I ordered these books from the Historical Museum. Because of my dreams. Twenty nights I was stabbed, butchered, a screaming bat pinned to a surgical mat, a thing rotting underground in a black box; bad, wicked dreams. Our whole crew dreamed of witch-things and were-things, vampires and phantoms, things they *couldn't* know anything about. Why? Because books on such ghastly subjects were destroyed a century ago. By law. Forbidden for anyone to own the grisly volumes. These books you see here are the *last* copies, kept for historical purposes in the locked museum vaults."

Smith bent to read the dusty titles:

"*Tales of Mystery and Imagination,* by Edgar Allan Poe. *Dracula,* by Bram Stoker. *Frankenstein,* by Mary Shelley. *The Turn of the Screw,* by Henry James. *The Legend of Sleepy Hollow,* by Washington Irving. *Rappaccini's Daughter,* by Nathaniel Hawthorne. *An Occurrence at Owl Creek Bridge,* by Ambrose Bierce. *Alice's Adventures in Wonderland,* by Lewis Carroll. *The Willows,* by Algernon Blackwood. *The Wizard of Oz,* by L. Frank Baum. *The Weird Shadow over Innsmouth,* by H. P. Lovecraft. And more! Books by Walter de la Mare, Wakefield, Harvey, Wells, Asquith, Huxley—all forbidden authors. All burned in the same year that Halloween was outlawed and Christmas was banned! But, sir, what good are these to us on the rocket?"

"I don't know," sighed the captain, "yet."

The three hags lifted the crystal where the captain's image flickered, his tiny voice tinkling out of the glass:

"I don't know," sighed the captain, "yet."

The three witches glared redly into one another's faces.

"We haven't much time," said one.

"Better warn *Them* in the City."

"They'll want to know about the books. It doesn't look good. That fool of a captain!"

"In an hour they'll land their rocket."

The three hags shuddered and blinked up at the Emerald City

by the edge of the dry Martian sea. In its highest window a small man held a blood-red drape aside. He watched the wastelands where the three witches fed their caldron and shaped the waxes. Farther along, ten thousand other blue fires and laurel incenses, black tobacco smokes and fir weeds, cinnamons and bone dusts rose soft as moths through the Martian night. The man counted the angry, magical fires. Then, as the three witches stared, he turned. The crimson drape, released, fell, causing the distant portal to wink, like a yellow eye.

Mr. Edgar Allan Poe stood in the tower window, a faint vapor of spirits upon his breath. ''Hecate's friends are busy tonight,'' he said, seeing the witches, far below.

A voice behind him said, ''I saw Will Shakespeare at the shore, earlier, whipping them on. All along the sea Shakespeare's army alone, tonight, numbers thousands: the three witches, Oberon, Hamlet's father, Puck—all, all of them—thousands! Good Lord, a regular sea of people.''

''Good William.'' Poe turned. He let the crimson drape fall shut. He stood for a moment to observe the raw stone room, the black-timbered table, the candle flame, the other man, Mr. Ambrose Bierce, sitting very idly there, lighting matches and watching them burn down, whistling under his breath, now and then laughing to himself.

''We'll have to tell Mr. Dickens now,'' said Mr. Poe. ''We've put it off too long. It's a matter of hours. Will you go down to his home with me, Bierce?''

Bierce glanced up merrily. ''I've just been thinking—what'll happen to us?''

''If we can't kill the rocket men off, frighten them away, then we'll have to leave, of course. We'll go on to Jupiter, and when they come to Jupiter, we'll go on to Saturn, and when they come to Saturn, we'll go to Uranus, or Neptune, and then on out to Pluto—''

''Where then?''

Mr. Poe's face was weary; there were fire coals remaining, fading, in his eyes, and a sad wildness in the way he talked, and a uselessness of his hands and the way his hair fell lankly over his amazing white brow. He was like a satan of some lost dark cause, a general arrived from a derelict invasion. His silky, soft, black mustache was worn away by his musing lips. He was so small his brow seemed to float, vast and phosphorescent, by itself, in the dark room.

"We have the advantages of superior forms of travel," he said. "We can always hope for one of their atomic wars, dissolution, the dark ages come again. The return of superstition. We could go back then to Earth, all of us, in one night." Mr. Poe's black eyes brooded under his round and luminant brow. He gazed at the ceiling. "So they're coming to ruin *this* world too? They won't leave *anything* undefiled, will they?"

"Does a wolf pack stop until it's killed its prey and eaten the guts?" said Bierce. "It should be quite a war. I shall sit on the sidelines and be the scorekeeper. So many Earthmen boiled in oil, so many Mss. Found in Bottles burnt, so many Earthmen stabbed with needles, so many Red Deaths put to flight by a battery of hypodermic syringes—ha!"

Poe swayed angrily, faintly drunk with wine. "What did we do? Be *with* us, Bierce, in the name of God! Did we have a fair trial before a company of literary critics? No! Our books were plucked up by neat, sterile, surgeon's pliers, and flung into vats, to boil, to be killed of all their mortuary germs. Damn them all!"

"I find our situation amusing," said Bierce.

They were interrupted by a hysterical shout from the tower stair.

"Mr. Poe! Mr. Bierce!"

"Yes, yes, we're coming!" Poe and Bierce descended to find a man gasping against the stone passage wall.

"Have you heard the news?" he cried immediately, clawing at them like a man about to fall over a cliff. "In an hour they'll land! They're bringing books with them—*old* books, the witches said! What're you doing in the tower at a time like this? Why aren't you acting?"

Poe said: "We're doing everything we can, Blackwood. You're new to all this. Come along, we're going to Mr. Charles Dickens' place—"

"—to contemplate our doom, our black doom," said Mr. Bierce, with a wink.

* * *

They moved down the echoing throats of the castle, level after dim green level, down into mustiness and decay and spiders and dreamlike webbing. "Don't worry," said Poe, his brow like a huge white lamp before them, descending, sinking. "All along the dead sea tonight I've called the others. Your friends and mine, Blackwood—Bierce. They're all there. The animals and the old women and the tall men with the sharp white teeth. The traps are waiting; the pits, yes, and the pendulums. The Red Death." Here he laughed quietly. "Yes, even the Red Death. I never thought—no, I never thought the time would come when a thing like the Red Death would actually *be.* But *they* asked for it, and they shall have it!"

"But are we strong enough?" wondered Blackwood.

"How strong is strong? They won't be prepared for us, at least. They haven't the imagination. Those clean young rocket men with their antiseptic bloomers and fish-bowl helmets, with their new religion. About their necks, on gold chains, scalpels. Upon their heads, a diadem of microscopes. In their holy fingers, steaming incense urns which in reality are only germicidal ovens for steaming out superstition. The names of Poe, Bierce, Hawthorne, Blackwood—blasphemy to their clean lips."

Outside the castle they advanced through a watery space, a tarn that was not a tarn, which misted before them like the stuff of nightmares. The air filled with wing sounds and whirring, a motion of winds and blacknesses. Voices changed, figures swayed at campfires. Mr. Poe watched the needles knitting, knitting, knitting, in the firelight; knitting pain and misery, knitting wickedness into wax marionettes, clay puppets. The caldron smells of wild garlic and cayenne and saffron hissed up to fill the night with evil pungency.

"Get on with it!" said Poe. "I'll be back!"

All down the empty seashore black figures spindled and waned, grew up and blew into black smoke on the sky. Bells rang in mountain towers and licorice ravens spilled out with the bronze sounds and spun away to ashes.

Over a lonely moor and into a small valley Poe and Bierce hurried, and found themselves quite suddenly on a cobbled street, in cold, bleak, biting weather, with people stomping up and down stony courtyards to warm their feet; foggy withal, and candles flaring in the windows of offices and shops where hung the Yuletide turkeys. At a distance some boys, all bundled up, snorting their pale breaths on the wintry air, were trilling, "God Rest Ye Merry, Gentlemen," while the immense tones of a great clock continuously sounded midnight. Children dashed by from the baker's with dinners all asteam in their grubby fists, on trays and under silver bowls.

At a sign which read SCROOGE, MARLEY AND DICKENS, Poe gave the Marley-faced knocker a rap, and from within, as the door popped open a few inches, a sudden gust of music almost swept them into a dance. And there, beyond the shoulder of the man who was sticking a trim goatee and mustaches at them, was Mr. Fezziwig clapping his hands, and Mrs. Fezziwig, one vast substantial smile, dancing and colliding with other merry-makers, while the fiddle chirped and laughter ran about a table like chandelier crystals given a sudden push of wind. The large table was heaped with brawn and turkey and holly and geese; with mince pies, suckling pigs, wreaths of sausages, oranges and apples; and there was Bob Cratchit and Little Dorrit and Tiny Tim and Mr. Fagin himself, and a man who looked as if he might be an undigested bit of beef, a blot of mustard, a crumb of cheese, a fragment of underdone potato—who else but Mr. Marley, chains and all, while the wine poured and the brown turkeys did their excellent best to steam!

"What do you want?" demanded Mr. Charles Dickens.

"We've come to plead with you again, Charles; we need your help," said Poe.

"Help? Do you think I would help you fight against those good men coming in the rocket? I don't belong here, anyway. My books were burned by mistake. I'm no supernaturalist, no writer of horrors and terrors like you, Poe; you, Bierce, or the others. I'll have nothing to do with you terrible people!"

"You are a persuasive talker," reasoned Poe. "You could go to meet the rocket men, lull them, lull their suspicions and then—then we would take care of them."

Mr. Dickens eyed the folds of the black cape which hid Poe's hands. From it, smiling, Poe drew forth a black cat. ''For *one* of our visitors.''

''And for the others?''

Poe smiled again, well pleased. ''The Premature Burial?''

''You are a grim man, Mr. Poe.''

''I am a frightened and an angry man. I am a god, Mr. Dickens, even as you are a god, even as we all are gods, and our inventions—our people, if you wish—have not only been threatened, but banished and burned, torn up and censored, ruined and done away with. The worlds we created are falling into ruin. Even gods must fight!''

''So?'' Mr. Dickens tilted his head, impatient to return to the party, the music, the food. ''Perhaps you can explain why we are here? How did we come here?''

''War begets war. Destruction begets destruction. On Earth, in the last half of the twentieth century they began to outlaw our books. Oh, what a horrible thing—to destroy our literary creations that way! It summoned us out of—what? Death? The Beyond? I don't like abstract things. I don't know. I only know that our worlds and our creations called us and we tried to save them, and the only saving thing we could do was wait out the century here on Mars, hoping Earth might overweight itself with these scientists and their doubtings; but now they're coming to clean us out of here, us and our dark things, and all the alchemists, witches, vampires, and were-things that, one by one, retreated across space as science made inroads through every country on Earth and finally left no alternative at all but exodus. You must help us. You have a good speaking manner. We need you.

''I repeat, I am not of you, I don't approve of you and the others,'' cried Dickens angrily. ''I was no player with witches and vampires and midnight things.''

''What of *A Christmas Carol?*''

''Ridiculous! *One* story. Oh, I wrote a few others about ghosts, perhaps, but what of that? My basic works had none of that nonsense!''

''Mistaken or not, they grouped you with us. They destroyed your books—your worlds too. You must hate them, Mr. Dickens!''

''I admit they are stupid and rude, but that is all. Good day!''

"Let Mr. Marley come, at least!"

"No!"

The door slammed. As Poe turned away, down the street, skimming over the frosty ground, the coachman playing a lively air on a bugle, came a great coach, out of which, cherry-red, laughing and singing, piled the Pickwickians, banging on the door, shouting Merry Christmas good and loud, when the door was opened by the fat boy.

Mr. Poe hurried along the midnight shore of the dry sea. By fires and smoke he hesitated, to shout orders, to check the bubbling caldrons, the poisons and the chalked pentagrams. "Good!" he said, and ran on. "Fine!" he shouted and ran again. People joined him and ran with him. Here were Mr. Coppard and Mr. Machen running with him now. And there were hating serpents and angry demons and fiery bronze dragons and spitting vipers and trembling witches like the barbs and nettles and thorns and all the vile flotsam and jetsam of the retreating sea of imagination, left on the melancholy shore, whining and frothing and spitting.

Mr. Machen stopped. He sat like a child on the cold sand. He began to sob. They tried to soothe him, but he would not listen. "I just thought," he said. "What happens to us on the day when the *last* copies of our books are destroyed?"

The air whirled.

"Don't speak of it!"

"We must," wailed Mr. Machen. "Now, now, as the rocket comes down, you, Mr. Poe; you, Coppard; you Bierce—all of you grow faint. Like wood smoke. Blowing away. Your faces melt—"

"Death! *Real* death for all of us."

"We exist only through Earth's sufferance. If a final edict tonight destroyed our last few works we'd be like lights put out."

Coppard brooded gently. "I wonder who I am. In what Earth mind tonight do I exist? In some African hut? Some hermit reading my tales? Is he the lonely candle in the wind of time and science? The flickering orb sustaining me here in rebellious exile? Is it him? Or some boy in a discarded attic finding me, only just in time! Oh, last night I felt ill, ill, ill to the marrows of me, for there is a body of the soul as well as a body of the body, and this soul body ached in all of its glowing parts, and last night I felt myself a candle, guttering. When suddenly I sprang up, given new light, as some child, sneezing with dust, in some yellow garret on Earth once more found a worn, time-specked copy of me! And so I'm given a short respite!''

A door banged wide in a little hut by the shore. A thin short man, with flesh hanging from him in folds, stepped out and, paying no attention to the others, sat down and stared into his clenched fists.

''There's the one I'm sorry for,'' whispered Blackwood. ''Look at him, dying away. He was once more real than we, who were men. They took him, a skeleton thought, and clothed him in centuries of pink flesh and snow beard and red velvet suit and black boot; made him reindeers, tinsel, holly. And after centuries of manufacturing him they drowned him in a vat of Lysol, you might say.''

The men were silent.

''What must it be on Earth?'' wondered Poe. ''Without Christmas? No hot chestnuts, no tree, no ornaments or drums or candles—nothing; nothing but the snow and wind and the lonely, factual people. . . .''

They all looked at the thin little man with the scraggly beard and faded red velvet suit.

''Have you heard his story?''

''I can imagine it. The glitter-eyed psychiatrist, the clever sociologist, the resentful, froth-mouthed educationalist, the anti-septic parents—''

''A regrettable situation,'' said Bierce, smiling, ''for the Yuletide merchants who, toward the last there, as I recall, were beginning to put up holly and sing Noel the day before Hallow-een. With any luck at all this year they might have started on Labor Day!''

Bierce did not continue. He fell forward with a sigh. As he lay upon the ground he had time to say only, ''How interest-ing.'' And then, as they all watched, horrified, his body burned into blue dust and charred bone, the ashes of which fled through the air in black tatters.

"Bierce, Bierce!"

"Gone!"

"His last book gone. Someone on Earth just now burned it."

"God rest him. Nothing of him left now. For what are we but books, and when those are gone, nothing's to be seen."

A rushing sound filled the sky.

They cried out, terrified, and looked up. In the sky, dazzling it with sizzling fire clouds, was the rocket! Around the men on the seashore lanterns bobbed; there was a squealing and a bubbling and an odor of cooked spells. Candle-eyed pumpkins lifted into the cold clear air. Thin fingers clenched into fists and a witch screamed from her withered mouth:

"Ship, ship, break, fall!
Ship, ship, burn all!
Crack, flake, shake, melt!
Mummy dust, cat pelt!"

"Time to go," murmured Blackwood. "On to Jupiter, on to Saturn or Pluto."

"Run away?" shouted Poe in the wind. "Never!"

"I'm a tired old man!"

Poe gazed into the old man's face and believed him. He climbed atop a huge boulder and faced the ten thousand gray shadows and green lights and yellow eyes on the hissing wind.

"The powders!" he shouted.

A thick hot smell of bitter almond, civet, cumin, wormseed, and orris!

The rocket came down—steadily down, with the shriek of a damned spirit! Poe raged at it! He flung his fists up and the orchestra of heat and smell and hatred answered in symphony! Like stripped tree fragments, bats flew upward! Burning hearts, flung like missiles, burst in bloody fireworks on the singed air. Down, down, relentlessly down, like a pendulum the rocket came. And Poe howled, furiously, and shrank back with every sweep and sweep of the rocket cutting and ravening the air! All the dead sea seemed a pit in which, trapped, they waited the sinking of the dread machinery, the glistening ax; they were people under the avalanche!

"The snakes!" screamed Poe.

And luminous serpentines of undulant green hurtled toward the rocket. But it came down, a sweep, a fire, a motion, and it lay panting out exhaustions of red plumage on the sand, a mile away.

"At it!" shrieked Poe. "The plan's changed! Only one chance! Run! At it! At it! Drown them with our bodies! Kill them!"

And as if he had commanded a violent sea to change its course, to suck itself free from primeval beds, the whirls and savage gouts of fire spread and ran like the wind and rain and stark lightning over the sea sands, down empty river deltas, shadowing and screaming, whistling and whining, sputtering and coalescing toward the rocket which, extinguished, lay like a clean metal torch in the farthest hollow. As if a great charred caldron of sparkling lava had been overturned, the boiling people and snapping animals churned down the dry fathoms.

"Kill them!" screamed Poe, running.

The rocket men leaped out of their ship, guns ready. They stalked about, sniffing the air like hounds. They saw nothing. They relaxed.

The captain stepped forth last. He gave sharp commands. Wood was gathered, kindled, and a fire leapt up in an instant. The captain beckoned his men into a half circle about him.

"A new world," he said, forcing himself to speak deliberately, though he glanced nervously, now and again, over his shoulder at the empty sea. "The old world left behind. A new start. What more symbolic than that we here dedicate ourselves all the more firmly to science and progress." He nodded crisply to his lieutenant. "The books."

Firelight limned the faded gilt titles: *The Willows, The Outsider, Behold This Dreamer, Dr. Jekyll and Mr. Hyde, The Land of Oz, Pellucidar, The Land That Time Forgot, A Midsummer Night's Dream,* and the monstrous names of Machen and Edgar Allan Poe and Cabell and Dunsany and Blackwood and Lewis Carroll; the names, the old names, the evil names.

"A new world. With a gesture, we burn the last of the old."

The captain ripped pages from the books. Leaf by seared leaf, he fed them into the fire.

A scream!

Leaping back, the men stared beyond the firelight at the edges of the encroaching and uninhabited sea.

Another scream! A high and wailing thing, like the death of a dragon and the thrashing of a bronzed whale left gasping when the waters of a leviathan's sea drain down the shingles and evaporate.

It was the sound of air rushing in to fill a vacuum, where, a moment before, there had been *something!*

The captain neatly disposed of the last book by putting it into the fire.

The air stopped quivering.

Silence!

The rocket men leaned and listened.

"Captain, did you hear it?"

"No."

"Like a wave, sir. On the sea bottom! I thought I saw something. Over there. A black wave. Big. Running at us."

"You were mistaken."

"There, sir!"

"What?"

"See it? There! The city! Way over! That green city near the lake! It's splitting in half. It's falling!"

The men squinted and shuffled forward.

Smith stood trembling among them. He put his hand to his head as if to find a thought there. "I remember. Yes, now I do. A long time back. When I was a child. A book I read. A story. Oz, I think it was. Yes. Oz. *The Emerald City of Oz* . . ."

"Oz?"

"Yes, Oz, that's what it was. I saw it just now, like in the story. I saw it fall."

"Smith!"

"Yes, sir?"

"Report to the ship's doctor."

"Yes, sir!" A brisk salute.

"Be careful."

The men tiptoed, guns alert, beyond the ship's aseptic light to gaze at the long sea and the low hills.

"Why," whispered Smith, disappointed, "there's no one here at all, is there? No one here at all."

The wind blew sand over his shoes, whining.

Here There Be Tygers

"You have to beat a planet at its own game," said Chatterton. "Get in and rip it up, kill its snakes, poison its animals, dam its rivers, sow its fields, depollinate its air, mine it, nail it down, hack away at it, and get the blazes out from under when you have what you want. Otherwise, a planet will fix you good. You can't trust planets. They're bound to be different, bound to be bad, bound to be out to get you, especially this far out, a billion miles from nowhere, so you get them first. Tear their skin off, I say. Drag out the minerals and run away before the nightmare world explodes in your face. That's the way to treat them."

The rocket ship sank down toward planet 7 of star system 84. They had traveled millions upon millions of miles; Earth was far away, her system and her sun forgotten, her system settled and investigated and profited on, and other systems rummaged through and milked and tidied up, and now the rockets of these tiny men from an impossibly remote planet were probing out to far universes. In a few months, a few years, they could travel anywhere, for the speed of their rocket was the speed of a god, and now for the ten-thousandth time one of the rockets of the far-circling hunt was feathering down toward an alien world.

"No," said Captain Forester. "I have too much respect for other worlds to treat them the way you want to, Chatterton. It's not my business to rape or ruin, anyway, thank God. I'm glad

I'm just a rocket man. You're the anthropologist-mineralogist. Go ahead, do your mining and ripping and scraping. I'll just watch. I'll just go around looking at this new world, whatever it is, however it seems. I like to look. All rocket men are lookers or they wouldn't be rocket men. You like to smell new airs, if you're a rocket man, and see new oceans and islands."

"Take your gun along," said Chatterton.

"In my holster," said Forester.

They turned to the port together and saw the green world rising to meet their ship. "I wonder what *it* thinks of us?" said Forester.

"It won't like me," said Chatterton. "I'll see to it it won't like me. And I don't care, you know, I'm out for the money. Land us over there, will you, Captain; that looks like rich country if I ever saw it."

It was the freshest green color they had seen since childhood. Lakes lay like clear blue water droplets through the soft hills; there were no loud highways, signboards or cities. It's a sea of green golf links, thought Forester, which goes on forever. Putting greens, driving greens, you could walk ten thousand miles in any direction and never finish your game. A Sunday planet, a croquet-lawn world, where you could lie on your back, clover in your lips, eyes half shut, smiling at the sky, smelling the grass, drowse through an eternal Sabbath, rousing only on occasion to turn the Sunday paper or crack the red-striped wooden ball through the wicket.

"If ever a planet was a woman, this one is."

"Woman on the outside, man on the inside," said Chatterton. "All hard underneath, all male iron, copper, uranium, black sod. Don't let the cosmetics fool you."

He walked to the bin where the Earth Drill waited. Its great screw-snout glittered bluely, ready to stab seventy feet deep and suck out corks of earth, deeper still with extensions into the heart of the planet. Chatterton winked at it. "We'll fix your planet, Forester, but good."

"Yes, I know you will," said Forester, quietly.

The rocket landed.

"It's too green, too peaceful," said Chatterton. "I don't like it." He turned to the captain. "We'll go out with our rifles."

"I give orders, if you don't mind."

"Yes, and my company pays our way with millions of dollars of machinery we must protect; quite an investment."

The air on the new planet 7 in star system 84 was good. The port swung wide. The men filed out into the greenhouse world.

The last man to emerge was Chatterton, gun in hand.

As Chatterton set foot to the green lawn, the earth trembled. The grass shook. The distant forest rumbled. The sky seemed to blink and darken imperceptibly. The men were watching Chatterton when it happened.

"An earthquake!"

Chatterton's face paled. Everyone laughed.

"It doesn't like you, Chatterton!"

"Nonsense!"

The trembling died away at last.

"Well," said Captain Forester, "It didn't quake for us, so it must be that it doesn't approve of your philosophy."

"Coincidence," Chatterton smiled weakly. "Come on now, on the double, I want the Drill out here in a half hour for a few samplings."

"Just a moment." Forester stopped laughing. "We've got to clear the area first, be certain there're no hostile people or animals. Besides, it isn't every year you hit a planet like this, very nice; can you blame us if we want to have a look at it?"

"All right." Chatterton joined them. "Let's get it over with."

They left a guard at the ship and they walked away over fields and meadows, over small hills and into little valleys. Like a bunch of boys out hiding on the finest day of the best summer in the most beautiful year in history, walking in the croquet weather where if you listened you could hear the whisper of the wooden ball across grass, the click through the wicket, the gentle undulations of voices, a sudden high drift of women's laughter from some ivy-shaded porch, the tinkle of ice in the summer tea pitcher.

"Hey," said Driscoll, one of the younger crewmen, sniffing the air. "I brought a baseball and bat; we'll have a game later. What a diamond!"

The men laughed quietly in the baseball season, in the good

quiet wind for tennis, in the weather for bicycling and picking wild grapes.

''How'd you like the job of mowing all this?'' asked Driscoll.

The men stopped.

''I *knew* there was something wrong!'' cried Chatterton. ''This grass; it's freshly cut!''

''Probably a species of dichondra; always short.''

Chatterton spat on the green grass and rubbed it in with his boot. ''I don't like it. I don't like it. If anything happened to us, no one on Earth would ever know. Silly policy: if a rocket fails to return, we never send a second rocket to check the reason why.''

''Natural enough,'' explained Forester. ''We can't waste time on a thousand hostile worlds, fighting futile wars. Each rocket represents years, money, lives. We can't afford to waste *two* rockets if one rocket proves a planet hostile. We go on to peaceful planets. Like this one.''

''I often wonder,'' said Driscoll, ''what happened to all those lost expeditions on worlds we'll never try again.''

Chatterton eyed the distant forest. ''They were shot, stabbed, broiled for dinner. Even as we may be, any minute. It's time we got back to work, Captain!''

They stood at the top of a little rise.

''Feel,'' said Driscoll, his hands and arms out loosely. ''Remember how you used to run when you were a kid, and how the wind felt. Like feathers on your arms. You ran and thought any minute you'd fly, but you never quite did.''

The men stood remembering. There was a smell of pollen and new rain drying upon a million grass blades.

Driscoll gave a little run. ''Feel it, by God, the wind. You know, we never have *really* flown by ourselves. We have to sit inside tons of metal, away from flying, really. We've never flown like birds fly, to themselves. Wouldn't it be nice to put your arms out like this—'' He extended his arms. ''And run.'' He ran ahead of them, laughing at his idiocy. ''And fly!'' he cried.

He flew.

* * *

Time passed on the silent gold wristwatches of the men standing below. They stared up. And from the sky came a high sound of almost unbelievable laughter.

"Tell him to come down now," whispered Chatterton. "He'll be killed."

Nobody heard. Their faces were raised away from Chatterton; they were stunned and smiling.

At last Driscoll landed at their feet. "Did you *see* me? I flew!"

They had seen.

"Let me sit down, oh, Lord, Lord." Driscoll slapped his knees, chuckling. "I'm a sparrow, I'm a hawk, God bless me. Go on, all you, try it!"

"It's the wind, it picked me up and flew me!" he said, a moment later, gasping, shivering with delight.

"Let's get out of here." Chatterton started turning, slowly in circles, watching the blue sky. "It's a trap, it wants us all to fly in the air. Then it'll drop us all at once and kill us. I'm going back to the ship."

"You'll wait for my order on that," said Forester.

The men were frowning, standing in the warm-cool air, while the wind sighed about them. There was a kite sound in the air, a sound of eternal March.

"I *asked* the wind to fly me," said Driscoll. "and it *did!*"

Forester waved the others aside. "I'll chance it next. If I'm killed, back to the ship, all of you."

"I'm sorry, I can't allow this, you're the captain," said Chatterton. "We can't risk you." He took out his gun. "I should have some sort of authority or force here. This game's gone on too long; I'm ordering us back to the ship."

"Holster your gun," said Forester, quietly.

"Stand still, you idiot!" Chatterton blinked now at this man, now at that. "Haven't you *felt* it? This world's alive, it has a look to it, it's playing with us, biding its time."

"I'll be the judge of that," said Forester. "You're going back to the ship, in a moment, under arrest, if you don't put up that gun."

"If you fools won't come with me, you can die out here. I'm going back, get my samples, and get out."

''Chatterton!''

''Don't try to stop me!''

Chatterton started to run. Then, suddenly, he gave a cry. Everyone shouted and looked up.

''There he goes,'' said Driscoll.

Chatterton was up in the sky.

Night had come on like the closing of a great but gentle eye. Chatterton sat stunned on the side of the hill. The other men sat around him, exhausted and laughing. He would not look at them, he would not look at the sky, he would only feel of the earth, and his arms and his legs and his body, tightening in on himself.

''Oh, wasn't it perfect!'' said a man named Koestler.

They had all flown, like orioles and eagles and sparrows, and they were all happy.

''Come out of it, Chatterton, it was fun, wasn't it?'' said Koestler.

''It's impossible.'' Chatterton shut his eyes, tight, tight. ''There's only one way for it to do it; it's alive. The air's alive. Like a fist it picked me up. Any minute now, it can kill us all. It's alive.''

''All right,'' said Koestler, ''say it's alive. And a living thing must have purpose. Suppose the purpose of this world is to make us happy.''

As if to add to this, Driscoll came flying up, canteens in each hand. ''I found a creek, tested and found pure water, wait'll you try it!''

Forester took a canteen, nudged Chatterton with it, offering a drink. Chatterton shook his head and drew hastily away. He put his hands over his face. ''It's the blood of this planet. Living blood. Drink that, put that inside and you put this world inside you to peer out your eyes and listen through your ears. No thanks!''

Forester shrugged and drank.

''Wine!'' he said.

''It can't be!''

''It *is!* Smell it, taste it! A rare white wine!''

''French domestic.'' Driscoll sipped his.

"Poison," said Chatterton.

They passed the canteens around.

They had idled on through the gentle afternoon, not wanting to do anything to disturb the peace that lay all about them. They were like very young men in the presence of great beauty, of a fine and famous woman, afraid that by some word, some gesture, they might turn her face away, avert her loveliness and her kindly attentions. They had felt the earthquake that had greeted Chatterton, and they did not want earthquake. Let them enjoy this Day After School Lets Out, this fishing weather. Let them sit under the shade trees or walk on the tender hills, but let them drill no drillings, test no testings, contaminate no contaminations.

They found a small stream which poured into a boiling water pool. Fish, swimming in the cold creek above, fell glittering into the hot spring and floated, minutes later, cooked, to the surface.

Chatterton reluctantly joined the others, eating.

"It'll poison us all. There's always a trick to things like this. I'm sleeping in the rocket tonight. You can sleep out if you want. To quote a map I saw in medieval history: 'Here there be tygers.' Some time tonight when you're sleeping, the tigers and cannibals will show up."

Forester shook his head. "I'll go along with you, this planet is alive. It's a race itself. But it needs us to show off to, to appreciate its beauty. What's the use of a stage full of miracles if there's no audience?"

But Chatterton was busy. He was bent over, being sick.

"I'm poisoned! Poisoned!"

They held his shoulders until the sickness passed. They gave him water. The others were feeling fine.

"Better eat nothing but ship's food from now on," advised Forester. "It'd be safer."

"We're starting work right now." Chatterton swayed, wiping his mouth. "We've wasted a whole day. I'll work alone if I have to. I'll show this infernal place!"

He staggered away toward the rocket.

"He doesn't know when he's well off," murmured Driscoll. "Can't we stop him, Captain?"

"He practically owns the expedition. We don't have to help

him, there's a clause in our contract that guarantees refusal to work under dangerous conditions. So . . . do unto this Picnic Ground as you would have it do unto you. No initial-cutting on the trees. Replace the turf on the greens. Clean up your banana peels after you.''

Now, below, in the ship there was an immense humming. From the storage port rolled the great shining Drill. Chatterton followed it, calling directions to its robot radio. ''This way, here!''

''The fool.''

''Now!'' cried Chatterton.

The Drill plunged its long screw-bore into the green grass. Chatterton waved up at the other men. ''Watch this!''

The sky trembled.

The Drill stood in the center of a little sea of grass. For a moment it plunged away, bringing up moist corks of sod which it spat unceremoniously into a shaking analysis bin.

Now the Drill gave a wrenched, metallic squeal like a monster interrupted at its feed. From the soil beneath it slow bluish liquids bubbled up.

Chatterton shouted, ''Get back, you fool!''

The Drill lumbered in a prehistoric dance. It shrieked like a mighty train turning on a sharp curve, throwing out red sparks. It was sinking. The black slime gave under it in a dark convulsion.

With a coughing sigh, a series of pants and churnings, the Drill sank into a black scum like an elephant shot and dying, trumpeting, like a mammoth at the end of an Age, vanishing limb by ponderous limb into the pit.

''Fool, Fool,'' said Forester under his breath, fascinated with the scene. ''You know what that is, Driscoll? It's tar. The fool machine hit a tar pit!''

''Listen, listen!'' cried Chatterton at the Drill, running about on the edge of the oily lake. ''*This* way, over here!''

But like the old tyrants of the earth, the dinosaurs with their tubed and screaming necks, the Drill was plunging and thrashing in the one lake from where there was no returning to bask on the firm and understandable shore.

Chatterton turned to the other men far away. "Do something, someone!'

The Drill was gone.

The tar pit bubbled and gloated, sucking the hidden monster bones. The surface of the pool was silent. A huge bubble, the last, rose, expelled a scent of ancient petroleum, and fell apart.

The men came down and stood on the edge of the little black sea.

Chatterton stopped yelling.

After a long minute of staring into the silent tar pool, Chatterton turned and looked at the hills, blindly, at the green rolling lawns. The distant trees were growing fruit now and dropping it, softly, to the ground.

"I'll show it," he said quietly.

"Take it easy, Chatterton."

"I'll fix it," he said.

"Sit down, have a drink."

"I'll fix it good, I'll show it it can't do this to me."

Chatterton started off back to the ship.

"Wait a minute now," said Forester.

Chatterton ran. "I know what to do, I know how to fix it!"

"Stop him!" said Forester. He ran, then remembered he could fly. "The A-bomb's on the ship, if he should get to that . . ."

The other men had thought of that and were in the air. A small grove of trees stood between the rocket and Chatterton as he ran on the ground, forgetting that he could fly, or afraid to fly, or not allowed to fly, yelling. The crew headed for the rocket to wait for him, the captain with them. They arrived, formed a line, and shut the rocket port. The last they saw of Chatterton he was plunging through the edge of the tiny forest.

The crew stood waiting.

"That fool, that crazy guy."

Chatterton didn't come out on the other side of the small woodland.

"He's turned back, waiting for us to relax our guard."

"Go bring him in," said Forester.

Two men flew off.

Now, softly, a great and gentle rain fell upon the green world.

''The final touch,'' said Driscoll. ''We'd never have to build houses here. Notice it's not raining *on* us. It's raining all around, ahead, behind us. What a world!''

They stood dry in the middle of the blue, cool rain. The sun was setting. The moon, a large one the color of ice, rose over the freshened hills.

''There's only one more thing this world needs.''

''Yes,'' said everyone, thoughtfully, slowly.

''We'll have to go looking,'' said Driscoll. ''It's logical. The wind flies us, the trees and streams feed us, everything is alive. Perhaps if we asked for companionship . . .''

''I've thought a long time, today and other days,'' said Koestler. ''We're all bachelors, been traveling for years, and tired of it. Wouldn't it be nice to settle down somewhere? Here, maybe. On Earth you sweat just to save enough to buy a house, pay taxes; the cities stink. Here, you won't even need a house, with this weather. If it gets monotonous you can ask for rain, clouds, snow, changes. You don't have to work here for anything.''

''It'd be boring. We'd go crazy.''

''No,'' Koestler said, smiling. ''If life got too soft, all we'd have to do is repeat a few times what Chatterton said: *'Here there be tygers.'* Listen!''

Far away, wasn't there the faintest roar of a giant cat, hidden in the twilight forests?

The men shivered.

''A versatile world,'' said Koestler dryly. ''A woman who'll do anything to please her guests, as long as we're kind to her. Chatterton wasn't kind.''

''Chatterton. What about him?''

As if to answer this, someone cried from a distance. The two men who had flown off to find Chatterton were waving at the edge of the woods.

Forester, Driscoll, and Koestler flew down alone.

''What's up?''

The men pointed into the forest. ''Thought you'd want to see this, Captain. It's eerie.'' One of the men indicated a pathway. ''Look here, sir.''

The marks of great claws stood on the path, fresh and clear.

"And over here."

A few drops of blood.

A heavy smell of some feline animal hung in the air.

"Chatterton?"

"I don't think we'll ever find him, Captain."

Faintly, faintly, moving away, now gone in the breathing silence of twilight, came the roar of a tiger.

The men lay on the resilient grass by the rocket and the night was warm. "Reminds me of nights when I was a kid," said Driscoll. "My brother and I waited for the hottest night in July and then we slept on the Court House lawn, counting the stars, talking; it was a great night, the best night of my life." Then he added, "Not counting tonight, of course."

"I keep thinking about Chatterton," said Koestler.

"Don't," said Forester. "We'll sleep a few hours and take off. We can't chance staying here another day. I don't mean the danger that got Chatterton. No. I mean, if we stayed on we'd get to liking this world too much. We'd never want to leave."

A soft wind blew over them.

"I don't want to leave now." Driscoll put his hands behind his head, lying quietly. "And it doesn't want us to leave."

"If we go back to Earth and tell everyone what a lovely planet it is, what then, Captain? They'll come smashing in here and ruin it."

"No," said Forester idly. "First, this planet wouldn't put up with a full-scale invasion. I don't know what it'd do, but it could probably think of some interesting things. Secondly, I like this planet too much; I respect it. We'll go back to Earth and lie about it. Say it's hostile. Which it would be to the average man, like Chatterton, jumping in here to hurt it. I guess we won't be lying after all."

"Funny thing," said Koestler. "I'm not afraid. Chatterton vanishes, is killed most horribly, perhaps, yet we lie here, no one runs, no one trembles. It's idiotic. Yet it's right. We trust *it* and *it* trusts us."

"Did you notice, after you drank just so much of the wine-water, you didn't want more? A world of moderation."

They lay listening to something like the great heart of this earth beating slowly and warmly under their bodies.

Forester thought, I'm thirsty.

A drop of rain splashed on his lips.

He laughed quietly.

I'm lonely, he thought.

Distantly, he heard soft, high voices.

He turned his eyes in upon a vision. There was a group of hills from which flowed a clear river, and in the shallows of that river, sending up spray, their faces shimmering, were the beautiful women. They played like children on the shore. And it came to Forester to know about them and their life. They were nomads, roaming the face of this world as was their desire. There were no highways or cities, there were only hills and plains and winds to carry them like white feathers where they wished. As Forester shaped the questions, some invisible answerer whispered the answers. There were no men. These women, alone, produced their race. The man had vanished fifty thousand years ago. And where were these women now? A mile down from the green forest, a mile over on the wine stream by the six white stones, and a third mile to the large river. There, in the shallows, were the women who would make fine wives, and raise beautiful children.

Forester opened his eyes. The other men were sitting up.

"I had a dream."

They had all dreamed.

"A mile down from the green forest . . ."

". . . a mile over on the wine stream . . ."

". . . by the six white stones . . ." said Koestler.

". . . and a third mile to the large river," said Driscoll, sitting there.

Nobody spoke again for a moment. They looked at the silver rocket standing there in the starlight.

"Do we walk or fly, Captain?"

Forester said nothing.

Driscoll said, "Captain, let's stay. Let's never go back to Earth. They'll never come and investigate to see what happened to us; they'll think we were destroyed here. What do you say?"

Forester's face was perspiring. His tongue moved again and

again on his lips. His hands twitched over his knees. The crew sat waiting.

"It'd be nice," said the captain.

"Sure."

"But . . ." Forester sighed. "We've got our job to do. People invested in our ship. We owe it to them to go back."

Forester got up. The men still sat on the ground, not listening to him.

"It's such a fine, nice, wonderful night," said Koestler.

They stared at the soft hills and the trees and the rivers running off to other horizons.

"Let's get aboard ship," said Forester, with difficulty.

"Captain . . ."

"Get aboard," he said.

The rocket rose into the sky. Looking back, Forester saw every valley and every tiny lake.

"We should've stayed," said Koestler.

"Yes, I know."

"It's not too late to turn back."

"I'm afraid it is." Forester made an adjustment on the port telescope. "Look now."

Koestler looked.

The face of the world was changed. Tigers, dinosaurs, mammoths appeared. Volcanoes erupted, cyclones and hurricanes tore over the hills in a welter and fury of weather.

"Yes, she was a woman all right," said Forester. "Waiting for visitors for millions of years, preparing herself, making herself beautiful. She put on her best face for us. When Chatterton treated her badly, she warned him a few times, and then, when he tried to ruin her beauty, eliminated him. She wanted to be loved, like every woman, for herself, not for her wealth. So now, after she had offered us everything, we turn our backs. She's the woman scorned. She let us go, yes, but we can never come back. She'll be waiting for us with *those* . . ." He nodded to the tigers and the cyclones and the boiling seas.

"Captain," said Koestler.

"Yes."

"It's a little late to tell you this. But just before we took off,

I was in charge of the air lock. I let Driscoll slip away from the ship. He wanted to go. I couldn't refuse him. I'm responsible. He's back there now, on that planet."

They both turned to the viewing port.

After a long while, Forester said, "I'm glad. I'm glad one of us had enough sense to stay."

"But he's dead by now!"

"No, that display down there is for us, perhaps a visual hallucination. Underneath all the tigers and lions and hurricanes, Driscoll is quite safe and alive, because he's her only audience now. Oh, she'll spoil him rotten. He'll lead a wonderful life, he will, while we're slugging it out up and down the system looking for but never finding a planet quite like this again. No, we won't try to go back and 'rescue' Driscoll. I don't think 'she' would let us anyway. Full speed ahead, Koestler, make it full speed."

The rocket leaped forward into greater accelerations.

And just before the planet dwindled away in brightness and mist, Forester imagined that he could see Driscoll very clearly, walking away down from the green forest, whistling quietly, all of the fresh planet around him, a wine creek flowing for him, baked fish lolling in the hot springs, fruit ripening in the midnight trees, and distant forests and lakes waiting for him to happen by. Driscoll walked away across the endless green lawns near the six white stones, beyond the forest, to the edge of the large bright river. . . .

The Strawberry Window

In his dream he was shutting the front door with its strawberry windows and lemon windows and windows like white clouds and windows like clear water in a country stream. Two dozen panes squared round the one big pane, colored of fruit wines and gelatins and cool water ices. He remembered his father holding him up as a child. "Look!" And through the green glass the world was emerald, moss, and summer mint. "Look!" The lilac pane made livid grapes of all the passers-by. And at last the strawberry glass perpetually bathed the town in roseate warmth, carpeted the world in pink sunrise, and made the cut lawn seem imported from some Persian rug bazaar. The strawberry window, best of all, cured people of their paleness, warmed the cold rain, and set the blowing, shifting February snows afire.

"Yes, yes! There—!"

He awoke.

He heard his boys talking before he was fully out of his dream and he lay in the dark now, listening to the sad sound their talk made, like the wind blowing the white sea-bottoms into the blue hills, and then he remembered.

We're on Mars, he thought.

"What?" His wife cried out in her sleep.

He hadn't realized he had spoken; he lay as still as he possibly could. But now, with a strange kind of numb reality, he saw his wife rise to haunt the room, her pale face staring through the small, high windows of their quonset hut at the clear but unfamiliar stars.

"Carrie," he whispered.

She did not hear.

"Carrie," he whispered. "There's something I want to tell you. For a month now I've been wanting to say . . . tomorrow . . . tomorrow morning, there's going to be . . ."

But his wife sat all to herself in the blue starlight and would not look at him.

If only the sun stayed up, he thought, if only there was no night. For during the day he nailed the settlement town together, the boys were in school, and Carrie had cleaning, gardening, cooking to do. But when the sun was gone and their hands were empty of flowers or hammers and nails and arithmetics, their memories, like night birds, came home in the dark.

His wife moved, a slight turn of her head.

"Bob," she said at last. "I want to go home."

"Carrie!"

"This isn't home," she said.

He saw that her eyes were wet and brimming. "Carrie, hold on awhile."

"I've got no fingernails from holding on now!"

As if she still moved in her sleep, she opened her bureau drawers and took out layers of handkerchiefs, shirts, underclothing, and put it all on top of the bureau, not seeing it, letting her fingers touch and bring it out and put it down. The routine was long familiar now. She would talk and put things out and stand quietly awhile, and then later put all the things away and come, dry-faced, back to bed and dreams. He was afraid that some night she would empty every drawer and reach for the few ancient suitcases against the wall.

"Bob . . ." Her voice was not bitter, but soft, featureless, and as uncolored as the moonlight that showed what she was doing. "So many nights for six months I've talked this way; I'm ashamed. You work hard building houses in town. A man who works so hard shouldn't have to listen to a wife gone sad on him. But there's nothing to do but talk it out. It's the little things I miss most of all. I don't know . . . silly things. Our front-porch swing. The wicker rocking chair, summer nights.

Looking at the people walk or ride by those evenings, back in Ohio. Our black upright piano, out of tune. My Swedish cut glass. Our parlor furniture—oh, it was like a herd of elephants, I know, and all of it old. And the Chinese hanging crystals that hit when the wind blew. And talking to neighbors there on the front porch, July nights. All those crazy, silly things—they're not important. But it seems those are things that come to mind around three in the morning. I'm sorry."

"Don't be," he said. "Mars is a far place. It smells funny, looks funny, and feels funny. I think to myself nights too. We came from a nice town."

"It was green," she said. "In the spring and summer. And yellow and red in the fall. And ours was a nice house; my, it was old, eighty-ninety years or so. Used to hear the house talking at night, whispering away. All the dry wood, the banisters, the front porch, the sills. Wherever you touched, it talked to you. Every room a different way. And when you had the whole house talking, it was a family around you in the dark, putting you to sleep. No other house, the kind they build nowadays, can be the same. A lot of people have got to go through and live in a house to make it mellow down all over. This place here, now, this hut, it doesn't know I'm in it, doesn't care if I live or die. It makes a noise like tin, and tin's cold. It's got no pores for the years to sink in. It's got no cellar for you to put things away for next year and the year after that. It's got no attic where you keep things from last year and all the other years before you were born. If we only had a little bit up here that was familiar, Bob, then we could make room for all that's strange. But when everything, *every single thing* is strange, then it takes forever to make things familiar."

He nodded in the dark. "There's nothing you say that I haven't thought."

She was looking at the moonlight where it lay upon the suitcases against the wall. He saw her move her hand down toward them.

"Carrie!"

"What?"

He swung his legs out of bed. "Carrie, I've done a crazy lame-brain thing. All these months I heard you dreaming away, scared, and the boys at night and the wind, and Mars out there, the sea-bottoms and all, and . . ." He stopped and swallowed. "You got to understand what I did and why I did it. All the money we had in the bank a month ago, all the money we saved for ten years, I spent."

"Bob!"

"I threw it away, Carrie, I swear, I threw it away on nothing. It was going to be a surprise. But now, tonight, there you are, and there are those blasted suitcases on the floor and . . ."

"Bob," she said, turning around. "You mean we've gone through all *this,* on Mars, putting away extra money every week, only to have you burn it up in a few hours?"

"I don't know," he said. "I'm a crazy fool. Look, it's not long till morning. We'll get up early. I'll take you down to see what I've done. I don't want to tell you, I want you to see. And if it's no go then, well, there's always those suitcases and the rocket to Earth four times a month."

She did not move. "Bob, Bob," she murmured.

"Don't say any more," he said.

"Bob, Bob . . ." She shook her head slowly, unbelievingly. He turned away and lay back down on his own side of the bed, and she sat on the other side, looking at the bureau where her handkerchiefs and jewelry and clothing lay ready in neat stacks where she had left them. Outside a wind the color of moonlight stirred up the sleeping dust and powdered the air.

At last she lay back, but said nothing more and was a cold weight in the bed, staring down the long tunnel of night toward the faintest sign of morning.

They got up in the very first light and moved in the small quonset hut without a sound. It was a pantomime prolonged almost to the time when someone might scream at the silence, as the mother and father and the boys washed and dressed and ate a quiet breakfast of toast and fruit juice and coffee, with no one looking directly at anyone and everyone watching someone in the reflective surfaces of toaster, glassware, or cutlery, where all their faces were melted out of shape and made terribly alien in the early hour. Then, at last, they opened the quonset door and let in the air that blew across the cold blue-white Martian seas, where only the sand tides dissolved and shifted and made ghost patterns, and they stepped out under a raw and staring cold sky and began their walk toward a town, which seemed no more than a motion-picture set far on ahead of them on a vast, empty stage.

"What part of town are we going to?" asked Carrie.

"The rocket depot," he said. "But before we get there, I've a lot to say."

The boys slowed down and moved behind their parents, listening. The father gazed ahead, and not once in all the time he was talking did he look at his wife or sons to see how they were taking all that he said.

"I believe in Mars," he began quietly. "I guess I believe someday it'll belong to us. We'll nail it down. We'll settle in. We won't turn tail and run. It came to me one day a year ago right after we first arrived. Why did we come? I asked myself. Because, I said, because. It's the same thing with the salmon every year. The salmon don't know why they go where they go, but they go, anyway. Up rivers they don't remember, up streams, jumping waterfalls, but finally making it to where they propagate and die, and the whole thing starts again. Call it racial memory, instinct, call it nothing, but there it is. And here we are."

They walked in the silent morning with the great sky watching them and the strange blue and steam-white sands sifting about their feet on the new highway.

"So here we are. And from Mars where? Jupiter, Neptune, Pluto, and on out? Right. *And on out.* Why? Someday the sun will blow up like a leaky furnace. Boom—there goes Earth. But maybe Mars won't be hurt; or if Mars is hurt maybe Pluto won't be, or if Pluto's hurt, then where'll *we* be, our sons' sons, that is?"

He gazed steadily up into that flawless shell of plum-colored sky.

"Why, we'll be on some world with a number maybe; planet 6 of star system 97, planet 2 of system 99! So darn far off from here you need a nightmare to take it in! We'll be gone, do you see, gone off away and safe! And I thought to myself, ah, ah. So that's the reason we came to Mars, so *that's* the reason men shoot off their rockets."

"Bob—"

"Let me finish; not to make money, no. Not to see the sights, no. Those are the lies men tell, the fancy reasons they give themselves. Get rich, get famous, they say. Have fun, jump around, they say. But all the while, inside, something else is ticking along the way it ticks in salmon or whales, the way it ticks, oh, Lord, in the smallest microbe you want to name. And that little clock that ticks in everything living, you know what it says? It says get away, spread out, move along, keep swimming. Run to so many worlds and build so many towns that *nothing* can ever kill man. You *see,* Carrie? It's not just us come to Mars, it's the race, the whole darn human race, depending on how *we* make out in our lifetime. This thing is so big I want to laugh, I'm so scared stiff of it."

He felt the boys walking steadily behind him, and he felt Carrie beside him and he wanted to see her face and how she was taking all this, but he didn't look there, either.

"All this is no different than me and Dad walking the fields when I was a boy, casting seed by hand when our seeder broke down and we'd no money to fix it. It had to be done, do you *remember* those Sunday-supplement articles. THE EARTH WILL FREEZE IN A MILLION YEARS! I bawled once, as a boy, reading articles like that. My mother asked why. I'm bawling for all those poor people up ahead, I said. Don't worry about them, Mother said. But, Carrie, that's my whole point; we *are* worrying about them. Or we wouldn't be here. It matters if Man with a capital M keeps going. There's nothing better than Man with a capital M in my books. I'm prejudiced, of course, because I'm one of the breed. But if there's any way to get hold of that immortality men are always talking about, this is the way—spread out—seed the universe. Then you got a harvest against crop failures anywhere down the line. No matter if Earth has famines or the rust comes in. You got the new wheat lifting on Venus or where-in-blazes-ever man gets to in the next thousand years. I'm crazy with the idea, Carrie, crazy. When I finally hit on it I got so excited I wanted to grab people, you, the boys, and tell them. But well, I knew that wasn't necessary. I knew a day or night would come when you'd hear that ticking in yourselves too, and then you'd see, and no one'd have to say anything again about all this. It's big talk, Carrie, I know, and big thoughts for a man just short of five feet five, but by all that's holy, it's true."

They moved through the deserted streets of the town and listened to the echoes of their walking feet.

"And this morning?" said Carrie.

"I'm coming to this morning," he said. "Part of *me* wants to go home too. But the other part says if we go, everything's lost. So I thought, what bothers us most? Some of the things we once had. Some of the boys' things, your things, mine. And I thought, if it takes an old thing to get a new thing started, why then, I'll use the old thing. I remember from history books that a thousand years ago they put charcoals in a hollowed out cow horn, blew on them during the day, so they carried their fire on marches from place to place, to start a fire every night with the sparks left over from morning. Always a new fire, but always something of the old in it. So I weighed and balanced it off. Is the Old worth all our money? I asked. No! It's only the things we *did* with the Old that have any worth. Well, then, is the New worth *all* our money? I asked. Do you feel like investing in the day after the middle of next week? Yes! I said. If I can fight this thing that makes us want to go back to Earth, I'd dip my money in kerosene and strike a match!"

Carrie and the two boys did not move. They stood on the street, looking at him as if he were a storm that had passed over and around, almost blowing them from the ground, a storm that was now dying away.

"The freight rocket came in this morning," he said, quietly. "Our delivery's on it. Let's go and pick it up."

They walked slowly up the three steps into the rocket depot and across the echoing floor toward the freight room that was just sliding back its doors, opening for the day.

"Tell us again about the salmon," said one of the boys.

In the middle of the warm morning they drove out of town in a rented truck filled with great crates and boxes and parcels and packages, long ones, tall ones, short ones, flat ones, all numbered and neatly addressed to one Robert Prentiss, New Toledo, Mars.

They stopped the truck by the quonset hut and the boys jumped down and helped their mother out. For a moment Bob sat behind the wheel, and then slowly got out himself to walk around and look into the back of the truck at the crates.

And by noon all but one of the boxes were opened and their contents placed on the sea-bottom where the family stood among them.

"Carrie . . ."

And he led her up the old porch steps that now stood uncrated on the edge of town.

"Listen to 'em, Carrie."

The steps squeaked and whispered underfoot.

"What do they say, tell me what they say?"

She stood on the ancient wooden steps, holding to herself, and could not tell him.

He waved his hand. "Front porch here, living room there, dining room, kitchen, three bedrooms. Most we'll build new, part we'll bring. Of course all we got here now is the front steps, some parlor furniture, and the old bed."

"All that money, Bob!"

He turned, smiling. "You're not mad, now, look at me! You're not mad. We'll bring it up, next year, five years! The cut-glass vases, that Armenian carpet your mother gave us in 1975! Just *let* the sun explode!"

They looked at the other crates, numbered and lettered: Front-porch swing, front-porch wicker rocker, hanging Chinese crystals . . .

"I'll blow them myself to make them ring."

And then they set the front door, with its little panes of colored glass, on the top of the stairs, and Carrie looked through the strawberry window.

"What do you see?"

But he knew what she saw, for he gazed through the colored glass, too. And there was Mars, with its cold sky warmed and its dead seas fired with color, with its hills like mounds of strawberry ice, and its sand like burning charcoals sifted by wind. The strawberry window, the strawberry window, breathed soft rose colors on the land and filled the mind and the eye with the light of a never-ending dawn. Bent there, looking through, he heard himself say:

"The town'll be out this way in a year. This'll be a shady street, you'll have your porch, and you'll have friends. You won't *need* all this so much, then. But starting right here, with this little bit that's familiar, watch it spread, watch Mars change so you'll know it as if you've known it all your life."

He ran down the steps to the last and as-yet unopened canvas-covered crate. With his pocket knife he cut a hole in the canvas. "Guess!" he said.

"My kitchen stove? My sewing machine?"

"Not in a million years." He smiled very gently. "Sing me a song," he said.

"Bob, you're clean off your head."

"Sing me a song worth all the money we had in the bank and now don't have, but who gives a blast in Hades," he said.

"I don't know anything but 'Genevieve, Sweet Genevieve!"

"Sing that," he said.

But she could not open her mouth and start the song. He saw her lips move and try, but there was no sound.

He ripped the canvas wider and shoved his hand into the crate and touched around for a quiet moment, and started to sing the words himself until he moved his hand a last time and then a single clear piano chord sprang out on the morning air.

"There," he said. "Let's take it right on to the end. Everyone! Here's the harmony."

The night blew in the short grass on the moor; there was no other motion. It had been years since a single bird had flown by in the great blind shell of sky. Long ago a few small stones had simulated life when they crumbled and fell into dust. Now only the night moved in the souls of the two men bent by their lonely fire in the wilderness; darkness pumped quietly in their veins and ticked silently in their temples and their wrists.

Firelight fled up and down their wild faces and welled in their eyes in orange tatters. They listened to each other's faint, cool breathing and the lizard blink of their eyelids. At last, one man poked the fire with his sword.

"Don't, idiot; you'll give us away!"

"No matter," said this second man. "The dragon can smell us miles off anyway. God's breath, it's cold. I wish I was back at the castle."

"It's death, not sleep we're after. . . ."

"Why? Why? The dragon never sets foot in the town!"

"Quiet, fool! He eats men traveling alone from our town to the next!"

"Let them be eaten and let us get home!"

"Wait now; listen!"

The two men froze.

They waited a long time, but there was only the shake of their horses' nervous skin like black velvet tambourines jingling the silver stirrup buckles, softly, softly.

"Ah." The second man sighed. "What a land of nightmares. Everything happens here. Someone blows out the sun; it's night. And then, and *then,* oh, sweet mortality, listen! This dragon, they say his eyes are fire. His breath a white gas; you can see him burn across the dark lands. He runs with sulfur and thunder and kindles the grass. Sheep panic and die insane. Women deliver forth monsters. The dragon's fury is such that tower walls shake back to dust. His victims, at sunrise, are strewn hither thither on the hills. How many knights, I ask, have gone for this monster and failed, even as we shall fail?"

"Enough of that!"

"More than enough! Out here in this desolation I cannot tell what year this is!"

"Nine hundred years since the Nativity."

"No, no," whispered the second man, eyes shut. "On this moor is no Time, is only Forever. I feel if I ran back on the road the town would be gone, the people yet unborn, things changed, the castles unquarried from the rocks, the timbers still uncut from the forests; don't ask how I know; the moor knows and tells me. And here we sit alone in the land of the fire dragon, God save us!"

"Be you afraid, then gird on your armor!"

"What use? The dragon runs from nowhere; we cannot guess its home. It vanishes in fog; we know not where it goes. Aye, on with our armor, we'll die well dressed."

Half into his silver corselet, the second man stopped again and turned his head.

Across the dim country, full of night and nothingness from the heart of the moor itself, the wind sprang full of dust from clocks that used dust for telling time. There were black suns burning in the heart of this new wind and a million burnt leaves shaken from some autumn tree beyond the horizon. The wind melted landscapes, lengthened bones like white wax, made the blood roil and thicken to a muddy deposit in the brain. The wind was a thousand souls dying and all time confused and in transit. It was a fog inside of a mist inside of a darkness, and this place was no man's place and there was no year or hour at all, but only these men in a faceless emptiness of sudden frost, storm and white thunder which moved behind the great falling pane of green glass that was the lightning. A squall of rain drenched the turf; all faded away until there was unbreathing hush and the two men waiting alone with their warmth in a cool season.

"There," whispered the first man, "Oh, *there* . . ."

Miles off, rushing with a great chant and a roar—the dragon.

In silence the men buckled on their armor and mounted their horses. The midnight wilderness was split by a monstrous gushing as the dragon roared nearer, nearer; its flashing yellow glare spurted above a hill and then, fold on fold of dark body, distantly seen, therefore indistinct, flowed over that hill and plunged vanishing into a valley.

"Quick!"

They spurred their horses forward to a small hollow.

"This is where it passes!"

They seized their lances with mailed fists and blinded their horses by flipping the visors down over their eyes.

"Lord!"

"Yes, let us use His name."

On the instant, the dragon rounded a hill. Its monstrous amber eye fed on them, fired their armor in red glints and glitters. With a terrible wailing cry and a grinding rush it flung itself forward.

"Mercy, mercy!"

The lance struck under the unlidded yellow eye, buckled, tossed the man through the air. The dragon hit, spilled him over, down, ground him under. Passing, the black brunt of its shoulder smashed the remaining horse and rider a hundred feet against the side of a boulder, wailing, wailing, the dragon shrieking, the fire all about, around, under it, a pink, yellow, orange sun-fire with great soft plumes of blinding smoke.

"Did you *see* it?" cried a voice. "Just like I told you!"

"The same! The same! A knight in armor, by the Lord Harry! We *hit* him!"

"You goin' to stop?"

'Did once; found nothing. Don't like to stop on this moor. I get the willies. Got a *feel,* it has."

"But we hit *something!*"

"Gave him plenty of whistle; chap wouldn't budge!"

A steaming blast cut the mist aside.

"We'll make Stokely on time. More coal, eh, Fred?"

Another whistle shook dew from the empty sky. The night train, in fire and fury, shot through a gully, up a rise, and vanished away over cold earth toward the north, leaving black smoke and steam to dissolve in the numbed air minutes after it had passed and gone forever.

Frost and Fire

I

During the night, Sim was born. He lay wailing upon the cold cave stones. His blood beat through him a thousand pulses each minute. He grew, steadily.

Into his mouth his mother with feverish hands put the food. The nightmare of living was begun. Almost instantly at birth his eyes grew alert, and then, without half understanding why, filled with bright, insistent terror. He gagged upon the food, choked and wailed. He looked about, blindly.

There was a thick fog. It cleared. The outlines of the cave appeared. And a man loomed up, insane and wild and terrible. A man with a dying face. Old, withered by winds, baked like adobe in the heat. The man was crouched in a far corner of the cave, his eyes whitening to one side of his face, listening to the far wind trumpeting up above on the frozen night planet.

Sim's mother, trembling now and again, staring at the man, fed Sim pebble-fruits, valley-grasses and ice-nipples broken from the cavern entrances, and eating, eliminating, eating again, he grew larger, larger.

The man in the corner of the cave was his father! The man's eyes were all that was alive in his face. He held a crude stone dagger in his withered hands and his jaw hung loose and senseless.

Then, with a widening focus, Sim saw the old people sitting in the tunnel beyond this living quarter. And as he watched, they began to die.

Their agonies filled the cave. They melted like waxen images, their faces collapsed inward on their sharp bones, their teeth protruded. One minute their faces were mature, fairly smooth, alive, electric. The next minute a desiccation and burning away of their fresh occurred.

Sim thrashed in his mother's grasp. She held him. "No, no," she soothed him, quietly, earnestly, looking to see if this, too, would cause her husband to rise again.

With a soft swift padding of naked feet, Sim's father ran across the cave. Sim's mother screamed. Sim felt himself torn loose from her grasp. He fell upon the stones, rolling, shrieking with his new, moist lungs!

The webbed face of his father jerked over him, the knife was poised. It was like one of those prenatal nightmares he'd had again and again while still in his mother's flesh. In the next few blazing, impossible instants questions flicked through his brain. The knife was high, suspended, ready to destroy him. But the whole question of life in this cave, the dying people, the withering and the insanity, surged through Sim's new, small head. How was it that he understood? A newborn child? Can a newborn child think, see, understand, interpret? No. It was wrong! It was impossible. Yet it was happening! To him. He had been alive an hour now. And in the next instant perhaps dead!

His mother flung herself upon the back of his father, and beat down the weapon. Sim caught the terrific backwash of emotion from both their conflicting minds. "Let me kill him!" shouted the father, breathing harshly, sobbingly. "What has he to live for?"

"No, no!" insisted the mother, and her body, frail and old as it was, stretched across the huge body of the father, tearing at his weapon. "He must live! There may be a future for him! He may live longer than us, and be young!"

The father fell back against a stone crib. Lying there, staring, eyes glittering, Sim saw another figure inside that stone crib. A girl-child, quietly feeding itself, moving its delicate hands to procure food. His sister.

The mother wrenched the dagger from her husband's grasp, stood up, weeping and pushing back her cloud of stiffening gray hair. Her mouth trembled and jerked. "I'll kill you!" she said, glaring down at her husband. "Leave my children alone."

The old man spat tiredly, bitterly, and looked vacantly into the stone crib, at the little girl. "One-eighth of *her* life's over already," he gasped. "And she doesn't know it. What's the use?"

As Sim watched, his own mother seemed to shift and take a tortured, smokelike form. The thin bony face broke out into a maze of wrinkles. She was shaken with pain and had to sit by him, shuddering and cuddling the knife to her shriveled breasts. She, like the old people in the tunnel, was aging, dying.

Sim cried steadily. Everywhere he looked was horror. A mind came to meet his own. Instinctively he glanced toward the stone crib. Dark, his sister returned his glance. Their minds brushed like straying fingers. He relaxed somewhat. He began to learn.

The father sighed, shut his lids down over his green eyes. "Feed the child," he said, exhaustedly. "Hurry. It is almost dawn and it is our last day of living, woman. Feed him. Make him grow."

Sim quieted, and images, out of the terror, floated to him.

This was a planet next to the sun. The nights burned with cold, the days were like torches of fire. It was a violent, impossible world. The people lived in the cliffs to escape the incredible ice and the day of flame. Only at dawn and sunset was the air breath-sweet, flower-strong, and then the cave peoples brought their children out into a stony, barren valley. At dawn the ice thawed into creeks and rivers, at sunset the day fire died and cooled. In the intervals of even, livable temperature the people lived, ran, played, loved, free of the caverns; all life on the planet jumped, burst into life. Plants grew instantly, birds were flung like pellets across the sky. Smaller, legged animal life rushed frantically through the rocks; everything tried to get its living done in the brief hour of respite.

It was an unbearable planet. Sim understood this, a matter of hours after birth. Racial memory bloomed in him. He would live his entire life in the caves, with two hours a day outside. Here, in stone channels of air he would talk, talk incessantly with his people, sleep never, think, think and lie upon his back, dreaming; but never sleeping.

And he would live exactly eight days.

* * *

The *violence* of this thought! Eight days. Eight *short* days. It was wrong, impossible, but a fact. Even while in his mother's flesh some racial knowledge of some strange far wild voice had told him he was being formed rapidly, shaped and propelled out swiftly.

Birth was quick as a knife. Childhood was over in a flash. Adolescence was a sheet of lighting. Manhood was a dream, maturity a myth, old age an inescapably quick reality, death a swift certainty.

Eight days from now he'd stand half-blind, withering, dying, as his father now stood, staring uselessly at his own wife and child.

This day was an eighth part of his total life! He must enjoy every second of it. He must search his parents' thoughts for knowledge.

Because in a few hours they'd be dead.

This was so impossibly unfair. Was this all of life? In his prenatal state hadn't he dreamed of *long* lives, valleys not of blasted stone but green foliage and temperate clime? Yes! And if he'd dreamed then there must be truth in the visions. How could he seek and find the long life? Where? And how could he accomplish a life mission that huge and depressing in eight short, vanishing days?

How had his people gotten into such a condition?

As if at a button pressed, he saw an image. Metal seeds, blown across space from a distant green world, fighting with long flames, crashing on this bleak planet. From their shattered hulls tumbled men and women.

When? Long ago. Ten thousand days. The crash victims hid in the cliffs from the sun. Fire, ice and floods washed away the wreckage of the huge metal seeds. The victims were shaped and beaten like iron upon a forge. Solar radiations drenched them. Their pulses quickened, two hundred, five hundred, a thousand beats a minute. Their skins thickened, their blood changed. Old age came rushing. Children were born in the caves. Swifter, swifter, swifter the process. Like all this world's wild life, the men and women from the crash lived and died in a week, leaving children to do likewise.

So this is life, thought Sim. It was not spoken in his mind, for he knew no words, he knew only images, old memory, an awareness, a telepathy that could penetrate flesh, rock, metal. Somewhere along the line, they *had* developed telepathy, plus racial memory, the only good gifts, the only hope in all this terror. So thought Sim, I'm the five-thousandth in a long line of futile sons? What can I do to save myself from dying eight days from now? Is there escape?

His eyes widened, another image came to focus.

Beyond this valley of cliffs, on a low mountain lay a perfect, unscarred metal seed. A metal ship, not rusted or touched by the avalanches. The ship was deserted, whole, intact. It was the only ship of all those that had crashed that was still a unit, still usable. But it was so far away. There was no one in it to help. This ship, then, on the far mountain, was the destiny toward which he would grow. There was his only hope of escape.

His mind flexed.

In this cliff, deep down in a confinement of solitude, worked a handful of scientists. To these men, when he was old enough and wise enough, he must go. They, too, dreamed of escape, of long life, of green valleys and temperate weathers. They, too, stared longingly at that distant ship upon its high mountain, its metal so perfect it did not rust or age.

The cliff groaned.

Sim's father lifted his eroded, lifeless face.

"Dawn's coming," he said.

II

Morning relaxed the mighty granite cliff muscles. It was the time of the Avalanche.

The tunnels echoed to running bare feet. Adults, children pushed with eager, hungry eyes toward the outside dawn. From far out, Sim heard a rumble of rock, a scream, a silence. Avalanches fell into valley. Stones that had been biding their time, not quite ready to fall, for a million years let go their bulks, and where they had begun their journey as single boulders they smashed upon the valley floor in a thousand shrapnels and friction-heated nuggets.

Every morning at least one person was caught in the downpour.

The cliff people dared the avalanches. It added one more excitement to their lives, already too short, too head-long, too dangerous.

Sim felt himself seized up by his father. He was carried brusquely down the tunnel for a thousand yards, to where the daylight appeared. There was a shining insane light in his father's eyes. Sim could not move. He sensed what was going to happen. Behind his father, his mother hurried, bringing with her the little sister, Dark. "Wait! Be careful!" she cried to her husband.

Sim felt his father crouch, listening.

High in the cliff was a tremor, a shivering.

"Now!" bellowed his father, and leaped out.

An avalanche fell down at them!

Sim had accelerated impressions of plunging walls, dust, confusion. His mother screamed! There was a jolting, a plunging.

With one last step, Sim's father hurried him forward into the day. The avalanche thundered behind him. The mouth of the cave, where mother and Dark stood back out of the way, was choked with rubble and two boulders that weighed a hundred pounds each.

The storm thunder of the avalanche passed away to a trickle of sand. Sim's father burst out into laughter. "Made it! By the Gods! Made it alive!" And he looked scornfully at the cliff and spat. "Pagh!"

Mother and sister Dark struggled through the rubble. She cursed her husband. "Fool! You might have killed Sim!"

"I may yet," retorted the father.

Sim was not listening. He was fascinated with the remains of an avalanche afront of the next tunnel. Blood trickled out from under a rise of boulders, soaking into the ground. There was nothing more to be seen. Someone else had lost the game.

Dark ran ahead on lithe, supple feet, naked and certain.

The valley air was like a wine filtered between mountains. The heaven was a restive blue; not the pale scorched atmosphere of full day, nor the bloated, bruised black-purple of night, a-riot with sickly shining stars.

This was a tide pool. A place where waves of varying and violent temperatures struck, receded. Now the tide pool was quiet, cool, and its life moved abroad.

Laughter! Far away, Sim heard it. Why laughter? How could any of his people find time for laughing? Perhaps later he would discover why.

The valley suddenly blushed with impulsive color. Plant life, thawing in the precipitant dawn, shoved out from most unexpected sources. It flowered as you watched. Pale green tendrils appeared on scoured rocks. Seconds later, ripe globes of fruit twitched upon the blade-tips. Father gave Sim to his mother and harvested the momentary, volatile crop, thrust scarlet, blue, yellow fruits into a fur sack which hung at his waist. Mother tugged at the moist new grasses, laid them on Sim's tongue.

His senses were being honed to a fine edge. He stored knowledge thirstily. He understood love, marriage, customs, anger, pity, rage, selfishness, shadings and subtleties, realities and reflections. One thing suggested another. The sight of green plant life whirled his mind like a gyroscope, seeking balance in a world where lack of time for explanations made a mind seek and interpret on its own. The soft burden of food gave him knowledge of his system, of energy, of movement. Like a bird newly cracking its way from a shell, he was almost a unit, complete, all-knowing. Heredity and telepathy that fed upon every mind and every wind had done all this for him. He grew excited with his ability.

They walked, mother, father and the two children, smelling the smells, watching the birds bounce from wall to wall of the valley like scurrying pebbles and suddenly the father said a strange thing:

"Remember?"

Remember what? Sim lay cradled. Was it any effort for them to remember, when they'd lived only seven days!

The husband and wife looked at each other.

"Was it only three days ago?" said the woman, her body shaking, her eyes closing to think. "I can't believe it. It is so unfair." She sobbed, then drew her hand across her face and bit her parched lips. The wind played at her gray hair. "Now it is my turn to cry. An hour ago it was you!"

"An hour is half a life."

"Come." She took her husband's arm. "Let us look at everything, because it will be our last looking."

"The sun'll be up in a few minutes," said the old man. "We must turn back now."

"Just one more moment," pleaded the woman.

"The sun will catch us."

"Let it catch me then!"

"You don't mean that."

"I mean nothing, nothing at all," cried the woman.

The sun was coming fast. The green in the valley burnt away. Searing wind blasted from over the cliffs. Far away where sun bolts hammered battlements of cliff, the huge stone faces shook their contents; those avalanches not already powdered down, were now released and fell like mantles.

'Dark!" shouted the father. The girl sprang over the warm floor of the valley, answering, her hair a black flag behind her. Hands full of green fruits, she joined them.

The sun rimmed the horizon with flame, the air convulsed dangerously with it, and whistled.

The cave people bolted, shouting, picking up their fallen children, bearing vast loads of fruit and grass with them back to their deep hideouts. In moments the valley was bare. Except for one small child someone had forgotten. He was running far out on the flatness, but he was not strong enough, and the engulfing heat was drifting down from the cliffs even as he was half across the valley.

Flowers were burnt into effigies, grasses sucked back into rocks like singed snakes. Flower seeds whirled and fell in the sudden furnace blast of wind, sown far into gullies and crannies, ready to blossom at sunset tonight, and then go to seed and die again.

Sim's father watched that child running, alone, out on the floor of the valley. He and his wife and Dark and Sim were safe in the mouth of their tunnel.

"He'll never make it," said father. "Do not watch him, woman. It's not a good thing to watch."

They turned away. All except Sim, whose eyes had caught a glint of metal far away. His heart hammered in him, and his eyes blurred. Far away, atop a low mountain, one of those metal seeds from space reflected a dazzling ripple of light! It was like one of his intra-embryo dreams fulfilled! A metal space seed, intact, undamaged, lying on a mountain! There was his future! There was his hope for survival! There was where he would go in a few days, when he was—strange thought—a grown man!

The sun plunged into the valley like molten lava.

The little running child screamed, the sun burned, and the screaming stopped.

Sim's mother walked painfully, with sudden age, down the tunnel, paused, reached up, broke off two last icicles that had formed during the night. She handed one to her husband, kept the other. "We will drink one last toast. To you, to the children."

"To *you,*" he nodded to her. "To the children." They lifted the icicles. The warmth melted the ice down into their thirsty mouths.

III

All day the sun seemed to blaze and erupt into the valley. Sim could not see it, but the vivid pictorials in his parents' minds were sufficient evidence of the nature of the day fire. The light ran like mercury, sizzling and roasting the caves, poking inward, but never penetrating deeply enough. It lighted the caves. It made the hollows of the cliff comfortably warm.

Sim fought to keep his parents young. But no matter how hard he fought with mind and image, they became like mummies before him. His father seemed to dissolve from one stage of oldness to another. This is what will happen to me soon, thought Sim in terror.

Sim grew upon himself. He felt the digestive-eliminatory movements of his body. He was fed every minute, he was continually swallowing, feeding. He began to fit words to images and processes. Such a word was love. It was not an abstraction, but a process, a stir of breath, a smell of morning air, a flutter of heart, the curve of arm holding him, the look in the suspended face of his mother. He saw the processes, then searched behind her suspended face and there was the word, in her brain, ready to use. His throat prepared to speak. Life was pushing him, rushing him along toward oblivion.

He sensed the expansion of his fingernails, the adjustments of his cells, the profusion of his hair, the multiplication of his bones and sinew, the grooving of the soft pale wax of his brain. His brain at birth was clear as a circle of ice, innocent, unmarked, was, an instant later, as if hit with a thrown rock, cracked and marked and patterned in a million crevices of thought and discovery.

His sister, Dark, ran in and out with other little hot-house children, forever eating. His mother trembled over him, not eating, she had no appetite, her eyes were webbed shut.

"Sunset," said his father, at last.

The day was over. The light faded, a wind sounded.

His mother arose. "I want to see the outside world once more . . . just once more. . . ." She stared blindly, shivering.

His father's eyes were shut, he lay against the wall.

"I cannot rise," he whispered faintly. "I cannot."

"Dark!" The mother croaked, the girl came running. "Here," and Sim was handed to the girl. "Hold to Sim, Dark, feed him, care for him." She gave Sim one last fondling touch.

Dark said not a word, holding Sim, her great green eyes shining wetly.

"Go now," said the mother. "Take him out into the sunset time. Enjoy yourselves. Pick foods, eat. Play."

Dark walked away without looking back. Sim twisted in her grasp, looking over her shoulder with unbelieving, tragic eyes. He cried out and somehow summoned from his lips the first word of his existence:

"Why . . . ?"

He saw his mother stiffen. "The child spoke!"

"Aye," said his father. "Did you hear what he said?"

"I heard," said the mother quietly.

The last thing Sim saw of his living parents was his mother weakly, swayingly, slowly moving across the floor to lie beside her silent husband. That was the last time he ever saw them move.

IV

The night came and passed and then started the second day.

The bodies of all those who had died during the night were carried in a funeral procession to the top of a small hill. The procession was long, the bodies numerous.

Dark walked in the procession, holding the newly walking Sim by one hand. Only an hour before dawn Sim had learned to walk.

At the top of the hill, Sim saw once again the far off metal seed. Nobody ever looked at it, or spoke of it. Why? Was there some reason? Was it a mirage? Why did they not run toward it? Worship it? Try to get to it and fly away into space?

The funeral words were spoken. The bodies were placed upon the ground where the sun, in a few minutes, would cremate them.

The procession then turned and ran down the hill, eager to have their few minutes of free time running and playing and laughing in the sweet air.

Dark and Sim, chattering like birds, feeding among the rocks, exchanged what they knew of life. He was in his second day, she in her third. They were driven, as always, by the mercurial speed of their lives.

Another piece of his life opened wide.

Fifty young men ran down from the cliffs, holding sharp stones and rock daggers in their thick hands. Shouting, they ran off toward distant black, low lines of small rock cliffs.

"War!"

The thought stood in Sim's brain. It shocked and beat at him. These men were running to fight, to kill, over there in those small black cliffs where other people lived.

But why? Wasn't life short enough without fighting, killing?

From a great distance he heard the sound of conflict, and it made his stomach cold. "Why, Dark, why?"

Dark didn't know. Perhaps they would understand tomorrow. Now, there was the business of eating to sustain and support their lives. Watching Dark was like seeing a lizard forever flicking its pink tongue, forever hungry.

Pale children ran on all sides of them. One beetlelike boy scuttled up the rocks, knocking Sim aside, to take from him a particularly luscious red berry he had found growing under an outcrop.

The child ate hastily of the fruit before Sim could gain his feet. Then Sim hurled himself unsteadily, the two of them fell in a ridiculous jumble, rolling, until Dark pried them, squalling, apart.

Sim bled. A part of him stood off, like a god, and said, "This should not be. Children should not be this way. It is wrong!"

Dark slapped the little intruding boy away. "Get on!" she cried. "What's your name, bad one?"

"Chion!" laughed the boy. "Chion, Chion, Chion!"

Sim glared at him with all the ferocity in his small, unskilled features. He choked. This was his enemy. It was as if he'd waited for an enemy of person as well as scene. He had already understood the avalanches, the heat, the cold, the shortness of life, but these were things of places, of scene—mute, extravagant manifestations of unthinking nature, not motivated save by gravity and radiation. Here, now, in this stridulant Chion he recognized a thinking enemy!

Chion darted off, turned at a distance, taunting:

"Tomorrow I will be big enough to kill you!"

And he vanished around a rock.

More children ran, giggling, by Sim. Which of them would be friends, enemies? How could friends and enemies come about in this impossible, quick lifetime? There was no time to make either, was there?

Dark, knowing his thoughts, drew him away. As they searched for food, she whispered fiercely in his ear. "Enemies are made over things like stolen foods; gifts of long grasses make friends. Enemies come, too, from opinions and thoughts. In five seconds you've made an enemy for life. Life's so short enemies must be made quickly." And she laughed with an irony strange for one so young, who was growing older before her rightful time. "You must fight to protect yourself. Others, superstitious ones, will try killing you. There is a belief, a ridiculous belief, that if one kills another, the murderer partakes of the life energy of the slain, and therefore will live an extra day. You see? As long as that is believed, you're in danger."

But Sim was not listening. Bursting from a flock of delicate girls who tomorrow would be tall, quieter, and who day after that would become shapely and the next day take husbands, Sim caught sight of one small girl whose hair was a violet-blue flame.

She ran past, brushed Sim, their bodies touched. Her eyes, white as silver coins, shone at him. He knew then that he'd found a friend, a love, a wife, one who would a week from now lie with him atop the funeral pyre as sunlight undressed their flesh from bone.

Only the glance, but it held them in mid-motion, one instant.

"Your name?" he shouted after her.

"Lyte!" she called laughingly back.

"I'm Sim," he answered, confused and bewildered.

"Sim!" she repeated it, flashing on. "I'll remember!"

Dark nudged his ribs. "Here, *eat,*" she said to the distracted boy. "Eat or you'll never get big enough to catch her."

From nowhere, Chion appeared, running by. "Lyte!" he mocked, dancing malevolently along and away. "Lyte! I'll remember Lyte, too!"

Dark stood tall and reed slender, shaking her dark ebony clouds of hair, sadly. "I see your life before you, little Sim. You'll need weapons soon to fight for this Lyte one. Now, hurry—the sun's coming!"

They ran back to the caves.

V

One-fourth of his life was over! Babyhood was gone. He was now a young boy! Wild rains lashed the valley at nightfall. He watched new river channels cut in the valley, out past the mountain of the metal seed. He stored the knowledge for later use. Each night there was a new river, a bed newly cut.

"What's beyond the valley?" wondered Sim.

"No one's ever been beyond it," explained Dark. "All who tried to reach the plain were frozen to death or burnt. The only land we know's within half an hour's run. Half an hour out and half an hour back."

"No one has ever reached the metal seed, then?"

Dark scoffed. "The Scientists, they try. Silly fools. They don't know enough to stop. It's no use. It's too far."

The Scientists. The word stirred him. He had almost forgotten the vision he had in the moments before and after birth. His voice was eager. "Where are the Scientists?"

Dark looked away from him, "I wouldn't tell you if I knew. They'd kill you, experimenting! I don't want you joining them! Live your life, don't cut it in half trying to reach that silly metal thing on the mountain."

"I'll find out where they are from someone else, then!"

"No one'll tell you! They hate the Scientists. You'll have to find them on your own. And then what? Will you save us? Yes, save us little boy!" Her face was sullen; already half her life was gone.

"We can't just sit and talk and eat," he protested. "And *nothing* else." He leapt up.

"Go find them!" she retorted acidly. "They'll help you forget. Yes, yes," she spat it out. "Forget your life's over in just a few more days!"

Sim ran through the tunnels, seeking. Sometimes he half imagined where the Scientists were. But then a flood of angry thought from those around him, when he asked the direction to the Scientists' cave, washed over him in confusion and resentment. After all, it was the Scientists' fault that they had been placed upon this terrible world! Sim flinched under the bombardment of oaths and curses.

Quietly he took his seat in a central chamber with the children to listen to the grown men talk. This was the time of education, the Time of Talking. No matter how he chafed at delay, or how great his impatience, even though life slipped fast from him and death approached like a black meteor, he knew his mind needed knowledge. Tonight, then, was the night of school. But he sat uneasily. Only *five* more days of life.

Chion sat across from Sim, his thin-mouthed face arrogant.

Lyte appeared between the two. The last few hours had made her firmer footed, gentler, taller. Her hair shone brighter. She smiled as she sat beside Sim, ignoring Chion. And Chion became rigid at this and ceased eating.

The dialogue crackled, filled the room. Swift as heartbeats, one thousand, two thousand words a minute. Sim learned, his head filled. He did not shut his eyes, but lapsed into a kind of dreaming that was almost intraembryonic in lassitude and drowsy vividness. In the faint background the words were spoken, and they wove a tapestry of knowledge in his head.

He dreamed of green meadows free of stones, all grass, round and rolling and rushing easily toward a dawn with no taint of freezing, merciless cold or smell of boiled rock or scorched monument. He walked across the green meadow. Overhead the metal seeds flew by in a heaven that was a steady, even temperature. Things were slow, slow, slow.

Birds lingered upon gigantic trees that took a hundred, two hundred, five thousand days to grow. Everything remained in its place, the birds did not flicker nervously at a hint of sun, nor did the trees suck back frightenedly when a ray of sunlight poured over them.

In this dream people strolled, they rarely ran, the heart rhythm of them was evenly languid, not jerking and insane. The grass remained, and did not burn away in torches. The dream people talked always of tomorrow and living and not tomorrow and dying. It all seemed so familiar that when Sim felt someone take his hand he thought it simply another part of the dream.

Lyte's hand lay inside his own. "Dreaming?" she asked.

"Yes."

"Things are balanced. Our minds, to even things, to balance the unfairness of our living, go back in on ourselves, to find what there is that is good to see."

He beat his hand against the stone floor again and again. "It does not make things fair! I hate it! It reminds me that there is something better, something I have missed! Why can't we be ignorant! Why can't we live and die without knowing that this is an abnormal living?" And his breath rushed harshly from his half-open, constricted mouth.

"There is purpose in everything," said Lyte. "This gives us purpose, makes us work, plan, try to find a way."

His eyes were hot emeralds in his face. "I walked up a hill of grass, very slowly," he said.

"The same hill of grass I walked an hour ago?" asked Lyte.

"Perhaps. Close enough to it. The dream is better than the

reality." He flexed his eyes, narrowed them. "I watched people and they did not eat."

"Or talk?"

"Or talk, either. And we always are eating, always talking. Sometimes those people in the dream sprawled with their eyes shut, not moving a muscle."

As Lyte stared down into his face a terrible thing happened. He imagined her face blackening, wrinkling, twisting into knots of agedness. The hair blew out like snow about her ears, the eyes were like discolored coins caught in a web of lashes. Her teeth sank away from her lips, the delicate fingers hung like charred twigs from her atrophied wrists. Her beauty was consumed and wasted even as he watched, and when he seized her, in terror, he cried out, for he imagined his own hand corroded, and he choked back a cry.

"Sim, what's wrong?"

The saliva in his mouth dried at the taste of the words.

"Five more days . . ."

"The Scientists."

Sim started. Who'd spoken? In the dim light a tall man talked. "The Scientists crashed us on this world, and now have wasted thousands of lives and time. It's no use. It's no use. Tolerate them but give them none of your time. You only live once, remember."

Where were these hated Scientists? Now, after the Learning, the Time of Talking, he was ready to find them. Now, at least, he knew enough to begin his fight for freedom, for the ship!

"Sim, where're you going?"

But Sim was gone. The echo of his running feet died away down a shaft of polished stone.

It seemed that half the night was wasted. He blundered into a dozen dead ends. Many times he was attacked by the insane young men who wanted his life energy. Their superstitious ravings echoed after him. The gashes of their hungry fingernails covered his body.

He found what he looked for.

A half dozen men gathered in a small basalt cave deep down

in the cliff lode. On a table before them lay objects which, though unfamiliar, struck harmonious chords in Sim.

The Scientists worked in sets, old men doing important work, young men learning, asking questions; and at their feet were three small children. They were a process. Every eight days there was an entirely new set of scientists working on any one problem. The amount of work done was terribly inadequate. They grew old, fell dead just when they were beginning their creative period. The creative time of any one individual was perhaps a matter of twelve hours out of his entire span. Three quarters of one's life was spent learning, a brief interval of creative power, then senility, insanity, death.

The men turned as Sim entered.

''Don't tell me we have a recruit?'' said the eldest of them.

''I don't believe it,'' said another, younger one. ''Chase him away. He's probably one of those warmongers.''

''No, no,'' objected the elder one, moving with little shuffles of his bare feet toward Sim. ''Come in, come in, boy.'' He had friendly eyes, slow eyes, unlike those of the swift inhabitants of the upper caves. Gray and quiet. ''What do you want?''

Sim hesitated, lowered his head, unable to meet the quiet, gentle gaze. ''I want to live,'' he whispered.

The old man laughed quietly. He touched Sim's shoulder. ''Are you a new breed? Are you sick?'' he queried of Sim, half seriously. ''Why aren't you playing? Why aren't you readying yourself for the time of love and marriage and children? Don't you know that tomorrow night you'll be almost grown? Don't you realize that if you are not careful you'll miss all of life?'' He stopped.

Sim moved his eyes back and forth with each query. He blinked at the instruments on the table top. ''Shouldn't I be here?'' he asked.

''Certainly,'' roared the old man, sternly. ''But it's a miracle you are. We've had no volunteers from the rank and file for a thousand days! We've had to breed our own scientists, a closed unit! Count us! Six! Six men! And three children! Are we not overwhelming?'' The old man spat upon the stone floor. ''We ask for volunteers and the people shout back at us, 'Get someone else!' or 'We have no time!' And you know why they say that?''

''No.'' Sim flinched.

''Because they're selfish. They'd like to live longer, yes, but they know that anything they do cannot possibly insure their *own* lives any extra time. It might guarantee longer life to some future offspring of theirs. But they won't give up their love, their brief youth, give up one interval of sunset or sunrise!''

Sim leaned against the table, earnestly. ''I understand.''

''You do?'' The old man stared at him blindly. He sighed and slapped the child's arm gently. ''Yes, of course, you do. It's too much to expect anyone to understand, anymore. You're rare.''

The others moved in around Sim and the old man.

''I am Dienc. Tomorrow night Cort here will be in my place. I'll be dead by then. And the night after that someone else will be in Cort's place, and then you, if you work and believe—but first, I give you a chance. Return to your playmates if you want. There is someone you love? Return to her. Life is short. Why should you care for the unborn to come? You have a right to youth. Go now, if you want. Because if you stay you'll have no time for anything but working and growing old and dying at your work. But it is good work. Well?''

Sim looked at the tunnel. From a distance the wind roared and blew, the smells of cooking and the patter of naked feet sounded, and the laughter of young people was an increasingly good thing to hear. He shook his head, impatiently, and his eyes were wet.

''I will stay,'' he said.

VI

The third night and third day passed. It was the fourth night. Sim was drawn into their living. He learned about that metal seed upon the top of the far mountain. He heard of the original seeds—things called ''ships'' that crashed and how the survivors hid and dug in the cliffs, grew old swiftly and in their scrabbling to barely survive, forgot all science. Knowledge of mechanical things had no chance of survival in such a volcanic civilization. There was only NOW for each human.

Yesterday didn't matter, tomorrow stared them vividly in their faces. But somehow the radiations that had forced their aging had also induced a kind of telepathic communication whereby philosophies and impressions were absorbed by the newborn. Racial memory, growing instinctively, preserved memories of another time.

"Why don't we go to that ship on the mountain?" asked Sim.

"It is too far. We would need protection from the sun," explained Dienc.

"Have you tried to make protection?"

"Salves and ointments, suits of stone and bird-wing and, recently, crude metals. None of which worked. In ten thousand more lifetimes perhaps we'll have made a metal in which will flow cool water to protect us on the march to the ship. But we work so slowly, so blindly. This morning, mature, I took up my instruments. Tomorrow, dying, I lay them down. What can one man do in one day? If we had ten thousand men, the problem would be solved. . . ."

"I will go to the ship," said Sim.

"Then you will die," said the old man. A silence had fallen on the room at Sim's words. Then the men stared at Sim. "You are a very selfish boy."

"Selfish!" cried Sim, resentfully.

The old man patted the air. "Selfish in a way I like. You want to live longer, you'll do anything for that. You will try for the ship. But I tell you it is useless. Yet, if you want to, I cannot stop you. At least you will not be like those among us who go to war for an extra few days of life."

"War?" asked Sim. "How can there be war here?"

And a shudder ran through him. He did not understand.

"Tomorrow will be time enough for that," said Dienc. "Listen to me, now."

The night passed.

VII

It was morning. Lyte came shouting and sobbing down a corridor, and ran full into his arms. She had changed again. She was older, again, more beautiful. She was shaking and she held to him. "Sim, they're coming after you!"

Bare feet marched down the corridor, surged inward at the opening. Chion stood grinning there, taller, too, a sharp rock in either of his hands. ''Oh, there you are, Sim!''

''Go away!'' cried Lyte, savagely whirling on him.

''Not until we take Sim with us,'' Chion assured her. Then, smiling at Sim. ''*If* that is, he is with us in the fight.''

Dienc shuffled forward, his eye weakly fluttering, his bird-like hands fumbling in the air. ''Leave!'' he shrilled angrily. ''This boy is a Scientist now. He works with us.''

Chion ceased smiling. ''There is better work to be done. We go now to fight the people in the farthest cliffs.'' His eyes glittered anxiously. ''Of course, you will come with us, Sim?''

''No, no!'' Lyte clutched at his arm.

Sim patted her shoulder, then turned to Chion. ''Why are you attacking these people?''

''There are three extra days for those who go with us to fight.''

''Three extra days! Of living?''

Chion nodded firmly. ''If we win, we live eleven days instead of eight. The cliffs they live in, something about the mineral in it that protects you from radiation! Think of it, Sim, three long, good days of life. Will you join us?''

Dienc interrupted. ''Get along without him. Sim is my pupil!''

Chion snorted. ''Go die, old man. By sunset tonight you'll be charred bone. Who are you to order us? We are young, we want to live longer.''

Eleven days. The words were unbelievable to Sim. Eleven days. Now he understood why there was war. Who wouldn't fight to have his life lengthened by almost half its total. So many more days of living! Yes. Why not, indeed!

''Three extra days,'' called Dienc, stridently, ''*if* you live to enjoy them. If you're not killed in battle. *If. If!* You have never won yet. You have always lost!''

''But this time,'' Chion declared sharply, ''we'll win!''

Sim was bewildered. ''But we are all of the same ancestors. Why don't we all share the best cliffs?''

Chin laughed and adjusted a sharp stone in his hand. 'Those who live in the best cliffs think they are better than us. That is always man's attitude when he has power. The cliffs there, besides, are smaller, there's room for only three hundred people in them."

Three extra days.

"I'll go with you," Sim said to Chion."

"Fine!" Chion was very glad, much too glad at the decision.

Dienc gasped.

Sim turned to Dienc and Lyte. "If I fight, and win, I will be half a mile closer to the Ship. And I'll have three extra days in which to strive to reach the Ship. That seems the only thing for me to do."

Dienc nodded, sadly. "It *is* the only thing. I believe you. Go along now."

"Good-bye," said Sim.

The old man looked surprised, then he laughed as at a little joke on himself. "That's right—I won't see you again, will I? Good-bye, then." And they shook hands.

They went out, Chion, Sim, and Lyte, together, followed by the others, all children growing swiftly into fighting men. And the light in Chion's eyes was not a good thing to see.

Lyte went with him. She chose his rocks for him and carried them. She would not go back, no matter how he pleaded. The sun was just beyond the horizon and they marched across the valley.

"Please, Lyte, go back!"

"And wait for Chion to return?" she said. "He plans that when you die I will be his mate." She shook out her unbelievable blue-white curls of hair defiantly. "But I'll be with you. If you fall, I fall."

Sim's face hardened. He was tall. The world had shrunk during the night. Children packs screamed by hilarious in their food-searching and he looked at them with alien wonder: could it be only four days ago he'd been like these? Strange. There was a sense of many days in his mind, as if he'd really lived a thousand days. There was a dimension of incident and thought so thick, so multicolored, so richly diverse in his head that it was not to be believed so much could happen in so short a time.

The fighting men ran in clusters of two or three. Sim looked ahead at the rising line of small ebon cliffs. This, then, he said to himself, is my fourth day. And still I am no closer to the Ship, or to anything, not even—he heard the light tread of Lyte beside him—not even to her who bears my weapons and picks me ripe berries.

One-half of his life was gone. Or a third of it—If he won this battle. *If.*

He ran easily, lifting, letting fall his legs. This is the day of my physical awareness, as I run I feed, as I feed I grow and as I grow I turn eyes to Lyte with a kind of dizzying vertigo. And she looks upon me with the same gentleness of thought. This is the day of our youth. Are we wasting it? Are we losing it on a dream, a folly?

Distantly he heard laughter. As a child he'd questioned it. Now he understood laughter. This particular laughter was made of climbing high rocks and plucking the greenest blades and drinking the headiest vintage from the morning ices and eating of the rock-fruits and tasting of young lips in new appetite.

They neared the cliffs of the enemy.

He saw the slender erectness of Lyte. The new surprise of her neck where if you touched you could time her pulse; the fingers which cupped in your own were animate and supple and never still; the . . .

Lyte snapped her head to one side. "Look ahead!" she cried. "See what is to come—look only ahead."

He felt that they were racing by part of their lives, leaving their youth on the pathside, without so much as a glance.

"I am blind with looking at stones," he said, running.

"Find new stones, then!"

"I see stones—" His voice grew gentle as the palm of her hand. The landscape floated under him. Everything was like a fine wind, blowing dreamily. "I see stones that make a ravine that lies in a cool shadow where the stone-berries are thick as tears. You touch a boulder and the berries fall in silent red avalanches, and the grass is very tender . . ."

"I do not see it!' She increased her pace, turning her head away.

He saw the floss upon her neck, like the small moss that grows silvery and light on the cool side of pebbles, that stirs if you breathe the lightest breath upon it. He looked upon himself, his hands clenched as he heaved himself forward toward death. Already his hands were veined and youth-swollen.

Lyte handed him food to eat.

"I am not hungry," he said.

"Eat, keep your mouth full," she commanded sharply, "so you will be strong for battle."

"Gods!" He roared, anguished. "Who cares for battles!"

Ahead of them, rocks hailed down, thudding. A man fell with his skull split wide. The war was begun.

Lyte passed the weapons to him. They ran without another word until they entered the killing ground.

The boulders began to roll in a synthetic avalanche from the battlements of the enemy!

Only one thought was in his mind now. To kill, to lessen the life of someone else so he could live, to gain a foothold here and live long enough to make a stab at the ship. He ducked, he weaved, he clutched stones and hurled them up. His left hand held a flat stone shield with which he diverted the swiftly plummeting rocks. There was a spatting sound everywhere. Lyte ran with him, encouraging him. Two men dropped before him, slain, their breasts cleaved to the bone, their blood springing out in unbelievable founts.

It was a useless conflict. Sim realized instantly how insane the venture was. They could never storm the cliff. A solid wall of rocks rained down. A dozen men dropped with shards of ebony in their brains, a half dozen more showed drooping, broken arms. One screamed and the upthrust white joint of his knee was exposed as the flesh was pulled away by two successive blows of well-aimed granite. Men stumbled over one another.

The muscles in his cheeks pulled tight and he began to wonder why he had ever come. But his raised eyes, as he danced from side to side, weaving and bobbing, sought always the cliffs. He wanted to live there so intensely, to have his chance. He would have to stick it out. But the heart was gone from him.

Lyte screamed piercingly. Sim, his heart panicking, twisted and saw that her hand was loose at the wrist, with an ugly wound bleeding profusely on the back of the knuckles. She clamped it under her armpit to soothe the pain. The anger rose in him and exploded. In his fury he raced forward, throwing his missiles with deadly accuracy. He saw a man topple and flail down, falling from one level to another of the caves, a victim of his shot. He must have been screaming, for his lungs were bursting open and closed and his throat was raw, and the ground spun madly under his racing feet.

The stone that clipped his head sent him reeling and plunging back. He ate sand. The universe dissolved into purple whorls. He could not get up. He lay and knew that this was his last day, his last time. The battle raged around him, dimly he felt Lyte over him. Her hands cooled his head, she tried to drag him out of range, but he lay gasping and telling her to leave him.

''Stop!'' shouted a voice. The whole war seemed to give pause. ''Retreat!'' commanded the voice swiftly. And as Sim watched, lying upon his side, him comrades turned and fled toward home.

''The sun is coming, our time is up!'' He saw their muscled backs, their moving, tensing, flickering legs go up and down. The dead were left upon the field. The wounded cried for help. But there was no time for the wounded. There was only time for swift men to run the gauntlet home and, their lungs aching and raw with heated air, burst into their tunnels before the sun burnt and killed them.

The sun!

Sim saw another figure racing toward him. It was Chion! Lyte was helping Sim to his feet, whispering helpfully to him. ''Can you walk?'' she asked. And he groaned and said, ''I think so.'' ''Walk then,'' she said. ''Walk slowly, and then faster and faster. We'll make it, I know we will.''

Sim got to his feet, stood swaying. Chion raced up, a strange expression cutting lines in his cheeks, his eyes shining with battle. Pushing Lyte abruptly aside he seized upon a rock and dealt Sim a jolting blow upon his ankle that laid wide the flesh. All of this was done quite silently.

Now he stood back, still not speaking, grinning like an animal from the night mountains, his chest panting in and out, looking from the thing he had done, to Lyte, and back. He got his breath. ''He'll never make it,'' he nodded at Sim. ''We'll have to leave him here. Come along, Lyte.''

Lyte, like a cat-animal, sprang upon Chion, searching for his eyes, shrieking through her exposed, hard-pressed teeth. Her fingers stroked great bloody furrows down Chion's arms and again, instantly, down his neck. Chion, with an oath, sprang away from her. She hurled a rock at him. Grunting, he let it miss him, then ran off a few yards. ''Fool!'' he cried, turning to scorn her. ''Come along with me. Sim will be dead in a few minutes. Come along!''

Lyte turned her back on him. ''I will go if you carry me.''

Chion's face changed. His eyes lost their gleaming. ''There is no time. We would both die if I carried you.''

Lyte looked through and beyond him. ''Carry me, then, for that's how I wish it to be.''

Without another word, glancing fearfully at the sun, Chion fled. His footsteps sped away and vanished from hearing. ''May he fall and break his neck,'' whispered Lyte, savagely glaring at his form as it skirted a ravine. She returned to Sim. ''Can you walk?''

Agonies of pain shot up his leg from the wounded ankle. He nodded ironically. ''We could make it to the cave in two hours, walking. I have an idea, Lyte. Carry me.'' And he smiled with the grim joke.

She took his arm. ''Nevertheless we'll walk. Come.''

''No,'' he said. ''We're staying here.''

''But why?''

''We came to seek a home here. If we walk we will die. I would rather die here. How much time have we?''

Together they measured the sun. ''A few minutes,'' she said, her voice flat and dull. She held close to him.

The black rocks of the cliff were paling into deep purples and browns as the sun began to flood the world.

What a fool he was! He should have stayed and worked with Dienc, and thought and dreamed.

With the sinews of his neck standing out defiantly he bellowed upward at the cliff holes.

''Send me down one man to do battle!''

Silence. His voice echoed from the cliff. The air was warm.

''It's no use,'' said Lyte. ''They'll pay no attention.''

He shouted again. ''Hear me!'' He stood with his weight on his good foot, his injured left leg throbbing and pulsating with pain. He shook a fist. ''Send down a warrior who is no coward! I will not turn and run home! I have come to fight a fair fight! Send a man who will fight for the right to his cave! Him I will surely kill!''

More silence. A wave of heat passed over the land, receded.

''Oh, surely,'' mocked Sim, hands on naked hips, head back, mouth wide, ''surely there's one among you not afraid to fight a cripple!'' Silence. ''No?'' Silence.

''Then I have miscalculated you. I'm wrong. I'll stand here, then, until the sun shucks the flesh off my bone in black scraps, and call you the filthy names you deserve.''

He got an answer.

''I do not like being called names,'' replied a man's voice.

Sim leaned forward, forgetting his crippled foot.

A huge man appeared in a cave mouth on the third level.

''Come down,'' urged Sim. ''Come down, fat one, and kill me.''

The man scowled seriously at his opponent a moment, then lumbered slowly down the path, his hands empty of any weapons. Immediately every cave above clustered with heads. An audience for this drama.

The man approached Sim. ''We will fight by the rules, if you know them.''

''I'll learn as we go,'' replied Sim.

This pleased the man and he looked at Sim warily, but not unkindly. ''This much I will tell you,'' offered the man generously. ''If you die, I will give your mate shelter and she will live as she pleases, because she is the wife of a good man.''

Sim nodded swiftly. ''I am ready,'' he said.

''The rules are simple. We do not touch each other, save with stones. The stones and the sun will do either of us in. Now is the time—''

VIII

A tip of the sun showed on the horizon. ''My name is Nhoj,'' said Sim's enemy, casually taking up a handful of pebbles and stones, weighing them. Sim did likewise. He was hungry. He had not eaten for many minutes. Hunger was the curse of this planet's peoples—a perpetual demanding of empty stomachs for more, more food. His blood flushed weakly, shot tinglingly through veins in jolting throbs of heat and pressure, his rib cage shoved out, went in, shoved out again, impatiently.

"Now!" roared the three hundred watchers from the cliffs. "Now!" they clamored, the men and women and children balanced, in turmoil on the ledges. "Now! Begin!"

As if at a cue, the sun arose. It smote them a blow as with a flat, sizzling stone. The two men staggered under the molten impact, sweat broke from their naked thighs and loins, under their arms and on their faces was a glaze like fine glass.

Nhoj shifted his huge weight and looked at the sun as if in no hurry to fight. Then, silently, with no warning, he snapped out a pebble with a startling trigger-flick of thumb and forefinger. It caught Sim flat on the cheek, staggered him back, so that a rocket of unbearable pain climbed up his crippled foot and burst into nervous explosion at the pit of his stomach. He tasted blood from his bleeding cheek.

Nhoj moved serenely. Three more flicks of his magical hands and three tiny, seemingly harmless bits of stone flew like whistling birds. Each of them fond a target, slammed it. The nerve centers of Sim's body! One hit his stomach so that ten hours' eating almost slid up his throat. A second got his forehead, a third his neck. He collapsed to the boiling sand. His knee made a wrenching sound on the hard earth. His face was colorless and his eyes, squeezed tight, were pushing tears out from the hot, quivering lids. But even as he had fallen he had let loose, with wild force, his handful of stones!

The stones purred in the air. One of them, and only one, struck Nhoj. Upon the left eyeball. Nhoj moaned and laid his hands in the next instant to his shattered eye.

Sim choked out a bitter, sighing laugh. This much triumph he had. The eye of his opponent. It would give him . . . Time. Oh, gods, he thought, his stomach retching sickly, fighting for breath, this is a world of time. Give me a little more, just a trifle!

Nhoj, one-eyed, weaving with pain, pelted the writhing body

of Sim, but his aim was off now, the stones flew to one side or if they struck at all they were weak and spent and lifeless.

Sim forced himself half erect. From the corners of his eyes he saw Lyte, waiting, staring at him, her lips breathing words of encouragement and hope. He was bathed in sweat, as if a rain spray had showered him down.

The sun was now fully over the horizon. You could smell it. Stones glinted like mirrors, the sand began to roil and bubble. Illusions sprang up everywhere in the valley. Instead of one warrior Nhoj he was confronted by a dozen, each in an upright position, preparing to launch another missile. A dozen irregular warriors who shimmered in the golden menace of day, like bronze gongs smitten, quivered in one vision!

Sim was breathing desperately. His nostrils flared and sucked and his mouth drank thirstily of flame instead of oxygen. His lungs took fire like silk torches and his body was consumed. The sweat spilled from his pores to be instantly evaporated. He felt himself shriveling, shriveling in on himself, he imagined himself looking like his father, old, sunken, slight, withered! Where was the sand? Could he move? Yes. The world wriggled under him, but now he was on his feet.

There would be no more fighting.

A murmur from the cliff told this. The sunburnt faces of the high audience gaped and jeered and shouted encouragement to their warrior. "Strand straight, Nhoj, save your strength now! Stand tall and perspire!" they urged him, and Nhoj stood, swaying lightly, swaying slowly, a pendulum in an incandescent fiery breath from the skyline. "Don't move, Nhoj, save your heart, save your power!"

"The Test, The Test!" said the people on the heights. "The test of the sun."

And this was the worst part of the fight. Sim squinted painfully at the distorted illusion of cliff. He thought he saw his parents; father with his defeated face, his green eyes burning, mother with her hair blowing like a cloud of gray smoke in the fire wind. He must get up to them, live for and with them!

Behind him, Sim heard Lyte whimper softly. There was a whisper of flesh against sand. She had fallen. He did not dare turn. The strength of turning would bring him thundering down in pain and darkness.

His knees bent. If I fall, he thought, I'll lie here and become ashes. Where was Nhoj? Nhoj was there, a few yards from him, standing bent, slick with perspiration, looking as if he were being hit over the spine with great hammers of destruction.

"Fall, Nhoj! Fall!" thought Sim. "Fall, fall! Fall so I can take your place!"

But Nhoj did not fall. One by one the pebbles in his half-loose left hand plummeted to the broiling sand and Nhoj's lips peeled back, the saliva burned away from his lips and his eyes glazed. But he did not fall. The will to live was strong in him. He hung as if by a wire.

Sim fell to one knee!

"Ahh!" wailed the knowing voices from the cliff. They were watching death. Sim jerked his head up, smiling mechanically, foolishly as if caught in the act of doing something silly. "No, no," he insisted drowsily, and got back up again. There was so much pain he was all one ringing numbness. A whirring, buzzing, frying sound filled the land. High up, an avalanche came down like a curtain on a drama, making no noise. Everything was quiet except for a steady humming. He saw fifty images of Nhoj now, dressed in armors of sweat, eyes puffed with torture, cheeks sunken, lips peeled back like the rind of a drying fruit. But the wire still held him.

"Now," muttered Sim, sluggishly, with a thick, baked tongue between his blazing teeth. "Now I'll fall and lie and dream." He said it with slow, thoughtful pleasure. He planned it. He knew how it must be done. He would do it accurately. He lifted his head to see if the audience was watching.

They were gone!

The sun had driven them back in. All save one or two brave ones. Sim laughed drunkenly and watched the sweat gather on his dead hands, hesitate, drop off, plunge down toward sand and turn to steam halfway there.

Nhoj fell.

The wire was cut. Nhoj fell flat upon his stomach, a gout of blood kicked from his mouth. His eyes rolled back into a white, senseless insanity.

Nhoj fell. So did his fifty duplicate illusions.

All across the valley the winds sang and moaned and Sim saw a blue lake with a blue river feeding it and low white houses near the river with people going and coming in the houses and among the tall green trees. Trees taller than seven men, beside the river mirage.

"Now," explained Sim to himself at last, "Now I can fall. Right—into—that—lake."

He fell forward.

He was shocked when he felt the hands eagerly stop him in mid-plunge, lift him, hurry him off, high in the hungry air, like a torch held and waved, ablaze.

"How strange is death," he thought, and blackness took him.

He wakened to the flow of cool water on his cheeks.

He opened his eyes fearfully. Lyte held his head upon her lap, her fingers were moving food to his mouth. He was tremendously hungry and tired, but fear squeezed both of these things away. He struggled upward, seeing the strange cave contours overhead.

"What time is it?" he demanded.

"The same day as the contest. Be quiet," she said.

"The same day!"

She nodded amusedly. "You've lost nothing of your life. This is Nhoj's cave. We are inside the black cliff. We will live three extra days. Satisfied? Lie down."

"Nhoj is dead?" He fell back, panting, his heart slamming his ribs. He relaxed slowly. "I won. I won," he breathed.

"Nhoj is dead. So were we, almost. They carried us in from outside only in time."

He ate ravenously. "We have no time to waste. We must get strong. My leg—" He looked at it, tested it. There was a swath of long yellow grasses around it and the ache had died away. Even as he watched, the terrific pulsings of his body went to work and cured away the impurities under the bandages. It *has* to be strong by sunset, he thought. It *has* to be.

He got up and limped around the cave like a captured animal. He felt Lyte's eyes upon him. He could not meet her gaze. Finally, helplessly, he turned.

She interrupted him. "You want to go on to the ship?" she asked, softly. "Tonight? When the sun goes down?"

He took a breath, exhaled it. "Yes."

"You couldn't possibly wait until morning?"

"No."

"Then I'll go with you."

"No!"

"If I lag behind, let me. There's nothing here for me."

They stared at each other a long while. He shrugged wearily.

"All right," he said, at last. "I couldn't stop you, I know that. We'll go together."

IX

They waited in the mouth of their new cave. The sun set. The stones cooled so that one could walk on them. It was almost time for the leaping out and the running toward the distant, glittering metal seed that lay on the far mountain.

Soon would come the rains. And Sim thought back over all the times he had watched the rains thicken into creeks, into rivers that cut new beds each night. One night there would be a river running north, the next a river running northeast, the third night a river running due west. The valley was continually cut and scarred by the torrents. Earthquakes and avalanches filled the old beds. New ones were the order of the day. It was this idea of the river and the directions of the river that he had turned over in his head for many hours. It might possibly—Well, he would wait and see.

He noticed how living in this new cliff had slowed his pulse, slowed everything. A mineral result, protection against the solar radiations. Life was still swift, but not as swift as before.

"Now, Sim!" cried Lyte.

They ran. Between the hot death and the cold one. Together, away from the cliffs, out toward the distant, beckoning ship.

Never had they run this way in their lives. The sound of their feet running was a hard, insistent clatter over vast oblongs of rock, down into ravines, up the sides, and on again. They raked the air in and out of their lungs. Behind them the cliffs faded into things they could never turn back to now.

They did not eat as they ran. They had eaten to the bursting point in the cave, to save time. Now it was only running, a lifting of legs, a balancing of bent elbows, a convulsion of muscles, a slaking in of air that had been fiery and was now cooling.

''Are they watching us?''

Lyte's breathless voice snatched at his ears above the pound of his heart.

''Who? But he knew the answer. The cliff peoples, of course. How long had it been since a race like this one? A thousand days? Ten thousand? How long since someone had taken the chance and sprinted with an entire civilization's eyes upon their backs, into gullies, across cooling plain. Were there lovers pausing in their laughter back there, gazing at the two tiny dots that were a man and woman running toward destiny? Were children eating of new fruits and stopping in their play to see the two people racing against time? Was Dienc still living, narrowing hairy eyebrows down over fading eyes, shouting them on in a feeble, rasping voice, shaking a twisted hand? Were there jeers? Were they being called fools, idiots? And in the midst of the name-calling, were people praying them on, hoping they would reach the ship?

Sim took a quick glance at the sky, which was beginning to bruise with the coming night. Out of nowhere clouds materialized and a light shower trailed across a gully two hundred yards ahead of them. Lightning beat upon distant mountains and there was a strong scent of ozone on the disturbed air.

''The halfway mark,'' panted Sim, and he saw Lyte's face half turn, longingly looking back at the life she was leaving. ''Now's the time, if we want to turn back, we still have time. Another minute—''

Thunder snarled in the mountains. An avalanche started out small and ended up huge and monstrous in a deep fissure. Light rain dotted Lyte's smooth white skin. In a minute her hair was glistening and soggy with rain.

''Too late, now,'' she shouted over the patting rhythm of her own naked feet. ''We've got to go ahead!''

And it was too late. Sim knew, judging the distances, that there was no turning back now.

His leg began to pain him. He favored it, slowing. A wind

came up swiftly. A cold wind that bit into the skin. But it came from the cliffs behind them, helped rather than hindered them. An omen? he wondered. No.

For as the minutes went by it grew upon him how poorly he had estimated the distance. Their time was dwindling out, but they were still an impossible distance from the ship. He said nothing, but the impotent anger at the slow muscles in his legs welled up into bitterly hot tears in his eyes.

He knew that Lyte was thinking the same as himself. But she flew along like a white bird, seeming hardly to touch ground. He heard her breath go out and in her throat, like a clean, sharp knife in its sheath.

Half the sky was dark. The first stars were peering through lengths of black cloud. Lightning jiggled a path along a rim just ahead of them. A full thunderstorm of violent rain and exploding electricity fell upon them.

They slipped and skidded on moss-smooth pebbles. Lyte fell, scrambled up again with a burning oath. Her body was scarred and dirty. The rain washed over her.

The rain came down and cried on Sim. It filled his eyes and ran in rivers down his spine and he wanted to cry with it.

Lyte fell and did not rise, sucking her breath, her breasts quivering.

He picked her up and held her. "Run, Lyte, please, run!"

"Leave me, Sim. Go ahead!" The rain filled her mouth. There was water everywhere. "It's no use. Go on without me."

He stood there, cold and powerless, his thoughts sagging, the flame of hope blinking out. All the world was blackness, cold falling sheaths of water, and despair.

"We'll walk, then," he said. "And keep walking, and resting."

They walked for fifty yards, easily, slowly, like children out for a stroll. The gully ahead of them filled with water that went sliding away with a swift wet sound, toward the horizon.

Sim cried out. Tugging at Lyte he raced forward. "A new channel," he said, pointing. "Each day the rain cuts a new channel. Here, Lyte!" He leaned over the floodwaters.

He dived in, taking her with him.

The flood swept them like bits of wood. They fought to stay

upright, the water got into their mouths, their noses. The land swept by on both sides of them. Clutching Lyte's fingers with insane strength, Sim felt himself hurled end over end, saw flicks of lightning on high, and a new fierce hope was born in him. They could no longer run—well, then they would let the water do the running for them.

With a speed that dashed them against rocks, split open their shoulders, abraded their legs, the new, brief river carried them. "This way!" Sim shouted over a salvo of thunder and steered frantically toward the opposite side of the gully. The mountain where the ship lay was just ahead. They must not pass it by. They fought in the transporting liquid and were slammed against the far side. Sim leaped up, caught at an overhanging rock, locked Lyte in his legs, and drew himself hand over hand upward.

As quickly as it had come, the storm was gone. The lightning faded. The rain ceased. The clouds melted and fell away over the sky. The wind whispered into silence.

"The ship!" Lyte lay upon the ground. "The ship, Sim. This is the mountain of the ship!"

Now the cold came. The killing cold.

They forced themselves drunkenly up the mountain. The cold slid along their limbs, got into their arteries like a chemical and slowed them.

Ahead of them, with a fresh-washed sheen, lay the ship. It was a dream. Sim could not believe that they were actually so near it. Two hundred yards. One hundred and seventy yards.

The ground became covered with ice. They slipped and fell again and again. Behind them the river was frozen into a blue-white snake of cold solidity. A few last drops of rain from somewhere came down as hard pellets.

Sim fell against the bulk of the ship. He was actually touching it. Touching it! He heard Lyte whimpering in her constricted throat. This was the metal, the ship. How many others had touched it in the long days? He and Lyte had made it!

Then, as cold as the air, his veins were chilled.

Where was the entrance?

You run, you swim, you almost drown, you curse, you sweat, you work, you reach a mountain, you go up it, you hammer on metal, you shout with relief, and then—you can't find the entrance.

He fought to control himself. Slowly, he told himself, but not too slowly, go around the ship. The metal slid under his searching hands, so cold that his hands, sweating, almost froze to it. Now, far around to the side. Lyte moved with him. The cold held them like a fist. It began to squeeze.

The entrance.

Metal. Cold, immutable metal. A thin line of opening at the sealing point. Throwing all caution aside, he beat at it. He felt his stomach seething with cold. His fingers were numb, his eyes were half frozen in their sockets. He began to beat and search and scream against the metal door. "Open up! Open up!" He staggered. He had struck something . . . A *click!*

The air lock sighed. With a whispering of metal on rubber beddings, the door swung softly sidewise and vanished back.

He saw Lyte run forward, clutch at her throat, and drop inside a small shiny chamber. He shuffled after her, blankly.

The air-lock door sealed shut behind him.

He could not breathe. His heart began to slow, to stop.

They were trapped inside the ship now, and something was happening. He sank down to his knees and choked for air.

The ship he had come to for salvation was now slowing his pulse, darkening his brain, poisoning him. With a starved, faint kind of expiring terror, he realized that he was dying.

Blackness.

He had a dim sense of time passing, of thinking, struggling, to make his heart go quick, quick. . . . To make his eyes focus. But the fluid in his body lagged quietly through his settling veins and he heard his pulses thud, pause, thud, pause and thud again with lulling intermissions.

He could not move, not a hand or leg or finger. It was an effort to lift the tonnage of his eyelashes. He could not shift his face even, to see Lyte lying beside him.

From a distance came her irregular breathing. It was like the sound a wounded bird makes with his dry, unraveled pinions. She was so close he could almost feel the heat of her; yet she seemed a long way removed.

I'm getting cold! he thought. Is this death? This slowing of blood, of my heart, this cooling of my body, this drowsy thinking of thoughts?

Staring at the ship's ceiling he traced its intricate system of tubes and machines. The knowledge, the purpose of the ship, its actions, seeped into him. He began to understand in a kind of revealing lassitude just what these things were his eyes rested upon. Slow. Slow.

There was an instrument with a gleaming white dial.

Its purpose?

He drudged away at the problem, like a man underwater.

People had used the dial. Touched it. People had repaired it. Installed it. People had dreamed of it before the building, before the installing, before the repairing and touching and using. The dial contained memory of use and manufacture, its very shape was a dream-memory telling Sim why and for what it had been built. Given time, looking at anything, he could draw from it the knowledge he desired. Some dim part of him reached out, dissected the contents of things, analyzed them.

This dial measured time!

Millions of hours of time!

But how could that be? Sim's eyes dilated, hot and glittering. Where were humans who needed such an instrument?

Blood thrummed and beat behind his eyes. He closed them.

Panic came to him. The day was passing. I am lying here, he thought, and my life slips away. I cannot move. My youth is passing. How long before I can move?

Through a kind of porthole he saw the night pass, the day come, the day pass, and again another night. Stars danced frostily.

I will lie here for four or five days, wrinkling and withering, he thought. This ship will not let me move. How much better if I had stayed in my home cliff, lived, enjoyed this short life. What good has it done to come here? I'm missing all the twilights and dawns. I'll never touch Lyte, though she's here at my side.

Delirium. His mind floated up. His thoughts whirled through the metal ship. He smelled the razor-sharp smell of joined metal. He heard the hull contract with night, relax with day.

Dawn.

Already—another dawn!

Today I would have been fully grown. His jaw clenched. I must get up. I must move. I must enjoy this time.

But he didn't move. He felt his blood pump sleepily from chamber to red chamber in his heart, on down and around through his dead body, to be purified by his folding and unfolding lungs.

The ship grew warm. From somewhere a machine clicked. Automatically the temperature cooled. A controlled gust of air flushed the room.

Night again. And then another day.

He lay and saw four days of his life pass.

He did not try to fight. It was no use. His life was over.

He didn't want to turn his head now. He didn't want to see Lyte with her face like his tortured mother's—eyelids like gray ash flakes, eyes like beaten, sanded metal, cheeks like eroded stones. He didn't want to see a throat like parched thongs of yellow grass, hands the pattern of smoke risen from a fire, breasts like desiccated rinds and hair stubbly and unshorn as moist gray weeds!

And himself? How did *he* look? Was his jaw sunken, the flesh of his eyes pitted, his brow lined and age-scarred?

His strength began to return. He felt his heart beating so slow that it was amazing. One hundred beats a minute. Impossible. He felt so cool, so thoughtful, so easy.

His head fell over to one side. He stared at Lyte. He shouted in surprise.

She was young and fair.

She was looking at him, too weak to say anything. Her eyes were like tiny silver medals, her throat curved like the arm of a child. Her hair was blue fire eating at her scalp, fed by the slender life of her body.

Four days had passed and still she was young . . . no, younger than when they had entered the ship. She was still adolescent.

He could not believe it.

Her first words were, "How long will this last?"

He replied, carefully, "I don't know."

"We are still young."

"The ship. Its metal is around us. It cuts away the sun and the things that came from the sun to age us."

Her eyes shifted thoughtfully. "Then, if we stay here—"

"We'll remain young."

"Six more days? Fourteen more? Twenty?"

"More than that, maybe."

She lay there, silently. After a long time she said, "Sim?"

'Yes."

"Let's stay here. Let's not go back. If we go back now, you know what'll happen to us . . . ?"

"I'm not certain."

"We'll start getting old again, won't we?"

He looked away. He stared at the ceiling and the clock with the moving finger. "Yes. We'll grow old."

"What if we grow old—instantly. When we step from the ship won't the shock be too much?"

"Maybe."

Another silence. He began to move his limbs, testing them. He was very hungry. "The others are waiting," he said.

Her next words made him gasp. "The others are dead," she said. "Or will be in a few hours. All those we knew back there are old."

He tried to picture them old. Dark, his sister, bent and senile with time. He shook his head, wiping the picture away. "They may die," he said. "But there are others who've been born."

"People we don't even know."

"But, nevertheless, *our* people," he replied. "People who'll live only eight days, or eleven days unless we help them."

"But we're *young,* Sim! We can *stay* young!"

He didn't want to listen. It was too tempting a thing to listen to. To stay here. To live. "We've already had more time than the others," he said. "I need workers. Men to heal this ship. We'll get on our feet now, you and I, and find food, eat, and see if the ship is movable. I'm afraid to try to move it myself. It's so big. I'll need help."

"But that means running back all that distance!"

"I know." He lifted himself weakly. "But I'll do it."

"How will you get the men back here?"

"We'll use the river."

"*If* it's there. It *may* be somewhere else."

"We'll wait until there *is* one, then. I've got to go back, Lyte. The son of Dienc is waiting for me, my sister, your brother, are old people, ready to die, and waiting for some word from us—"

After a long while he heard her move, dragging herself tiredly to him. She put her head upon his chest, her eyes closed, stroking his arm. "I'm sorry. Forgive me. You have to go back. I'm a selfish fool."

He touched her cheek, clumsily. "You're human. I understand you. There's nothing to forgive."

They found food. They walked through the ship. It was empty. Only in the control room did they find the remains of a man who must have been the chief pilot. The others had evidently bailed out into space in emergency lifeboats. This pilot, sitting at his controls, alone, had landed the ship on a mountain within sight of other fallen and smashed crafts. Its location on high ground had saved it from the floods. The pilot himself had died, probably of heart failure, soon after landing. The ship had remained here, almost within reach of the other survivors, perfect as an egg, but silent, for—how many thousand days? If the pilot had lived, what a different thing life might have been for the ancestors of Sim and Lyte. Sim, thinking of this, felt the distant, ominous vibration of war. How had the war between worlds come out? Who had won? Or had both planets lost and never bothered trying to pick up survivors? Who had been right? Who was the enemy? Were Sim's people of the guilty or innocent side? They might never know.

He checked the ship hurriedly. He knew nothing of its workings, yet as he walked its corridors, patted its machines, he learned from it. It needed only a crew. One man couldn't possibly set the whole thing running again. He laid his hand upon one round, snoutlike machine. He jerked his hand away, as if burnt.

"Lyte!"

"What is it?"

He touched the machine again, caressed it, his hand trembled violently, his eyes welled with tears, his mouth opened and closed, he looked at the machine, loving it, then looked at Lyte.

"With this machine—" he stammered, softly, incredulously. "With— With this machine I can—"

"What, Sim?"

He inserted his hand into a cuplike contraption with a lever inside. Out of the porthole in front of him he could see the distant line of cliffs. "We were afraid there might never be another river running by this mountain, weren't we?" he asked, exultantly.

"Yes, Sim, but—"

"There *will* be a river. And I *will* come back, tonight! And I'll bring men with me. Five hundred men! Because with this machine I can blast a river bottom all the way to the cliffs, down which the waters will rush, giving myself and the men a swift, sure way of traveling back!" He rubbed the machine's barrellike body. "When I touched it, the life and method of it burnt into me! Watch!" He depressed the lever.

A beam of incandescent fire lanced out from the ship, screaming.

Steadily, accurately, Sim began to cut away a riverbed for the storm waters to flow in. The night was turned to day by its hungry eating.

The return to the cliffs was to be carried out by Sim alone. Lyte was to remain in the ship, in case of any mishap. The trip back seemed, at first glance, to be impossible. There would be no river rushing to cut his time, to sweep him along toward his destination. He would have to run the entire distance in the dawn, and the sun would get him, catch him before he'd reached safety.

"The only way to do it is to start *before* sunrise."

"But you'd be frozen, Sim."

"Here?" He made adjustments on the machine that had just finished cutting the riverbed in the rock floor of the valley. He lifted the smooth snout of the gun, pressed the lever, left it down. A gout of fire shot toward the cliffs. He fingered the range control, focused the flame end three miles from its source. Done. He turned to Lyte. "But I don't understand," she said.

He opened the air-lock door. "It's bitter cold out, and half an hour yet till dawn. If I run parallel to the flame from the machine, close enough to it, there'll not be much heat, but enough to sustain life, anyway.''

''It doesn't sound safe,'' Lyte protested.

''*Nothing* does, on this world.'' He moved forward. ''I'll have a half-hour start. That should be enough to reach the cliffs.''

'But if the machine should fail while you're still running near its beam?''

''Let's not think of that,'' he said.

A moment later he was outside. He staggered as if kicked in the stomach. His heart almost exploded in him. The environment of his world forced him into swift living again. He felt his pulse rise, kicking through his veins.

The night was cold as death. The heat ray from the ship sliced across the valley, humming, solid and warm. He moved next to it, very close. One misstep in his running and—

''I'll be back,'' he called to Lyte.

He and the ray of light went together.

In the early morning the people in the caves saw the long finger of orange incandescence and the weird whitish apparition floating, running along beside it. There was muttering and moaning and many sighs of awe.

And when Sim finally reached the cliffs of his childhood he saw alien peoples swarming there. There were no familiar faces. Then he realized how foolish it was to expect familiar faces. One of the older men glared down at him. ''Who're you?'' he shouted. ''Are you from the enemy cliff? What's your name?''

''I am Sim, the son of Sim!''

''Sim!''

An old woman shrieked from the cliff above him. She came hobbling down the stone pathway. ''Sim, Sim, it *is* you!''

He looked at her frankly bewildered. ''But I don't know you,'' he murmured.

''Sim, don't you recognize me? Oh, Sim, it's me! Dark!''

''Dark!''

He felt sick at his stomach. She fell into his arms. This old, trembling woman with the half-blind eyes, his sister.

Another face appeared above. That of an old man. A cruel,

bitter face. It looked down at Sim and snarled. "Drive him away!" cried the old man. "He comes from the cliff of the enemy. He's lived there! He's still young! Those who go there can never come back among us. Disloyal beast!" And a rock hurtled down.

Sim leaped aside, pulling the old woman with him.

A roar came from the people. They ran toward Sim, shaking their fists. "Kill him, kill him!" raved the old man, and Sim did not know who he was.

"Stop!" Sim held out his hands. "I come from the ship!"

"The ship?" The people slowed. Dark clung to him looking up into his young face, puzzling over its smoothness.

"Kill him, kill him, kill him!" croaked the old man, and picked up another rock.

"I offer you ten days, twenty days, thirty more days of life!"

The people stopped. Their mouths hung open. Their eyes were incredulous.

"Thirty days?" It was repeated again and again. "How?"

"Come back to the ship with me. Inside it, one can live forever!"

The old man lifted high a rock, then, choking, fell forward in an apoplectic fit, and tumbled down the rocks to lie at Sim's feet.

Sim bent to peer at the ancient one, at the raw, dead eyes, the loose, sneering lips, the crumpled, quiet body.

"Chion!"

"Yes," said Dark behind him, in a croaking, strange voice. "Your enemy. Chion."

That night two hundred men started for the ship. The water ran in the new channel. One hundred of them were drowned or lost behind in the cold. The others, with Sim, got through to the ship.

Lyte awaited them, and threw wide the metal door.

The weeks passed. Generations lived and died in the cliffs, while the scientists and workers labored over the ship, learning its functions and its parts.

On the last day, two dozen men moved to their stations within the ship. Now there was a destiny of travel ahead.

Sim touched the control plates under his fingers.

Lyte, rubbing her eyes, came and sat on the floor next to him, resting her head against his knee, drowsily. "I had a dream," she said, looking off at something far away. "I dreamed I lived in caves in a cliff on a cold-hot planet where people grew old and died in eight days."

"What an impossible dream," said Sim. "People couldn't possibly live in such a nightmare. Forget it. You're awake now."

He touched the plates gently. The ship rose and moved into space.

Sim was right.

The nightmare was over at last.

Uncle Einar

"It will take only a minute," said Uncle Einar's sweet wife.

"I refuse," he said. "And that takes but a *second.*"

"I've worked all morning," she said, holding to her slender back, "and you won't help? It's drumming for a rain."

"Let it rain," he cried, morosely. "I'll not be pierced by lightning just to air your clothes."

"But you're so quick at it."

'Again, I refuse." His vast tarpaulin wings hummed nervously behind his indignant back.

She gave him a slender rope on which were tied four dozen fresh-washed clothes. He turned it in his fingers with distaste. "So it's come to this," he muttered, bitterly. "To this, to this, to this." He almost wept angry and acid tears.

"Don't cry; you'll wet them down again," she said. "Jump up, now, run them about."

"Run them about." His voice was hollow, deep, and terribly wounded. "I say: let it thunder, let it pour!"

"If it was a nice, sunny day I wouldn't ask," she said, reasonably. "All my washing gone for nothing if you don't. They'll hang about the house—"

That *did* it. Above all, he hated clothes flagged and festooned so a man had to creep under on the way across a room. He jumped up. His vast green wings boomed. "Only so far as the pasture fence!"

Whirl: up he jumped, his wings chewed and loved the cool

air. Before you'd say Uncle Einar Has Green Wings he sailed low across his farmland, trailing the clothes in a vast fluttering loop through the pounding concussion and backwash of his wings!

"Catch!"

Back from the trip, he sailed the clothes; dry as popcorn, down on a series of clean blankets she'd spread for their landing.

"Thank you!" she cried.

"Gahh!" he shouted, and flew off under the apple tree to brood.

Uncle Einar's beautiful silk-like wings hung like sea-green sails behind him, and whirred and whispered from his shoulders when he sneezed or turned swiftly. He was one of the few in the Family whose talent was visible. All his dark cousins and nephews and brothers hid in small towns across the world, did unseen mental things or things with witch-fingers and white teeth, or blew down the sky like fire-leaves, or loped in forests like moon-silvered wolves. They lived comparatively safe from normal humans. Not so a man with great green wings.

Not that he hated his wings. Far from it! In his youth he'd always flown nights, because nights were rare times for winged men! Daylight held dangers, always had, always would; but nights, ah, nights, he had sailed over islands of cloud and seas of summer sky. With no danger to himself. It had been a rich, full soaring, an exhilaration.

But now he could not fly at night.

On his way home to some high mountain pass in Europe after a Homecoming among Family members in Mellin Town, Illinois (some years ago) he had drunk too much rich crimson wine. "I'll be all right," he had told himself, vaguely, as he beat his long way under the morning stars, over the moon-dreaming country hills beyond Mellin Town. And then—crack out of the sky—

A high-tension tower.

Liked a netted duck! A great sizzle! His face blown black by a blue sparkler of wire, he fended off the electricity with a terrific back-jumping percussion of his wings, and fell.

His hitting the moonlit meadow under the tower made a noise like a large telephone book dropped from the sky.

Early the next morning, his dew-sodden wings shaking violently, he stood up. It was still dark. There was a faint bandage of dawn stretched across the east. Soon the bandage would stain and all flight would be restricted. There was nothing to do but take refuge in the forest and wait out the day in the deepest thicket until another night gave his wings a hidden motion in the sky.

In this fashion he met his wife.

During the day, which was warm for November first in Illinois country, pretty young Brunilla Wexley was out to udder a lost cow, for she carried a silver pail in one hand as she sidled through thickets and pleaded cleverly to the unseen cow to please return home or burst her gut with unplucked milk. The fact that the cow would have most certainly come home when her teats really needed pulling did not concern Brunilla Wexley. It was a sweet excuse for forest-journeying, thistle-blowing, and flower chewing; all of which Brunilla was doing as she stumbled upon Uncle Einar.

Asleep near a bush, he seemed a man under a green shelter.

"Oh," said Brunilla, with a fever. "A man. In a camp-tent."

Uncle Einar awoke. The camp-tent spread like a large green fan behind him.

"Oh," said Brunilla, the cow-searcher. "A man with wings."

That was how she took it. She was startled, yes, but she had never been hurt in her life, so she wasn't afraid of anyone, and it was a fancy thing to see a winged man and she was proud to meet him. She began to talk. In an hour they were old friends, and in two hours she'd quite forgotten his wings were there. And he somehow confessed how he happened to be in this wood.

"Yes, I noticed you looked banged around," she said. "That right wing looks very bad. You'd best let me take you home and fix it. You won't be able to fly all the way to Europe on it, anyway. And who wants to live in Europe these days?"

He thanked her, but he didn't quite see how he could accept.

"But I live alone," she said. "For, as you see, I'm quite ugly."

He insisted she was not.

''How kind of you,'' she said. ''But I am, there's no fooling myself. My folks are dead, I've a farm, a big one, all to myself, quite far from Mellin Town, and I'm in need of talking company.''

But wasn't she afraid of him? he asked.

''Proud and jealous would be more near it,'' she said. ''*May* I?'' And she stroked his large green membraned veils with careful envy. He shuddered at the touch and put his tongue between his teeth.

So there was nothing for it but that he come to her house for medicaments and ointments, and my! what a burn across his face, beneath his eyes! ''Lucky you weren't blinded,'' she said. ''How'd it happen?''

''Well . . .'' he said, and they were at her farm, hardly noticing they'd walked a mile, looking at each other.

A day passed, and another, and he thanked her at her door and said he must be going, he much appreciated the ointment, the care, the lodgings. It was twilight and between now, six o'clock, and five the next morning, he must cross an ocean and a continent. ''Thank you; good-bye,'' he said, and started to fly off in the dusk and crashed right into a maple tree.

''Oh!'' she screamed, and ran to his unconscious body.

When he waked the next hour he knew he'd fly no more in the dark again ever; his delicate night-perception was gone. The winged telepathy that had warned him where towers, trees, houses and hills stood across his path, the fine clear vision and sensibility that guided him through mazes of forest, cliff, and cloud, all were burnt forever by that strike across his face, that blue electric fry and sizzle.

''How?'' he moaned softly. ''How can I go to Europe? If I flew by day, I'd be seen and—miserable joke—maybe shot down! Or kept for a zoo perhaps, what a life *that'd* be! Brunilla, tell me, what shall I do?''

''Oh,'' she whispered, looking at her hands. ''We'll think of something . . .''

They were married.

The Family came for the wedding. In a great autumnal avalanche of maple, sycamore, oak, elm leaf they hissed and rustled, fell in a shower of horse chestnut, thumped like winter apples on the earth, with an overall scent of farewell-summer on the wind they made in their rushing. The ceremony? The ceremony was brief as a black candle lit, blown out, and smoke left still on the air. Its briefness, darkness, upside-down and backward quality escaped Brunilla, who only listened to the great tide of Uncle Einar's wings faintly murmuring above them as they finished out the rite. And as for Uncle Einar, the wound across his nose was almost healed and, holding Brunilla's arm, he felt Europe grow faint and melt away in the distance.

He didn't have to see very well to fly straight up, or come straight down. It was only natural that on this night of their wedding he take Brunilla in his arms and fly right up into the sky.

A farmer, five miles over, glanced at a low cloud at midnight, saw faint glows and crackles.

"Heat lightning," he observed, and went to bed.

They didn't come down till morning, with the dew.

The marriage took. She had only to look at him, and it lifted her to think she was the only woman in the world married to a winged man. "Who else could say it?" she asked her mirror. And the answer was: "No one!"

He, on the other hand, found great beauty behind her face, great kindness and understanding. He made some changes in his diet to fit her thinking, and was careful with his wings about the house; knocked porcelains and broken lamps were nerve-scrapers, he stayed away from them. He changed his sleeping habits, since he couldn't fly nights now anyhow. And she in turn fixed chairs so they were comfortable for his wings, put extra padding here or took it out there, and the things she said were the things he loved her for. "We're in our cocoons, all of us. See how ugly I am?" she said. "But one day I'll break out, spread wings as fine and handsome as you."

"You broke out long ago," he said.

She thought it over. "Yes," she had to admit. "I know just which day it was, too. In the woods when I looked for a cow and found a tent!" They laughed, and with him holding her she felt so beautiful she knew their marriage had slipped her from her ugliness, like a bright sword from its case.

They had children. At first there was fear, all on his part, that they'd be winged.

"Nonsense, I'd love it!" she said. "Keep them out from under foot."

"Then," he exclaimed, "they'd be in your *hair!*"

"Ow!" she cried.

Four children were born, three boys and a girl, who, for their energy, seemed to have wings. They popped up like toadstools in a few years, and on hot summer days asked their father to sit under the apple tree and fan them with his cooling wings and tell them wild starlit tales of island clouds and ocean skies and textures of mist and wind and how a star tastes melting in your mouth, and how to drink cold mountain air, and how it feels to be a pebble dropped from Mt. Everest, turning to a green bloom, flowering your wings just before you strike bottom!

This was his marriage.

And today, six years later, here sat Uncle Einar, here he was, festering under the apple tree, grown impatient and unkind; not because this was his desire, but because after the long wait, he was still unable to fly the wild night sky; his extra sense had never returned. Here he sat despondently, nothing more than a summer sun-parasol, green and discarded, abandoned for the season by the reckless vacationers who once sought the refuge of its translucent shadow. Was he to sit here forever, afraid to fly by day because someone might see him? Was his only flight to be as a drier of clothes for his wife, or a fanner of children on hot August noons? His one occupation had *always* been flying Family errands, quicker than storms. A boomerang, he'd whickled over hills and valleys and like a thistle, landed. He had always had money; the Family had good use for their winged man! But now? Bitterness! His wings jittered and whisked the air and made a captive thunder.

"Papa," said little Meg.

The children stood looking at his thought-dark face.

"Papa," said Ronald. "Make more thunder!"

''It's a cold March day, there'll soon be rain and plenty of thunder,'' said Uncle Einar.

''Will you come watch us?'' asked Michael.

''Run on, run on! Let papa brood!''

He was shut of love, the children of love, and the love of children. He thought only of heavens, skies, horizons, infinities, by night or day, lit by star, moon, or sun, cloudy or clear, but always it was skies and heavens and horizons that ran ahead of you forever when you soared. Yet here he was, sculling the pasture, kept low for fear of being seen.

Misery in a deep well!

''Papa, come watch us; it's March!'' cried Meg. ''And we're going to the Hill with all the kids from town!''

Uncle Einar grunted. ''What hill is that?''

''The Kite Hill, of course!'' they all sang together.

Now he looked at them.

Each held a large paper kite, their faces sweating with anticipation and an animal glowing. In their small fingers were balls of white twine. From the kites, colored red and blue and yellow and green, hung caudal appendages of cotton and silk strips.

''We'll fly our kites!'' said Ronald. ''Won't you come?''

''No,'' he said, sadly. ''I mustn't be seen by anyone or there'd be trouble.''

''You could hide and watch from the woods,'' said Meg. ''We made the kites ourselves. Just because we know how.''

''How do you know how?''

''You're our father!'' was the instant cry. ''That's why!''

He looked at his children for a long while. He sighed. ''A kite festival, is it?''

''Yes, sir!''

''I'm going to win,'' said Meg.

''No, *I'm!*'' Michael contradicted.

''Me, *me!*'' piped Stephen.

''Wind up the chimney!'' roared Uncle Einar, leaping high with a deafening kettledrum of wings. ''Children! Children, I love you dearly!''

''Father, what's wrong?'' said Michael, backing off.

''Nothing, nothing, nothing!'' chanted Einar. He flexed his wings to their greatest propulsion and plundering. Whoom! they slammed like cymbals. The children fell flat in the backwash! "I have it, I *have* it! I'm free again! Fire in the flue! Feather on the wind! Brunilla!" Einar called to the house. His wife appeared. "I'm free!" he called, flushed and tall, on his toes. "Listen, Brunilla, I don't need the night anymore! I can fly by day! I don't need the night! I'll fly *every* day and *any* day of the year from now on!—but I waste time, talking. Look!"

And as the worried members of his family watched, he seized the cotton tail from one of the little kites, tied it to his belt behind, grabbed the twine ball, held one end in his teeth, gave the other end to his children, and up, up into the air he flew, away into the March wind!

And across the meadows and over the farms his children ran, letting out string to the daylit sky, bubbling and stumbling, and Brunilla stood back in the farmyard and waved and laughed to see what was happening; and her children marched to the far Kite Hill and stood, the four of them, holding the ball of twine in their eager, proud fingers, each tugging and directing and pulling. And the children from Mellin Town came running with *their* small kites to let up on the wind, and they saw the great green kite leap and hover in the sky and exclaimed:

"Oh, oh, what a kite! What a kite! Oh, I wish I'd a kite like that! Where, where did you *get* it!"

"Our father made it!' cried Meg and Michael and Stephen and Ronald, and gave an exultant pull on the twine and the humming, thundering kite in the sky dipped and soared and made a great and magical exclamation mark across a cloud!

The Time Machine

"Seems like the town is full of machines," said Douglas, running. "Mr. Auffmann and his Happiness Machine, Miss Fern and Miss Roberta and their Green Machine. Now, Charlie, what you handing me?"

"A Time Machine!" panted Charlie Woodman, pacing him. "Mother's, scout's, Injun's honor!"

"Travels in the past and future?" John Huff asked, easily circling them.

"Only in the past, but you can't have everything. Here we are."

Charlie Woodman pulled up at a hedge.

Douglas peered in at the old house. "Heck, that's Colonel Freeleigh's place. Can't be no Time Machine in there. He's no inventor, and if he was, we'd known about an important thing like a Time Machine years ago."

Charlie and John tiptoed up the front-porch steps. Douglas snorted and shook his head, staying at the bottom of the steps.

"Okay, Douglas," said Charlie. "Be a knucklehead. Sure, Colonel Freeleigh didn't *invent* this Time Machine. But he's got a proprietary interest in it, and it's been here all the time. We were too darned dumb to notice! So long, Douglas Spaulding, to you!"

Charlie took John's elbow as though he was escorting a lady, opened the front-porch screen and went in. The screen door did not slam.

Douglas had caught the screen and was following silently.

Charlie walked across the enclosed porch, knocked, and opened the inside door. They all peered down a long dark hall toward a room that was lit like an undersea grotto, soft green, dim, and watery.

"Colonel Freeleigh?"

Silence.

"He don't hear so good," whispered Charlie. "But he told me to just come on in and yell. *Colonel!*"

The only answer was the dust sifting down and around the spiral stairwell from above. Then there was a faint stir in that undersea chamber at the far end of the hall.

They moved carefully along and peered into a room which contained but two pieces of furniture—an old man and a chair. They resembled each other, both so thin you could see just how they had been put together, ball and socket, sinew and joint. The rest of the room was raw floorboards, naked walls and ceiling, and vast quantities of silent air.

"He looks dead," whispered Douglas.

"No, he's just thinking up new places to travel to," said Charlie, very proud and quiet. "Colonel?"

One of the pieces of brown furniture moved and it was the colonel, blinking around, focusing, and smiling a wild and toothless smile. "Charlie!"

"Colonel, Doug and John here came to—"

"Welcome, boys; sit down, sit down!"

The boys sat, uneasily, on the floor.

"But where's the—" said Douglas. Charlie jabbed his ribs quickly.

"Where's the what?" asked Colonel Freeleigh.

"Where's the point in *us* talking, he means." Charlie grimaced at Douglas, then smiled at the old man. "We got nothing to say. Colonel, *you* say something."

"Beware, Charlie, old men only lie in wait for people to ask them to talk. Then they rattle on like a rusty elevator wheezing up a shaft."

"Ching Ling Soo," suggested Charlie casually.

"Eh?" said the colonel.

"Boston," Charlie prompted, "1910."

"Boston, 1910 . . ." The colonel frowned. "Why, Ching Ling Soo, of course!"

"Yes, sir, Colonel."

"Let me see now . . ." The colonel's voice murmured, it drifted away on serene lake waters. "Let me see . . ."

The boys waited.

Colonel Freeleigh closed his eyes.

"October first, 1910, a calm cool fine autumn night, the Boston Variety Theatre, yes, there it *is.* Full house, all waiting. Orchestra, fanfare, curtain! Ching Ling Soo, the great Oriental Magician! There he is, on stage! And there I am, front row center! 'The Bullet Trick!' he cried. 'Volunteers!' The man next to me goes up. 'Examine the rifle!' says Ching. 'Mark the bullet!' says he. 'Now, fire this marked bullet from this rifle, using my face for a target, and,' says Ching; 'at the far end of the stage I will catch the bullet in my *teeth!*' "

Colonel Freeleigh took a deep breath and paused.

Douglas was staring at him, half puzzled, half in awe. John Huff and Charlie were completely lost. Now the old man went on, his head and body frozen, only his lips moving.

" 'Ready, aim, fire!' cries Ching Ling Soo. Bang! The rifle cracks. Bang! Ching Ling Soo shrieks, he staggers, he falls, his face all red. Pandemonium. Audience on its feet. Something wrong with the rifle. 'Dead,' someone says. And they're right. Dead. Horrible, horrible . . . I'll always remember . . . his face a mask of red, the curtain coming down fast and the women weeping . . . 1910 . . . Boston . . . Variety Theatre . . . poor man . . . poor man . . ."

Colonel Freeleigh slowly opened his eyes.

"Boy, Colonel," said Charlie, "that was fine. Now how about Pawnee Bill?"

"Pawnee Bill . . . ?"

"And the time you was on the prairie way back in seventy-five."

"Pawnee Bill . . ." The colonel moved into darkness. "Eighteen seventy-five . . . yes, me and Pawnee Bill on a little rise in the middle of that prairie, waiting. 'Sh!' says Pawnee Bill. 'Listen.' The prairie like a big stag all set for the storm to come. Thunder. Soft. Thunder again. Not so soft. And across that prairie as far as the eye could see this big ominous yellow-dark cloud full of black lightning, somehow sunk to earth, fifty miles wide, fifty miles long, a mile high, and no more than an inch off the ground. 'Lord!' I cried, 'Lord!'—from up on my hill—'Lord!' The earth pounded like a mad heart, boys, a heart gone to panic. My bones shook fit to break. The earth shook: rat-a-tat rat-a-tat, boom! Rumble. That's a rare word: rumble. Oh, how that mighty storm rumbled along down, up, and over the rise, and all you could see was the cloud and nothing inside. 'That's them!' cried Pawnee Bill. And the cloud was dust! Not vapors or rain, no, but prairie dust flung up from the tinder-dry grass like fine cornmeal, like pollen all blazed with sunlight now, for the sun had come out. I shouted again! Why? Because in all that hell-fire filtering dust now a veil moved aside and I saw them, I swear it! The grand army of the ancient prairie: the bison, the buffalo!''

The colonel let the silence build, then broke it again.

''Heads like giant Negroes' fists, bodies like locomotives! Twenty, fifty, two hundred thousand iron missiles shot out of the west, gone off the track and flailing cinders, their eyes like blazing coals, rumbling toward oblivion!''

''I saw that the dust rose up and for a little while showed me that the sea of humps, of dolloping manes, black shaggy waves rising, falling . . . 'Shoot!' says Pawnee Bill. 'Shoot!' And I cock and aim. 'Shoot!' he says. And I stand there feeling like God's right hand, looking at that great vision of strength and violence going by, going by, midnight at noon, like a glinty funeral train all black and long and sad and forever and you don't fire at a funeral train, now do you, boys? *Do* you? All I wanted then was for the dust to sink again and cover the black shapes of doom which pummeled and jostled on in great burdensome commotions. And, boys, the dust came down. The cloud hid the million feet that were drumming up the thunder and dusting out the storm. I heard Pawnee Bill curse and hit my arm. But I was glad I hadn't touched that cloud or the power within that cloud with so much as a pellet of lead. I just wanted to stand watching time bundle by in great trundlings all hid by the storm the bison made and carried with them toward eternity.

"An hour, three hours, six, it took for the storm to pass on away over the horizon toward less kind men than me. Pawnee Bill was gone, I stood alone, stone deaf. I walked all numb through a town a hundred miles south and heard not the voices of men and was satisfied not to hear. For a little while I wanted to remember the thunder. I hear it still, on summer afternoons like this when the rain shapes over the lake; a fearsome, wondrous sound . . . one I wish you might have heard. . . ."

The dim light filtered through Colonel Freeleigh's nose which was large and like white porcelain which cupped a very thin and tepid orange tea indeed.

"Is he asleep?" asked Douglas at last.

"No," said Charlie. "Just recharging his batteries."

Colonel Freeleigh breathed swiftly, softly, as if he'd run a long way. At last he opened his eyes.

"Yes, *sir!*" said Charlie, in admiration.

"Hello, Charlie." The colonel smiled at the boys puzzledly.

"That's Doug and that's John," said Charlie.

"How-de-do, boys."

The boys said hello.

"But—" said Douglas. "Where is the—?"

"My gosh, you're dumb!" Charlie jabbed Douglas in the arm. He turned to the colonel. "You were saying, sir?"

"*Was* I?" murmured the old man.

"The Civil War," suggested John Huff quietly. "Does he remember that?"

"Do I remember?" said the colonel. "Oh, I do, I do!" His voice trembled as he shut up his eyes again. "Everything! Except . . . which side I fought on. . . ."

"The *color* of your uniform—" Charlie began.

"Colors begin to run on you," whispered the colonel. "It's gotten hazy. I see soldiers with me, but a long time ago I stopped seeing color in their coats or caps. I was born in Illinois, raised in Virginia, married in New York, built a house in Tennessee and now, very late, here I am, good Lord, back in Green Town. So you see why the colors run and blend. . . ."

"But you remember which side of hills you fought on?" Charlie did not raise his voice. "Did the sun rise on your left or right? Did you march toward Canada or Mexico?"

"Seems some mornings the sun rose on my good right hand, some mornings over my left shoulder. We marched all directions. It's most seventy years since. You forgot suns and mornings that long past."

"You remember winning, don't you? A battle won, somewhere?"

"No," said the old man, deep under. "I don't remember anyone winning anywhere any time. War's never a winning thing, Charlie. You just lose all the time, and the one who loses last asks for terms. All I remember is a lot of losing and sadness and nothing good but the end of it. The end of it, Charles, that was a winning all to itself, having nothing to do with guns. But I don't suppose that's the kind of victory you boys mean for me to talk on."

"Antietam," said John Huff. "Ask about the Antietam."

"I was there."

The boys' eyes grew bright. "Bull Run, ask him Bull Run . . ."

"I was there." Softly.

"What about Shiloh?"

"There's never been a year in my life I haven't thought, what a lovely name and what a shame to see it only on battle records."

"Shiloh, then. Fort Sumter?"

"I saw the first puffs of powder smoke." A dreaming voice, "So many things come back, oh, so many things. I remember songs. 'All's quiet along the Potomac tonight, where the soldiers lie peacefully dreaming; their tents in the rays of the clear autumn moon, or the light of the watchfire, are gleaming.' Remember, remember . . . 'All quiet along the Potomac tonight; no sound save the rush of the river; while soft falls the dew on the face of the dead—the picket's off duty forever!' . . . After the surrender, Mr. Lincoln, on the White House balcony asked the band to play, 'Look away, look away, look away, Dixie land . . .' And then there was the Boston lady who one night wrote a song will last a thousand years: 'Mine eyes have seen the glory of the coming of the Lord; He is trampling out the vintage where the grapes of wrath are stored.' Late nights I feel my mouth move singing back in another time. 'Ye Cavaliers of Dixie! Who guard the Southern shores . . .' 'When the boys come home in triumph, brother, with the laurels they shall gain . . .' So many songs, sung on both sides, blowing north, blowing south on the night winds. 'We are coming, Father Abraham, three hundred thousand more . . .' 'Tenting tonight, tenting tonight, tenting on the old camp ground.' 'Hurrah, hurrah, we bring the Jubilee, hurrah, hurrah, the flag that makes us free . . .' "

The old man's voice faded.

The boys sat for a long while without moving. Then Charlie turned and looked at Douglas and said, "Well, is he or isn't he?"

Douglas breathed twice and said, "He sure *is*."

The colonel opened his eyes.

"I sure am *what?*" he said.

"A Time Machine," murmured Douglas. "A Time Machine."

The colonel looked at the boys for a full five seconds. Now it was his voice that was full of awe.

"Is that what you boys call me?"

"Yes, sir, Colonel."

"Yes, sir."

The colonel sat slowly back in his chair and looked at the boys and looked at his hands and then looked at the blank wall beyond them steadily.

Charlie arose. "Well, I guess we better go. So long and thanks, Colonel."

"What? Oh, so long, boys."

Douglas and John and Charlie went on tiptoe out the door.

Colonel Freeleigh, though they crossed his line of vision, did not see them go.

In the street, the boys were startled when someone shouted from a first-floor window above, "Hey!"

They looked up.

"Yes, sir, Colonel?"

The colonel leaned out, waving one arm.

"I thought about what you said, boys!"

"Yes, sir?"

"And—you're right! Why didn't I *think* of it before! A Time Machine, praise heaven. A Time Machine!"

"Yes, sir."

"So long, boys. Come aboard any time!"

At the end of the street they turned again and the colonel was still waving. They waved back, feeling warm and good, then went on.

"Chug-a-chug," said John. "I can't travel twelve years into the past. Wham-chug-ding!"

"Yeah," said Charlie, looking back at that quiet house, "but you can't go a hundred years."

"No," mused John. "I can go a hundred years. That's really traveling. That's really some machine."

They walked for a full minute in silence, looking at their feet. They came to a fence.

"Last one over this fence," said Douglas, "is a girl."

All the way home they called Douglas "Dora."

The Sound of Summer Running

Late that night, going home from the show with his mother and father and his brother Tom, Douglas saw the tennis shoes in the bright store window. He glanced quickly away, but his ankles were seized, his feet suspended, then rushed. The earth spun; the shop awnings slammed their canvas wings overhead with the thrust of his body running. His mother and father and brother walked quietly on both sides of him. Douglas walked backward, watching the tennis shoes in the midnight window left behind.

"It was a nice movie," said Mother.

Douglas murmured, "It was . . ."

It was June and long past time for buying the special shoes that were quiet as a summer rain falling on the walls. June and the earth full of raw power and everything everywhere in motion. The grass was still pouring in from the country, surrounding the sidewalks, stranding the houses. Any moment the town would capsize, go down and leave not a stir in the clover and weeds. And here Douglas stood, trapped on the dead cement and the red-brick streets, hardly able to move.

"Dad!" He blurted it out. "Back there in that window, those Cream-Sponge Para Litefoot Shoes . . ."

His father didn't even turn. "Suppose you tell me why you need a new pair of sneakers. Can you do that?"

"Well . . ."

It was because they felt the way it feels every summer when

you take off your shoes for the first time and run in the grass. They felt like it feels sticking your feet out of the hot covers in wintertime to let the cold wind from the open window blow on them suddenly and you let them stay out a long time until you pull them back in under the covers again to feel them, like packed snow. The tennis shoes felt like it always feels the first time every year wading in the slow waters of the creek and seeing your feet below, half an inch further downstream, with refraction, than the real part of you above water.

"Dad," said Douglas, "it's hard to explain."

Somehow the people who made tennis shoes knew what boys needed and wanted. They put marshmallows and coiled springs in the soles and they wove the rest out of grasses bleached and fired in the wilderness. Somewhere deep in the soft loam of the shoes the thin hard sinews of the buck deer were hidden. The people that made the shoes must have watched a lot of winds blow the trees and a lot of rivers going down to the lakes. Whatever it was, it was in the shoes, and it was summer.

Douglas tried to get all this in words.

"Yes," said Father, "but what's wrong with last year's sneakers? Why can't you dig *them* out of the closet?"

Well, he felt sorry for boys who lived in California where they wore tennis shoes all year and never knew what it was to get winter off your feet, peel off the iron leather shoes all full of snow and rain and run barefoot for a day and then lace on the first new tennis shoes of the season, which was better than barefoot. The magic was always in the new pair of shoes. The magic might die by the first of September, but now in late June there was still plenty of magic, and shoes like these could jump you over trees and rivers and houses. And if you wanted, they could jump you over fences and sidewalks and dogs.

"Don't you see?" said Douglas. "I just *can't* use last year's pair."

For last year's pair were dead inside. They had been fine when he started them out, last year. But by the end of summer, every year, you always found out, you always knew, you couldn't really jump over rivers and trees and houses in them, and they were dead. But this was a new year, and he felt that this time, with this new pair of shoes, he could do anything, anything at all.

They walked up on the steps to their house. "Save your money," said Dad. "In five or six weeks—"

"Summer'll be over!"

Lights out, with Tom asleep, Douglas lay watching his feet, far away down there at the end of the bed in the moonlight, free of the heavy iron shoes, the big chunks of winter fallen away from them.

"Reasons. I've got to think of reasons for the shoes."

Well, as anyone knew, the hills around town were wild with friends putting cows to riot, playing barometer to the atmospheric changes, taking sun, peeling like calendars each day to take more sun. To catch those friends, you must run much faster than foxes or squirrels. As for the town, it steamed with enemies grown irritable with heat, so remembering every winter argument and insult. *Find friends, ditch enemies!* That was the Cream-Sponge Para Litefoot motto. *Does the world run too fast? Want to be alert, stay alert? Litefoot, then! Litefoot!*

He held his coin bank up and heard the faint small tinkling, the airy weight of money there.

Whatever you want, he thought, you got to make your own way. During the night now, let's find that path through the forest. . . .

Downtown, the store lights went out, one by one. A wind blew in the window. It was like a river going downstream and his feet wanting to go with it.

In his dreams he heard a rabbit running running running in the deep warm grass.

Old Mr. Sanderson moved through his shoe store as the proprietor of a pet shop must move through his shop where are kenneled animals from everywhere in the world, touching each one briefly along the way. Mr. Sanderson brushed his hands over the shoes in the window, and some of them were like cats to him and some were like dogs; he touched each pair with concern, adjusting laces, fixing tongues. Then he stood in the exact center of the carpet and looked around, nodding.

There was a sound of growing thunder.

One moment, the door to Sanderson's Shoe Emporium was empty. The next, Douglas Spaulding stood clumsily there, staring down at his leather shoes as if these heavy things could not be pulled up out of the cement. The thunder had stopped when his shoes stopped. Now, with painful slowness, daring to look only at the money in his cupped hand, Douglas moved out of the bright sunlight of Saturday noon. He made careful stacks of nickels, dimes, and quarters on the counter, like someone playing chess and worried if the next move carried him out into sun or deep into shadow.

"Don't say a word!" said Mr. Sanderson.

Douglas froze.

"First, I know just what you want to buy," said Mr. Sanderson. "Second, I see you every afternoon at my window; you think I don't see? You're wrong. Third, to give it its full name, you want the Royal Crown Cream-Sponge Para Litefoot Tennis Shoes: 'LIKE MENTHOL ON YOUR FEET!' Fourth, you want credit."

"No!" cried Douglas, breathing hard, as if he'd run all night in his dreams. "I got something better than credit to offer!" he gasped. "Before I tell, Mr. Sanderson, you got to do me one small favor. Can you remember when was the last time you yourself wore a pair of Litefoot sneakers, sir?"

Mr. Sanderson's face darkened. "Oh, ten, twenty, say, thirty years ago. Why . . . ?"

'Mr. Sanderson, don't you think you owe it to your customers, sir, to at least try the tennis shoes you sell, for just one minute, so you know how they feel? People forget if they don't keep testing things. United Cigar Store man smokes cigars, don't he? Candy-store man samples his own stuff, I should think. So . . ."

"You may have noticed," said the old man, "I'm wearing shoes."

"But not sneakers, sir! How you going to sell sneakers unless you can rave about them and how you going to rave about them unless you know them?"

Mr. Sanderson backed off a little distance from the boy's fever, one hand to his chin. "Well . . ."

"Mr. Sanderson,"said Douglas, "you sell me something and I'll sell you something just as valuable."

"Is it absolutely necessary to the sale that I put on a pair of the sneakers, boy?" said the old man.

"I sure wish you could, sir!"

The old man sighed. A minute later, seated panting quietly, he laced the tennis shoes to his long narrow feet. They looked detached and alien down there next to the dark cuffs of his business suit. Mr. Sanderson stood up.

"How do they *feel?*" asked the boy.

"How do they feel, he asks; they feel fine." He started to sit down.

"Please!" Douglas held out his hand. "Mr. Sanderson, now could you kind of rock back and forth a little, sponge around, bounce kind of, while I tell you the rest? It's this: I give you my money, you give me the shoes, I owe you a dollar. But, Mr. Sanderson, *but*—soon as I get those shoes on, you know what *happens?*"

"What?"

"Bang! I deliver your packages, pick up packages, bring you coffee, burn your trash, run to the post office, telegraph office, library! You'll see twelve of me in and out, in and out, every minute. Feel those shoes, Mr. Sanderson, *feel* how fast they'd take me? All those springs inside? Feel all the running inside? Feel how they kind of grab hold and can't let you alone and don't like you just *standing* there? Feel how quick I'd be doing the things you'd rather not bother with? You stay in the nice cool store while I'm jumping all around town! But it's not me really, it's the shoes. They're going like mad down alleys, cutting corners, and back! There they go!"

Mr. Sanderson stood amazed with the rush of words. When the words got going the flow carried him; he began to sink deep in the shoes, to flex his toes, limber his arches, test his ankles. He rocked softly, secretly, back and forth in a small breeze from the open door. The tennis shoes silently hushed themselves deep in the carpet, sank as in a jungle grass, in loam and resilient clay. He gave one solemn bounce of his heels in the yeasty dough, in the yielding and welcoming earth. Emotions hurried over his face as if many colored lights had been switched on and off. His mouth hung slightly open. Slowly he gentled and rocked himself to a halt, and the boy's voice faded and they stood there looking at each other in a tremendous and natural silence.

A few people drifted by on the sidewalk outside, in the hot sun.

Still the man and boy stood there, the boy glowing, the man with revelation in his face.

"Boy," said the old man at last, "in five years, how would you like a job selling shoes in this emporium?"

"Gosh, thanks, Mr. Sanderson, but I don't know what I'm going to be yet."

"Anything you want to be, son," said the old man, "you'll be. No one will ever stop you."

The old man walked lightly across the store to the wall of ten thousand boxes, came back with some shoes for the boy, and wrote up a list on some paper while the boy was lacing the shoes on his feet and then standing there, waiting.

The old man held out his list. "A dozen things you got to do for me this afternoon. Finish them, we're even Stephen, and you're fired."

"Thanks, Mr. Sanderson!" Douglas bounded away.

"Stop!" cried the old man.

Douglas pulled up and turned.

Mr. Sanderson leaned forward. "How do they *feel?*"

The boy looked down at his feet deep in the rivers, in the fields of wheat, in the wind that already was rushing him out of the town. He looked up at the old man, his eyes burning, his mouth moving, but no sound came out.

"Antelopes?" said the old man, looking from the boy's face to his shoes. "Gazelles?"

The boy thought about it, hesitated, and nodded a quick nod. Almost immediately he vanished. He just spun about with a whisper and went off. The door stood empty. The sound of the tennis shoes faded in the jungle heat.

Mr. Sanderson stood in the sun-blazed door, listening. From a long time ago, when he dreamed as a boy, he remembered the sound. Beautiful creatures leaping under the sky, gone through brush, under trees, away, and only the soft echo their running left behind.

"Antelopes," said Mr. Sanderson. "Gazelles."

He bent to pick up the boy's abandoned winter shoes, heavy with forgotten rains and long-melted snows. Moving out of the blazing sun, walking softly, lightly, slowly, he headed back toward civilization. . . .